ROAR OF THE JAGUAR

To Austin

[signature]

11/10/2012

Novels by
DONALD FREDERICKSON

Dakharo Heist
To Steal a Priate's Treasure

Roar of the Jaguar
The Legacy of a Mayan Prince

ROAR OF THE JAGUAR

THE LEGACY OF A MAYAN PRINCE

Donald Frederickson

Hiawatha Publishing
Clinton Township, Michigan

Published in Clinton Township, Michigan, by Hiawatha Publishing

www.hiawatha publishing@gmail.com

Publisher's Note: This novel is a work of fiction. Names, characters, places, and incidents are either products of the author's imagination or used fictitiously . All characters are fictional and any similarity to people living or dead is purely coincidental.

Cover Design by Donald W. Frederickson

Page Design by Donald W. Frederickson

Edited by Priscilla Mangold

ISBN 978-0-9846722-8-8

Dedicated to my Mother
Minnie Viola Frederickson
(1922—1983)
who took the time and patience to give the gift of her love
of reading to me.

Foreword
Dr. John Telford

Once in a great while a book comes along that encompasses an historical period with a fictional perspective where the work has merit from an academic standpoint. Don Frederickson's novel, *The Roar of the Jaguar—The Legacy of a Mayan Prince,* is such a work. The novel involves a prominent archaeologist who, during an excavation, uncovers a drug used in ancient ceremonies, takes it and is transported back in time to the ancient Maya city of Yaxchilan, the time 759 A.D.

The book is the result of Mr. Frederickson's interests in ancient cultures, primarily in the new world. He holds an undergraduate degree from the University of Wisconsin in economics and anthropology, which was emphasized with studies and field work in archaeology. Earning a master's degree in industrial management from the University of Central Michigan, he had a successful career and is now retired from the auto industry. Over the years he maintained active involvement in his first academic love—archaeology. Mayan studies have been a focal point of his interests which are supported by his substantial library in the field. He has traveled extensively in Mexico and Central America visiting archaeological sites to further his knowledge and understanding of ancient America.

Mr. Frederickson's novel, *Roar of the Jaguar—The Legacy of a Mayan Prince*, utilizes the culmination of knowledge gained over decades of study and places it in a story about the Maya in the Eighth Century, during the height of their civilization. The narrator of the novel is a prominent archaeologist who travels back in time where he observes an ancient culture and describes it within a story about a young prince's obsession to become king and his actions to gain his objective. Written as historical fiction, he brings the ancient culture to light before our eyes. Historical events, recorded by the ancient Mayan kings on their stone hieroglyphs, serve as cornerstones anchoring the story in a sound historical basis.

The characters are real persons recorded as prominent figures living during that time period. Around this empirical knowledge, he describes life in the royal court and political intrigue as powerful men vie for position against a backdrop of an aggressive society in a state of perpetual warfare with their neighbor cities. Battles, rituals, ceremonies, and sacrifices, all significant to their culture, are depicted as Shield Jaguar III drives in his quest for the throne.

The novel, *Roar of the Jaguar—The Legacy of a Mayan Prince,* is a book that will entertain both young and old alike. Its historical basis is suitably sufficient to use it in an educational environment within the library system or as a supplemental reading in anthropology or history. As a novel, an ancient world that thrived thirteen hundred years ago is brought to life with a provocative narrative and fast-paced action scenes. The book provides a basis for understanding the human side of historical events as they are placed within the context of a primitive society vastly different from the one in which we live today.

John Telford, Ph.D.
Author, social commentator, retired educator
He formerly held positions in the field of education:
- Executive director of Detroit Public Schools
- Director of Division of Basic Education, Macomb College
- Superintendent of Detroit Madison District Schools
- Deputy Superintendent of Schools, Rochester Michigan

The Roar of the Jaguar—Historical Preface

The height of the splendor for the Maya civilization, during the end of the Late Classical Period (700-800 A.D.), was characterized by sharply increased building activity in their ceremonial centers, the heightened sophistication of their monumental art, improved agricultural techniques, a sharp increase in population, and increased presence and sophistication in warfare.

The ancient Maya city, Yaxchilan, located in the Guatemalan lowlands on the banks of the Usumacinta River, stands out as one of the finest examples reminiscent of the Maya culture during this late classical era. The massive building programs and subsequent ceremonial dedications from 700 to 800 A.D spanning the reign of the three great kings has left science with a comprehensive picture of their majestic culture and indications of the turn toward its eventual downfall. The reigning kings were:

- Shield Jaguar II (681—742 A.D.)

- Bird Jaguar IV (752—768 A.D.)

- Shield Jaguar III (769—800 A.D.)

They were grandfather, father and son.

The Roar of the Jaguar is the story of the rise of Shield Jaguar III from a prince to a king as observed by a world-renowned Mayan archaeologist, who goes back in time.

The story takes place from roughly 759-771 A.D. and is historically accurate with respect to events and characters. The underlying premise of the story is that the genealogy of Shield Jaguar III, as understood by the archaeological community, is incorrect and is subject to reinterpretation. Current knowledge indicates that upon the death of his father, Bird Jaguar IV, Chel-Te' his son, at the age of sixteen, ascended to the throne and changed his name to Shield Jaguar III after his grandfather. In this story, Chel-Te' ascends to the throne but shortly thereafter is displaced by Shield Jaguar III, the half brother of the king Bird Jaguar IV.

This is the type of change to historical interpretation of the ancient records that would happen as new information comes to light and is evaluated. In effect, as we view the historical account in the book, only our perception of who the players are has changed and the royal lineage is still based upon birthright; history remains constant. In the book, the newly postulated theory is presented to the archaeological community the same as it would be in the real world and meets the same critique and challenges.

Historical Figures who are characters in the novel

- *Bird Jaguar IV,* reigning king of Yaxchilan

- *Chel-Te' chan K'inich,* prince of Yaxchilan. Succeeds his father Bird Jaguar IV to the throne at the age of sixteen

- *Shield Jaguar III* (Itzamnaaj B'alam III), half brother of Bird Jaguar IV who seizes the throne from Chel-Te' shortly after he ascends

- *Little Rabbit,* princess of Yaxchilan and sister to Shield Jaguar III. Later in history she is recorded as Lady Rabbit, queen of Bonampak and mother to the child who is dedicated heir to the throne on the famous Bonampak murals

- *Lord Great Skull Zero,* chief counselor to the king Bird Jaguar IV, brother to the queen Lady Great Skull Zero, and chief counselor to Shield Jaguar III after he becomes king

- *Chan Muwaan II*, prince of Bonampak and Later in history will become the king.

- *Lady Great Skull Zero*, primary (but second) wife of Bird Jaguar IV and mother to Chel-Te', designated heir to the throne.

- *Ha'k'in Xook*, prince of Piedras Negras. Later in history will become the king of Piedras Negras.

Referenced Historical Figures described in context of their function in society

- *Shield Jaguar II,* (Itzamnaaj B'alam II) (ancestor)—past king of Yaxchilan. 681-742 A.D.

- *Lady K'ab'al Xook,* (ancesto—primary wife of Shield Jaguar II, considered to have been instrumental in keeping Bird Jaguar IV from ascending to the throne for ten years after his father's death

- *Lady Ik' Skull* also known as Lady Eveningstar (ancestor)— second wife of Shield Jaguar II, a royal princess from Calakmul, mother of the king Bird Jaguar IV

- *Lady Sak B'iyann (*ancestor)—Third wife of Shield Jaguar II, referred to as an ixik ch'ok, a young woman. In this story she is the mother of Shield Jaguar III

- *Yoaat B'alam II*—assumed to be an insignificant interregnum term ruler of Yaxchilan (742-752 A.D.) between the reigns of Shield Jaguar II and Bird Jaguar IV.

- *Yo'nal Ahk III*—King of Piedras Negras

- *K'an Tok Wayib*—Chief counselor to Bird Jaguar IV along with

Lord Great Skull Zero

- *K'an-Tok and Mi Kimi*—nobles who are renowned ball players

- *Aj Uk*—first recorded captive of Bird Jaguar IV in 752 A.D.

- *Jeweled Skul*—second recorded captive of Bird Jaguar IV. Taken with the help of *K'an Tok Wayib,* the king's counselor

- *K'inil ajaw (a high lord) T'ul Chiik*—captive from Preidras Negras in 759, taken with the help of *Baah Saval Tillom,* the ruler of Pasadita, vassal city

- *K'inich Tatb'u Skull III*—son of Shield Jaguar III, the last recorded king of Yaxchilan

Fictional Characters that interact with the historical figures

- *Dr. Alan Johnson*—world renowned archaeologist, also known as the Maya character *Lightning Sky*

- *Phoebe Grant*—associate of Dr. Johnson's, a doctoral candidate in Maya glyph interpretation, also known as the Maya character *Running Deer*

- *Smoking Squirrel*—cousin to Shield Jaguar III, and brother to Lightning Sky

- *Broken Monkey*—evil Maya hunchback

Reference Note: *The Chronicle of Maya Kings and Queens* by Simon Martin and Nkolia Grube (2000) is the reference for names

Chapter 1

The cave was just a little opening, hardly more than a crevice hidden on the hillside in a grove of trees, behind a large boulder. If his old hound dog had led him there while chasing a coon, he might take note of it, but otherwise would pass it without a thought. There were lots of caves in the area, many were large and spectacular. This was just a hole in the earth behind a rock, hardly worth consideration.

He and the old man had driven many miles up a dirt road in an old pickup truck to reach it. They came to the end of the road and then continued on foot. For an hour they had followed a faint animal trail up into the hills. The old man's demeanor changed as they got closer. When they left the village in the truck, he had been ecstatic about their trip. It had been a long time since he had been to the cave. Now he was uneasy and quiet, pensively glancing from place to place. He was bringing a stranger to the sacred cave. *Will the gods approve?*

"This is the entrance to the Xibalba, the underworld," said the old man, a shaman and spiritual leader for the present-day Maya living in Chiapas, Mexico. He ministered to those who held on to the old ways and performed the rituals demanded by the gods, just as they had been done for over two thousand years.

It was the ancient gods who still watched over his people and provided the annual rains to make the crops grow. If they weren't worshiped properly, they could become angry and send storms, or insects, or drought to ruin their crops. The new Catholic religion claimed that if the people were good and reverent they would one day live with their God in paradise. But the people knew they had to live today, they had to feed their children and shelter them. If no crops grew, they would suffer.

He knew it was better to worship the ancient gods. The old gods helped them today. Perhaps the new god would help them tomorrow. But, tomorrow was tomorrow. The Knowledge of the Ancients and the old gods was passed from shaman to shaman every generation. The Catholic Church had converted most of the people to the new ways, but the old ways were still practiced.

The old man pointed to the hole and spoke. "The Progenitors of Man, the Hero Twins, emerged from here to build a home for our people on the outside. It is here my ancestors, those shamen before me, came and performed our most sacred ceremonies. We must perform the ritual here."

Dr. Alan Johnson, leader of the archaeological team from the University of Wisconsin excavating the Yaxchilan ruins in Mexico, followed the old shaman as he crawled into the hole and through a narrow tunnel which led to a small chamber. The old man found some firebrands stored there—sticks with rags wound around them held together by dark oil pitch. No battery powered lights would be used. This was the sacred place of the ancients. Modern conveniences were not welcome.

Carrying the torches of fire, they silently followed the tunnels of the cave deeper and deeper into the bowels of the earth until they came to a large chamber with a small stream running through it. The walls were rough and the ceiling black from the smoke of centuries of fires that had been made there.

There were a few bowls and some broken pottery on the floor, left by predecessors. In a flat, level space beside the stream, on the blackened scorched floor, the shaman made a small fire. It gave off an eerie light as it bounced off the walls. Johnson could faintly see pictures of animals painted long ago. It was a place of the spirits of the ancestors. It felt like they were still there and he was being watched.

Dr. Johnson was trembling from both fear and anticipation. He was about to enter a new realm of discovery. For many years he had been an archaeologist living vicariously with the ghosts of the past as he excavated old ruins. He studied the occasional artifacts and hypothesized what the prehistoric past was like yet never knowing for sure. That would change tonight. Tonight he would follow in the footsteps of a king, the physical and spiritual leader of an ancient civilization, a deity in the eyes of his people. Tonight, with the old Shaman's help, he would travel on a quest for a vision.

The ritual would begin soon. Johnson held the jar to his chest, careful not to spill any of the powder it contained. Inside was a thirteen-hundred-year-old drug used by ancient Maya kings in their blood sacrifice rituals, ceremonies so special that they could only be performed by the king or a member of the royal personage. He thought that ingesting this powder, believed to be an hallucinogen, would put the ancients into a trance where they communicated with the spirit world, received visions, and determined direction for their people. Tonight, with the guidance of one of the surviving shaman, a follower of the old Maya religion, he would soon use the powder as part of the ancient ritual.

The fire burnt down to embers leaving just a small flame. Barely touching the walls, the flickering light held them in a dark sphere, a capsule of dim illumination deep in the underground. It became a pinpoint in the universe where man and the gods came together for a brief encounter.

At the old man's direction, Dr. Johnson sat cross-legged on the floor, the fire between them. The shaman solemnly chanted the ritual phrases calling the gods into their presence. A tear rolled down his face. This would be one of the last of these sessions. He was an old man, not much longer for this world. When he died a younger man would take his place and keep the old traditions alive.

He lit a cigar with a stick from the fire and blew a large puff of smoke in each of the four directions of the compass and then threw the cigar into the fire. Then he lifted a small bottle of tequila, took a mouthful and spit it in each of the four directions, and poured the remainder into the fire. Taking the bottle of powder and a wooden tube from Johnson, he carefully placed a portion of the powder inside the tube and offered it into the four directions. Chanting the words imploring the gods to carry Johnson to the spirit world, he slowly placed one end of the tube into Dr. Johnson's nose. With a quick burst of air from his lungs, he blew the powder through the tube and into Johnson.

§

Everything exploded in a blinding flash of light; a sunburst infinite white, as his eyes dissolved. Next came the pain, searing pain from deep inside, and he felt his head vaporize. Suddenly he was being transported past the sun, past the stars, and into the black tunnel in the center of the galaxy, the spiraling road to Xibalba. Across his mind flashed pictures of strange beings, not men but humanoid in resemblance. They were calling to him to come to them. They were fearsome but something was protecting him. He didn't know what, but he felt it was there.

And then it was quiet and he floated weightlessly in the dark aware only of a faint trace of illumination. He felt at peace, a gentle peace coming from the center of his being, encompassing the world. It radiated around him and everything in the world was right, like he was back in the womb warm and comfortable, a place he never wanted to leave.

"Why are you here?" asked a voice. He didn't hear the voice but it was there, he felt it. It was in the Maya tongue, not like the Maya he used daily when talking with the locals, but with more of an accent, like a southern accent would be in English.

"I'm here to talk to the gods," he responded, "the gods of the ancient ones."

"Here you will find the gods of the people," the voice said. "You are not one of them. Why have you come?"

"To learn of the people, to know them as they were," Johnson replied.

"You will be sent to the ancients," the voice responded. "Tell them to come back to us."

§

"Wake up, little brother." The voice was commanding. "Wake up and tell us what the gods said."

Johnson opened his eyes, looked around and could see three pyramids in a line facing a large plaza. He was sitting cross-legged on a raised platform at the top of a fourth pyramid. On the opposite side of the plaza was a row of buildings that looked like temples and a hill rose behind them. Darkness was starting to set in. To the west the sun was just a ray of fading light. Deep shadows covered the buildings. On the hill above the temples were large structures, a palace and another very large temple still visible in the fading light. The stairway running up to them was illuminated by long rows of torchlights on each side.

There were hundreds of people below, many carrying lit torches. In the middle of the plaza was a row of stone markers with colorfully painted figures on them, and a small ceremonial ball court like those used for ritual games, but the ball court wasn't in ruins. It appeared to be functional, covered with red plaster and adorned with painted pictures. As an archaeologist, he always saw just the vertical sidewalls of the ruins of ancient ball courts, with crumbling platforms above where the royal spectators sat and watched. Something was strange here. The pyramids were red too, and the plaza was paved. And what were all the people doing here?

"What did the gods say?" he heard someone above him ask.

Johnson turned and looked up at the voice. He shrank back in horror. Looking down at him was the most ferocious creature he had ever seen. A man, covered in a jaguar-skin cloak and wearing an immense headdress consisting of an animal skull with an outlandish array of colorful feathers, was staring intently at him. His face was covered in symmetric tattoos and there was a bone running through his nose. In his earlobes were large jade spools enlarging and stretching them. Around his neck and over his shoulders was a breastplate made of jade stones fitted together. It hung loosely over his bare chest and over it was a large necklace of jade from which hung a shrunken head.

Transfixed, Johnson stared at the head. It stared back, watching him through the slits where its eyes had once been. There was a twisted grin on its face. Tearing his eyes away from the head, he strained to look up at the man who was looking back at him. His eyes were almost black; his head looked deformed. It was stretched, elongated in the back, and there was a predominate arch to his nose. His hair was cropped short and he was scowling, revealing teeth that had been filed into geometric patterns with small precious stones inlaid in them.

As the man looked down at him, a fierce scowl crossed his face. "What did the gods tell you, little brother?" the man demanded in a slightly familiar dialect of Maya, his voice containing a guttural accent. "Is it time to fight? Will we win the battles?"

"What?" Johnson asked dumbly, not understanding. *What is*

happening? Where am I? In a daze he looked around again, then back up at the man who was talking and saw two others behind him who looked just as ferocious. All were staring expectantly at him waiting for an answer.

"The astronomer says Venus is in position when the sun peeks from behind the trees in the morning. Do the gods favor us for battle?" the man shouted down at him. His eyes gleamed madly making him look even more intimidating. "What did the gods say, little brother? Will we take many captives?"

"What?" Johnson asked slowly in Maya as he started to tremble. "Where am I?"

"You've been talking to the gods," the man answered. "You were to ask them if we will be victorious in battle tomorrow. What did they say?" The man searched his eyes, seeking an answer.

Johnson looked around. He felt panic. *I shouldn't be here. I have to get out of here.* Fear gripped him and his body tightened. He wanted to flee, but where? The place he found himself in didn't exist. His eyes told him he was in the ceremonial center of Yaxchilan, the Mayan city his archaeological team was excavating. But what he saw was intact, not a city in ruins. And it was occupied. His brain said it couldn't be. The site had been deserted for over a thousand years. He trembled harder, and the spasms increased until he was shaking uncontrollably.

The man knelt down and steadied his shoulder with a strong grip.

"Come back to our world slowly, my brother," he said in a gentler tone. "You've been on a long journey."

Johnson's mind raced. *It's the powder, it must be the powder. It's a vision. It isn't real, just my imagination. It's just a vision.* Again he looked out over the plaza. Hundreds of faces looked back.

Turning toward the man beside him, Johnson searched for an

appropriate response. Weakly he whispered, "The gods favor us."

Quickly the man stood up and raised his arms, holding them outstretched over the plaza, and shouted in a booming voice, "The gods favor us!"

The crowd roared back. "The gods favor us! The gods favor us!"

The man looked again at Johnson and smiled. "We go to fight tomorrow and the gods are on our side. It will be a glorious day!"

Johnson forced a smile as he took closer note of his surroundings. He was obviously engaged in some type of ceremony, but what? On the pyramid behind him was a small temple with three entry doors. Three men were with him. Two were dressed in jaguar-skin capes, fine-spun cloth shorts, soft animal-skin sandals with sides rising to their calves, and wrist cuffs matching their capes. Bare-chested, they were arrayed with heavy, gem-encrusted breastplates overlaid with heavy jade jewelry. Their heads supported ornate headpieces richly adorned with bright multi-colored bird feathers. The third man was standing at the temple door with his arms folded in front of him. He was dressed in a robe of fine white cloth adorned with only a simple neck ring consisting of jade stones and a smaller headdress. Images of warriors and a priest flashed through Johnson's mind.

Then he noticed that the wrist cuffs he was wearing were made of jaguar fur. Looking down, he saw that he was dressed the same as the men standing above him. He felt the weight of the string of jade stones around his neck. Fingering them, he noticed the large tattoos adorning his arms. They were inked with brilliant geometric designs and his arms were muscular, thick and strong, too strong. Something was seriously wrong. His chest tightened and his body constricted as he felt himself unable to breathe.

It's not possible, vision or not, it's not physically possible. It was then he realized he was not in his own body. He was another person, just like the one on the pyramid who was now screaming to the crowd below enticing them to scream back, "We're going to reclaim our honor! We're going to reclaim our honor, over and over

Then he noticed the two young women, one sitting on each side of the stairs just below the landing. The one to his right moved closer to him, her large brown eyes stared inquisitively at him. She was lovely, a vision of pure beauty. Long jet-black hair, large almond-shaped eyes sparkling in the torchlight, full lips formed like a heart. She wore only a loin cloth and was covered with gold dust. Only her brown eyes, black hair and the brown nipples of her breasts shown through. The effect took his breath away. There was a purity that seemed to radiate from her.

More than a child, she was the budding essence of the transition to womanhood. She was gorgeous. Never in his life had he seen a more beautiful woman. She was leaning over the landing and staring intently into his eyes, searching.

A look of desperation came over her face. "Lightning Sky, what did the gods say about us?" she whispered cautiously under the noise of the shouting man above.

Johnson just stared back feebly. It was too much. His mind raced desperately. *What's happening?* He had to be in some type of ceremony. *Is she a priestess?* Everything started to spin, and darkness slowly enveloped him as he was transfixed on the girl.

A scared look came over her face and the last thing he heard was, "Will the gods bless us, Lightning Sky? Will they bless our love?"

Chapter 2

The artifacts were displayed on the table, remnants of the ancient culture they were studying. Students from the University of Wisconsin were excavating the archaeological site of Yaxchilan, Mexico, a Maya classical city. The site was considered to be a premier example of a city that was occupied at the height of the Maya civilization, just before its catastrophic collapse during the Ninth Century.

Tonight, Dr. Alan Johnson, the expedition leader and head of the Department of Archaeology from the University of Wisconsin, would hold a review session to discuss the artifacts and their function and importance in the ancient society. He touted the session as informal, but the students knew that the quality of their responses would be noted. An endorsement from Dr. Johnson at the end of their coursework could mean the difference in the direction of their careers. He was considered the leading expert of the Maya in the United States and possibly the world.

The artifacts consisted of a kit for a blood-sacrifice ceremony, four bowls with scene paintings including glyphs, a little stone box containing jade jewelry, an ornamental breastplate, a headpiece with an animal skull and inlaid jade, two ornamental obsidian knives, and a little jar of powder.

The team had arrived a little over a week ago. Almost immediately it seemed they had uncovered a major find—a cache of offerings dedicating a king's throne room placed in a hidden chamber beneath the king's bench, a stone platform in the palace where the king sat when in royal session. They knew it was a royal chamber in the temple from paintings on ceremonial bowls found during previous excavations. The paintings depicted the king in audience receiving gifts from dignitaries of other cities and various people in attendance. The king always sat on a raised bench.

The Maya were known to make ceremonial dedications to building structures, such as new rooms, or perhaps the addition of an upper level of a building. Dr. Johnson thought they might have done the same in the throne room. Starting here proved to be a good decision. Almost immediately they found a dedication offering under the king's bench. Over the next week painstakingly slow work was done to extract it properly so no damage would be done. They had taken an additional two days to clean the artifacts to the extent a field team could.

§

That evening the students were sitting around the table admiring the displayed items. They were all graduate students in archaeology. For almost a week there had been many discussions about the relevance of their find.

It was a competitive group. The students considered themselves to be fortunate to be studying on an excavation lead by Dr. Johnson. Considered a gifted scientist and theorist, his discoveries and publications on the classical Maya culture was held in the highest regard in the archaeological community. He had received his doctoral degree at age twenty-two, and ten years later, with three books to his credit and eight field expeditions, he was the youngest department head at the University of Wisconsin.

During tonight's session they were going to place the artifacts into a real life context looking for a deeper understanding of the people who lived thirteen hundred years earlier. The students were psyched up for the session.

"What do you think is the most important piece?" mused Jim, as he looked over the artifacts on display.

"I think the jewelry, breastplate and headgear," said one of the girls. "We see these objects in the stone reliefs showing they were worn by the kings, but seeing it up close, holding it, and even putting some of them on really blows the mind."

"Obviously," another student offered. "I saw you put that jade necklace on. It looked like you took a liking to it."

"Sure did," she answered. "I can see why private collectors provide tomb robbers with a good living. I'd bet someone with a lot of money would pay a real price for that necklace."

"I think the bowls are the most important," said Phoebe Grant, a post-grad student working on her doctoral degree. She was specializing in deciphering Maya glyphs and was already considered an expert in her field. As a member of the team, she was interested in studying the glyph stairway leading to the 'Temple Major' with hopes of providing further decipherment.

"I'll bet the inscriptions on them will give us a lot of information. Two of them were showing ceremonies where the king was in session. I'm sure they were important events and sometimes those bowls give the names of the owners," Phoebe continued. "They were often made as special commemorations of an historic event."

"Something like souvenirs," the girl who admired the jewelry said.

"That's not a bad way of looking at it," Phoebe said, "and both of them have dates on them. I haven't deciphered them but they are real dates. That means we can pinpoint the time and administration during the period where we are digging."

"I thought you were an expert," said Bill. "Dates are straight forward, aren't they?"

"The bowls have been buried a long time. The glyphs are still encrusted, marring the figures. We're going to have to clean them in the lab if we expect to identify them accurately. The Maya had a number of ways of writing the same thing," Phoebe replied. "There is a lot of variation even in the same symbols."

§

"The question I put to you," stated Dr. Johnson to the team when they were assembled for their formal review, "is what do these artifacts tell us about Yaxchilan when it was inhabited? We are excavating to find out more about how the Maya lived. Placing our finds in the context of where we found them is very important. The site was inhabited from about 350 A.D. to 800 A.D. That's just where we have some records from the stone monuments. It was undoubtedly occupied for much longer. Still the question is, in what period are we working?"

"We found them in the palace under the king's bench. That's important, right Dr. Johnson?"

"Yes, Dan, but which king and when did he reign?"

"The palace was dedicated sometime after 700 A.D. I think," said Kim.

"That's a good start. You're getting closer. Now again, which king?" Johnson challenged. "There were three of them in the Eighth Century, all three were very important. They were the ones that ruled during the time when Yaxchilan was in the state of its greatest glory. At that time it would rival anything you would find in Egypt."

"This is getting more difficult," said Dan.

"Yes, it usually goes that way, but we aren't pot hunters just looking for artifacts. We need to extract everything we can to tell us about the society we are studying."

"So we are digging in the West Acropolis. We need to know when it was built, right?" asked Dan.

"Yes, now you are going in the right direction. The West Acropolis, where we are excavating, was built and expanded over a long period of time," explained Johnson, "at least fifty years, probably quite a bit longer. But if you look closely there were two buildings with a number of stele and lintels which provide us dates. One is obviously older than the other and was dedicated around 700 A.D. The other was around 750 A.D. Different kings ruled during those two periods. Our excavation and find was in context with the later building. And who was the king at that time?"

"That would be Bird Jaguar IV," said Kim.

"You've got it," said Johnson. "I think that this may be a dedication that the king Bird Jaguar IV may have made to the gods. It puts it at the height of the classical period, just before the civilization collapsed. During the classical period Yaxchilan was one of the most prosperous Maya cities. It is a prime example of the height of the Maya civilization before its downfall, which started around 800 A.D."

§

Later that evening, when the students went to their rooms to sleep, Dr. Johnson went back to the workroom where they kept the artifacts. He was holding a jar filled with powder found with the other artifacts when Phoebe Grant entered.

She had a brilliant mind but she didn't quite fit the model he envisioned as a field archaeologist. Long blond hair and big blue eyes reflected her Norwegian heritage. Slim and shapely with great legs, she was one of the few women on campus who habitually wore a skirt. It emphasized her legs. His male students fell all over themselves to be near her. She loved to flirt and was good at it. As he looked at her, he noted that at the excavation site her tight shorts and hiking boots still emphasized her legs.

When she turned her subtle charm on Johnson, he became uncomfortable and not sure how to react. She seemed to enjoy putting him in this position. He thought it was her feminine feline quality, something like a cat with a mouse, and she was toying with him. She was a student and he the professor, but she never let him forget he was a man and she a woman.

A couple of years prior they went out for a casual dinner one evening. It led to dating and eventually to a brief affair. They found they were socially compatible but not in love. Phoebe wanted more from a relationship, and he agreed she deserved it. They decided to break it off and maintain a professional relationship. Over time they became close friends.

"And what do you think is the most important artifact that we found Alan?" Phoebe said eyeing him coyly.

"Perhaps it's this," said Johnson as he held up the jar with the powder inside.

"What are you going to do with it?" asked Phoebe as she took the jar from him to examine it closer.

"I'm not sure," Johnson said while staring reflectively, deep in thought. When they dug it up, it was included with a blood sacrifice kit. It was part of the kit which included a bowl to catch the blood, the string with the stingray barbs used to draw the blood, the paper the blood was dripped onto before it was burned as an offering to the gods, and the little jar with the powder inside.

The ceremony was obviously painful. Stone reliefs indicated that when the queen sacrificed blood she drew the string with the barbs through her tongue. The king, on the other hand, pulled the string and barbs through the skin on his penis. No trace of drugs was ever found or referred to, but conventional thinking had always considered them to be there.

"It looks like it's still in good shape," he said as he looked wistfully at the jar in her hand.

"Yes it does, doesn't it?" she replied suddenly, watching him closer. "You've been staring at that jar all evening with a bit of a faraway look in your eyes. Something is working in you. What are you thinking?"

"What do you mean, Pheb? We dig them up, clean them up, study them and publish our findings."

"I mean the powder," she replied. "No one has ever found any before. You seem to be taking a strong interest it."

"Yes, it is something new isn't it?" he said as he held the jar up, eyeing it.

"You seem overly concerned with it. Every time I look at you, your eyes are on that powder. When you see me, you avert them, and you have been quiet all night like you are somewhere else."

"It is a curiosity," he replied, taking the jar and putting it on the table.

"And it's potentially dangerous," she replied beginning to get the idea.

"It's just a drug, Pheb. The Maya kings took it during ceremonies and we don't know about it adversely affecting them," he replied, a mechanical smile crossing over his face.

"Until this week we didn't even know they had some type of drug used in their ceremonies, and now you're considering it didn't affect them." She stood a little taller and looked him straight in the eye. "Alan, I know you. When I see that tight-lipped little smile you have and the gleam in your eyes, I know you're on the move and about one step ahead of the posse."

"Just think, Pheb," he said as he looked back at her with the hope of convincing her of his assumptions, "It was probably used to induce visions of their gods. The Maya culture had a thousand years of ceremonies before they even got to the point where this drug was used. Think of all the potions they must have experimented with to gain their visions. This isn't just a couple of herbs put together to dull the pain. It has to be the product of a millennium of evolution in the communication with their gods, the most important communication of their society. Just consider the possibilities of what we have here."

She stared at him. He was giddy, like a young school boy who had just caught a frog. It was precious, something special. He looked like he wanted to shout, "Look, see what I've got," knowing it was not likely to be his for long.

Normally he looked every bit the professor on an expedition, serious and conservative. Medium in height and build, he wore the proverbial felt explorer's homburg to cover his flyaway brown hair, a button-down khaki shirt, cargo shorts and ankle high boots. When he was intent on something, his deep brown eyes shone with curiosity, introducing an intellect that needed to be fed, and he had an enchanting shy smile she loved when she flirted or teased him.

"You want to take it, don't you?" she asked as she picked up the jar, removed the stopper and peered inside. "You found a thousand-year-old drug and you want to try it."

"The thought has come to mind."

"It could be dangerous. It should be analyzed in a lab to find out what is in there."

"And it will be sequestered by the university and destroyed or put on a shelf for eternity unless some enterprising graduate student, looking for a quick trip, stumbles across it and figures out he or she can get high on it."

"You're really going to do it, aren't you?" she asked as she put the bottle back on the table and sat down in a chair. "You're going to try it."

"Phoebe, look at it as a scientific experiment. I'm a scientist. Perhaps I owe it to the archaeological community to do the research and bring the results to them for their consideration."

"Experiment hell, Alan, you're just looking for an excuse to get high. I may be one of your students but don't pull that scientific crap with me. I don't buy it."

"Okay, we'll do it in context. The old ways are still practiced by the present-day Maya in this area alongside of the Christian religion. We'll talk to the old man, the shaman who lives by himself along the river a couple of miles south. The people claim he is one of the ancient ones. Let's approach him about how to do it the right way, the way it would have been done by a Maya king during a ceremony. If he can put it in context, would that make you happy?"

"No, but knowing you, what else can I do?"

"You can carry the body back home."

Chapter 3

Dawn would be breaking soon. The birds were singing, making more of a racket than usual, Johnson thought as he awoke. The singing of the birds woke him every morning and often he was unable to get back to sleep. He'd lie there a few more minutes cherishing the solitude before getting up and facing the new day. Almost dozing, he was abruptly jarred back by the roar of a howler monkey, followed by another and another. The troop was on the move, announcing their presence to the world as they sought their morning meal. *They sure are close this morning,* he thought. *The students would probably be getting up to watch them.*

As the morning light crept in, Johnson could see the room he was in. He started to shake again as he tried to hold back his fear. He wasn't in his room at the lodge in the little pueblo in Frontera Corozol where the team stayed. In the gloom he could see the outlines of a narrow room a few feet wide. The walls were made of stone blocks. It had an open doorway, no windows and a ceiling that was highly arched to a sharp point. He recognized it as a sleeping room, a room in a Maya palace. But it couldn't be.

His guts tightened pulling at every muscle in his body as a

termer ran through him. The paralyzing fear was returning. He shouldn't be here. He should be back at the camp getting ready to organize the day's work for the students. He stared at the open doorway. It was the only way out. He felt trapped in the room. Maybe he was still here in the past. What if that wasn't a dream last night. It had to be a dream caused by the powder. It was the effect of the powder. Yes, the old shaman had blown the powder up his nose, and he had a vision of being in the past as part of an ancient ceremony. But why was he here now in this stone building with the narrow room like the ones built by the ancient Maya?

"Time to wake up," the old woman said as she came through the door. "You've got to get ready. Shield Jaguar won't wait for you, and your old mother will get whipped for not taking proper care of you."

"Ready for what?" Johnson asked as he shrank back against a wall staring at the woman who entered the room. She didn't look dangerous, an old woman wearing a simple cloth shift and sandals. She apparently knew him. Her manner was familiar and friendly, but if she'd knew for sure he wasn't the man who was supposed to be here, what would happen then?

"You're going this time," she said as a big smile crossed her face. "Today you go to fight those monkey-fornicating heathens who captured your brother three years ago, and tortured and sacrificed him at their mid-period ceremony."

"I'm what?" Johnson asked as he braced himself against the wall like he could push back through it.

"You are going with the warriors this time. Your brother Shield Jaguar insists."

"What?" Johnson said, trying to get a grasp of what was happening.

"He says it's time for you to be a man. Even a scholar needs to know how to fight."

"Going to fight?" Johnson cautiously replied following the drift of the conversation. "I can't do that." He had never been in a fight in his life.

"Say no to the king's brother? No one says no to Shield Jaguar except the king."

"And he can say no?"

"Silly boy, the words from the king's lips are law. Even your brother has to listen to him. He doesn't like it but he does it."

"Really," Johnson said transfixed as he watched the woman walk around him to the back of the room and pick up clothes laying there. She was obviously familiar with their relationship or perhaps it was a process she was following.

"Now stand and let me dress you," she said as she came over and laid the clothes next to him on the sleeping platform. "A warrior is always dressed by his woman before going into battle."

"And you're my woman?" Johnson asked, amazed she didn't know he was an imposter.

"Silly boy, you tease me this morning," said the old woman kindly. "I'm your old mother, the woman who has taken care of you since you were a child. Your birth mother was too busy being a royal lady, so I'm your mother. It gives meaning to my life."

Over simple brown cotton shorts she placed a shirt tunic of jaguar fur held at the bottom by a belt with a narrow, ornate celt hanging down in front of his legs. Next were jade jewelry cuffs and a jade stone necklace. A skull made of jade hung from a leather band around his neck reaching to his waist. On his feet she placed soft sandals with high backs tied at the calf. On his head she placed a headdress made of a jaguar head with jewels for eyes and adorned with a jade neck band.

Johnson stood there silently trying to compose himself as she dressed him. Curiosity started to set in as his thoughts went to the reliefs, the stone pictures of the Maya kings that survived over millenniums. As she placed each piece on him, he became more awed. He was obviously dressed in a ceremonial fashion reserved for royalty, dressed as a warrior. Only a royal personage was allowed to wear jaguar skins. He smiled at the thought. *.If my colleagues back at the university could see me now.* He wished he had a mirror to be able to see what he looked like; better yet a camera.

"Come now," she said as she handed him his spear, also adorned with jaguar fur and jade. She tied the war club with inlaid obsidian blades to his belt. "They are waiting for you."

"No cape?" he asked as he saw the jaguar-skin cape and another more ornate headdress still on the sleeping mat.

"Now I know you are teasing me this morning. You know they are for the ceremony when you come back with your prisoners and present them to the king."

She put her hand on his arm and looked gently into his eyes. "Don't worry my son, Shield Jaguar will make sure nothing happens to you, not on your first raid," she whispered as she turned and walked out the door.

Johnson watched her go. *Now what? She doesn't seem to think there is anything wrong with me. That's is a good sign.* Johnson looked at the doorway. What was on the other side? His stomach tightened again as new fear started to grip him, but he resisted it. He looked at his clothes again and his heart started to pound. He looked out the door, his portal into the past. His fear was mixed with anticipation. During his entire career he had led archaeological expeditions into the jungles only to wonder and speculate what it would be like to be part of the ancient Maya society. And now he was about to find out. He had only to walk through the doorway.

There were white spots before his eyes as he stepped out of the dark room into the sunlight. He squinted, trying to adjust his eyes to the light. As he focused, he found himself to be in a courtyard surrounded by a long, low building. On one side of the courtyard, the building was elevated and a long porch-like platform ran in front of it. In a back corner of the courtyard, fires were burning on small stone hearths and women were cooking. Standing in front of him, backlit by the early morning sun, was a fuzzy looking group of men surrounded by a white halo.

Looking hard, his eyes cleared and twenty young men, all carrying spears, materialized. On their heads were large headpieces in the form of fearsome monsters. Numerous people, bearing a cautious demeanor, stood around the edges of the courtyard watching the men. The women held their children to keep them from approaching. Johnson slowly looked around trying to take everything in. The men were clad in loin cloths and sandals. Each carried a large square shield and two spears, one short and one long. Hanging from their belts were war clubs with inset obsidian blades. Their gruesome headgear of monsters looked down on him.

A gang of wild primitives, heartless killers without conscience, their faces, dark and foreboding, were covered with tattoos and painted streaks, and symbols, all of which added to their ferocity.

Johnson stood there, feet frozen in place, his whole body trembling again. *They'll undoubtedly kill me if they find out,* he thought as he tried to control his fear. *They will find out I am not the man they know and they will kill me. What am I supposed to do? I can't just stand here.*

In front of the group were two men, lavishly attired. One was the man from the ceremony on the pyramid from the night before. He appeared to be the leader. Standing there he was an imposing figure wearing a fitted leopard skin tunic with lots of jade, wrist bands, a large jade stone necklace and an ornate headdress consisting of a decorated jaguar head. Half of his face was blue and the other half white. When he opened his mouth his teeth were filed into points or squared and inlaid with bits of jade. His dark eyes sparkled as he saw Johnson emerge from the doorway and he beamed a broad smile.

"Come along little brother," he said in a booming voice, "it's time to make you a man."

Johnson stood fast and just stared. He needed to take it all in. *What is this guy talking about? The man who says he is my brother says "They are going to make a man out of me," and the old woman talked of a raid. This looks like an American Plains Indian war party. It doesn't look good. I am supposed to be a scientist, removed and observing. That's the way it's supposed to work. This doesn't look like it fits the criteria for field observation.*

Make me a man? Johnson stood there, trying to think. The 'making of a man' was normally signified by a rite of passage involving pain. Fear ran up his back as his shoulders and stomach tightened harder. He wanted to run—anywhere. *I shouldn't be here. It's a mistake.*

"Hurry up Lightning Sky," said the other man, standing next to the leader. "You look like a girl saying no when you want to say yes. It's time to lose your boyhood, taste some blood and become a man."

Johnson stared blankly at him. He was obviously a companion to the leader. His status appeared lower because he wore a simpler tunic of jaguar-skin fur and the headdress of a monster from Xibalba. It looked somewhat like a crocodile. There was a palm print on one side of his face and streaks on the other.

Johnson remained motionless trying to fathom everything. Standing in front of him appeared to be a Maya war party. During her prattle, the old woman mentioned to him it would be led by Shield Jaguar. But which one? Johnson knew of three Shield Jaguars from classical Maya times. They were all recorded by history to be great kings. The old woman said that this one's brother was the king. That didn't compute. He knew the royal line as a linear line with alternating generations being lead by kings named Shield Jaguar. The order was father/son, father/son.

Brother didn't fit in.

"Lightning Sky," the leader said as he stepped up to him, "you sleep too long. We are ready to leave. Today is the day we've been waiting for."

Johnson, unable to believe what he was seeing, just stood and stared at the leader. For years he had seen the stone reliefs with the Maya kings wearing their beautiful costumes and the murals depicting Maya warriors in jaguar skin and lavish monster helmets. Here was a noble Maya warrior, obviously from the royal line, standing in front of him. The effect stunned him. He could never have imagined the immense presence radiating from the man. He exuded an awesome power, a power over life and death.

Johnson shivered as he took in the scene. He knew every eye in the courtyard was on him. He could feel them. *They know, they all know I am an imposter.* He stood there glued to the spot still unable to move. *What am I to do? What is expected of me? What if I do something wrong?*

The fierce warrior smiled with his wide grin, stepped forward and took Johnson's arm grasping it tight with a grip like iron just below the elbow. Johnson responded with the same embrace, obviously a greeting.

"Come," Shield Jaguar said. "We're late. We must go to the temple to make an offering to the gods asking them to come with us and lead us to a glorious victory. Then we are off to the canoes. The gods are on our side now. It's time to pay those ass-sniffing dogs back." He turned to walk away motioning Johnson beside him. The other lavishly dressed man walked on the other side of the leader. Johnson hurried to catch up. The group of men with the fearsome headgear fell in behind them. People in the courtyard hurried out of their way and lowered their heads and averted their eyes as the warriors passed.

§

"Oh my God," gasped Johnson as he turned to follow the warrior. He was on the side of a hill and the ceremonial center lay below him. He had only seen the shadows of it the night before. The Great Plaza stretched away from them with rows of pyramids and temples strung out along it. From the hilltop palace he could see the whole complex. The great masses of people participating in the ceremony from the previous night were gone. It was early morning but it appeared to be quickly filling.

Dozens of men were sweeping the plaza of debris; leaves the jungle trees dropped continually dropped. People were going up and down from the temples while white-robed priests and their assistants stood at the landings to greet the entrants. Two new temples were under construction. Scores of men were working, carrying stone blocks and making plaster for the walls. Others were doing the building. There was a market at one edge of the complex and vendors were already selling their wares. A stream of people appeared to be coming and going. It was a busy place.

As Shield Jaguar and his warriors entered the Great Plaza, a horn sounded three times from atop a pyramid to alert everyone that a member of the royal family was entering the center. Everyone stopped what they were doing to watch them. As the group passed, the people moved back making way and lowered their heads.

"Come along Lightning Sky," the warrior commanded as he walked briskly forward. "What's the matter with you? We've been looking forward to this day, your first battle." As they walked along, the warriors took up two long rows behind them trailing in formation.

"It's amazing," Johnson said as he came alongside the warrior. His head was swiveling back and forth trying to take everything in at once. The temples terraced on the hill along the edge of the plaza were beautiful, works of art by the best artisans the society had to offer.

"Yes it is amazing," confirmed the warrior. "The day has finally come for you to become a warrior. You can't study forever. Learning and building temples is good but fighting is better. Glory is in the battle."

"The battle?" Johnson murmured.

"Men of courage make war. Today you join my brother and me as a warrior. It is a good day."

They walked along the Great Plaza to a row of temples at the opposite end. Johnson had seen artists' renderings of what temples were supposed to have looked like when they were originally built but they weren't even close. Each was a distinctive work of art. The detail in the carvings, the composition, the color, it all came together in a symmetric beauty. They were exquisite beyond comparison.

The group came to the end of the plaza and stopped in front of a temple.

"My mother's temple," Shield Jaguar said as the three started up the steps. "Stopping here will undoubtedly get the palace riled up."

"You think so?" Johnson stated noncommittally.

"Of course. My brother the king wants petitions to the gods made in the memory of Lady Eveningstar, his mother, in her new temple. He says she needs to receive her due. But I make mine in my mother's temple."

My god, thought Johnson quickly deciphering his location. This was Temple 11 dedicated to Lady Sak B'iyaan, third wife of the great Shield Jaguar II from the early Eighth Century. He had built this temple and dedicated it to her. She was a very young wife when he was an old man. Archaeology made little mention of Lady Sak B'iyaan. Her place in history was overshadowed by a rivalry between the great king's other two wives, a rivalry straddling decades and generating intense speculation by the archaeologists on their respective places in history.

Johnson looked to the opposite side of the plaza at the other temples dedicated to the great king's other wives. On the adjacent terrace was Temple 23 built in honor of the king's primary wife, Lady K'ab'al Xook, a wife from a prominent aristocratic family of Yaxchilan. Two structures away was Temple 21, the temple dedicated to Lady Ik' Skull normally referred to as Lady Eveningstar. She was the great Shield Jaguar II's second wife,from Calakmul, who bore him the child, Bird Jaguar IV, his eventual successor.

The archaeological community theorized that there had been a rivalry between the two women and a conflict ensued over the lineage and succession of the royal blood line when the great Shield Jaguar II died. The conflict had blocked his son Bird Jaguar IV's ascension to kingship for ten years.

As the three young men continued up the stairs, Shield Jaguar's personal guard of warriors took up positions in front of the pyramid. No one would enter it while Shield Jaguar was there.

When they neared the top of the stairs the Maya leader said, "We need to call the gods to come with us and give you a great battle. Then you can come home and sing about it to let the people know what a great warrior you are."

Johnson looked at the other man, seemingly hearing him for the first time. *Warrior, he keeps talking about me becoming a warrior and the gods are coming with us to a battle.* Johnson looked behind him. Twenty men with spears, war clubs and shields were standing at the bottom of the stairs watching them. His knees started to tremble again, his step faltering. *This can't be happening.* He was with a war party that was going to attack an enemy. He had never been in a fight in his life, not even a verbal confrontation. *I can't go into a battle. No, never. I'd be killed in an instant.*

The warrior noted his hesitation. "Come, let's go. The gods are waiting for their blood. Last night in the ceremony the gods told you they favor us. It will be a great battle."

Entering the temple, Johnson noted a change in the warrior leader. His arrogance diminished, his haughty air faded, his position no longer appeared threatening. The gods held the power here and they were fickle. They wanted their due. In this case a blood offering was required to call them and still they might play tricks. A man must always be reverent, even a king, or his brother.

Johnson watched Shield Jaguar, who was obviously royalty, as he conversed with the temple priest. He looked around at the temple they were in. He knew it as Temple 11 built by Shield Jaguar II, so it had to be after 700 A.D., and Temple 21 across the plaza seemed to be complete. It was built by Bird Jaguar IV for his mother when he was king, so it had to be after 750 A.D. He had a son who was known to have changed his name to Shield Jaguar after he became king. Could this man be him?

But Johnson was confused. This man called the king his brother, yet the archaeological interpretation considered Shield Jaguar to be the son of the king Bird Jaguar. The son was supposedly only sixteen when Bird Jaguar died. This man was almost double that, and he said this was his mother's temple.

Then it hit him. This had to be Shield Jaguar III who would be the next king. The archaeologists had the genealogical kingship succession wrong. This man had to be the present king's half brother born to the old great king's third and very young wife.

Johnson's head whirled in thought. *I have the answer.* The implication stunned him. *The archaeological records must have been interpreted wrong. The time period had to be after 750 A.D. when Bird Jaguar the current king ascended to the throne. This meant he was back in time at exactly the height of the splendor of the Maya civilization, just before its catastrophic collapse. And this man talking to the priest would eventually reign during a turn of events resulting in the collapse of their civilization.*

Johnson, and the other warrior who was dressed like he was, stood behind Shield Jaguar watching the priest and the warrior as the ceremony started. Facing the altar, the priest chanted to the statues of the gods seated there. Turning, while holding a small bowl and knife, he came forward to Shield Jaguar.

After chanting again to call the gods to their presence, the priest picked up the obsidian knife. Shield Jaguar held his arm out and the priest cut the top of his arm, inflicting a small wound, enough to bleed lightly. The gods required an offering of blood; it didn't have to be a lot. Blood was the essence of life and they demanded it as the only sacrifice. The priest held the sacred paper as they turned his arm so the blood could drop onto it.

He then turned back to the altar where a small fire was burning. He placed the blood splattered paper into it, watched it burn to a cinder and chanted words petitioning the spirits of the gods into their presence to accompany the war party and ensure their victory.

§

When they left the temple a second group of men were waiting in the plaza in front of Lady Eveningstar's temple. Johnson surveyed them. They were dressed the same as the group he was in: breechcloths topped by padded vests, solid sandals and the wonderfully garish headpieces of monsters.

"Where's my brother, the king?" Shield Jaguar called as they approached.

"In the temple of his mother calling upon the gods to provide us with good fortune," one of the men said.

As they waited, Johnson looked intently over the plaza, the stepped terraces with the temples, the pyramids, the acropolis toward the end in the distance. People were everywhere but they made wide berth for these men. They appeared to have a special status within this society. As he looked up at the temple, admiring the frescoed and painted murals, three men came out of the temple. One obviously was the leader, the jaguar skin, jade jewelry and helmet the most ornate of all of them. He was followed closely by two men carrying spears who looked like guards.

"Ready brother?" Shield Jaguar called as the other man came down the stairs.

"The gods bless us," said the other man as he approached. Everyone bowed their heads in respect when he stopped. *The king,* Johnson thought. *This must be Bird Jaguar IV, one of the most controversial men in Maya history. He came out of Temple 21, known as Lady Eveningstar's temple, the one he built in honor of his mother.*

"The seer cast the bones and he says the raid will be good."

"Did he use the bones of a young chicken this time?" Shield Jaguar asked. "That old priest doesn't give you the proper reverence. He buys old chickens from his brother-in-law. You should make an example of him."

"Have him beaten perhaps." the king said.

"No", spat Shield Jaguar, "kill him. Do it on a feast day to let the other priests know that they will not tamper with the benevolence of the gods."

The king smiled and said nothing. The discussion ended. He held up his hand, a horn sounded three times and the king started walking away, two guards off to both sides of him.

"To the canoes", the king called as the procession formed. Shield Jaguar took a place beside him and the one they called Smoking Squirrel followed. The clothes Johnson was wearing were much the same as Smoking Squirrel's so he took a place beside him. So far no one seemed to notice a difference.

Johnson scanned back and forth. This couldn't be happening. Here he was in Yaxchilan, at the height of the city's glory, somewhere around 752 A.D. and he was part of a party of warriors that appeared to be going off on a raid.

The crowd split apart as the group of men approached and people bowed their heads. This was royalty; the king and his brother. The king was a deity and his brother was placed by the common man into the same category.

There were canoes at the river, along with another large party of men. Johnson looked around. The king and his brother each had around twenty men who must be their personal guard, and another eighty or so were waiting for them. Twelve large canoes were ready, each holding ten men.

They launched the canoes and paddled up river. In the lead were two canoes, the king's and Shield Jaguar's. The other ten followed closely behind.

§

The two men watched the canoes as they paddled up the river. They didn't say anything until the boats were nearly out of sight.

"There goes Shield Jaguar and the king," Lord Great Skull said to his eldest son with disdain. "They are off to raid the Piedras Negras river outpost."

"So," the young man mused, "they are always going on a raid somewhere. They love making raids."

"But this time there is supposed to be a high lord from Piedras Negras there."

"What? How do you know that?" The young man looked up at his father inquisitively. He was full of surprises. He had spies all over the kingdom and always seemed to know things before anyone else.

"I heard that the Baah Sajal Tiloom, the ruler of La Pasadita, gave Shield Jaguar the information that T'ul Chiik, a high-ranking lord would be at the outpost tomorrow or the next day. I believe he has the Sajal as a supporter now."

"How did he manage that?" asked the young man. He looked at his father and admired the richness of the great lord's attire and his badges of office. Someday he'd be a lord too. He was of the appropriate bloodline, the first son of a noble family, and his father was the chief counselor to the king. People feared him now the same as they did his father and he liked it.

"He's quietly making bargains," Lord Great Skull replied. "I don't know what he promised the Baah Sajal but you can bet it was a stiff price. The gall of the man, attempting to snatch Lord T'ul Chiik of Piedras Negras out from under their noses. It is likely to start a war again."

"Did the king approve?" asked his son.

"Shield Jaguar told him he was going, and asked if the king wanted to come along."

"What? He can get away with that, telling the king he is going and asking if he wants to come along?" the younger man asked in amazement.

"He thinks he can and I tend to agree with him."

"What? He's the king. No one talks to the king that way."

"Son, the king is just a man, a man in a very powerful position, and Shield Jaguar is blood. The king listens to him, especially when counseling of war."

"Shield Jaguar is becoming a problem isn't he?" the young man asked, as he looked for confirmation from his father. He was a teen now and his father was teaching him the basics of politics.

"More than I would have thought," replied the Great Lord, eyeing his son closely. He had seldom discussed Shield Jaguar with his son before, but the young man was developing a good sense for people and he learned quickly. Being a young man of rank and privilege, he was sought out by others. He had learned early on how to manipulate them to his advantage.

"Yes, I think he may become a problem," the great lord mused. "He has ambition. He never lets anyone forget that he is the son of Shield Jaguar II, the same as the king is. He wants the throne and his brother the king is weak."

"But the king wants his son, your sister's child, Chel-Te', to succeed him," the young man replied. "This is his wish."

"When the king is gone, anything can happen. Shield Jaguar knows that," claimed the great lord. "His birthright and the power of his position as half brother to the king lend credibility to his claim. He is making strong political connections."

"So what will that do for him?" asked the younger man.

"He might be in a position to resist Chel-Te's claim when the king dies. He leads the Eagle Warriors and now this alignment with the Baah Sajal of La Pasadita—he's a good one to have on your side—and I've also heard Shield Jaguar is a friend of Chan Muwaan the prince of Bonampak, too."

"How can anyone be Chan Muwaan's friend?" the young man gasped. "He's the most arrogant monkey's ass I ever met."

"And also one of the most powerful ones," replied his father. "He may well be a king some day and he's a fighter like Shield Jaguar, fearless, and he has an attitude of no backing away from anything. They would make quite a team."

"You can't be serious; those two?"

"Stranger things have happened."

"What are you going to do?" his son asked.

"I'm not sure, but whatever I do I won't advertise it. It's best not to let others know your plans," Lord Great Skull said as he watched the canoes disappear from sight. "It is something the Shield Jaguar may have to learn the hard way. But I think they know he is coming."

The young man looked up with surprise. Many times his father didn't explain how to accomplish his goals, but left an example for him to wrestle with. Slowly he formulated his response, almost daring not to mouth it.

"You mean they might catch him?"

"Perhaps; captives are taken all the time," the great lord laughed. "Perhaps the hunter will become the prey this time."

The young man stood silent and thoughtful for a moment as he looked closely at his father. "With Shield Jaguar gone," he speculated cautiously, "Chel-Te', your sister's son, will be guaranteed the throne."

"Yes, and we will be the first noble family," the great lord replied as he watched his son and motioned with his hand for him to continue.

"And then if something happens to Chel-Te'...," the young man thought aloud.

Lord Great Skull smiled to himself as he looked at his son. He had a lot to learn about politics and eliminating his enemies, but he had a devious mind and ambition. He'd go far.

"Then as the chief regent, with control of the warriors, I would become the king," Lord Great Skull Zero said as he completed the thought. "Who could stop me?"

Chapter 4

It was near sundown when the canoes stopped. They had been paddling upriver most of the day. Under other circumstances it would have been a pleasant trip. Johnson had felt the tenseness of the men increase as the day progressed and they came closer to their objective. He tried to act the same as they did by doing his share of the rowing. Fear gripped him throughout the day. They were sure to notice.

He maintained a low profile and was amazed they didn't see anything different about him. He was just their companion Lightning Sky, a little quiet they mentioned, but just Lightning Sky. As the day progressed, Johnson started to feel more secure in his position. If he kept quiet, perhaps they wouldn't notice. The warriors talked and joked as they paddled tirelessly together.

Men the world over always talk about the same thing—how tough they are and their sexual prowess. They looked tough, and to Johnson, talked tough. They recounted past battles, the men they had killed, and who was the fiercest. It appeared all were veterans. Bets were placed between individual warriors on who would do better in the upcoming battle.

Their talk about women indicated that chastity was generally expected of a woman of noble blood, but it was significantly different for a common woman. Men of noble birth could pretty much travel the countryside and take what they wanted from the common women, but among their own class care was supposed to be taken. A noble woman was to be a virgin when she came to her husband's bed. If she wasn't, by convention the husband could nullify the marriage.

Listening, he found the rules seemed to be, *just don't get caught*. The younger generation considered it a private matter whether a noble woman was a virgin or not on her wedding night and it was not usually a point of consideration. They had found a practical solution to an age-old problem.

For the first hour Johnson had noticed a stream of people, often carrying bundles, walking along the path by the riverbank. The boat traffic on the river was constant. Numerous small dugouts carrying people or goods were constantly in sight. Larger canoes piled high with produce were frequent. The Usumacinta River was a water highway, an easy way to transport people and wares from one place to another. It enabled a lively commerce. Tolls were charged by the cities along its path, providing lucrative funds or resources. The more toll stations a city could command the wealthier it became. Wars were waged regularly between cities competing for control of the trade. Yaxchilan and Piedras Negras had been fighting over it for four hundred years.

"We'll stay here tonight and leave before dawn," the king told the men as they pulled up to shore. "It's just a short march to the outpost." There would be no fires tonight, nothing to alert the enemy they were there. They made a hurried camp. The king's servants erected a shelter for him then broke out the food they had brought along—a simple dinner of corn meal, tortilla-type corn bread, and chilies washed down with water.

"Scared, little brother?" Shield Jaguar asked as he came down by the water where Johnson had found a spot a little away from the group and sat down on the log next to him. He began eating his food.

"No," Johnson lied. "I'll be ready." Inside he was quaking. He was beginning to understand the nature of their undertaking. It seemed unreal, but these men were going on a raid. It was actually happening. People were going to get hurt, perhaps killed. Johnson knew nothing of fighting. He was sure it wasn't something he could bluff his way through. There was no place to run and Shield Jaguar assured them during the trip that he would personally run a spear through any man who so much as took a step backward.

"You will do okay," replied Shield Jaguar. "Anyway, my Eagle Warriors will watch out for you. They are the best. I can't have you getting captured on your first raid. That old woman who calls herself your mother would skin me alive."

"She does have her way, doesn't she?" Johnson replied trying to stay vague.

"I don't know why you keep her around. Her sharp tongue and arrogant attitude is going to cause her to lose her life one day. She'll piss someone off and get whipped to death. I'm sure of it. You could have a number of younger, prettier women minister to you."

"And lose a supporter who will stand up to you?" Johnson said as he watched the man closely to calculate his response. Shield Jaguar looked a little surprised. Maybe he had stepped too far.

"Best keep her on a leash if you like her," he commanded. "I know at least five men who would kill her in a second thinking they would be gaining your favor."

Johnson laughed lightly and nodded as he waited to see how the conversation would unfold.

The other man who appeared to be the companion to Shield Jaguar came with his food and sat down near them.

"It's a fine evening," he said. "The gods favor us."

"Smoking Squirrel, the gods always favor you. That's why I keep you around," Shield Jaguar said.

"We'll be lucky if we capture the lord tomorrow and get away with our heads," replied Smoking Squirrel. "They are sure to be chasing after us with many warriors."

"That's the sport of it, capturing him and getting away. What fun would it be if there wasn't a little challenge to it?"

"Your brother the king will claim the right to capture the prisoner for himself," said Smoking Squirrel.

"He can try, but I might just get there first."

"But he's the king."

"And I'm his brother. We're both sons of the same father. I have a claim to the throne too. If I catch the prisoner, I will show off at the celebration and my brother can claim him and torture him later. During the celebration of his capture, the people will know who caught him."

"It amazes me how you get away with it."

"It's balls, Smoking Squirrel," said Shield Jaguar. "You have to have the balls of a jaguar for it."

"Aren't you worried that Lord Great Skull will raise the issue if you bring back the captive, even if the king would let you? Great Skull is the king's chief counselor. He's a shrewd man and he has the king's support in whatever he does."

"We must stand up to Great Skull," spat Shield Jaguar. "He's not the king and he's not of the royal family. It's about time he learns his place."

"He has the king's ear. His sister is the king's wife and she has bore the king a son."

"When the king dies, and he will, we will take care of Lord Great Skull," Shield Jaguar replied. "Right now it's the three of us against him. We need to be known as a powerful force, one to be reckoned with if we can ever stand up to him and have the support of the nobles."

"When the king dies the lord will try to stop you," replied Smoking Squirrel. "It's said he stood against the Xook family and swung the balance of power to make your brother king. That's quite an obligation your brother has to him. And he's pushing for Chel-Te', his nephew, to become the next king."

"Yes, but marrying Great Skull's sister was a smart move for my brother. When she had the baby, it brought the lord to my brother's side. He will do everything in his power to make Chel-Te' the next king."

Shield Jaguar sat in thoughtful contemplation. His face turned hard as he considered his words. "Right now he is an adversary, and he is a strong man, both politically and personally. In the future, when the king dies, that will change. He'll have to face me and it will be on my terms. I promise you, one day he will bow down before me."

Shield Jaguar became more intent. "The gods willing, tomorrow we get our opportunity to show the nobles our strength. "I need to take the captive; he's very high ranking. Lord T'ul Chiik will be traveling on his way to La Mara. I want him. I want the king of Yo'k'ib in Piedras Negras to know we don't like being under his thumb and we are going to do something about it."

"Does the king, Bird Jaguar, know your plans?" Smoking Squirrel asked.

"No, he doesn't know," Shield Jaguar laughed. "He thinks it's a raid to punish them for taking too much tariff on the river."

"He might not be too happy when he finds what you are up to this time."

"By the balls of the god Chalk, no, he won't be happy."

"But he's the king," Smoking Squirrel gasped.

"He's my brother and he wears a crown, that's all."

"But his word is law. Yaxchilan is allied with them. He went to Yo'k'ib for Yo'nal Ahk's coronation ceremony."

"He was summoned to it as a vassal. My father never would have gone."

"What will the king do?" asked Smoking Squirrel.

"If we get Lord T'ul Chiik as a captive he'll be happy."

"Yo'nal 'Ahk, their king, will be mad. He'll demand the captive back. Will Bird Jaguar stand up to him?"

"What choice will he have?" Shield Jaguar laughed "Really, what choice will he have?" and he laughed again.

Johnson sat and stared at them. *Yo'k'ib,* he thought. *What city is Yo'k'ib?* It sounded familiar. He ran through the sites in his memory. There were numerous cities in the area whose names were not known. And there were references to names of cities that they were unable to locate. Perhaps Yo'k'ib was one of those. And then it hit him. They had been paddling upriver all day.

The age-old enemy of Yaxchilan was Piedras Negras. Yo'k'ib was its name in ancient times. Yaxchilan and Piedras Negras had been feuding for almost four hundred years by now. If he was right, Piedras Negras had the upper hand. During this time period, Yaxchilan was subservient to it. History said there was a change of fortunes and Yaxchilan eventually shed its yoke, but it had to be some time in the future.

Johnson searched his mind. He recollected that archaeologists recently recovered a lintel denoting the capture of a major lord from Piedras Negras in 759 A.D.. The Baah Sayal, leader of the town of La Pasadita, made the stone lintel to record his assisting Yaxchilan in the capture. Perhaps it was a record of the capture during this raid.

Johnson looked out over the river. The water flowed slowly by. The setting felt peaceful. Across the river was a tree with numerous white spots covering it. As he watched, white birds flew in and landed on its branches, a nesting tree where they would spend the night. "What's going to happen in the morning?" Johnson asked as casually as he could.

"In the morning we are going to hit them hard and fast just as the sun comes up," replied Shield Jaguar. "The outpost is a tenth of a sun's hike up the river from here. Lightning Sky, when we go in I want you to stay next to me. My Eagle Warriors will be around you. They will help if necessary. Don't take unnecessary chances. You don't have to capture someone on your first time out. A good fight will do."

Shield Jaguar went back to the camp. Johnson continued to sit and look out over the water. He needed to think. So much had happened so fast that he felt he was on overload. He sat quietly watching the slow current of the river. The birds in the nesting tree quieted down. The sun was setting as evening arrived with its soft light. The world was, for the moment, peaceful and he felt a part of it. A calmness came over him. It shouldn't be there but it was. Something had changed. He had paddled with these men all day and wasn't tired, not even a little. The body he was in was strong and powerful, not like his. It was a comfort. Tomorrow he was to go into battle with these fierce men. He should be scared, but somehow he wasn't. The debilitating fear had left. Something replaced it, anticipation yes, concern yes, a tension like all his muscles were contracting into strength, a strength he had never known. He had never been in a fight in his life, and tomorrow it could be to the death, and he still wasn't afraid. *Most unusual,* he thought.

As he watched, a group of forty men came to the camp and were welcomed by Shield Jaguar.

"Who are they?" Lightning Sky asked Smoking Squirrel.

"It's the Sajal of Tiloom from La Pasadita. He is the one who found out about the lord being here. He is looking for favor from the king and helping to capture a high level lord will give it to him. La Pasadita is our first line of defense against the oppressors. We will need their help when war starts again."

"Will war start again?" Lightning Sky asked.

"If Shield Jaguar has anything to say about it, it will."

As the sun settled, Johnson looked back at the camp and sighed. He had managed to make it through the day without the men finding out who he really was. He hoped that tomorrow it would go as well. The scene looked so peaceful. Men were talking together in small groups that seemed to fade into the background as the light diminished. Sound carried easily through the jungle at night so they spoke softly. They could be any group of men on an outing, a fishing or hunting trip. They looked benign, rough on the surface but average Joe's on the inside. Then he pictured tomorrow and what it may bring. Shield Jaguar said these men were battle hardened veterans, the best. Tomorrow they would become the monsters their lavish head gear portrayed and there would be a lot of blood spilled; and he was now part of them.

§

The birds were just starting to sing. A faint glow radiated in the east. Venus was low in the sky. The night before, Shield Jaguar told them the gods would gather on Venus in the morning and watch them. They would reward bravery and courage and give them captives if they did well. A man who left the group when they beached the canoes had returned at dark and told them that three officials were at the station with a body of guards and one of them was dressed like a lord. Shield Jaguar was ecstatic; "*A lord,*" he kept saying to himself. He beamed with the anticipation of the next day and claimed he was in the gods' favor.

§

As dawn broke, a hundred warriors from Yaxchilan were hiding in two groups in the jungle behind the outpost. There was a low defense wall between them and the camp. The front of the outpost faced the river where toll keepers stopped canoes and charged a fee for transporting goods along the water highway.

No one moved or made a sound. If the birds stopped singing it would give them away.

The warriors were hunters now, in position and waiting for their quarry to come into their trap. Shield Jaguar would give the signal to attack. They all knew he was waiting for the high official, a lord of the Piedras Negras royal court. When he located his quarry he didn't want the man to escape. Men started to come out of the shelters and head to the bushes to relieve themselves. The camp was starting to awaken. The night guards left their posts, no longer needed.

The time for the attack was close. Johnson's chest tightened and a spasm ran up his back. His heart was pounding wildly and he could hardly breathe. His hands were sweating so bad the spear he held felt slippery. What was he doing here? Last night Shield Jaguar had said that the warriors would watch out for him. As he looked around at them, he hoped it would be so.

He looked over at Shield Jaguar who was intently watching the compound, searching for his prey, missing nothing, everything else pushed from his mind.

As they watched, three men came from a thatched-roof hut and headed for the bushes.

"Look," Shield Jaguar whispered softly, "the hair is different on the one in front. The gods favor us today. It's Lord T'ul Chiik and he's in my grasp."

The king motioned with his hand, and two men stood up and threw their spears. Johnson watched as they slowly arced through the air and down toward their targets. The two men with the official were hit in their chests. The warriors jumped up and ran toward the outpost screaming war cries. A mass of monsters floated on the headdresses above the warriors, monsters going fiercely into battle. Johnson stood there frozen, mesmerized at the sight. No longer men, they were the monsters of the underworld charging their hapless victims, waging death and destruction on any who opposed them.

Bird Jaguar and Shield Jaguar both leapt to their feet and ran hard, side by side, with Johnson right behind them. The king caught the lord, striking him with the wood shaft of his spear, knocking him to the ground. As the others charged the huts to engage the enemy, Shield Jaguar looped a rope around the scared man's neck and pulled it tight choking him.

Johnson stood next to the warrior brothers, his heart pounding. He didn't know what he was supposed to do. All around him men were fighting, many were laying on the ground dead or wounded. Blood seemed to be everywhere. A morbid fascination replaced his tenseness. This couldn't be real, yet it was.

Suddenly they were facing a large force. Men were streaming out of the buildings. Shield Jaguar's warriors were being driven back out of the compound by the superior numbers of opposing warriors. Another large group of men came charging out of the jungle, hurling spears.

"A trap!" screamed one of the warriors as they were being pushed back. "They were waiting for us. It's a trap!"

"There must be three hundred of them!" Smoking Squirrel shouted.

The king's guard immediately circled the king, his brother, and Johnson. The guards were the defender's now. Their job was to keep the king and Shield Jaguar from being captured. The fighting was heavy.

Shield Jaguar roughly pulled the choking official to his feet as an opposing warrior broke through the line, club held high. He charged. Johnson reacted, swinging the point of his spear toward the man. The warrior couldn't stop as it embedded in his chest. Two more warriors followed. Johnson grabbed his club and swung a roundhouse as hard as he could. The second warrior blocked, but the force was too much and Johnson's club broke his arm and slammed into the side of his head. His forward momentum carried him past Johnson as he fell to the ground.

The last man came on hard and swung his club down at Johnson. Holding his club up with both hands, Johnson braced and warded off the blow. The warrior crashed into him landing on top, pinning him, as they hit the ground. Johnson struggled to free himself. He saw the obsidian knife streaking toward his face and managed to grab the wrist with both hands. The warrior put the strength of his whole body behind the blade. Johnson was about to die. Fear arose in him but was suddenly replaced with a strength he had never known. His entire being was centered on the knife. It was him or the knife, and the knife wasn't going to win. Suddenly the weight was taken off him and he saw Shield Jaguar lift the man up and slit his throat. He gave his hand to Johnson and pulled him up.

"Run," Shield Jaguar shouted, as he raced off, holding the rope dragging the official behind.

The warriors ran back the way they had come, their pursuers close behind them. As they topped a small hill, those with spears suddenly stopped, turned, and threw them back at the enemy. Their aims were accurate. Many were hit. The enemy warriors stopped. Shield Jaguar's men started running again leaving their enemy further behind with the gap widening.

The canoes were waiting, bows pointed toward the river. The men piled in and pushed them off the shore and started paddling hard. The king's canoe was the first one launched and led the retreat. The first duty of the warriors was to protect the king.

As they pulled into the river's flow, the warriors behind them reached the water. They threw their spears. All but two fell short. A man in the last canoe was hit in the back and fell over the side into the water.

"They were waiting for us," Shield Jaguar screamed in a rage. "It was a trap, a monkey-fornicating trap!"

"There must have been two or three hundred men there,"

claimed Smoking Squirrel.

"That was close," Johnson gasped as he panted from the exertion. The adrenaline continued pumping through his veins, unable to stop. He was wired, every fiber of his body on fire waiting for the next danger.

"Close hell," screamed Shield Jaguar louder than before. "Those dung-eaters were waiting for us. Someone set us up."

"I can guess who, too," was Smoking Squirrel's reply.

"Great Skull, huh."

"Who else?" growled Smoking Squirrel, "or maybe that miserable son of his."

"No, not him," Shield Jaguar responded. "He's an arrogant little mouse's prick, but that field rodent doesn't have the balls to stand up to a little dog, let alone a Jaguar."

"You know he'll never face you head on," claimed Smoking Squirrel.

Shield Jaguar looked at his friend and his face broke into a grin and suddenly he laughed. He laughed uncontrollably. His mood changed as he looked back at the force of warriors standing on the shore. They were safe now. They had pulled it off. And he laughed harder, unable to stop. They had avoided the trap set for them and had taken a captive.

"I'll bet the little mouse will shit in front of everybody when we show up with the prisoner," Smoking squirrel concluded.

They both roared with laughter.

Johnson stared blankly at them, watching them laugh. Savages, he thought. The surge of adrenaline running through him produced a high he never felt before. A feeling of well-being washed over him; he had survived. He had fought and survived. He was invincible. And he chuckled at the realization. The chuckle turned into a laugh and soon he was laughing uncontrollably like the others. The other guys were dead and he was alive. Life was sweet. Never in his life had he felt this way.

"We pulled it off," Shield Jaguar hollered hoarsely. "The gods are with us. Look at those monkeys standing back there with their pricks in their hands as they watch their lord sail away with us." The entire force of warriors laughed with abandon at the joke. As the laughter died down, Shield Jaguar announced to the men, "It's a good day. You have done well. We will go home with our heads held high."

Johnson looked around at the warriors. The mood was festive. They had pulled it off. He trembled and noted that it was now in the aftermath of the fight. The fear he had, left when he stabbed the warrior with his spear. Every fiber of his being had gone into the fight. It consumed him. Nothing else mattered. It was him or the enemy and he won. Now he was one of the victors and was entitled to part of their glory. He smiled. *I am one of them now*, he thought. *I am a warrior and it feels good.*

"It's going to be a good night tonight," Shield Jaguar exclaimed as he pulled the captive off the bottom of the boat, holding him by his hair. The man's face was deep red. Shield Jaguar held the head up like it was separated from the body and stared into the man's glassy eyes. "I'm going to enjoy seeing you scream, you little rabbit, waiting in the trap for the Jaguar. The Jaguar got you this time and you're going to die slowly and painfully. Word will get back to your sons and daughters and your brothers and sisters and father and mother and all your friends that you don't fornicate with Shield Jaguar. His enemies quake at his name and suffer at his hand, and you're going to tell them that from Xibalba, little rabbit."

§

It was late afternoon when the canoes arrived at the bend in the river, the point of the peninsula where Yaxchilan was located. Scouts had watched them as they came down the river and sent word forward. Shield Jaguar had held the captive up by the hair for them to see. News of them bringing a captive, a high ranking captive, traveled fast. A group of people followed them, waving and cheering, as they paddled down the river. When they came to the landing, the crowd gathered to watch them.

Shield Jaguar pulled the captive out of the canoe before it beached, and roughly dragged him by his hair up to the shore. He motioned for Lightning Sky and Smoking Squirrel to follow on either side. Stopping in front of the crowd, Shield Jaguar held his hand up, full of the man's hair, supporting the captive's head as his body appeared to dangle.

"It's a great day," he shouted. "The gods favor my brothers and me. We have a captive, a great lord of Piedras Negras for sacrifice." The crowd cheered. There would be a great festival tonight in their honor.

The king came over and held the hair too and laughed at Shield Jaguar. "It looks like we both got him. It's been a good day brother. Tonight you can dance the conquest story dance and then he is mine to torture and sacrifice at the Period Ending ceremonies.

With his other hand, Shield Jaguar grabbed Johnson's wrist and held it high. "My brother Lightning Sky fought well today. He killed two men. We must honor him at our feast tonight!"

The crowd cheered again. The king and his brother had come back victorious again.

A crier called, "Make way, make way, for Lord Great Skull." A hush came over the people. The crowd parted leaving a wide opening. The king's entourage led by Lord Great Skull came to greet the king. It was not right for the king to move from place to place without his entourage. His counselors, the great Lords and a warrior contingent came forward, even his dwarf was there. They stopped in front of the three young warriors.

"It's a great day," the king proclaimed proudly to Lord Great Skull. "We bring a captive from Piedras Negras to add to the glory of Yaxchilan. And Lightning Sky killed two warriors in his first battle today. Tonight we will feast and rejoice in his bravery and courage."

Lord Great Skull looked ashen. "That's K'inil Ajaw T'ul Chiik," he said feebly, "of Piedras Negras. Their king will be incensed. He will want him back and compensation for taking him." Looking at the king, he continued, "He'll never allow this. We'll just have to let him go."

"My brother and I caught him and we are not giving him back," the king snapped, angered at being addressed as an underling.

Lord Great Skull said nothing as he glared at Shield Jaguar, hate showing in his eyes.

Shield Jaguar glared back and said, "You look surprised Lord Great Skull. Are you surprised to see me or surprised that I'm capable of sacrificing a lord?" He laughed openly and pushed past them dragging his captive behind.

Chapter 5

A large fire illuminated the courtyard where the young woman danced. Torches placed around the perimeter of the area burned brightly. Their light, flickering off the walls of the palace, lent a radiating glow to the festivities.

"Beautiful isn't she?" Smoking Squirrel remarked as he watched the dancer. "If she can move those hips on the sleeping mat the way she does when she dances it would be a night to remember."

"I could handle that," responded Shield Jaguar. "How about you little brother, think you could handle her?"

"Her?" Johnson responded with a chuckle. "That would be a night worth remembering, wouldn't it?"

The woman, clad only in a brief loin cloth, twirled and gyrated to the beat of the music. As she came out of each twirling movement she glanced seductively at the three young men and a sly smile crossed her face. They were nobility and she liked their attention.

The fermented brew they were drinking was making Johnson light-headed. He was still basking in the high from the battle and it enhanced the feeling. He had actually been there and fought; and they had pulled it off. They captured the lord and escaped. He looked at the two warriors, his new friends, and felt a sense of camaraderie. The drink helped. He laughed at the thought. They were brothers, Shield Jaguar, Smoking Squirrel and him. People called them 'The Trio'. They were held in awe when they passed by; royalty and seasoned warriors, they held a special place in society's mind-set.

He held up the drink, eyeing the cup, studying the liquid within. Dark brown in color, it carried the sweet taste of diluted cocoa but left an aftertaste of corn that clung heavily to the taste buds. If it was anything like chorte, a corn-based fermented drink that included fermented cocoa beans, it would have a hell of a kick and leave the drinker with a nasty hangover in the morning.   It was passable and tasting better with each cup.

The feast hadn't started. It wouldn't start until the king arrived. As they waited, the three young men were recounting their adventure to all who would listen, their bravery heightened with each telling and each drink

Johnson looked over the scene before him. He took another sip and held up the cup again, not sure if he was admiring it or what it was doing to him. *Damn it's good*. He was more than a little mellow. It felt comfortable. He looked at the other two. They were feeling it too. He tried to tell himself he was a scientist. He'd have to remember all of this and tried to concentrate. It was a banquet. He looked over the arrangements. In the courtyard five long low benches just above ground level were aligned side by side in front of the palace, perpendicular to the porch running along the face of the building. On them, groups of flowers were arranged every few feet.

There appeared to be a strict hierarchy in the seating arrangement. The king would set at the head of the center table, his principle wife, Lady Great Skull, and Chel-Te' their son, to his right, followed by his other wives and children. Shield Jaguar, Lightning Sky and Smoking Squirrel would sit to his left, with each noble family at a separate table with seating also based on status. The noble families favored by the king had tables closer to him and the less favored further away. Lord Great Skull, the head of his family line, would occupy the table to the king's right.

The people were sitting at the tables talking while the music played and the girl danced. Suddenly horns loudly sounded and the music stopped, the girl sank to the ground as if lifeless, and the people turned to look at the palace. King Bird Jaguar slowly emerged from his palace doorway, which was framed with drapes, and stopped on the front porch to view the crowd. His personal guard of seasoned warriors were standing on each side of the doorway. Johnson looked in awe. *What an entrance. Hollywood couldn't have set a better stage.* It became quiet. All eyes were on the king.

Dressed in splendid royal attire, he emulated the regal presence of a god/king. A loincloth and cape of jaguar fur adorned his body. Over it laid a heavy belt and a kilt with a jade god's head on it. A heavy jade shoulder piece adorned his shoulders and upper chest, accented by elaborate jade wrist bands. On his head he wore an immense headdress with hasaw-ka'an staffs in it, personified wings, mat and reed decorations, and long feathers arching above and behind them. He looked regal and in charge, like the pictures Johnson had seen on ceremonial bowls in museums. Shield Jaguar, a royal prince was similarly adorned but with a more conservative headdress. Johnson noted that he and Smoking Squirrel were dressed a little less opulently. They must be at a lower station even though Shield Jaguar called them brothers. He wondered just how he fit into this hierarchy.

How fortunate that he had the old woman as a servant, thought Johnson as he watched the king and noted a similarity in their attire. Different outfits were worn depending on the ceremony.

Earlier she had laid the ceremonial garments to be worn that evening on his sleeping platform. As she dressed him she prattled constantly on how he should behave during dinner. He may have done well in his first battle, but the glory of taking a captive was Shield Jaguar's, and proper reverence was always to be paid to the king.

Quiet reigned as the people waited for the king. He stood there quietly, and looked around saying nothing, letting a little tension build. He knew how to make an entrance. No one was to address the king unless first addressed by him. After several minutes he came down the steps and walked over to the head of the center table, sat down and raised his hand. Once again the horns sounded announcing the start of the banquet. People resumed talking and slaves started to bring out the food. The participants sat on the ground cross-legged. The head of the table was served first and each member followed according to their position.

"Brother," said the king looking over at Shield Jaguar, "our capturing the prisoner from Piedras Negras will make King Yo'nal Ahk mad."

"That's the idea," replied Shield Jaguar.

"It will cause retaliation."

"Then we stop them and send them home. You like a captive you can torture, don't you?"

"Of course I do. Having a captive is always good. It's too bad we couldn't have gotten another one," the king laughed. "The Kantun Period Ending is coming up in another three moons and we will sacrifice him then. He is high ranking and that will make the gods happy. Meanwhile, we will play with him."

"So, if you like the captive what is the problem?" Shield Jaguar asked.

"I went to King Yo'nal Ahk III's ascension ceremonies two years ago."

"And you were commanded to go, like a mere subject of the

king," retorted Shield Jaguar. "That relationship should have been broken long ago."

"It has been a long time without fighting. We have been able to use the time and energy elsewhere. They are very strong. It will take a lot to remove their burden."

"Always the politician, aren't you brother," claimed Shield Jaguar. "Buy them off, and since you don't have to battle them, you can plunder from the smaller cities."

"It works well. It allows me to spend my time building and adding to the glory of our city."

"But we have been paying them a large tribute for a long time and they want more. They consider it their right to just command and we give. We pay them and they dictate to us. They should be paying the tribute to us," said Shield Jaguar.

"Perhaps," replied the king. "We shall see."

"It's a wise man who can balance the needs of the people and the gods against the aggression of our enemies," continued the king as he picked up a pepper and bit into it.

"Brother," replied Shield Jaguar, "you do the building and administration, let me do the fighting, and Yaxchilan will be glorious."

At the next table Lord Great Skull heard the conversation. He leaned toward his son sitting next to him and whispered, "See, we are going to have trouble with him. I can see it coming. Now that he is old enough, he is starting to challenge my power."

As they were eating, Johnson noticed a young woman watching him. She was the young woman who was on the pyramid when he arrived. She was sitting further down at his table and part of the royal family. Every time he looked back, her eyes were on him. The words she said the night before came back, "What did the gods say Lightning Sky? Will they bless our love?" *Who is she? How can I find out?*

The meal was almost over when a loud scream came from

outside the palace complex. The prisoner was dragged into the courtyard by two warriors. Two more followed and poked him repeatedly with their spears. Blood flowed from the small wounds in his back, buttocks and legs. They stopped in front of the diners and tied the prisoner to a log. He squatted down crouched in fear with his back against the log, he whimpered and stared through glassy eyes, horrified at his tormentors.

The king's eyes got big and a broad smile crossed his face. He chuckled lightly in anticipation of the entertainment they were about to see. "Whip him, but don't kill him," the king commanded one of his personal guards. "He got caught. Let the people see his humiliation."

The warrior pulled out a long whip and proceeded to slowly and methodically flay the man. A roar came from the crowd with each blow. They chattered excitedly with one another at each scream. Horrified, Johnson watched the scene hardly believing what he saw. *This is entertainment for them; the pain to the captive is not a consideration.* Women remarked on the severity of the blows, "Oh that's a good one" and laughed at the prisoner's screams. Men called across tables making bets on how long the captive would last until he broke. As the prisoner slumped over unable to resist any longer, the winners cheered as the losers groaned.

Smoking Squirrel looked over at Johnson as he pointed to a man at another table. The man looked ashen, stunned that he lost, as he assessed the ramifications of his actions. "He's going to have to work a long time to pay that wager."

"Really?" Johnson exclaimed.

"He bet the next harvest from his cornfield by the river. It will be poor eating for his family until the next planting comes in."

"Do they always bet that much?" Johnson asked.

"What is the use of a wager if it isn't worthy? I don't have the means yet of accepting that heavy of a bet but I would have taken it," Smoking Squirrel replied. "This captive is a weakling. He's soft. He screams when he should clench his teeth in anger and curse his captors. Then when he hurts enough to kneel in front of the king and beg for mercy he will mean it. He's not much of a man. See the way he snivels. He never would have lasted the fifty strokes. A warrior would, but never a lord."

Lord Great Skull, the winner of the large bet was watching the three closely. "Hey little puppies," he called over, "there are lords and then there are lords."

"And you could have done better?" Shield Jaguar asked across the tables, a smirk on his face. "I'd like to see that."

"Fifty strokes? I think I could handle it," the lord said as he smiled back at them. "The question is, do you think you would do better?"

"Better than a lord, and may the god Cizin, the evil god of death, keep me forever in the underworld if I couldn't," Shield Jaguar shot back.

"Maybe someday you will get the chance to demonstrate just how strong you are," the great lord replied.

"Perhaps," Shield Jaguar replied. "Disappointed that it isn't tonight?"

Lord Great Skull looked at him and smiled. This cocky young prince knew. He'd have to be more careful next time.

The prisoner was left tied to the log by a length of rope. During the course of the evening, people were expected to go over and hit or kick him. It promised to be a painful night.

§

When the dinner ended, slaves removed the remains from the tables and then carried the tables away. The king held his hand up and a dozen horns sounded three strong notes announcing the king was moving. Bird Jaguar IV rose and walked out of the courtyard with his primary wife, Lady Great Skull, beside him, his other two wives behind. Next, came Shield Jaguar, followed by the great lords, the heads of the major noble families.

Slowly the king's entourage moved down the stairs to the ceremonial center. The diners followed in loose groups. Lightning Sky and Smoking Squirrel joined the diners. As they got to the palace entrance, the young woman from the pyramid joined them taking a place between the men. Johnson tensed. She obviously knew the man who was actually Lightning Sky very well. Johnson was sure she would be able to tell the difference. He stared straight ahead walking mechanically, certain the charade was up.

At the bottom of the hill, along one side of the Great Plaza, was a large two-story temple topped with a stone comb. A large patio spread out in front of it. A dais had been placed in front of the temple for the king. Behind and off to the sides stood his personal guards holding their spears butt to the ground. His wives sat on one side of him and the great lords on the other. Two bonfires were lit, one on either side of the plaza. The people who had been at the banquet were entitled to seats along the sides of the plaza. Beyond them were hundreds of spectators seated like an audience.

Johnson stared at the scene unfolding before him. He was intrigued. The arrangements appeared grandiose. He knew it must be something special. The people found places to sit around the perimeter of the palace plaza. Johnson noted that the social strata, so strict at the banquet, seemed to disappear as people gathered with friends.

When they reached the plaza, the young men joined Shield Jaguar and took seats in a place near the king. The young woman from the pyramid the night before sat down between Shield Jaguar and Johnson. He tightened at the sudden nearness of her presence. Her scent permeated his senses. She exuded an exotic sweetness that wrapped itself around him and pulled him in. She looked up into his eyes, probing, and he felt weak and overpowered. Suddenly scared, he wondered what he was to do.

"What's your problem tonight?" she asked Johnson as she elbowed him in the ribs. "You're quiet."

"He can't get his mind off the dancer," Smoking Squirrel answered for him.

"Oh yeah," the girl said as she looked up at Johnson and glared. "The dancer, huh?"

"Anyone want to take bets on who ends up with her tonight?" Shield Jaguar asked.

"It won't be me," Johnson said, hoping it would be the right answer. The girl wasn't happy hearing about his interest in the dancer.

"Little Rabbit, what do you see happening tonight?" Smoking Squirrel asked.

"I see people having fun and perhaps, if he doesn't drink too much, Shield Jaguar sleeping with the dancer."

"Are you ever wrong?" Smoking Squirrel asked.

"Sometimes, but not tonight," she replied a sly smile on her face. "She wants him, and I'll bet she'll gets him."

§

"Time to tell the story of the battle," Shield Jaguar screamed as he jumped into the middle of the courtyard with the young woman who was dancing. He danced around the fires, she followed him move for move. When he hopped forward like he was rowing the canoe, she hopped and rowed right behind him. As he crept cautiously through the forest, one hand over his eyes looking in all directions, she scouted with him. When he stopped to sing the part of the battle where he captured the lord, she danced in circles around him rubbing against him to emphasize his presence.

Johnson looked over at Smoking Squirrel and asked, "The girl, what is she doing?"

"What girl?"

"The one with Shield Jaguar."

"That's not a girl," replied Smoking Squirrel looking at him strangely. "That's his spirit animal, his owl. It was his owl who guided us into battle and helped us get away. Shield Jaguar has a powerful spirit watching over him."

Three other girls in the background danced and twirled on the outskirts of Shield Jaguar's dance.

"And the other dancers?" Johnson asked.

"They are spirits of the woods: the trees, the grass, the animals and the birds. All of the spirits viewed our journey."

Johnson watched in fascination. He saw dancers, they saw spirits. He knew the nobles danced and the ceremonies held special importance from the paintings on the few artifacts found from this period, but the meaning of the dances was not known.

As Shield Jaguar danced, the spectators clapped in rhythm to the drums. The music became louder and they clapped harder. The gyrations were wilder, the dancing faster as everyone became consumed with the pageant. Suddenly it ended as Shield Jaguar dragged the captive up from the ground by his hair and held him high for all to see, everyone cheered.

The horns sounded again. All became silent as the king rose and entered the center of the courtyard. The bonfires gave off an eerie light. A slave came into the yard carrying a large snake, a white boa constrictor, and gave it to the king. Then music started playing and the king began to dance. The large white snake slithered and coiled around his arms. Johnson watched the scene unfolding. A snake dance. Dances were an important part of their culture. He knew this was an important type of dance, but that was about all. A large portion of the artifacts with pictures had scenes of the king and lords dancing. It was a communication, the gods with the people. The pageants taught and reinforced their ideology.

The king was dancing for his people. He was communicating

with the gods. The people watched in silence as he danced to the beat of the drums telling a story, the story of a snake god, a god of life from Xibalba. All eyes were glued on the king as he danced. The snake coiled itself around him tighter. Three young women joined the dance as the snake god ascended from the underworld embodied in the snake into the world of the spirits and man. Was he god or man? Johnson couldn't tell. He heard two people whisper, "The god is coming."

The crowd clapped as the three young girls danced around him, darting in and out of his grasp, tantalizing and seductive. The people, enchanted with the dance swayed with the drums and flutes. A god was dancing for them, celebrating with them, rejoicing in their regained honor, the honor of their city. The people clapped and chanted louder expressing their reverence. They were being honored as descendents of the First Father.

The music changed as did the king's steps. He held the head of the snake toward the people as he danced, pushing it out toward them. Faster and faster he twirled as he followed intricate steps. The people clapped harder and harder.

"Come forth," the king shouted. "Come into the world of the people." A hush came over the crowd. Johnson glanced over at Little Rabbit. She was staring, eyes wide as she bit her lip.

He looked at the king, now dancing a little slower and with different steps. He looked around at the other people. They were all watching the king, mesmerized. Johnson turned toward the girl again. "It's KuKulkan, the plumed serpent, the creator god," she whispered reverently. "He came to dance and celebrate with us tonight."

Johnson turned back to the dancer. It was the king, the king and the snake. Again he looked back at Little Rabbit who was staring in awe at the dancer. And it hit him. They were seeing two different beings; he saw the king with a snake, she saw a god.

Throughout the night, dance followed dance. Johnson knew

they had cultural significance but couldn't make sense of most of them. Some appeared to be Wayob dances where the individual's companion spirit takes control of the body and dances with abandon. Others appeared to be dances recounting and enacting past events in their history that they honored and remembered. As the story-dances were performed, spirits of past kings were summoned to dance with the people and the people rejoiced as their ancestors joined the celebration.

Johnson watched the change in the people as the dances continued. Their celebration, he observed, consisted of the people of Yaxchilan, their spirit animals, summoned gods from Xibalba, and ancestors who lived over two hundred years before. As he watched, he noted the peoples' responses. To him the various dancers were just in different costumes and masks, but to the people of Yaxchilan they were different beings and they were real. The people, the spirits, the ancestors and the gods were of one community living together in a state of perfect balance.

The dancing continued long into the night. Hour after hour the horns called out and the drums beat rhythmically. The intoxicating brew flowed freely. Some people appeared to be in a trance, overwhelmed by the presence of the gods. Others caught up in the rapture of the celebration were dancing with wild abandonment. The bonfires were fading. Many people appeared to be sleeping or just passed out as much from the drink as from the rapture.

Couples silently stole off looking for places in the dark for their sexual liaisons. Some couplings were in dark corners of the courtyard, seemingly ignored by the other people. Shield Jaguar and Smoking Squirrel had long since disappeared. Johnson thought he saw Shield Jaguar leave with the dancer who had accompanied him as his spirit.

Finally Johnson and Little Rabbit were alone. The intoxicating drink was strongly affecting him and he was starting to doze.

"Good stuff," he mumbled to himself as he poured another cupful and took a sip.

"What's the matter Lightning Sky? You didn't come to see me last night," she said softly as she slipped her hand around his arm pulling him close. "And I waited for you long into the night."

What could he say? "The vision tired me," he meekly replied as he looked into her eyes, deep celestial pools reflecting the firelight. Mesmerized, he watched the delicate hair of the black lashes sweep gracefully across them. His breath shortened and his heart beat louder. The aroma of her scent had affected him all evening making him ever conscious of her presence. It now pulled at the core of his being. He wanted to be with her.

"I fell asleep," he said sounding noncommittal. "It was a long journey."

"And what did the gods say?" she asked, fear showing as she peered into his eyes.

"They didn't say," he replied.

"Nothing, after all the sacrifices we have made to them?"

"Maybe they will say something in the future," he tried to reassure her.

"We don't have much time. The time is not too far away and I will have to marry."

"When will that happen?"

"I don't know for sure, but I'm sure it's not too long. I have seen it come to pass."

"You have seen it?" he asked.

"My brother, Shield Jaguar, will be the king. The gods have told me. Is he not the son of Shield Jaguar the Great? Soon his half brother, the king, will die. When Shield Jaguar becomes king he will promise me in marriage to another king."

"But why?"

"He needs the power of political alliances. A bad time is coming. The strong shall survive and the weak perish."

"Doesn't Chel-Te' ascend to the throne? Isn't he the heir?" Johnson asked. To his knowledge history indicated Chel-Te' succeeded King Bird Jaguar and then took the name 'Shield Jaguar' after his illustrious grandfather.

"For a short time," she responded, "but just a short time. Shield Jaguar is the rightful heir. It is the will of the gods."

"Is there no way to get out of it?" he asked, following the conversation.

"Why ask? You know there isn't. He loves you like a brother. He'd give you almost anything, but in this he won't move. He can't. He'll wait his time, but when the time comes there will be a wedding."

They sat there quietly watching the dancers, both lost in thought. The beverage was affecting him more now. His lips were thick and numb. As he watched the dancers everything started to spin. *My god, what was in this drink?* He held on to the bench to try to steady the effect. His voice was heavy and slurred, talking difficult. His thoughts wouldn't line up right and he kept losing some of them. He was having trouble focusing, even with one eye, and he wanted to sleep. Yes sleep, peaceful gentle sleep. His head fell off to the side and he abruptly jerked it back.

What about Little Rabbit? He couldn't go to sleep now. She was here, her captivating aroma filling him with desire, longing to be enveloped in it, ever closer until they were one. He had to have her and she was sitting next to him, touching him, enticing him, close and feminine and wanting him too. He couldn't sleep, not now. And the last thing he remembered was her saying, "Come with me," as she took his arm to help him up.

Chapter 6

He felt cold and he had a splitting headache. As sleep slowly left him, he remembered the drinking and dancing, and that enchanting young woman. It must be near dawn. The monkeys should be howling soon. Johnson lay back, tightly closing his eyes against the pain and listened for the sounds of the jungle—nothing, just a babbling of water.

Something was wrong. He couldn't place it. Slowly it came to him. He was in the cave again. Opening his eyes he could see the little fire, just embers now, and in its dim light the outline of the shaman. Silently sitting there, hunched forward for the little warmth the fire gave, he was watching Johnson closely.

"You're back," he said solemnly.

"Was I gone long?"

"About two hours," was the reply.

"It was two days," Johnson said. "I was there for two days. How could it have been for just two hours?"

"Time is different on the other side," the old shaman said. He added a couple of sticks to the fire and a flame caught making the cave brighter. He looked at Johnson curiously. The man seemed just a little different. He looked around like a cat, taking in everything at once, feral, cautious. He seemed more aware than before. "Did you talk to the gods?" the shaman asked.

"It was amazing," said Johnson. "I traveled somewhere, somewhere not of this earth. It must have been to the gods. They wanted to know why. They sent me back to the old ones, back in time to Yaxchilan. I saw the city the way it was. I saw it when it was at the height of its glory."

"And the old ones?" asked the shaman. "What of the old ones?"

"I saw them too. I saw King Bird Jaguar IV, and I believe Shield Jaguar III, and the nobles and the people—just the way they lived. At least I think I saw them. Was it a vision?"

"I don't know. Only you can tell, but I believe that the old gods have the power to send you back in time. They are very powerful, but they are also very deceitful."

Johnson felt exhausted as they left the cave. His body felt tight and tense. The headache was terrible. It felt like a hangover. It was obvious he had been through an ordeal, but what kind of an ordeal? Was the pain from the drug and a vision, or from the drinking in the past? It had felt so real.

§

Phoebe was sitting at a picnic table on the veranda when the pick-up truck pulled up in front of the lodge. Johnson had been gone most of the day and it was getting dark. She thought he was on a fool's mission and probably just got stoned. Johnson hurried from the truck and called to her.

"Phoebe, you wouldn't believe it," he said as he came up the walk. "I saw it, I really saw it!"

"Saw what?"

"The drug took me back in time. I was there when it was occupied. I met Bird Jaguar IV, the king!" Johnson was ecstatic. He wanted to tell the world but the world wasn't there. He needed to tell someone. When he woke up in the cave and told the shaman he had gone back to the ancient city the old man claimed he was most fortunate that the gods favored him. There was no doubt in the man's mind that he had traveled back in time.

"Phoebe, it was mind blowing!" Johnson came up and grabbed her by the hands, looking wildly into her eyes. "I was there. I was really there!"

"Where?"

"Yaxchilan. Yaxchilan when it was occupied. I was there."

"Easy now, hold on. You went where?" she asked.

"You wouldn't believe it Pheb. I hardly believe it myself and I experienced it."

"Believe what?"

"I traveled back in time. I went back to Yaxchilan to the middle of the Eighth Century. I saw it. I saw the site as it was in its height of glory."

"Come on, Alan. When you left here you and that old man were going up into the hills to smoke some dope you found. That's a far cry from time travel," she said looking at him skeptically.

"We went up into the hills and into an old cave, a very sacred cave, he claimed. He performed a ritual and blew the powder up my nose and I went back in time."

"You mean you took a trip. Drugs can do that to you."

"I really went back in time. I know it."

"It must have been a dream. You took a drug-induced trip. Maybe it felt like a vision but that would still be a stretch."

"The old man said I went back in time too," Johnson claimed. "He said the ancient gods could do that—send me back."

"Alan, it's physically impossible to travel in time. It just can't be done."

They sat down at the picnic table on the patio, his eyes pleading for understanding. "But I saw it. I saw the city, not in ruins, but with new buildings and people. There were hundreds of them.

It was a functioning city. I saw the temples as they were. The detail in Lady Xook's temple and the painted relief pictures were beyond anything we could have ever imagined. It was gorgeous. I couldn't have seen that or envisioned it without having been there."

She leaned forward over the table across from him, squeezed his hands and looked compassionately into his eyes. He looked tired, like he hadn't slept in days. "Alan, I do believe you experienced something but going back in time? Really. You're a scientist trained to look at the physical world rationally. It must have been a dream induced by the drugs. Dreams can seem to be real. Slowly, now tell me just what did you see."

"I became a Maya, the nephew of King Bird Jaguar IV and cousin to Shield Jaguar III."

"You became a Maya? Then it had to be a dream. Even if you could go back in time you couldn't enter someone else's body."

"But it was real, Pheb. I was there. I was involved in a ceremony petitioning the gods for victory a coming battle. I went on a raid with a band of warriors where Shield Jaguar captured a lord from Piedras Negras. I attended the victory ceremonies and actually saw the king dancing just like in the pictures on the bowls in the museums. I saw it all."

"Alan, you're exhausted. You need sleep," she replied in a conciliatory manner. He looked exhausted, out on his feet and mumbling, fleeting from topic to topic as images flashed through his mind. "Go in the lodge and sleep and we can talk about it in the morning," she ordered.

He looked at her with glazed eyes, staring but not quite seeing. "I need to record what I saw. I need to write it down. I can't forget anything. I must sit at the computer tonight. I need to remember. It's a scientific breakthrough." He got up and went to his room.

An hour later, Phoebe looked in his room to see him hunched over his computer asleep in the chair. She went in and peered over his shoulder at the computer screen. He had written only a few lines before he fell asleep. She read them.

Deep in the Jungles of Southern Mexico and Guatemala, along the Usumacinta River lies the great Maya city of Yaxchilan. I traveled back in time to that location to a point somewhere around 760 A.D. and became part of the royal family, nephew of the king, Bird Jaguar IV.

During the Eighth Century two sons were born to Shield Jaguar II who reigned from 680 to 742 A.D. History only recorded one, Bird Jaguar IV, who was born of Lady Ik' Skull of Calakmul, referred to as Lady Eveningstar.

A second son, Shield Jaguar III was born during the great king's elderly years by Lady Sak B'iyaan a very young wife. This second son's proper designation was never recorded in history. The record has been interpreted that Chel-Te', the son of Bird Jaguar IV, changed his name to Shield Jaguar III upon ascension to the throne around 769/772 A.D. and that Chel-Te' and Shield Jaguar III, were in fact, different people.

During this time period political intrigue abounded. The aristocratic families were jockeying for royal favor. The family of Lady K'ab'al Xook appeared to be in the forefront of putting a king from their family line on the throne. After ten years, with the help of the Lord Great Skull Zero, the head of the Great Skull family, Bird Jaguar IV ascended to the throne.

Lord Great Skull Zero was the queen's brother and became the chief counselor to the king. He is also the maternal uncle to the king's son, Chel-Te'. He appeared to have a strong influence over the king and there was talk that the king was indebted to him for his throne. The real Shield Jaguar appeared to be an adversary of the great lord. I believe he may have been vying for political power.

§

"Can you believe that guy?" said Jim to the group as he glanced back over his shoulder to see if Dr. Johnson was near enough to hear them talk. The students were sitting along the bank of the river eating their lunch, just a bag lunch and a bottle of water.

"Was he wound up this morning, or what?" replied Kim. "I've never seen him like that."

"You mean Old Stuffed Shirt Johnson?" asked one of the girls.

"He wasn't Old Stuffed Shirt this morning," Kim exclaimed. "Those stories about the Mayas dancing and all, he really got into it."

"I kind of liked it," said one of the other girls. "In class back at the university he would hold up one of the ceremonial dedication bowls for us to see and drone on and on about how it was made, who was painted on it and how they came to know something about ancient times. They were always important finds and blah, blah, blah. Everything came out so technical you could fall asleep. But the stories of the dancing in the palace courtyard were different; they were interesting."

"He broke his own rules," replied Jim and added solemnly in a deeper voice, "An archaeologist can never speculate without empirical evidence to support his contentions," as he imitated Johnson's admonishments to his classes when they proposed claims he considered too speculative.

"What did you think when he demonstrated hopping and paddling the canoe?" the girl said. "Didn't he look funny?"

"And that spirit woman who was supposed to be jumping with him, where did he come up with that?" Jim asked.

"It was funny, but it really makes sense," Kim added. "Spirits were important to the Maya. Every living thing had a spirit. Why shouldn't the dancers emulate them too?"

"I wonder what made him change," mused Jim. "He seems like a different man."

"He went off the other day and Phoebe said he went to visit the local shaman," Kim replied. "Maybe that has something to do with it."

"It must be something. When he described the dances, his eyes took on a gleam and he got all fired up. He wasn't the same man we've seen before."

"I liked it," said another student. "I really felt like I was watching it happen. He really made me feel it."

"Me too," claimed another student. "I really got into it. I hope he keeps it up."

"We'll see about that this afternoon," Kim said. "We're going over to Temples 21 and 23 and he's going to tell us about how temple sacrifices were made and compare them and their effect on the community."

"Yeah, Lady Xook and Lady Eveningstar and their temples," replied Jim. "I wonder what he will come up with about that, probably a hell of a catfight."

§

"The students really loved your stories today," Phoebe said as they strolled among the ruins just before sundown. I listened to them as they were waiting for the boat to take them back to the lodge. They think you are a different man."

"I am a different man, Pheb. I'll never be the same."

"You are the same man Alan, but you are seeing things differently now," she said as they walked along the remnants of the Great Plaza.

"It's because I've seen it, I've seen Yaxchilan as it was in the time of its greatest glory. Now when I look at the site, it's like I'm looking at something else. Look out over the site Phoebe. At this time of day the light is starting to fade, temple servants are lighting torches. The plaza is taking on a different glow.

"People may come to the plaza tonight if something is

happening. There might be a woman with a little stand over there off to the side of that temple cooking corn tortillas filled with a little meat and spices to sell. It's near the end of her day but a couple of priests are eating. Maybe some men are sweeping the ball court for tonight's game. The king's warriors would be standing guard at various stations, and priests and nobles are walking in little groups, perhaps in discussion."

"And the common people?" she asked. "All of the people you talked about. Where are they? The ruins are so empty now I never envisioned them filled with people."

"For the most part the ceremonial center was for the privileged classes," he replied, "roughly ten to twenty percent of the population. At its height there were fifty thousand people in the area. That would give five to ten thousand upper-class people access to all of this. They would be members of the wealthy who owned the large farms, or perhaps merchants, artisans, scribes, priests and such. The society had two distinct classes; those who had and those who didn't, and a line that wasn't to be crossed."

"It sounds plausible when you talk about it, but Alan, it's still just speculation."

"Phoebe, I have seen it, I have a story to tell. The world is entitled to know what they were really like."

"Alan you're a scientist. You show the world as it is from facts, verifiable facts and conclusions from your research. You've always told us that."

"But I've seen it. That's research, and I want to see more of it. I need to know them better. I'm going back. I'm going to take the drug again."

"Alan, you can't. This isn't right."

"Pheb, I must. I've been thinking about it all day. I can't put it out of my mind. It's pulling at me. I have to go back. I have to know more about them."

"I'm scared Alan. It scares the hell out of me."

Chapter 7

As they traveled to the cave, Johnson's anticipation grew. He hadn't told Phoebe about the battle and killing two men. He wasn't sure he believed it himself. Maybe it was a dream. He had to be sure. It was a great adventure; he was going on an adventure like no modern man ever had. His mind dwelt on the last trip. By nature he was a mild-mannered professor, an academic. He never even played sports or did anything exciting until two days ago. The boldest competition he had ever been in was a chess game.

As Lightning Sky, he was different, and it felt strangely accelerating. He was strong, confident and powerful, all things Johnson wasn't, and all the things he wanted to be. There had been more excitement in one day than Johnson had seen in his entire lifetime. It was strongly compelling. He was unsure of what he would find this time. As he dwelt on it, he tensed. *But what if something goes wrong? What if something bad happens when I am back in time, then what?* Fear started to return. *Be brave like Lightning Sky. Be brave.*

The shaman was concerned. He didn't want to go back again. "You don't beseech the gods," he said. "They give gifts to man;

they are not to be commanded. Coming back so soon might make them angry."

Johnson was insistent. The old man relented when he offered the services of the students to assist the community in digging a new well. It would be part of the university program, their giving back for invading the sacred site. Water tables had dropped. Many of the individual family wells had gone dry. A new well would help them all. It was a bribe, but it worked. The old man's concern for helping his people overrode his fears.

The shaman said nothing to Johnson as they descended into the cave. He mumbled prayers and shook a rattle before him as they continued along the narrow passages. He appeared scared and was apprehensive, glancing back and forth as if something might come out of the walls. As they got closer to the chamber he moved slower and slower. It was obvious he didn't want to go further.

"Something is wrong," he said to Johnson. "We must go back."

"We can't, we've come too far to turn around."

"The gods aren't happy."

"I'll take my chances," Johnson responded.

"The gods are deceitful. They will lead you in then devour you just like they did the Hero Twins," the old man said, referencing the creation myths concerning the gods and the first men.

"I'll have to take the chance," Johnson responded chuckling at the thought. He looked at the old man, just another farmer in the community, but held in respect by the others. The man believed in the gods and that Johnson had seen and talked to them. Deep inside he felt he should listen to the shaman, but he couldn't. He had to go ahead.

They came to the little chamber where the ceremony was to take place. The shaman made the little fire as Johnson sat and watched. He pleaded with Johnson not to go through with the ceremony again. Johnson wouldn't listen. He had the powder, the drug. He clutched it tight against his chest and knew he had to take it again. His entire being depended on it. He could no more stop now than to stop breathing. He knew to deny it would tear a void in him. He couldn't stop even if he wanted to.

The craving was stronger than anything he ever felt before. He started to sweat and then to shake. His eyes became dilated and fixed on the shaman. Saliva drooled from the corner of his lip and the shaking got worse. His guts constricted as every fiber of his body strained to be free of this world. He needed to be fed the essence of the drug to be sedated. Only then would peace come to him. It would liberate him and take him to another plane of existence. Anger rose within him. *What is taking that man so long? His preparations should be done by now. Doesn't he understand? The 'blood of past life' must enter my veins again. It demands to be released. I need it, without it there is nothing.*

§

"Why have you come?" the voice said. Johnson looked around. He knew the voice. It was the same one as before. He couldn't see anything, just a dim twilight of illumination. Once again he was floating in the center of the universe. The effect of the drug had left him at peace.

"Who are you?" Johnson asked.

"I am the watcher of the gateway to Xibalba," was the reply. "I greet those who come to see the gods. Why have you come here?" the voice asked again.

"I came to return to the ancient ones," he responded to the voice. "I want to learn more about them."

"You have seen the ancient ones," the voice said. "What more do you want to know?"

"I want to know about the life of Shield Jaguar III. I want to know how he won, how he gained the throne."

"He won because he was of his father's loins and he carried the blood of kings all the way back to the beginning. He won because he was a great warrior in all things."

"I need to know him," Johnson said. "I need to know my brother."

"Are you ready to face the truth? The truth will consume you. It may destroy you."

"I am ready."

§

"Stand still," the old woman said as she held up the breastplate to his chest and tied it around the back. "You're awfully fidgety today."

Johnson looked around, he was in the same sleeping room he had been in before. The old woman who called herself his old mother was dressing him. He could see the low light coming through the doorway . It must be early morning. If it were evening he figured she would be helping him out of his clothing.

He looked at the garment he was to wear today. It looked important. Perhaps something special was happening. "So what am I doing today?" he asked hoping the woman would provide an idea of what to expect.

"Silly boy," she replied smiling while exposing her missing teeth. "You know the delegation from Piedras Negras comes today. You and your brother are to meet them and escort them to the royal court."

This must be an important meeting. Ceremonial protocol would be required. He began to tremble. He wouldn't know what it was. They would find out he was an imposter. Then what would happen? Maybe he shouldn't have come back again. It was too late, he was here. Once again he had to face the unknown. Taking the drug sounded so good when I told Phoebe I was going back. But was it?

After he was dressed he took a moment to collect his thoughts. He looked out the doorway. It was his portal to the past. On the other side he would again be Lightning Sky. He'd have to act like Lightning Sky, not Johnson. He'd be a young Maya noble. Cautiously Johnson stopped in the doorway and looked over the palace grounds. He needed to get a feel for what was outside before he faced it.

He saw small cooking fires located together in the center of the courtyard and women were cooking cornmeal tortillas on them. Breakfast was being prepared. People were gathering in small groups to eat. He noticed a woman motion to him to come. She held out a stack of fried corn tortillas filled with peppers and some type of meat he didn't recognize, which he gratefully took and started to casually eat. *Where to from here?*

"Fornicating monkey penises," he heard someone behind him say loudly. The voice sounded familiar. "That's all they are, fornicating monkey penises. I say we turn them around, kick them in their asses and send them on their way."

Johnson turned and looked at Shield Jaguar sitting on the steps to the palace dressed in ceremonial garments. He was glaring at another man, older and stockier, who was dressed in a long white robe with a neck piece holding the badges of his office, signifying he was a lord. Even under the robe Johnson could see he was a strong, powerful man, and his demeanor indicated he was not accustomed to being challenged. His long hair was braided together to the top of his head and held with a small headdress, the length of it trailing down his back. His eyes were narrow and shone black, and his nose appeared too big. Breaking up the symmetrical tattoo on his face was a long thick scar running from temple to jaw.

"These men are ambassadors from the king of Piedras Negras," the man in the white robe said.

"They are monkey penises," retorted Shield Jaguar as he took a bite of a tortilla and talked while chewing.

"Easy my brother," stated a third man, the king. He had been quietly watching the conflict with interest. "Lord Great Skull Zero has a point. We need to hear them out and see what they want."

"We know what they want," Shield Jaguar shot back. "They want us to give Lord T'ul Chiik back and then they want you to kneel in homage to their king. And, by the way, while you're kneeling there he'd like you to suck his little monkey penis, and tell him how good he is to let you do it."

"Diplomacy isn't your strong point, is it?" said the man identified as Lord Great Skull.

"You want to show diplomacy to a man when he wants you to kneel down and suck his penis?" retorted Shield Jaguar. "I say kill the fornicating maggot, and if you can't do that, bite it off. What kind of a counselor are you? You're not a war counselor."

"And we are not at war," the lord snapped back.

"We will be and it will be a good thing too, unless you're ready to open your mouth and start sucking." Shield Jaguar stood glaring at the other man. "They will see to that."

"What do you think little brother," Shield Jaguar asked as Johnson walked up to them. "Suck or fight?"

"That's a loaded question," Johnson remarked.

"Answer me," demanded Shield Jaguar. "Suck or fight, which would you rather do?"

"I don't like the sucking part," Johnson cautiously responded. He was going to stick close to this man. Arrogant or confident he couldn't be sure, but he was a fighter.

"We will have enemies on both sides if we fight them," Lord Great Skull shot back. "Tikal on one side and Piedras Negras on the other. That puts us in the middle and spreads our warriors too thin. The heathens from Tikal are warring with everyone again. The ring of the cities of the True People, descendents of the Hero

Twins, can't hold them back any longer. "Those heathens with the northern blood," he continued, "staged the destruction of Dos Pilas by instigating the revolt by the people of Tamarindito. And we're just down the river, next in line. They overran the town and the royal family ran for their lives. They reign no more and never will. If Tikal comes after us we should have strong allies on our side. We should be making truces to strengthen our position."

"May the gods shit on alliances with Piedras Negras," spat Shield Jaguar. "If we were blocked in, they wouldn't be coming here with a delegation. They would demand we come to them. Their power is weakening."

"And what do you think they will do today," Lord Great Skull replied, "ask politely?" Since you captured their K'inil Ajaw, (high lord) T'ul Chiik' two moons ago, they have made two raids on our people and...."

"And got sent running back home like a pack of scared little piglets," broke in Shield Jaguar, "just what they deserved."

Johnson watched, fascinated at the discourse and was suddenly shaken as it dawned on him: Lord Great Skull had said it has been two months since they took the captive. But they only captured him two days ago in Johnson's time. How long has the interval been since he was last here? He assumed time would be consistent between the two worlds, but it wasn't. It appeared he could be placed here at any time in the past. Were the gods playing with him? His reverie was broken by Lord Great Skull's reply.

"Tikal will be coming," he said. "Since they overran Calakmul and captured Jaguar Paw their king, the city isn't strong enough to stop them anymore. Calakmul was supposed to be aiding Dos Pilas against Tikal and it didn't help. Calakmul is no more able to help us than it was able to help Dos Pilas.

"And don't forget, when Tikal goes to war they are not looking to take captives for sacrifices or subjugate the king as a vassal.

They have no honor. They are destroyers. They destroy towns, kill the royal family and put their own people in charge. We need Piedras Negras to help stand up to them or they may destroy us too."

The king watched the argument closely, saying nothing. *What is he thinking?* Johnson wondered as he studied the man. *Here are two men giving him conflicting advice; the counselor who appears to have a hammer over him and his power, and his arrogant outspoken brother. The king is supposed to be a god, sanctified and deified. His word is law, totally and completely, not to be contested. It appears that the king is a thoughtful man, one who takes the counsel of others seriously. Who would I follow?*

"Lightning Sky," he heard someone call his name as Smoking Squirrel came up to the group. "Where have you been? We haven't seen much of you lately."

"He's got a girl," said Shield Jaguar, a big smile emerging on his face.

"You finally found one, huh? It's about time. We were starting to wonder if we should still be hanging around with you, maybe you like boys. What's she like?"

"You know," Johnson said cautiously, "Long black hair, big brown eyes."

"It's a commoner," interrupted Shield Jaguar. "He keeps disappearing at night so it must be a commoner."

"She got big breasts?" asked Smoking Squirrel. "I like the ones with big breasts."

"Humph," growled Great Skull. "All you three think about is sex and war." He turned and walked over to one of the cooking fires to get more tortillas, beans and hot peppers.

"What's he all upset about this morning?" asked Smoking Squirrel.

"I told him he couldn't suck a monkey's penis today," replied Shield Jaguar.

"I think that it bothered him," Johnson followed up.

"You shouldn't ride him like that," the king said with irritation. "He's a powerful man, a good one to have on your side."

"You keep him, brother," Shield Jaguar replied. "I don't want him."

"He can also be a powerful enemy. You should think about that," the king replied.

"It takes a powerful man to conquer powerful enemies," Shield Jaguar said as he shoved a large portion of tortilla in his mouth. He turned his head to follow the man. "And one day he's going to find that out."

Lord Great Skull returned with a large stack of tortillas and a bowl of hot peppers, and handed some to the others. The king motioned the men to move to the side of the patio and sit together where they couldn't be overheard.

"We need to come to an understanding," he said. "Like it or not, the delegation from Piedras Negras is going to come here, and we must listen to them."

"Let the…," Shield Jaguar started to say.

"No," burst the king. His face got hard as he stared at his brother. "It's time to plan, not fight. I don't like them either but we need a strategy to handle them today, not a battle plan. That may be for later. Right now I need to know what to expect and how best to respond to them. I solicit your advice, but I will make the decision on which way to go."

"Our father wouldn't have knelt to them if he didn't have to. Why should you?" retorted Shield Jaguar. "We don't have to be vassals to them anymore. It has been over thirty years since they defeated us and put us in this position. Our father was an old man at the time and he got careless. It is time to lift the burden, brother. Send them home with nothing. Tell them they will get nothing more. We can't afford to give them the corn tribute again this year and have enough left over for our use. The rains haven't come like before, and they are taking more of the tribute from the river merchants, leaving less for us. The crops will be small again, not enough for our people to eat. Many will go hungry, many will die. Better their people die than ours."

"I couldn't disagree with you more," Great Skull replied authoritatively. "I think the greater risk is Tikal. I'm your brother's counselor and it's my responsibility to advise him as I see fit. I think continuing our alliance with Piedras Negras would be in our best interest. We need their support."

Shield Jaguar glared at the great lord. "Support provided by Piedras Negras you say. I piss on their support. Piedras Negras is our enemy and has been for generations. It's best you not forget that." He glared into the lord's eyes long and unwavering. Then he turned and walked away as he called over his shoulder, "Come on brothers, it's time we go to meet those devils."

§

Johnson, Shield Jaguar and Smoking Squirrel headed down the hill followed by Shield Jaguar's Eagle Warrior Guards. As they left the center, another hundred warriors joined them. Formally dressed now as young royal lords, the three men looked like the noblemen in the stone pictures. All the warriors were wearing headdresses with a bird skull pointing forward, the Eagle Warriors. To Johnson it seemed like a lot of men just to meet a delegation from another city.

As they moved out of the city, people stood aside to make way for them, others came from their houses and stood and watched them pass. They were a spectacle. The people knew Shield Jaguar and liked the wild young prince who was so much like his father When he was going somewhere with a lot of men it often meant something was going to happen. Excitement seemed to follow him. Any new adventures became stories that were relished and told over and over again. His fame grew and they speculated upon his future and whether he would become the next king.

He was half brother to the reigning king and the son of the great ancestor king, Shield Jaguar II. He was fearless and arrogant, even to the king. He demanded respect as the son of the great king at all times. As a great warrior they said, he lived to fight and vanquish his enemies. He was courageous in battle and deadly when provoked.

He led the Eagle Warriors, a society of superior fighters. Admittance was only by invitation with the candidate's qualifications assessed by Shield Jaguar himself, and his standards were high. A minimum of four kills was necessary to even be considered, and they had to be combined with superior aggressiveness. He bragged that he would kill any of his warriors that moved a step backward on the battlefield. The slightest sign of cowardice from anyone was dealt with harshly, no second chances were given.

Each of his Eagle Warriors was correspondingly arrogant within the community. They were placed above the norm and society expected them to flaunt their position. An Eagle Warrior was always met with difference. He could demand it and if slighted, administer punishment on the spot. As they passed, it looked like another war party but without the face paint and strange headdresses. But the men looked just as ferocious.

"Where are we to meet them?" Smoking Squirrel asked.

"By the large blue water hole with the red rocks, a morning's walk near where the farms and the jungle come together. That's as far as they come with an escort."

"Do they know that?" Smoking Squirrel laughed.

"No, it's something new. They will know it when we get there," Shield Jaguar answered.

"They won't they like it, will they?" Johnson questioned.

"Not when I get done with them," Shield Jaguar laughed. "They think they own us and Ha' K'in Xook, the king's brother, will be leading them. He's an arrogant little mouse's prick who will probably be their next king. He'll have a lot of men with him expecting to intimidate us, but he's in for a surprise."

As they walked out of the town center they passed through the commoners' neighborhoods consisting of one room homes with thatched roofs adjacent to small fields under cultivation. The rainy season was beginning and farmers were starting to plant their land.

They walked for two hours. The trail narrowed and the warriors strung out in a long line. They came upon a small group of capybara and they cornered and killed two of them. The rest were let go. As they watched them run off, Shield Jaguar thanked the spirits of the two animals imploring them to go with the others letting their bodies be food for the men. The two they killed were tied to a pole and carried between two of the warriors.

The party came to the place of the red rocks and the hole with blue water, a large cenote eighty feet across. A path wound around the sides going down to a landing by the water.

Picturesque perfect, Johnson thought as he felt the tranquility and understood why it was considered a place where the gods' spirits dwelt. As others stood ready, small groups of men went down to drink the cool fresh water.

Then without warning, half the warriors formed a defense line facing the west. The other half split apart and disappeared into the jungle, a group to each side of the line. Johnson had heard no order given. From the corner of his eye he saw a hand signal from Shield Jaguar. Johnson smiled to himself. *This was no mere group of Paleoindians running around the jungle with stone-tipped spears looking for trouble.*

The Eagle Warriors were well trained. They moved fast, with purpose, and made no sound. From their position they could either spring a trap or guard a flank and in either case they were not obvious. Jaguar Shield motioned and the three young nobles took their place just ahead of the defense line.

§

The delegation from Piedras Negras came out of the forest. Shield Jaguar's presence was unexpected. Ha' K'in Xook, the prince from Piedras Negras, came into the clearing, stopped about one hundred feet from them and looked at the line. Johnson could hear his laugh as his warriors spread out behind him. He had the larger force and these underlings were going to get out of his way. To Johnson it looked like a standoff.

Shield Jaguar, Lightning Sky and Smoking Squirrel walked out into the middle between the two lines and waited. They watched the leader stand motionless, looking angry.

"Good morning," Shield Jaguar called and waited for a response. The Piedras Negras prince appeared even angrier. He was here to demand respect and being met with an armed force wasn't acceptable. A delegation of twenty warriors would have been correct, enough to demonstrate subservience to his superior status. A quick count indicated at least fifty warriors were there opposing his eighty.

"You meet me with force?" he shouted. "You dare to meet me with force?"

"I'm here to greet you," Shield Jaguar called back. "You are a guest in our land."

"Greet me with a war party?" Johnson could see him shaking with anger. They were going to charge. He just knew it.

"What? We are a hunting party. We have killed fresh meat for the banquet tonight," Shield Jaguar claimed as the two men brought the rodents around the ends of the line for them to see.

"I'm so glad we were hunting in this area. It's fortunate for you to have run into us. Now we can proceed back to the city together. It will give us a chance to get to know one another."

"Get out of my way," screamed the opposing prince. "I am

bringing a delegation to see the king, and I'll not be interfered with."

"You want to see my brother?" Shield Jaguar called back. "He mentioned that he was expecting an official from Piedras Negras who was coming our way. You must be him. You're a couple of days early aren't you?"

"I am Prince Ha' K'in Xook, heir to the throne of Piedras Negras, and I command you to stand aside." His warriors spread out behind him showing their superior numbers.

Shield Jaguar raised his arms outward and his concealed warriors stood up, spears held back in a launch position. At the same time the line behind him also raised their spears to throw.

"Let one man raise a spear and I'll turn them loose," Shield Jaguar said quietly, the authority of his voice ringing in the silence, "and Piedras Negras will be looking for another heir."

The young prince was caught. He knew it. How dare this dung-eating fornicator do this to him? He needs to be whipped to death for his arrogance, and before this was over he would see that it was done.

He looked closer at the warriors and noted the headdresses with the eagle skulls. They all had eagle skulls, seasoned warriors, the best. He recognized them. Their reputation preceded them. If they charged he would be dead or even worse captured. This had to be Shield Jaguar, the uncontrollable one. They said he didn't give a damn about the consequences of his actions and the gods supported him for it. He was the one who captured their high lord T'ul Chiik and he did it out of the mouth of a trap they set for him.

Johnson watched the situation play out. He felt a mixture of anticipation and elation. This man standing before him, who was facing down the opposing prince, had balls. Johnson realized he was a part of it and a feeling of pride grew in his chest, something he had never felt before. He was here in the Eighth Century facing an enemy preparing to charge, drawing him into a battle. He felt no fear and he smiled to himself. Deep down inside he was hoping it would happen and it felt good.

The procession back to the city center allowed Shield Jaguar to show he was in control of the entourage. A group of Shield Jaguar's Eagle Warriors preceded the group. Then came the two princes, the two ambassadors who were with Ha' K'in Xook, and Lightning Sky and Smoking Squirrel. Behind the nobles was another group of Shield Jaguar's warriors, and further back were the remainder of the Piedras Negras warriors followed by more of the Yaxchilan warriors. Anyone looking at the procession obviously understood that Shield Jaguar was fully in command and the prince from Piedras Negras appeared to be a captive.

As they passed from village to village, the people came out and stared in awe at the procession. It was the prince Shield Jaguar, and he had taken the Piedras Negras ambassador as a prisoner they thought, and a new story sprang to life to glorify his honor adding to his hero status. It was only when they got back to the ceremonial center that Shield Jaguar allowed the prince the official protocol entitled to a visiting dignitary.

Chapter 8

The blowing of horns announced their arrival. The Piedras Negras prince and his ambassadors entered the Great Plaza and were greeted by a cheering crowd. Receiving official state visitors was an occasion. Even those from an enemy state were provided a dignified welcome. The people who did the cheering had been ordered to be there. Appearances must be kept.

They entered the city in a formal procession. Shield Jaguar and Ha' K'in Xook headed the parade, followed by their closest retainers. All the nobles were wearing ceremonial attire. The princes wore jaguar-skin capes and large ornate headdresses decorated with brilliant feathers. They were followed by a group of lords of Yaxchilan who wore long white capes with embroidered red borders. Three medallions of gold, marking their station, hung by chains from their necks and on their heads were smaller but ornate headdresses. Two small groups of warriors of token guards followed closely; one from Piedras Negras and one from Yaxchilan. The young princes waved to the crowd. They moved slowly across the plaza in a dignified manner signifying the solemn nature of the visit.

From the hill overlooking the plaza on the opposite side, was a small group of Yaxchilan's family heads, senior lords, watching the procession. A delegation from Piedras Negras was not a welcome sight. For over four hundred years they had been adversaries and fought periodic wars. During the reign of the king's father, Yaxchilan had been defeated by Piedras Negras, and since that time were a subservient state to them.

"Look at them," exclaimed one of the lords as he pointed to the group crossing the plaza, "entering our city like they owned it."

"Humiliating," said another.

"What do they want here?"

"They want Lord T'ul Chiik, and a severe payment for taking him."

"Think they will get him?" the first one asked.

"Not if Shield Jaguar has anything to say about it. He took him and he'll keep him."

"But he's not the king," another lord injected.

"Think that will stop the prince?" the first lord asked with a laugh. "He's like his father, Shield Jaguar the Great. He'll fight until there is nothing left to fight with."

"He sure acts like he's the king sometimes," the other lord said.

Lord Great Skull who had been listening to the conversation said, "Well he's not the king and never will be. The king wants his successor to be from his own loins."

"And his son, your nephew, is to be the next king?"

"Perhaps," said Great Skull with an inward smile. "Who knows what the gods favor? Don't they play tricks on man? My sister is the king's primary and favorite wife and her child is heir."

"Shield Jaguar is still the half brother to the king and the son of the Great Shield Jaguar. He has a claim to the throne," replied another lord.

"He's never been officially designated as heir," replied Great Skull harshly. "That leaves a lot open. The king wants his son to follow him."

"You'd never know that listening to the prince," replied the other lord. "He invokes his father's name every chance he gets. Even the people are starting to say, 'there goes Shield Jaguar a great warrior, the son of the great Shield Jaguar'."

"Look at him down there," Lord Great Skull said as they looked over the plaza at the procession of men entering it. "You'd think he was the king now with all his airs."

"He does get the people aroused doesn't he?" the other lord replied.

"I can't worry about what he does," Great Skull snapped as he started down the hill from the palace. "I have to get down there and welcome the delegation and arrange to take them to the king."

"Think he will pull it off?" asked one of the other lords as they watched Lord Great Skull walk down the stairs to meet the delegation.

"Maybe," replied the other man. "I don't think I'd like to be on the receiving end of one of his schemes. He'll stop at nothing to get what he wants."

"I wonder what he has on the king," the first lord mused. "He sure has a hold on him."

"It's best not talked about," the other lord replied. "He'd be a bad man to have as an enemy and that's a subject he doesn't want in the open."

§

The king, Bird Jaguar, sat immobile and observed the procession coming toward him. It was a hot day, but he was in the shade of the door to his palace reception room. A thatched roof was positioned above him. There was a soft breeze and it would have been a nice day if not for the arrival of the Piedras Negras delegation..

Runners had informed him earlier that Ha' K'in Xook, the brother to the king, was the lead dignitary. He may well be the next reigning king of Piedras Negras. The prince coming here was unusual. It indicated that the prince was coming to make demands with the expectation they will be received and acted on immediately. It was an insult. A long time had passed since their defeat by Piedras Negras. Yaxchilan should have shed the yoke of burden long ago but his father was an old man when defeated, and feeble. After he died, the council of families who ruled was impotent. Now it was up to him, even if it meant war.

The royal session for the audience was held in the courtyard instead of inside the palace, enabling more nobles to observe the proceedings. Normally, high level lords of the king attended meetings to promote alliances or settle disputes between city states, at least in the initial stages

The palace buildings were placed in a rectangular pattern with the courtyard in the center. Along the inside of one wall of the building ran a porch-like landing a few feet above the courtyard, the king's residence. Many doorways opened to it, rooms of the king and his close family members. Sitting in front of the largest opening, the one to the king's royal chamber, was an intricately carved stone dais. Carved glyphs adorned the bench identifying the king and his status as a descendent of the First Father and conduit to the gods. Behind the dais around the opening were red curtains framing the seated king.

Bird Jaguar sat cross-legged solemnly waiting in silence. He was attired simply—a white breechcloth, soft leather boots and an ornate headpiece signifying his royal status. Around his neck was a heavy jade-stone necklace and on his wrists inlaid jade cuffs. Clutched to his chest he held a god effigy. No special ceremonies were being made to honor these visitors. As dignitaries from a rival city state it was an insult, but they weren't welcome.

On the landing below the dais, to the king's left, sat the

three great lords of Yaxchilan—the heads of three of the five aristocratic families making up the nobility, the fourth and fifth being Lord Great Skull's family and the royal family. Kneeling on the ground in front of the steps on the king's right were his three wives. Lady Great Skull, his main wife, was holding Chel-Te' the king's young son.

Three steep stairs rose up to the landing. When introduced, the visitors would stand at the bottom of the stairs looking up to the king, never to be above him. Shield Jaguar and Lightning Sky came across the courtyard to stand behind the king's dais. They were dressed as young royal nobles in fine jaguar-skin capes. Red loincloths supported with ornate belts and a long celt decorated with a god's head. Matching red shirts were overlain with heavy jade neckpieces stretching down over their chests Jade wrist cuffs were accented by large rings set with colored stones. Large headpieces with ornate feathers complemented the costume. On the same political level as the visitor, they were not to be outdone by the prince from Piedras Negras in dress or manner.

As they moved into position, Johnson looked at the scene in awe, the formal court of a Maya king. He had seen pictures on bowls depicting settings like these. There was an air of formality as the scene took on a sacred tone. Everyone knew where to go. They took their places in silence. The king looked regal, different from the earlier informal meetings with his advisors. He was transformed into another being, deified and commanding. Sitting on his dais, the world was his to command.

The process of bringing petitioners before him was administered by the lords of Yaxchilan, with Lord Great Skull having the final approval. The king only decided important matters. If Lord Great Skull decided the petition was not significant enough he would route it in the proper direction. The system allowed every petition to be met on the level deemed necessary for its resolution.

A troupe of musicians standing along the landing started

playing. Horns sounded announcing the arrival of the visiting dignitaries and drums were rhythmically beaten to call the gods to join the ceremonial gathering; flutes carried a melody.

Lord Great Skull was dressed simply but wore the woven white cotton robe with the red border and necklace holding the badges which designated his esteemed office as the king's first counselor. He stepped forward and announced the visitors, the Piedras Negras prince and the two ambassadors. He announced a lengthy formal dialogue expounding on the prince's titles and achievements.

After the announcement of the visitors, the lord presented the "Great King Bird Jaguar, Holy Lord of Yaxchilan, Guardian of Aj Uk', He of Twenty Captives, Holy Lord of the Split Sky Place, is receiving petitions." Upon completion he walked up the stairs careful to always keep his head below the king's and took his place, sitting with the other lords to the right beside the king's dais.

"With the blessing of the gods I greet you today as a friend from the great city of Piedras Negras," said Prince Ha' K'in Xook loudly for all in the courtyard to hear.

The presentation of gifts was made as slaves brought forward sacks of cocoa beans and a box of jade jewelry, obsidian blades and a polished stone mirror. The king motioned to his left on the landing and the Piedras Negras prince and ambassadors took seats sitting cross-legged beside the king's dais.

Shield Jaguar leaned toward Lightning Sky and whispered, "That monkey's ass coming here. I tell you, he's up to no good. I should have run him off as soon as he stepped foot in our province. I don't know why my brother let him come to his court. I've tried to tell him that his politicking won't work with Piedras Negras. I say run a spear up his ass and send him home. That's the way to deal with those heathens."

"Perhaps he'll do that before it's over," replied Lightning Sky.

"He pisses me off," Shield Jaguar replied glaring at the visiting prince. "An arrogant monkey's penis and he will be a king someday."

"Yeah, I noticed you weren't looking happy about it."

Shield Jaguar leaned forward and cupped his hand around the king's ear. "Here it comes, brother. That arrogant monkey's penis is about to ask you to 'open wide'. He's got something for you to suck on."

The king looked over his shoulder, smiled with a silent little chuckle and said, "Maybe he wants you to do it. You're his rival—both princes. You might consider it an obligation of the office."

"I'd take my knife and cut the fornicating thing off first," snarled Shield Jaguar.

"Best let me handle this then," the king said with a laugh. "I can't send him back to his brother without his manhood, can I?"

The king turned back and looked hard at the young prince. He was in no hurry. *Let the little whelp know who is in charge.* He watched the prince become uncomfortable with the silence.

"How is your brother, the king of Piedras Negras, these days?" the king opened.

"The great king rules with a strong hand and a gentle heart. He is a benefactor to his friends and a destroyer of his enemies," the prince stated as he launched into a loud speech extolling the virtues of Piedras Negras and its king.

Bird Jaguar sat back and waited. Protocol was protocol. When the prince finished, he sat quietly letting the silence settle in.

"Yaxchilan has a glorious history too," he said softly. "I'm sure you are aware our enemies kneel at my feet, as they did with my father and grandfather and those before them, and beg for mercy. You are sitting at my feet young prince, what are you begging for?"

"Begging? Why you...," the prince exclaimed as he started

to rise. From across the courtyard ten warriors moved forward, spears held ready to launch. Shield Jaguar grabbed a war club and stepped beside the dais.

"Sit," commanded the king, glaring down at the young man.

The young prince shrunk back down, obviously shook at his error in protocol.

"Now, young prince, what do you want with Yaxchilan?" the king said softly, as he watched the man's face closely.

"You forget who the lord and master of your city is. You owe us servitude."

"Really?" replied the king. "Your claim was a long time ago. Perhaps it is no longer valid."

"We want Lord T'ul Chiik back," said the prince ignoring the king's reply.

"Really," replied the king after a long pause.

"And compensation of two thousand bags of corn for the inconvenience."

"The lord and two thousand bags of corn you say," the king mused.

"That's in addition to this year's tribute," replied the prince confidently.

"Anything else that comes to mind while we are talking?" asked the king.

"The king, as your friend, would like to take your sister as a fourth wife as a show of good faith in our being your benefactor. In return he would give you his sister as a fourth wife."

"My sister now. Really, he wants my sister as a wife, a fourth wife," replied the king as he scratched his chin in thought. "She won't make much of a wife you know. She has a mean disposition, especially in the mornings. That can be hard on a man. I'm not sure I want to inflict that on a friend."

The king sat in silence staring blankly into the prince's eyes. To accept would hold him as a vassal to Piedras Negras. Wives from other cities were often used for political alliances. His mother was a princess from Calakmul. He had two political wives now. He didn't want another, especially from Piedras Negras. And no, sending his sister to Piedras Negras wasn't going to happen. To refuse would place their military strength against him. This was a veiled threat. His body tensed as his anger rose.

He looked at the young man sternly. *He'll be a king some day, but not this day. The arrogant little mouse's turd has a lot of gall to come in front of me, a true king with ancestors traceable back to the First Father, and pompously demand my sister as a wife, a hostage. It's absurd.*

If I wasn't under an oath of protection, I'd send the little turd's head back to his father impaled on a spear. To kill this little fornicator wouldn't be enough, even slowly and painfully. Did the king of Piedras Negras think I'd just abandon my mother's people who came from Calakmul and come and serve him?

Jaguar Shield, standing behind the king, gasped under his breath. "That fornicating little wasp," he mumbled. "A marriage alliance, he has the nerve." Everyone waited for the king who sat there silent as he slowly rocked his head back and forth in thought.

Shield Jaguar stepped forward and cupped his hand over the king's ear in a way that indicated he wanted to say something private. "Perhaps brother, if you swap wives," he said loud enough for everyone to hear. "Ask for the king's daughter instead of his sister. She's sixteen now, a woman, and I hear she's a good fornicator, insatiable in bed, wants it day and night." Shield Jaguar looked at the visiting prince to see how his insult was received. "Perhaps," he continued, "you could take her for a while, try her out and then give her back since she's been used before."

The king turned his head and smiled, then chuckled. Leave it up to his brother. "Lady Great Skull might have a problem with that."

"Eat lots of peppers and clams. Then you will be strong enough to service both of them."

"And if I'm not?"

"Then perhaps I can help you with that little wildcat. Give her to me. I think I could tame her." Shield Jaguar looked hard at the Piedras Negras prince. "Think I could tame your brother's daughter Ha' K'in Xook?"

The prince's face turned red at the insult, then hard as he started to rise.

"Sit," the king commanded the prince as he waved his hand back to shut Shield Jaguar up.

Shield Jaguar nudged Lightning Sky, looked over and smiled.

"The king's in good form today," he whispered softly.

"It does look like the prince is having a hard time of it, doesn't it?" was the reply.

"And look at Great Skull," said Shield Jaguar. "He's not too happy about it. I wonder what he has up his sleeve this time. He isn't afraid of Piedras Negras, but he's pushing for staying subservient to them. My brother's tone doesn't indicate he's going to get it."

"I must consider your generous offer," the king continued. "Tell your brother the king, I will take it under advisement."

"I have instructions to escort Lord T'ul Chiik back with me."

"That may be difficult," the king responded. Now was the time to make the break.

"Explain 'difficult'," the prince said tersely, turning red with anger.

"I like him," replied the king. "He's entertaining. My dwarf likes playing with him."

"You exceed your position," the prince said harshly. "My brother, King *Yo' Nal Ahk III*, has made a generous offer for restitution. You would be well advised to take it. It will not be repeated."

"I'll consider that," the King replied.

"I'll take Lord T'ul Chiik back now. This is a command from my brother, your reigning king."

The king's body tightened noticeably, a scowl crossed his face as he glared at the young prince. "Shield Jaguar, go prepare Lord T'ul Chiik for travel," he commanded. "He wants to go home."

Shield Jaguar left the palace. Returning a few minutes later, he gave a small cloth bag to the king. The king looked in the bag, nodded and handed it to Lord Great Skull who also looked into the bag. He closed it and handed it to the prince. As the prince opened the bag, the king said. "I'll send him home a piece at a time. This time the ears go with you. They can listen to your useless prattle."

§

The light from the torches blanketed the courtyard behind the men with a soft flickering light. Evening was setting in and the king, his chief counselors and the heads of the other families, were sitting on the top of the hill at the edge of the king's palace compound overlooking the Great Plaza. The palace, a series of buildings and courtyards housing the royal family, was a large and prominent structure with a commanding view of the area. Similar compounds were arranged in close proximity for each of the other aristocratic families. Each lord reigned as the head of his family and their enterprises, and pledged fidelity to the king.

The king held audiences and conducted business in his palace throne room daily. There he was a god, listening, deciding and commanding. There was no discussion. The king spoke and it was law. A formal protocol was strictly observed and the king commanded absolute obedience. He was the leader of the people, held divine power and was the community's conduit to the gods.

However, the evenings around sundown often found the

king and his advisors gathering on the hill to discuss the day's events and other issues of importance. It appeared to be a casual gathering with give and take as they discussed matters of importance. However, protocol was still maintained for both seating and conversation. The king was still the king, never to be addressed casually. There was a distinct difference in the approach to governing.

Johnson realized that Bird Jaguar was a ruler with divine power but he was also a cautious and thoughtful man who regularly sought the advice of his counselors and tended to follow it. Historians thought this king was a political man with insecurities about his position. The noble families had power and though he had wrested it from them, they could still cause him inconveniences.

Earlier in the day the prince, Ha' K'in Xook of Piedras Negras, left the audience with the king and started back home in defiance of formal protocol. A dinner had been arranged. The visit by a royal personage of another city required a formal banquet and festivities no matter what the subject of the visit. Angry at the response he received from the king, *Ha' K'in Xook*, vowed that the enemies of Piedras Negras would one day bow down in subjugation to him. The implication was that Yaxchilan was now to be considered an enemy once again.

That evening the king called the lords together to discuss the audience and its implications. As Shield Jaguar and Lightning Sky walked up to the group and took their places, they heard Lord Great Skull say, "That arrogant little prick, he actually came here and asked for your sister as a bride to the king. Did he really think you would give her to him?"

"It wasn't a request," replied the king. "It was a command from his brother, the king; remain his vassal or become his enemy. Giving my sister in marriage to their king would keep me his vassal."

"If you went for the trade," said Shield Jaguar laughing. "I still think I could have negotiated to get you the king's daughter. Then you'd have a young wife in your bed. She's good looking and perhaps she likes to fornicate. That's not all bad. Think of the rodents your other two political wives are. They sure didn't send their best when you demanded hostage wives."

"Lady Mut-B'alam doesn't look too bad. She'd do on the night of a full moon," said Smoking Squirrel slyly as he cautiously peered at the king. Sometimes he went along with their levity, sometimes not. Shield Jaguar, being the arrogant brother, could get by saying almost anything, but Smoking Squirrel could not. He had to be careful.

"The king comes to the first meal of the day looking well spent some mornings," said Shield Jaguar.

"Maybe Lady Great Skull does that," Smoking Squirrel followed the drift.

"Not on those mornings," Shield Jaguar said with authority.

"He looks grouchy the morning after a Lady Great Skull night."

"Okay, my marital affairs aren't your concern," the king spat out, showing his irritation. We came here to discuss the meeting with Prince Ha' K'in Xook and the issues arising from it."

"So the issue," claimed Shield Jaguar looking at the king as he openly laughed, "is fornicate or fight, and this morning I thought it was suck or fight. How can a man be so wrong?"

"Sounds like a better offer, doesn't it?" The king laughed at the thought, and at his brother. He could always count on him to take a major problem and make something humorous out of it. But when it came down to facing an adversary, he'd turn hard and put it all on the line, and at those times he could be a very determined man. "However," he continued, "the result would be about the same. I'd be subordinate to them."

"This time you have it right," replied Lord Great Skull to the king as he sat back studying the king's brother. He was becoming a formidable opponent. Was he going to become a problem? "The word is fight," the lord responded. "I'm afraid we have incited an old enemy."

"We never were friends," responded Shield Jaguar. "It doesn't look like we've lost much."

"They will be coming after us now and we have to be ready for them," concluded Lord Great Skull.

"When we put your warriors and those of the other families together with mine," said Shield Jaguar, "we'll have enough to stop them."

Great Skull's strength was vested in his command of the military. The stronger it was, the stronger he was, and controlling both that of his family and the king's, put him in a position of power over the other families. Now this young whelp was going to run off with over half of his command, maybe more. The lord quietly fumed. Not if he could help it.

"I think," started Lord Great Skull cautiously, "that perhaps you should lead a group of one hundred Eagle Warriors for a while longer, and gain more experience before you command a larger force."

"I have been trained my whole life for war," retorted Shield Jaguar. "Now you say I need more experience? The warriors of the royal family are my brothers, and I will lead them. It is my birthright."

"My brother is no longer a boy," broke in the king. "He has been making attacks against our enemies and defending against their attacks on us. Yes, he is young, but he has killed his enemies and taken a prisoner as a demonstration of his power and skill as a warrior. Perhaps it is time for him to take on the responsibility."

"But...," stated the lord.

"He will still have you as a counselor, as I have," continued the king, "which will continue to ensure his success."

Shield Jaguar broke into a big smile. *What's happening to my brother today?* he thought. *He always followed Great Skull's advice before, always. You'd think Lord Great Skull was the king from the way he struts around in his aloof manner. All the other lords are afraid of him.* Today was the first time Shield Jaguar saw the king stand up to the lord on a major issue and in his favor.

First he kicked the Piedras Negras prince out and then supported Shield Jaguar on taking command of the warriors. This is new. If Shield Jaguar controlled the warriors, Lord Great Skull wouldn't have quite the same control over the king.

"The problem we face is: what is Piedras Negras going to do?" stated the king.

"They will attack us hard this time, I think," said another lord.

"I think it's going to be bad," responded Lord Great Skull. They will want to destroy us this time. It will be a new kind of war, one without honor. Like Tikal, they will try to overrun our vassal towns and cities and kill the high nobles and their families when Venus appears brightest as the morning star. I think there will be hard times."

"Then we must fight them their way," replied Shield Jaguar. "We must be destroyers too. And we must destroy them before they can destroy us."

"I'm afraid you are right," replied the king. "The old ways are leaving us and we must adapt the new."

§

The group broke up. The king and lords drifted back to their compounds. Shield Jaguar, Smoking Squirrel and Lightning Sky remained sitting in the quiet setting, reflecting on the discussion.

"It's been a good day," Shield Jaguar said.

"You think so?" replied Johnson.

"Did you see the look on old Great Skull's face when that monkey's ass demanded the king's sister as a wife for an alliance?" Shield Jaguar laughed heartily at the memory. "He never saw it coming. I can just see her and Lady Great Skull under the same roof."

"Problems?" Johnson responded hoping to gain an insight into the political workings of the kingdom.

"If it were the Piedras Negras princess, yes, she's a wild cat all right. You could wager that there'd be problems."

"You know her?"

"Only by reputation. She's supposed to be beautiful, spoiled and a real bitch. She and Lady Great Skull in the same house." Shield Jaguar again laughed heartily. "They are two of a kind, but Lady Great Skull is probably worse. My brother would never know peace."

"Really, why don't you think so?" Johnson cautiously asked.

"It was that way with our father, the great Shield Jaguar II. He had to put up with Lady Xook his first wife and Bird Jaguar's mother, a political wife from Calakmul. Lady Xook made his life hell. He erected that temple down there to make her happy and she still made his life miserable," he said pointing toward a temple at the bottom of the hill.

"After he died she did everything she could to keep my brother from the throne. She lived in a world of hate for Lady Eveningstar. Bird Jaguar couldn't gain power until after she died."

"Her family was strong though, wasn't it?" Johnson questioned. One of the great mysteries of the Maya was about to be revealed. How could the great Bird Jaguar IV have been stopped from ascending to his father's throne for ten years?

Shield Jaguar looked at the young man and said, "You should know his claim to being a king ascended from the ancestors was in doubt. My father wasn't a direct descendent of the male line. The line had been broken when my grandfather and mother had no surviving son. Grandfather Bird Jaguar III arranged for his mother's line to connect to the gods which gave credibility to the Xook family. After my father died, Lady Xook claimed her brother was now a direct descendent of the First Father, and demanded that he become king. She got her way for a while. Later Lord Great Skull opposed her and a few years after that gained the support of the other families. The price for his support was for Bird Jaguar IV to marry Great Skull Zero' sister, have a male child by her, and designate him as heir to the throne."

"I thought taking a captive was included." said Johnson. Contemporary anthropological thinking claimed it was the primary requirement.

"It helped, I think. He captured others before but not prisoners of any consequence."

§

Later that evening, Johnson stood in the center of the Great Plaza and slowly turned in a circle. He felt a shiver run down his spine. Throughout the plaza area, torches burned, sculpturing the buildings with eerie lines and shadows adding to their mystique. It was quiet and there was a peacefulness at this time of the evening. Only a few priests passed, breaking his reverie. He sensed a feeling of harmony in this place. Perhaps the ancestors were watching over him. Pyramids stood majestically ringing the plaza; man-made structures, the mountains of the outer world rising from the plaza: the primordial watery world of Xibalba home of the gods, birthplace of man.

As he slowly turned, taking in everything, he marveled anew. The ceremonial complex was a jewel that rivaled anything found in the ancient world. *It's a shame that they aren't in the desert like Egypt where the dry climate would have preserved them so much better. I need to study each one in turn and commit their features to memory. Will there be time? The last time I was here for two nights and a day. How long would it be this time? There is so much to do and so little time, where do I start?*

He walked along the plaza viewing the buildings until he came to Lady Sak B'iyann's temple, Temple 11 as he knew it. Stopping in front he looked up the stairs, studying the structure and reliefs. It was beautiful. He looked back at the temples dedicated to Lady Xook and Lady Eveningstar. The archaeological world was fascinated with the rivalry between the two, almost ignoring the significance of this temple. For decades the two women fought to be mothers of the royal line, while Lady Sak B'iyann of this temple bore children to an old man. *The old king must have been eighty at the time.* Johnson chuckled. *If what Shield Jaguar said about the rivalry between the great ladies was true, the king must have enjoyed the company of this younger one.*

A woman appeared in the doorway of the temple. She stood there watching Johnson. Cautiously she looked around at the plaza and buildings. Who else was watching? Only some priests and a priestess and a few guards are still here. It was bold of him to come here. Someone could see him. She smiled. *He must love me desperately to take the chance. My heart aches at the sight of him and I long to be in his arms again.*

As he came past the temple she stepped into the light. "Lightning Sky, here," she called softly and stepped back into the shadows.

Johnson looked up the steps trying to make out the woman in the dim light. He started up the steps. It sounded like the young girl who had been on the pyramid when he first arrived.

"Little Rabbit, is that you?"

"Come," she replied

As Johnson reached the top of the stairs, she stepped into the faint light flickering from the torches inside the temple. Johnson's heart pounded at the sight of her. She waited silently, longingly watching him come to her. The subtle beauty of her features held a radiant glow. She stood immobile, like a statue chiseled by a master. Her thin white shift clung to the contours of her body, accenting her slim youthful figure. Her long black hair glistened and her shining eyes sparkled. She stood there motionless, a haunting beauty. She appeared a goddess, the temple a sanctuary. He stopped. He could go no further. He couldn't enter this sacred space. She was an apparition. Yes, an apparition from another world, a daughter of the gods.

Then her face broke into a broad smile, and the spell was broken. The exotic goddess disappeared before his eyes to be reincarnated a woman, young, beautiful and enraptured by his presence. She beamed, and her eyes sparkled and she became full of life.

"Lightning Sky, oh Lightning Sky," she said as she wrapped her arms around his waist and held her head against his chest.

He placed his arms around her and held her close.

"I was so worried when you didn't come last night," she said.

"It couldn't be helped," he said noncommittally

"Does Shield Jaguar suspect?" she asked, fear creeping into her voice.

"I'm not sure; I don't know," He replied. *Suspect, what was he to supposed to suspect? Was this Shield Jaguar's woman?*

"What are we going to do?"

"What do you think we should do?" Johnson asked slowly.

"The gods are against us. How can we resist their wishes?" she cried.

"Maybe they will change," Johnson said. *What the hell is this woman talking about? On the pyramid during the first trip she had asked if the gods blessed our love. Then at the victory celebration she wanted me to go with her,* he thought, *but the evening's drinking took me instead. And now she wants to know what we are supposed to do.*

"You know the gods favor Shield Jaguar," she said. "He is strong and he demands their respect. Sometimes the gods listen to men. They listen to him," she replied tearfully as she held him tighter.

"Why can't they listen to both of you?" he asked. "Gods can do that you know."

"You know I am to be wed to another. I will be betrothed to a prince or a king and am expected to marry him and bear him a son to carry on his line. My blood is sacred. It goes back to the beginning. The gods have told me this is to be. They command it. Lightning Sky, what are we to do?"

What would the real Lightning Sky say, reasoned Johnson. He was obviously enamored with this woman. Slowly, he said, "I would think we must take the time we have and make the best use of it."

"Come with me," she said as she took his hand and held it tightly to her breast. "Let's go to our special place. I need you."

§

The river was dark and the current lazy as they paddled the canoe to the opposite shore. Even with the light of a half moon he could barely see her as she pointed the direction. They put in at a little cut covered with brush where the canoe could be beached and not seen from the river. The night was still, not a sound was heard. Stepping from the canoe she threw her arms around his neck and kissed him hard.

"I can't wait," she whispered desperately. "I need you," and she kissed him again and again. "When you didn't come last night I thought I was going to die. Each day brings renewed dread that it may be the last. Each minute with you is a precious gift. The gods can't forsake us, but my love, they do. They tease us with a few minutes of bliss and punish us with hours of pain for our actions. But I don't care. For only a minute of bliss with you I would endure a lifetime of pain, and eventually that will be my lot in life."

Johnson held her tightly. How was he to act? She obviously loved Lightning Sky but it was a love based on desperation. He felt like a voyeur. Yet this exquisite young woman was wrapped up in his arms. Her scent intoxicated his senses. Through the thin shift she wore he could feel the softness of her skin. She felt warm; he felt her yielding as he became enveloped in her aura. And something stirred within his loins; basic, primal, a need coming from the depths of his soul. And he knew he wanted her. No, he needed her, more than anything in this world. He needed to be one with her.

"Come," she said as she took his hand pulling him into the jungle. Running before him, she appeared a spirit flitting through the forest. She'd disappear behind a tree, vanish from his sight. He'd stop and look; the forest, dark and quiet, became empty without her presence, then she'd reappear, pulling him, teasing him, so close yet just out of reach. He was chasing an enchanting forest sprite who mesmerized him as she clutched at his soul. Ten minutes later they came to a small mound.

"What is this?" he asked.

"You know. It is a temple of the ancient ones. We found it when we were children. No one else knows it is here. It just looks like a little hill. It has been our secret place ever since."

She cleared some brush piled in front of the mound and stepped through the doorway into a small room and lit a lamp. A room appeared in the soft glow with a dirt floor and stone walls, the doorway the only opening. Along one side was a stone altar, along another a sleeping mat covered with soft animal skins.

He turned back from his investigation and she stood in front of him, the shift settling around her feet. The light low, her pensive gaze enchanting, she once again became the goddess of the temple, standing before him. She held out her hand, took his and led him to the sleeping mat. Slowly she undressed him, caressing and kissing him as each piece of clothing was removed. When completed she lay down on the bed. As she looked up at him, a tear rolled down her cheek. "Come my love," she said, "the gods have given us another gift. Maybe they don't hate us. They rejoice in our love as desperate as it may be. Tonight I am yours. Always I will be yours."

As he settled beside her, Little Rabbit held him tightly. Her body trembled and she wept softly. "The time is not long now. How am I going to live without you?" she wept. "How can I see you every day and not be with you?"

"We have tonight," Johnson answered. What else could he say? "Tonight I am yours as you are mine." He raised himself up on an elbow and looked into her eyes. "All that matters is tonight and our love," he said as he leaned down and kissed her softly. "Tonight you are my woman and I have all that I want in this world." He kissed the tears that rolled down her cheeks.

"I love you," she responded and kissed him back softly.

They held each other gently and kissed tenderly over and over. Passion fueled by desperation enveloped them as their lovemaking become harder, almost brutal. Each became wrapped up in the other; giving, taking, demanding more as the passion rose, needing more in return, fueling the never-ending cycle spiraling them into oblivion. From two they became one, joined at the soul, no longer of this world, each lost in the other as the moment of release approached and claimed them. Spent, they held each other tightly, afraid to be apart, each belonging to the other, an affirmation of their love.

Later, he lay beside her on the pallet. Small and delicate, she nestled against him as he held her close. Her scent intoxicated him and her aura enveloped him. As he held her in his arms, his whole being wrapped itself around her and he was filled with an exquisite joy.

She was the core of his essence. He knew it always had been and always would be. Instinctively he knew as he lay there holding her tightly that from this time on she would be the only thing in the world that would ever mean anything to him. A deep pain washed over him as he suddenly realized that he was only a visitor in this dark jungle thirteen hundred years before his own time, only to be here for a short while. He held her tighter as despair gripped his soul and he remembered the admonishment of the gods that the truth would destroy him.

Chapter 9

You have come back from your trip," the old shaman said as Johnson started to stir. Disoriented from the drug, Johnson stared blankly. It was dark and cold, the faint light flickering off the walls illuminated only by the small fire. He was in the cave again. The old man, sitting cross-legged on the other side of the fire, was watching him intently. Johnson looked around like he had never seen the place before. What was happening?

"You have come back," the old man said again. "Did you travel to the ancient world like before?"

Johnson stared blankly at the old man. *I can't be in the cave again. I only had a day in the past. Last time it had been two days. What was going to happen in response to Piedras Negras' demands? And what of Little Rabbit?* The joy he felt upon waking was turning to an ache in his heart. *I expected to see her this morning.* His soul had rejoiced with the anticipation of it. He looked around the cave and again at the old man. *This is real. The cave is real. I knew it's real. My life's work has led me here. But going to the past; was it real or not? Could it have only been a dream? It didn't feel like it had been a dream. I can't tell.*

"What did the gods tell you?" the old man asked.

"That Shield Jaguar is descended from the beginning."

"What else?" demanded the old man sharply. His face turned hard as he looked at Johnson. "The gods would demand a price for your return to the past."

"They said the truth would destroy me."

"Then you must never go back. It was a warning."

§

"Alan, you need some rest," Phoebe said as she came into the makeshift office at the archaeological site. "You look like you're dead on your feet."

He sat hunched over a computer on a table set up in a small work area, just inside the door to a temple. Situated in the shade, he could look out over the plaza. He sat back and watched for a reaction as Phoebe picked up the pages and read them. He had been typing since early morning.

"I need to get it recorded," he said. "I need to write down everything I saw and did, before I forget any of it. I've found a new way to view the past and need to share it with the archaeological community."

"Alan, you actually think that you really did these things?" she asked as she continued reading. "You went on a raid to kill people and when it went bad you were chased by savage warriors through the jungle. It doesn't sound like you."

"It wasn't. I was Lightning Sky, a warrior. I was in his body. It was exhilarating. He was strong, confident, people looked up to him. I only did what was expected of him."

"It seems like they expected a lot."

"Yes it does, doesn't it?"

"But Alan, it wasn't real."

"It sure felt real, still does for that matter."

"Alan, you had a vision, a dream induced by drugs. That's not scientific research," Phoebe said.

"Phoebe, look out there," he said as he pointed toward the plaza. Last night I stood right there, right there where that tourist is standing, and slowly turned in a circle trying to memorize everything I saw. It was real I tell you. It was real. And on that pyramid," he shifted his finger and pointed at Temple 11, "on top there was a beautiful temple. A young priestess called to me to come to her. She had to be real. You have to believe me."

"Alan, I believe the same thing I did after the first time you took the drug. I believe you saw something, a dream perhaps, maybe even a trance, but it couldn't be anything more than that. You've been studying this culture for years. You are the leading expert. You know it better than anyone. Your subconscious probably developed a picture of what it thinks it was like and the drug brought it forward for you."

"And the young woman, what about her?"

"You lucky guy, you," she said as she put the papers in her lap and broke into a big smile. "Some dreams are a lot better than others. Two years ago I'd have been jealous as hell, dream or not."

"It was real, Pheb."

"You wish," she said as she scanned the pages again. "From this you'd think you had a hell of a time. I'd say it was a damn good dream."

§

Each day as the students worked on the excavation, Dr. Johnson wandered around the site seemingly lost in thought, always looking for something, never seeming to be able to find it. During the day he spent time around the palace, mostly just a crumbling foundation now.

He'd picture the courtyard with family activities in it, the women cooking, children playing, full of the sounds of people talking and laughing, recalling the strange smells, the reverence given to the king even in his own house, and the laughter. Yes, the laughter. He smiled to himself. They were a happy people; the palace housed a large extended family with the joys and sorrows any close family has.

They lived together mostly in the plaza. Modern day people are accustomed to having houses that they live inside, and going outside from time to time. The Maya lived outside and the houses had rooms to go into for sleeping and getting out of bad weather.

At night he would go down and sit in the plaza and stare at the pyramid and temple where he met the young priestess. He could picture her up there: young, beautiful, an exotic enchantress who brought an excitement to him beyond anything he had ever felt. Was she real? As he lay back and closed his eyes he could smell her scent, sweet and musky. He longed to be immersed in it again. Was it a dream? Phoebe said it was and logic agreed with her. He closed his eyes and his heart ached and he resolved himself to accept her conclusion.

§

Dan Perry, a reporter for Globe News was on the story. At the end of last week he got the assignment to travel to the University of Wisconsin in Madison. A rumor was going around the Internet about an archaeologist who claimed to have gone back in time and lived with the Maya Indians during the period they were building pyramids.

It was just the type of story his paper liked. They were known for their off-the-wall, wild style of reporting. The world was full of crazy people, and it was his job to find them and bring their stories to light. It was news of sorts but people bought the paper more for entertainment.

"Do you think the professor really went back in time?" Perry asked as he watched the students, looking closely for signs that this might be a prank. University students were known for such things, especially if they could get a national newspaper involved in reporting it. They were sitting in the student union. Perry had been on campus all morning beating the bush looking for students who were on last summer's excavation. It all seemed so casual as he approached two of them in the student union, identified himself as a reporter and asked if they had been on the dig and might be so kind as to answer a couple of questions.

"There is a story going around the internet that says the department head of archaeology, Dr. Johnson, claims to have gone back in time," Perry said as an opener.

"He thinks so," responded Dan. "I was working on the excavation and we found an ancient drug. Dr. Johnson took it and claims it transported him back in time."

"And what do you think?" Perry pushed.

"I don't know what to think. I've been a student of his for three years now and I have the highest respect for the man. He's brilliant and a leader in his field."

"He was different after he took it," Susan said. "We both saw a change in him."

"So the guy found a drug, lit up a joint and back in time he went," Perry recapped casually. This sounded like a prank and a poor one at that.

"No," replied Dan, "a local shaman performed a ritual and administered the drug to him. It was done as close to the way it would have been used in ancient times, as far as they could determine. It allowed him to communicate with the ancient gods and they sent him back in time."

"And this shaman, he was a Maya?" Perry asked with a little more interest. He had the elements of a story: a reputable professor, an ancient drug, a modern witch doctor performing ancient rites and the intervention of ancient gods. *I might be able to pull a story out of it after all, even if it was a prank. It all depends on what type of nutcase this professor is.*

"He was a modern day Quiche Maya shaman," Dan replied, "a descendent of the ancient Maya priests whose traditions were handed down to successive shaman from generation to generation. Their beliefs today are a blend of Christianity and the old ways. The old gods and the new one stand side by side."

"And you say he was different when he came back?" Perry led with an open-ended question.

"He told the most wonderful stories about what the site looked like in ancient times," Susan shared, "like it was when it was occupied thirteen hundred years ago. The way he described it made it seem to come to life before our eyes and he told us about the king's court and festivals and the warriors."

"Warriors?" Perry asked.

"He claimed to have taken on the body of a royal warrior when he was there," she replied. "Isn't that wild?"

§

Later that afternoon Perry was wandering around the faculty office building. He learned long before that making an appointment to see people didn't work. As soon as the name of his paper was mentioned, they clammed up. He usually just showed up and flashed a card saying he was from an independent news agency who supplied feature and special interest stories to the bigger papers. It was a cover that was usually well received.

"Your students really like you," Perry said as he sat down across the desk from Dr. Alan Johnson. I ran into a couple of them in the student union while you were in class. They claimed you are a good teacher."

"I try," replied Johnson as he looked the man over. There was a buzz on the Internet about his claim to have traveled through time that was more than just a little skeptical. Now a reporter for some news service just walked into his office. He wasn't sure what to think. Perhaps he could clarify the situation.

"What brings you here?" he asked cautiously.

"Time travel, professor; I'm here looking for a story about time travel."

"It sounds incredulous on the surface doesn't it?" Johnson said.

"Not one of my routine assignments," Perry replied with a smile. The man didn't look like the usual crackpot he was accustomed to interviewing.

"Yes, time travel," Johnson opened. "I believe I've incurred a situation where I may have traveled through time."

"May have?" Perry asked. "A rumor abounds that you have claimed you actually did go back in time."

"I feel I have. However, my colleagues have offered alternative explanations. I can't conclusively discount that they may be right. Their arguments make sense and they certainly have the laws of physics on their side."

"What makes you think that you actually went back in time professor, your side of the argument?" Perry asked.

"It felt so real. It felt like I was actually back in the city's ceremonial center witnessing the splendor of it all. The beauty of the work of their artisans was magnificent. And the people, they were real, true to character. The king was omnipotent in manner and bearing. The warriors were fierce, their leaders revered as heroes. Their celebrations came alive with the people, their gods and ancestors, all together in a state of balance. It was the most amazing thing I have ever seen."

"Your students claim you took on the body of a warrior while you were there," Perry said, "Isn't that a little bizarre?"

Johnson laughed at the memory. "Not as bizarre as what happened when I was in the body."

Perry perked up. *Here it comes.* "Really?"

"I went on a raid with a war party."

"A raid?"

"Yes. Yaxchilan raided an outpost of a rival city, Piedras Negras, to capture a high-ranking lord to be used for a sacrifice. I was with them during the fight."

"You took part in a battle?" Perry looked closer at the other man. Medium in height and healthy in figure, he was just average. There was no indication of anything more.

"Yes, I was in the body of Lightning Sky, a young warrior who went with his first war party."

"Yeah, how did he do?" Perry asked with a chuckle. The guy looked good but the story was becoming more fantastical as it was told.

"I killed two men and the Yaxchilan prince I was with kept another from killing me."

"That must have been scary," Perry said to humor the man. *This is becoming one of the better stories I've heard in a while.*

"Initially it was scary," Johnson replied enthusiastically, "but all said and done, by the time it was over, it was the most amazing thing that has ever happened to me."

Perry looked at the man. Johnson obviously believed what he said was true. All the crackpots did. Experience told him that sometimes at this point the interviewee became belligerent if confronted with his fallacy. It was time to wrap it up. He had a wild story for his readers this time. The editor could handle any adverse response after it was run.

§

"What the hell is this?" Dave Stron, the president of the university asked as threw the paper down on Johnson's desk. The caption read. *Renowned University of Wisconsin Archaeologist Takes Ancient Drug And Is Transported Back In Time.*

Johnson looked at the paper, the Globe, a scandal sheet of sensationalism considered to be a publication of outlandish stories or outright wild lies.

"A reporter came in here a couple of weeks ago asking about the expedition to Yaxchilan last summer. He didn't say he was from the Globe."

"Well, he was from the Globe. And this article makes the university look like we support witch doctors and drug-induced dreams to promote academic understanding. You actually told the guy this crap?"

"Crap?" Johnson exclaimed his irritation building as he rose to meet the challenge. "I haven't read the article but I assure you what I told him wasn't crap."

"It says you were given a drug by a witch doctor, went back in time and joined a war party where you killed two men."

"That's out of context," Johnson retorted with a flash of anger. *Why am I being questioned? Aren't I an honorable man? It was an experiment done under scientific conditions. I am a qualified scientist. That should be sufficient.*

"Is this what you told him or not?" the university president asked as he pointed to the paper.

"Yes, I told him that, and a lot of other things too."

"Well it comes out in here that you are quite the crackpot."

"Believe what you will, Dave," Johnson shot back. "I haven't done anything here that I feel should be questioned, by you or by anyone else." Johnson glared at the president. "What gives you the right? It's my honor he's questioning and it is beyond reproach."

Stron stopped, taken aback. This man, a colleague and friend for years, was a calm and gentle man. To his knowledge he had never raised his voice to anyone in anger, and here he was standing in front of him acting like he wanted to fight.

"Alan," he said with a shaky voice. "This is serious."

"It's just the Globe," Johnson replied as his anger abated enough to wonder, fleetingly, where the anger had come from. "In a week it will blow over and I'll catch a little residue, that's all."

"We can't have the university laughed at," Stron mumbled.

"And it won't be. I'll take care of it. I'm writing a paper now on my experiences. The *Archaeology Review* has accepted my proposal for consideration and requested a draft. It will explain everything in context and will be read by the people who really count."

§

Five months passed since the article in the Globe hit the newsstands. Requests had come in from the late night talk shows for interviews, but Johnson tactfully turned them down. Stron had convinced him to maintain a low key. He didn't like it. Phoebe was in his corner and that helped. The *Quarterly Archaeology Review* accepted his paper with disclaimers, and the information went out into the academic community.

§

"Once again your brilliance and dedication to your field reward you," said Dave Stron raising his glass.

"Here here," said Dan, "a toast to the man." They all raised their drinks. Friday afternoon at the Congress Bar was a regular occasion for Johnson and Stron for years. The bar was a favorite of students at the university, and known for hosting wild parties especially after Saturday's football games. On Friday afternoon the bar was a little over half full with students wrapping up their week. The buzz of conversation competed with the music. The transition to the weekend had started. Today Phoebe and Dan were invited along for the celebration. Dr. Johnson's paper had just been published by the *Quarterly Archaeology Review*.

"They had a big party here last Saturday night," Johnson said as he took a sip of his scotch and water, "and the Badgers lost again. It doesn't make sense."

"It's been a bad year on the gridiron," was the president's reply. "If no wins make for no parties, you get a dull fall semester. This way it supports the winning-isn't-everything concept."

"Perhaps it supports this school's wild party reputation," countered Johnson.

"Sure, that too. All work and no play make Jack and Jill dull boys and girls," the president replied as he took a sip of his martini and contemplated it appreciatively.

"We couldn't have that now, could we?"

"Nope, considering that parties support the learning of new social skills," replied the president sarcastically as he took the olive out of his drink and ate it.

"Aren't you supposed to finish the drink before you eat the olive?" asked Johnson.

"What's the problem Al? Students like parties, I like olives. We've been going out for Friday afternoon cocktails deep in the heart of student-land for years now letting the students know we aren't complete prudes. This is supposed to be a celebration."

"The paper was brilliant Alan," Phoebe said. "I never thought you could have handled it that way, putting your response to the drug into the context of a scientific experiment."

"It was quite a trip," Dan said, "but I'm disappointed. You could have told us about it when we were down there."

"And I suppose you'd have wanted to take the drug too," Alan responded.

"Hey, sure, I'd love to take a trip with you. Go back in time and see some real Maya Indians, all in the interest of science. It sounds like the ultimate adventure."

"Experiment," Johnson said as he took a sip of his drink, twirled the ice with a swizzle stick, and put the glass on the table between them. "It was an experiment. It was done under controlled conditions."

"With a witch doctor," the president said. "That's what the

Globe reported."

"A shaman, Dave, there is a difference. And the information in the Globe was skewed to make it look as bad as they could."

"It looked pretty bad."

"And it blew over, just as I said it would," Johnson replied.

"It's the principle, Alan. What if that stuff had killed you? I can just see me announcing to the world that I lost my Archaeology Department Head from a drug overdose. And by the way, the supplier was a thirteen-hundred-year-old Maya king."

"The tabloids would love it," Phoebe said. "You'd get all sorts of press for the university. But as luck would have it, the paper made the *Quarterly Archaeology Review*, and the story came out the way Alan here wanted to tell it. I think that's wonderful. Any feedback yet?"

"I've gotten a number of calls, mostly good. I'm not sure how good of a sample that is when only your friends call. Time will tell."

"*In Quest of a Vision.* It's a catchy title," Dan said.

"It makes taking a drug so scientific sounding."

"It was scientific."

"You and the old shaman, a real science team," injected Phoebe.

"Field work, my dear; you don't usually have clinical settings in field work."

"You should have asked one of us to go along," said Dan. "I'd have been a good volunteer." He held up his beer.

"Your problem, Dan," said Phoebe, "is that you are a lot like him. You don't think of the consequences of your actions before you act."

"We'd make a good team, then wouldn't we? Can I go next time?"

"There won't be a next time," Alan said as he stared at the front window. Its light was strangely like the light in the open door of the palace sleeping chamber where he woke up in the Eighth

Century. A young woman looked in briefly, caught his eye and disappeared. Long black hair, dark eyes, tan complexion; was he seeing things? He was looking into the light. His heart leaped. It looked like her. He got up quickly and went to the door. Looking out, he saw no one who would fit the description of the young woman. *Is my mind was playing tricks on me?*

"Something wrong?" Phoebe asked when he returned. "You look pale."

"No, I just thought I saw someone I knew," he replied.

"I heard that you had a costume made up to look like a Maya king and wore it to class," the university president said.

"What?" Johnson said his mind still on the woman at the window. *She looked directly at me, but she wasn't there when I got to the door. Where is she? There wasn't anywhere she could have gone in that amount of time.*

"I said I heard stories about you dressing as a Maya king and coming to class that way. Are they true?" asked the university president.

"I've had two costumes made from that time period. One is a warrior costume worn when Shield Jaguar presented a prisoner to the king. The other was one used during ceremonies at royal palace functions. Perhaps I should wear one the next time I make a presentation at one of our conferences."

"Which one?" asked Dan. "I'd wear the war costume."

"How macho," said Phoebe, "just like a guy."

"Probably the ceremonial one," countered Johnson. "The presentation is more like a ceremony. Anyway it is more ornate and resembles the ones found on the Yaxchilan lintels."

"I've got to leave," Stron said, standing up. "Friday night fish fry at the VFW again. The wife would be upset if I was late."

"Can I catch a ride back to the dorm?" Dan asked. "I've got to get ready for a date."

"Once again, Alan," the president said, "congratulations on

the paper in the *Quarterly Archaeological Review*. It's another feather in our school's cap."

"It's been a long week, Phoebe," Johnson said as they watched the two leave the bar. "I didn't mention it to Dave, but the paper wasn't quite as well received as I let on."

"No. I thought it was very good," she replied, "perhaps a little radical in approach, but still within reason."

"My colleagues might not agree with that. They are a conservative lot.   They like baby steps built upon stable foundations."

"Hang in there Alan. The initial reaction will pass," she counseled.

"I'm sure glad to have you on my side. You're my strong pillar of support," he said as he looked at her legs now coming out of a short skirt instead of khaki shorts with dirty knees from kneeling in the dirt of an excavation. Back in civilization she once again took on the feminine wiles that seemed to effortlessly draw men to her.

"Always willing to help," she replied with a broad smile.

"Do you ever miss them, Pheb," Johnson asked, "the old times?" He waited for a reaction.

The smile vanished, her mood quieted. She sat there staring into her drink, quietly thinking. "Sometimes; it was good at the time. I was in love then. I like you better now. Our relationship is more comfortable. Sometimes I miss the sex. The sex was good."

"If you want we could still have sex," he said with a smile.

"You guys never stop thinking about it, do you? No, I have to have either special feelings for the man or perhaps no feelings at all, for a quick fling. I think I still love you, but not the same way."

"So the sex is out?" he teased.

"Well, maybe if you take me out and get me drunk enough some night, I might reconsider it." She looked into his eyes with a coquettish smile.

"How do you feel about us, now, at this time?"

"That's a strange question," she said looking at him trying to fathom his feelings from his eyes.

"No. How do you picture me? It's a good question."

"Are you trying to tell me you want to go back to being lovers Alan?"

"No. But your answer is important to me."

"I don't know Alan. You're more than a brother and less than a lover. I cherish the time we were lovers. It's a part of us I want to remember and hold on to, but not a part I want to go back to. And it has nothing to do with you. We just don't have those feelings for each other anymore, but I want you in my life just as much as I did when we were lovers. You are very special to me."

He looked out the window, lost in thought, torn, wondering the direction he was going to go in. *Should I confide in her?*

"Why, Alan, do you need to know how I feel about you? Something's bothering you isn't it? I saw it earlier when you went to the door."

He looked at her, saying nothing, carefully collecting his thoughts, struggling to reply. "Something happened when I went back in time. I can't explain it. Something happened when I was with that girl."

"The hot date, huh?"

"Yes, the hot date. Something happened inside of me. I don't know what it was. It was only a dream, but I seem to be preoccupied over it. I keep thinking about her."

"Sounds like a school boy crush to me."

"Phoebe, look at me. I'm serious. I think I've seen her twice since we've come back, but when I try to go to her she isn't there. This afternoon, she looked through the window directly into my eyes. When I got to the door seconds later no one was there."

"Probably just a coincidence, your mind playing tricks on you."

"It doesn't feel that way. It feels strange but I can't explain how or why."

"Alan, take it easy. Don't trouble yourself over this. Give it a little more time and it will pass. I'm sure of it."

§

The first day of the meeting of the Central U.S. Region of the Archaeological Society had finished an hour ago. The bar in the Hilton Hotel in Chicago was filled with the day's participants. It was a time for meeting old colleagues and making new friends. Presentations at the conference were formal, the questions professional and polite. However, outside of the presentations, in the company of trusted old friends having a few drinks, discussions became more personal, less professional and aptly more honest.

"I saw your paper on the Maya's social structure in the last *Quarterly Archaeology Review*," Gerhardt Weber from the University of Chicago said. "It was a considerable piece of work."

"Considerable," said Bill Jefferies from the University of Michigan. "That's an ambiguous term."

"Considerable is a good word," mused Weber. "Its strength is in its ambiguity."

"So you think the paper is ambiguous," said Jefferies.

"I think it was from a refreshingly new perspective, but an unprecedented one."

"You're on a roll today Gerhardt," returned Jim Harper, from Penn State. "You have a rare talent for using a lot of words when you don't want to say much. The question put to you is: did you like it or not?"

Johnson sat and listened to the dialogue unfold. They were sparring now, but given a short time and perhaps a couple of drinks, the gloves would come off and he expected a beating. His paper was definitely unique, as Phoebe had told him. Archaeological papers were normally based upon empirical studies, supported by lots of statistical data, expanding current theories, and adding to the body of scientific knowledge. Normally it was a rather straight-forward process but the approach taken in his paper would be considered radical.

To support his presentation of going back in time and observing an ancient culture, Johnson claimed to have used the recognized ethnographic field methods, the process of observation and recording. Feedback had been mixed. He had been told by a number of colleagues that you can't mix apples and oranges. He was broaching the world of unethical reporting in the same vein as unprofessional self-proclaimed sensationalists do to get their stories and films sold on the National Geographic TV channel.

The opinions of these men sitting here were crucial to him. They were the leading experts in the field of ancient Mesoamerican archaeology. Their opinions carried considerable weight in the archaeological academic community.

"I liked it," Gerhardt Weber replied as he sat back and interlocked his hands over his stomach. With head held high he peered through the bottom half of his glasses as he closely watched Johnson. "It was entertaining, but really, a scientific paper on taking a drug? It sounds like we are back in the sixties."

"But," replied Johnson, "my paper 'In Quest of a Vision' was about taking an ancient drug, used by Maya Kings, most probably in ceremonies."

"All the more reason to consider it out of context," Weber responded. "They used it in special public ceremonies, you didn't."

"Perhaps he should have performed a blood sacrifice ceremony like the one the drug was designed for," interrupted Harper. "He could have taken the drug then pulled a string with attached stingray barbs through the foreskin of his penis, caught the resulting blood on paper and burned it. That would have put it in context." He smiled at Johnson. "By the way, are you circumcised?" he asked. "If so, no foreskin. God that must hurt. I give you my condolences." He raised his glass in mock salute.

"No," replied Gerhardt again, always serious. "In context, it means the drug was obviously intended to reduce pain. A string with stingray spines pulled through a penis or a tongue is obviously painful."

"How do you know that?" returned Jefferies. "Maybe it was just an hallucinogen, a communication device allowing them to talk to their gods."

"That's the way it worked for me," injected Johnson.

"But your process, it's not scientific," said Weber, picking up his shot of schnapps and downing it in one gulp. "Reporting the results of taking a drug and a resulting dream or hallucination as a scientific process does not meet strict academic criteria. I'm quite surprised they published it for you."

"But that's the way it happened," replied Johnson. "I took the drug and went back in time."

"You can't go back in time. It's not possible," countered Weber.

"Perhaps it was an hallucination," said Jefferies.

"Then it's all in the mind," Weber responded. "If it's all in the mind, it isn't real, and therefore is just speculation."

"It felt real," Johnson replied. "It felt like I was there and the memory of it feels like I was there. I met the king, the nobles and the warriors. I saw the king in chamber as the head of state. I attended festivals and banquets and saw the ritual dances. These were things I couldn't have made up."

"But your experience and conclusions, they don't fit the record as we know it," Weber replied. "You have come up with what appears to be some very interesting observations, if I might stretch the term, but it doesn't fit with what we know about that time period."

"What's got your craw Gerhardt? Spit it out," Harper said. "Something is bothering you. Let us know what it is. Alan here is dying for some honest feedback. We've been colleagues for years, and we owe it to him."

"Speculation and imagination is my concern," voiced Gerhardt as he picked up his beer and took a sip washing down the flavor of his schnapps, "Not like a good German beer," he mumbled in distaste, holding the glass up to the light. "As I was saying," he continued looking back at them, "speculation and imagination. I believe you saw something under the influence of the drug, but nothing more than your imagination could conjure up.

"You're making a lot of conjecture to fit into a very scanty record, alluding to your seeing something, call it a vision, a dream, or something on that order. I'll admit that Piedras Negras and Yaxchilan were adversaries for centuries. But to hinge the turning point of the mighty city of Piedras Negras' downfall at the hands of Yaxchilan on the taking of a single captive, well I can't buy that. Yaxchilan's capturing Lord T'ul Chiik, the high-ranking lord from Piedras Negras, is of course an historic event and recorded as such. We know that because the Baah Sajal of Tiloom, the leader of La Pasadita, made a record of proudly assisting Yaxchilan in the capture. It was a big event for him to be included. But claiming it threw off the yoke of the overlord king of the city at the crown of its glory, is more than I can support."

"Gerhardt," responded Johnson, "I'm postulating it was the hinge point that led to increased warfare that contributed to their downfall. Consider ten years earlier in 749 A.D., a king of Yaxchilan, probably an interim leader, Yoaat B'alam II, attended a Period Ending anniversary at Piedras Negras. These weren't social calls, but events where homage was paid to the superior king. It indicates Yaxchilan was subservient to Piedras Negras at that time.

"And twenty years before we know there was fighting between

them when a lieutenant of Bird Jaguar II was captured by Piedras Negras warriors. Obviously Piedras Negras asserted their dominance at that time or somewhere soon after. Piedras Negras had the upper hand.

"I'm saying that the capture of T'ul Chiik by Yaxchilan in 759 A.D., marks the point where they threw off the yoke. The result was the resumption of the wars between the two cities."

"Those are the records, of course," Weber said, "but it's part of their pattern of ritualistic war; the usual fighting, lulls, and fighting again. It's the Maya way throughout the life of their civilization. They were fighting all of the time. Every forty or fifty years the guy on the bottom switched places with the guy on the top. It happened that way over and over."

"My take is more specific than that," replied Johnson quickly. "The food supply was starting to decline soon after the early Eighth Century spike in population. They were short-cutting their agricultural system of crop rotation for short term crop increases, which eventually led to the production of less food. Tribute from a subservient town to the dominate town consisted of food, mostly corn and lots of it.

"Production of food was dwindling. It could no longer support both the upper class and lower class. The strain on their sociopolitical structure was immense. Their response was to go to war over tribute-food. The strongest shall survive. Combine this with the increase of the destructive Venus Tlaloc Wars and you have the elements to their downfall.

"For Yaxchilan this was the turning point on their attitude and behavior of making war. It turned from ritual-based war to economic-based war. I'm hinging the capture of T'ul Chiik with Yaxchilan throwing off the yoke of servitude to Piedras Negras and reasserting their influence in the area and ultimately using the Venus Tlaloc Warfare process to do so.

"We also know that a few years later, during the reign of Shield

Jaguar III, a severe blow was struck against Piedras Negras. It was most probably near the end of his reign when the fighting became much heavier. And finally in 810 A.D., his son K'inich Tatb'u Skull III captured their king and ended the dynastic line resulting in the subsequent downfall of Piedras Negras' political and economic system and ultimately the abandonment of their city."

"Perhaps Doctor, I might be inclined to agree with you if there were a little more concrete information," Gerhardt said. "I try to keep an open mind, but I still contend that you are speculating. There were fewer records of wars and conflict during the latter part of the Eighth Century indicating that war was on the decline. You are advocating there were more wars."

"Less wars, Gerhardt, or less records of wars? I think it's a vital question. Perhaps recording their history of wars declined along with the building of ceremonial structures."

"Gentlemen," injected Jefferies, "food for thought, food for thought. Johnson here has challenged us to think on a different level."

"I think," said a flustered Gerhardt looking from Jefferies to Johnson, "Alan has entertained us with speculation advocating it as higher-level thinking, as opposed to following conservative scientific principles." He looked at Johnson. "Alan, this is a dangerous practice. As much as I want to, I can't support it."

He finished his schnapps with a flourish and washed it down with the last of his beer and leaned forward. "Alan, you know I like and respect you. For years we have challenged each other's theories often to the benefit of both of us. I want to believe what you wrote, but I think you are too far out now. You are stretching the scientific process. I am very opposed to that."

Shortly after, Johnson took his leave, apologizing, saying he needed to contact the school on a business issue before it was too late in the day. He tried not to show his disappointment. He thought surely these men would understand.

§

Later that evening Johnson was in the bar when his close friend Jim Harper from Penn State came in and sat down next to him.

"I don't know why they don't believe me," Johnson said. "I am a reigning expert in my field with an impeccable record of achievements. I feel I have reached another level of scientific observation but my colleagues don't appear to support me. You have the ear of most of the archaeologists in the country Jim. I know this paper made me the talk of the community. This isn't a normal response. Is it really that bad?"

"Alan," said Harper, "its one thing to excavate a site, find a drug and experiment with it. I'm not sure if it is ethical but we'll excuse that. I'd probably have taken it too. Your explanation of their civic activities is great. The description of the king in council is outstanding. I felt like I was there watching it and it's in a reasonable line with pictures that have survived on the pottery.

"But, as you are aware, some of the experiences you describe don't fit with the archaeological record as we know it. You know how it works. It's hard to concur with your conclusions without supporting evidence. Your colleagues feel that you are too enterprising in insisting the descriptions of some activities were the actual practices and haven't provided the burden of proof for challenging the historical record."

"The response is that bad?" Johnson asked thoughtfully.

"It's polite," the other archaeologist answered. "You command a lot of respect in the field. But the talk coming out is 'the guy's got quite an imagination'. If I were you I'd tone it down a little."

§

"Merry Christmas," Phoebe said as she and Dan entered the office. She carried a decorated, foot-high artificial tree. Dan carried two wrapped presents. Placing the tree in the center of his desk, Phoebe leaned over and kissed Johnson on the cheek and said, "And a Happy New Year."

"No kiss from me," Dan said putting out his hand.

"You two look happy," Alan said as they sat down. "What's the occasion?"

"It's Christmas Alan, we get two weeks off."

Dan pulled a hip flask out of his pocket and three Dixie cups from under his coat. "Here's to a good year," he said with a beaming smile on his face as he poured a little scotch into each cup.

"The university frowns on that," said Johnson.

"I won't tell," replied Dan. "Anyway, it's Christmas."

"And what are you so happy about," asked Johnson picking up his cup and looking at the smiling student.

"He's got a new girlfriend," Phoebe responded.

"And that's good?"

"You should see her," Dan responded. "A real knockout."

"Freshman?"

"Of course," said Phoebe. "Who else do you think our fine outstanding upper classman would be chasing?"

"Figures," Johnson responded.

"She's a knockout," Dan repeated.

"What are you going to do for Christmas, Alan?" Phoebe asked as she tore the paper off her present.

"I'm going back, Pheb."

A look of fear crossed her face as she stopped and looked at him. "You can't Alan."

"I've made up my mind; I have to. I have to know what happened."

"What am I missing here?" Dan asked as he sat up in his chair expecting an immediate answer.

"He's going back to Mexico to take that drug again," Phoebe

spat without taking her eyes off Johnson.

"Really," said Dan, "can I come along?"

"No!" said Phoebe and Johnson at the same time.

"Bummer. Why do you want to do it?" Dan said to Johnson.

"I have to. There are answers to questions I have. I need to find them."

"Bullshit Alan. All you have talked about since we came back is how it feels to be a warrior like Lightning Sky and raving about that girl."

"What?" said Dan, "a warrior, and a girl? I've listened to your lectures, the presentations, and read your paper. There was no mention of a warrior and a girl."

"She's a knockout Dan," Johnson said.

"She's an apparition," injected Phoebe, "just a dream."

"I'm not so sure about that," Johnson tersely replied.

"What?" Phoebe shot back. "Alan you're a scientist. You know it's not possible. You took a drug and had an experience of the mind. Call it a dream, call it a vision. It doesn't matter. It was all in your head."

"It's done something to me Pheb. I sit at my desk here and suddenly I feel like I am mentally preparing for a battle. Not to dress up or to go somewhere, but inside. A change happens.

"I sit here in fear-gripped anticipation ready for something to explode. My heart is pounding, muscles tight, I find myself staring intently past that wall. I'm sitting here yet I'm back in the jungle along the Usumacinta River again, waiting for the attack to start. I become someone else."

"Alan, you're scaring me."

"A warrior," said Dan. "I don't see you as a warrior; maybe on the chessboard but not in real life. What else happened that you aren't telling us about?"

"I became someone else. I took the body of Lightning Sky, a warrior and the cousin of Shield Jaguar III before he became king."

"And you loved it," said Phoebe, "being someone else."

"Yes Pheb, I loved it. I never experienced anything like it before. I want to experience being him again. I want to feel strong, confident and capable of facing anything. I want to walk among the masses with the arrogance of a superior being. I want to express the hate I have for my enemies, and feel the strength and confidence to face them to the death, preferably theirs. I want to feel I'm a man among men and deserving of the love of a goddess. For the briefest of time I experienced what life can be, and I want to feel it again."

"Alan, it isn't real."

"Isn't it, Phoebe? It is to me."

Chapter 10

Dr. Johnson was impatient. The last week of classes before Christmas break had been trying. He couldn't keep his focus on his work and was preoccupied with his pending trip back to Mexico. He kept telling himself that he was again venturing on a scientific process and he was only continuing it to gather more information. He was convinced he had a unique insight into the lives and culture of the classic period Maya, and kept telling himself he had to know more. It was his scientific duty.

For years, as an archaeologist studying the Maya civilization, he had a foggy perception of what life could have been like in the Eighth Century. But it was just perception and speculation, foggy at best, neither of which came close to reality, if reality is what he had seen. He convinced himself he was a scientist and needed to know more about the Maya culture and the workings of their society.

But deep down inside he knew better. He wanted to experience the lifestyle again. During his time since returning to the university, his mind continually drifted back. The facts about the society he so vociferously touted as examples of his research were of little importance to him. He wanted to see and hear and feel what he had when he took the drug before.

The thought of being a warrior and the camaraderie of being a part of those fierce men again called to him. He yearned for it. And the woman, that exotic woman, never had he met a woman like her. He wanted to hold her in his arms again, be enveloped in her scent and feel her warmth. His thoughts turned to desire then to yearning, and he knew he had to go back. It was pulling at his soul.

Finally the Christmas break came and classes let out for two weeks, the cherished holidays. Classes finished on the Friday before Christmas and Johnson caught a plane out early Saturday morning. The layover in Mexico City seemed forever before the short flight to Villahermosa. The closer he got, the more restless he became.

In Villahermosa he rented a room in the Hotel Villahermosa Cencali with a balcony overlooking *Laguna de las Ilusiones*. He was getting closer to Yaxchilan and his body was tight with nervous anticipation. It felt good to be in Mexico near the archaeological site again. Tomorrow he would rent a 4x4 vehicle and drive the rest of the way.

"The Lagoon of Illusions," Johnson translated as he sat on the balcony overlooking the water, sipping a scotch and water from the room's bar and watching the sun set over the lagoon. Was it all an illusion? His two trips to the past seemed real. Physically it was impossible but what else could explain the vivid experience. His conversations with Phoebe just before leaving continued to haunt him. She insisted he was chasing a drug-induced vision. Was he? Is that all it was?

§

"No," said the old shaman. "You can't go back. It's too dangerous."

"I have to go back," Johnson pleaded. "I have to find out what happened."

"It will change nothing. The past is the past. It is gone." The man was adamant, he felt there would be consequences and they would be bad.

"I'm a scientist. To find how their civilization crashed is my life's work."

"And I'm a doer," replied the old man, "a follower of the ways of the ancients. The gods will play tricks on you. They are deceitful. They will draw you in and destroy you just as they did the first Hero Twins."

For three days Johnson visited the shaman's home begging but the shaman was adamant. As keeper of the gateway he had his responsibilities. He couldn't bother the gods so soon. They would become angry and vengeful. They might make life harder for the villagers. Life was hard enough now. The gods might come to them, invade their bodies bringing disease or keep the rain from falling on time again this year. It was better to appease the gods instead of antagonizing them. Make sacrifices to them and don't bother them with needless requests. It was the best way.

On the fourth day Johnson convinced the shaman that he would petition the gods for the favor of the village asking for ample rain and sun and ask them to provide a bountiful harvest. Last year's rain had been sparse, the harvest poor. This year they needed a good crop or many would go hungry. He told the shaman that the gods had spoken to him before and they would speak to him again and he would petition them for more rain. The drug allowed him to do that. If the gods didn't want him to return to the past they would tell him. The shaman finally reluctantly agreed.

As they traveled in the old man's pickup truck to the cave, there was tension. The shaman didn't speak for the entire trip. Remorseful that he made the wrong decision, he worried about the consequences. The gods would be mad at this imposter. They would blame him and the village. It would be bad for the village. But, he agreed to help this man and he had to uphold his honor. He would keep his promise and do his part. Perhaps the gods would understand.

§

"Why have you come?" said the voice. It was not the same voice as before. It must not be the gatekeeper. Johnson was floating, feeling the euphoria of being back in Xibalba, the womb. It was comfortable. He was confident they would accept his return and send him into the past. He turned and looked toward the voice. A form looked back at him. It was out of focus. It appeared to be in a fog of some sort. Behind the it were three other forms. Johnson squinted and stared. What did they look like? He couldn't tell.

"Why have you come?" the voice asked again.

"I've come to petition the gods for the village, asking they be provided adequate rain for their crops, and health and prosperity this season."

"The villagers respect the ancient ways and honor us. They make sacrifices but not like the old ones," the god replied. It is not the same. We sent you to the ancient ones and you were to ask them to come back. They have not come back to us."

"The ancient ones are gone," replied Johnson. "Their civilization died. Some survived but the big cities are gone, only ruins now. I need to go back. I need to know how they lived and why the cities died. I need to go back to find this out."

"If they are gone, they are gone. They are not worshipping us anymore," claimed the form. "Your going back won't change that."

"I can teach the old ways to the ones that are now living in the villages, the ones that are left. Yes, I can go back and learn, then return and teach them the old ways. They have forgotten their past. I can tell them of it and give them pride in their heritage.

Then they will worship you in the old ways."

§

Johnson looked around. He felt disoriented and dizzy. *Where am I?* It appeared he was on the remnants of a battlefield. Dead warriors were laying everywhere, many with grotesque looks on their faces as death had suddenly taken them. A few men were walking through the carnage picking up fallen weapons. On occasion one of them would spear a fallen man who was severely wounded. On the hill overlooking the carnage was a group of men all sitting with their hands tied behind their backs, the prisoners.

Johnson looked around. Obviously a battle had just taken place and he was again in Lightning Sky's body. Smoking Squirrel came up to him. His arm was in a sling. "You were lucky," he whispered. "You almost came through it without a scratch." He touched Lightning Sky's arm.

Looking down, Johnson noticed a bloody cloth wrapped around it. As Smoking Squirrel lifted the cloth, Lightning Sky saw a long cut and abrasion. It looked horrible; the arm was various shades of black with the gash still oozing blood. As he looked at it, pain suddenly reached him. It hurt. There was more pain than he ever known in his life.

"Just a scratch," said Smoking Squirrel looking at the wound then smiling at him. "I thought that guy had you for sure. If Shield Jaguar hadn't stopped him, your old woman would be crying for you now."

"I guess I am lucky," said Johnson.

"That was a hell of a fight you put up, you and Shield Jaguar together; it was a sight. You two mowed them down. Your arms should still hurt from swinging the club."

Johnson looked around to get his bearings. He was standing with a group of men. The king and Lord Great Skull were talking with other men dressed as captains, or so he thought.

"We were lucky; we found them as they were coming," Johnson heard Lord Great Skull say. "We beat them, but it could have been the other way around if they had managed to surprise us."

Johnson looked at the men. They were splattered with blood and mud. Each had abrasions on their arms and legs where they had taken blows. The king had a lacerated arm and was being attended by a physician as they talked. The great lord had numerous cuts, some bound in cloth, others open yet to be attended. Both men looked tired but elated. They had won a great battle against their age-old enemy.

"We are going to have to watch closer now," the king responded. "They will come again."

"And we will turn them around again," the great lord responded.

The king gave orders to his captains to help the wounded and prepare the dead to be brought back to the city. They backed away with reverence, then turned and left, running.

"Where is Shield Jaguar?" Johnson said. He wasn't with the king.

"He's laying over there," Smoking Squirrel answered," pointing to a place where the wounded were being taken. "He's wounded, but if the gods favor it he will live."

"How bad?"

"A cut along the ribs, the bones stopped the knife, and he can't move his left arm very well. He got hit with a club."

"And you?" Johnson asked. "How about your wound?"

"Arm's broken. A healer can pull it straight it and bind it. Maybe it will stay that way and if the gods favor me I'll be able to use it again."

The two men went over to see Shield Jaguar. Johnson looked down at the man on the ground being tended by a physician.

"Tend to the others first," Shield Jaguar commanded the physician.

"But Prince, you need to be sewn. The wound needs tending."

"And who will die while you become a sewing woman? Just wrap the wound to stop the blood and it can be sewn later. Bind it and be off with you," Shield Jaguar commanded.

"Brothers," he said smiling up at Lightning Sky and Smoking Squirrel, "it was a good fight."

Johnson chuckled. He had finally figured he was a cousin to this man but he was called brother. In many primitive societies with extended families, the distinction between brother and cousin isn't made until they are older. The prince's use of brother at this age showed the special place he held for them.

"Yes, a good one," replied Smoking Squirrel. "We put them to flight didn't we? I hope they run all the way home."

"And you, how are you, Smoking Squirrel?" Lightning Sky asked.

"It's just a scratch. It will heal fast enough."

The wound didn't look good to Johnson, but he had never seen wounded men before except for a couple in the canoes when they returned from the last raid. How could the man be so cavalier about it? He looked at his own arm. Someone had wrapped it for him. There was blood oozing from the wound but there was no dangerous flow. How could these men be so brave? It was all he could do to bear the pain. There was no pain reliever here, just guts. You either fought it or succumbed to it. Fighting was better he concluded.

The war party left the battlefield. Those who were injured and who could walk, did. Those who couldn't were carried on litters. Those who were dead were also on litters—the last to leave the field. They would be taken home to be buried. The enemy's dead were left to lay where they fell. Later that day or the next the enemy would come to claim the bodies and remove them for burial. They would not be interfered with. All warriors deserved to be properly prepared to travel to the afterlife.

Lighting Sky and Smoking Squirrel walked on each side of Shield Jaguar's litter. Those Eagle Warriors not helping with the wounded and the dead were stationed both before and behind them. Following them were the other wounded. As they left the battlefield Johnson looked back, disappointed. He had missed the fight. The gods had played a trick on him—share in the spoils, not in the glory. It felt unfair.

§

An old woman was sitting outside of one of the many doors to the palace. She was wailing loudly. She wore a sackcloth type shift; her face and hair were smeared with ashes. Tears streaking stripes through the ashes stretched down under her eyes. Three young women were sitting near her trying to console her. Seeing Lightning Sky standing in the plaza she started crying louder.

"My son is gone," she wailed. "He lives no more." Johnson stood there staring. Two other women were doing the same thing in other doorways. The wails of sadness permeated the air. He heard other mournful crying the distance, from other family compounds grouped around the royal palace. No one else spoke above a low whisper. They moved quietly to wherever they were headed. Only the young women sitting with the criers offered comfort.

"Lightning Sky, Lightning Sky," he heard his name being called softly.

Little Rabbit ran across the yard to the two of them. There was a frightened look on her face. "I was so worried about you. I saw the warriors coming back and I asked what happened. They said many were dead. My heart stopped but now I see you are alive, it has started again."

He stood there staring at her, his heart racing. As she looked at him, her eyes sparkled and she was radiant in her joy that he had returned. She beamed and he felt her smile was only for him.

Warmth enveloped him and the world was right again for the first time in months, the pain of his wound no longer a concern. She was close to him, even lovelier than before, and he felt comfort in her presence.

"Was it bad?" she asked.

"It wasn't good," he responded casually.

"Shield Jaguar said you held them off. You stopped the attack and sent them back," she said.

"And where is he now?" Johnson asked.

She turned and pointed to a doorway, "In the palace being tended."

Johnson, Little Rabbit and Smoking Squirrel hurried to the other side of the courtyard. As he followed her inside, he wondered if he should be seen with her. What was their arrangement? During the last trip she was concerned about them being seen in the temple together. Now she seemed to be a close friend in public. Was their affair still a secret?

"There you are Lightning Sky," said Shield Jaguar from his sleeping platform, a big smile coming across his face. "We stopped them, didn't we?" He was sitting and talking to them as a woman was sewing up the laceration along the rib cage. A physician was watching for a response as he moved and examined the arm. After a brief examination he claimed that the shoulder was bruised but the arm would be able to be used in a couple of days.

"Smoking Squirrel said you were badly injured," said Johnson looking from Shield Jaguar to Smoking Squirrel.

"He's always exaggerating," said Shield Jaguar. "It's just a little inconvenience. The gods don't want me getting too confident. They think they run the heavens, the world of man, and the underworld, and I'm supposed to follow them."

"Looks like they are making themselves heard," replied Johnson.

"Perhaps they don't like the fact that one day I will be a god too, like my ancestors before me."

"They don't?" Johnson asked, his curiosity picking up. He looked closely at Shield Jaguar, studying him. He had never met anyone who was to be deified as a god before.

"The gods are jealous of man. They must stay in Xibalba, held there by the First Father. They can't walk the outer world. But I am able to walk the land as a man and still be a god. My spirit is strong and protects me, even from the vengeance of the gods."

"And what makes you so sure you will succeed your brother?" Johnson asked in astonishment. The archaeological records indicated that Chel-Te', the son of Bird Jaguar, would be the next king and upon ascending to the throne he changed his name to Shield Jaguar.

"Chel-Te' will never be the king," snapped Shield Jaguar. "I, like my brother, am the son of the great Shield Jaguar II. I have as much right as my brother to be the king."

"Wasn't Chel-Te' dedicated by your brother to be the next king?"

"Dedicated or not, I will be the next king. Our seer has told us."

"Our seer?" Johnson responded. *Best tread carefully here*, he thought. Something was going on he didn't see. They lived in a different world where the metaphysical and physical were one. He could only see one dimension. His education trained him to believe that those who could conjure were most often considered evil and detrimental to society. What did this man have going for himself?

"Our seer," Shield Jaguar said looking at Little Rabbit, "and she's never wrong, are you?"

"No my Lord," she replied shyly with a noticeable bow of her head. "One day you will be a great king, a great warrior king. You will vanquish your enemies and take many captives. You will deliver great blows, shaking the reign of Piedras Negras and from your loins will come their end."

Johnson looked at the woman. Both Shield Jaguar and Smoking Squirrel were suddenly contrite in her presence. She had spoken. She was believed. Getting up she walked to the doorway and looked out.

He watched her. 'From the loins of Shield Jaguar would come the downfall of Piedras Negras' she had said. That would happen, but not for forty years or so. History indicated that in 810 A.D. Shield Jaguar III's son would conquer Piedras Negras and capture their king, ending their dynasty, never to rise again.

Johnson looked back at Shield Jaguar. Strength appeared to radiate from him. A man of self-determination and self-confidence, he was in command of all around him. As Johnson watched, he could see why people gravitated to Shield Jaguar. Even the strongest man would kneel to him. It seemed the only right thing to do, part of the natural order of things.

Johnson looked back at Little Rabbit standing by the door, a seer they said. He knew her as a priestess, now a seer. Were they interchangeable in this society? Ethnographic studies indicated that shamen in general could conjure up things and interpret the will of the gods for the future. The people they administered to believed it without question. Perhaps it was the same here. Hell of a prediction though.

He looked at her again, longingly this time. She was so beautiful to look at, it almost hurt his eyes. He wanted her near to him. He needed her. Didn't he come back for her? Sure he was a scientist, on a quest for knowledge beyond anything ever found in archaeology before. But in his heart he knew he came back for her.

Johnson quickly stepped back mentally to assess the situation. Evidently being with Little Rabbit in public wasn't a concern. Their social standing must allow it. She is acting like he was a friend, just a friend. Hadn't she told him they had been friends since childhood? He longed to be closer to her. Still it would be better to be reserved, to see where his place was. Society always had its norms. He had to learn them quickly.

She said Shield Jaguar was to marry her off for a political alliance. Did she see that too? What was their present relationship? It seemed casual. She said she would be a queen someday. It seemed important to her. It sounded like something she accepted as a given.

"You did well today," Shield Jaguar said to Johnson, interrupting his thoughts. "You made a name for yourself. Two kills. The people will talk of you as a warrior now. With the two from the raid on the outpost you have four. You will be invited to join the Eagle Warrior Society."

"It was a good day, wasn't it?" Johnson responded wishing he had come back sooner. The praise was good but he missed the fight. *Imagine,* he thought, *sorry to have missed the fight. Who would have thought? The mild-mannered Professor Johnson is bothered about missing a battle where they fought hand to hand to the death."*

He felt strong inside, a primal physical strength radiating from his being. He was a man to be reckoned with, cousin of Shield Jaguar, the prince and future king. He chuckled to himself. He had the height of privilege in this ancient society, but that wasn't important. What really amazed him was that he was a warrior. His chest swelled as a smile crossed his face, and to hear it, a very successful one.

"We stopped them, and we stopped them hard," continued Shield Jaguar. "Yo'nal Ahk III, Piedras Negras' king will think twice before attacking us again. He took the worst of it this time."

"I guess," Johnson responded.

"He isn't the king his father was. The old man was good. He was like my father was, a great warrior-king feared for his wrath. Yes, it's a good day. We've shown he can be stopped. Now we have to bring him to his knees. He's an administrator like my brother, not a warrior. He likes his building and governing his provinces. He's getting soft."

"Lightning Sky, you're bleeding," Little Rabbit suddenly said changing the subject. "We need to sew you up," she said as she picked up a needle and thread from the basket of the woman sewing Shield Jaguar.

Johnson paled. *Sew me up with no anesthetic; this can't be happening.* She noted a scared look pass across his face.

"Don't be a child," she chided as she plunged the bone needle roughly into the flesh alongside the wound.

He looked at Shield Jaguar being sewn up as if he didn't have a care in the world. He saw him wince but no one else did. He was expected not to show pain. Could he do less than Shield Jaguar in front of this woman he was captivated by? He grit his teeth and smiled through closed lips as he looked down at Little Rabbit. He couldn't let her see the pain.

§

"Stand aside," shouted the caller. "Stand aside for Lord Great Skull."

Hearing the commotion, Lightning Sky moved to the doorway to look. People were moving off to the side as a group of warriors carrying spears and shields entered the compound. Floating above them was an array of monsters, apparitions from the headgear they were wearing. In the lead was Lord Great Skull with his eldest son at his side.

"The presence of the bear," Little Rabbit said as she looked past him.

"What?"

"It's the presence of the bear. Can't you feel it? The great lord's spirit animal is the be—strong, determined, ready to stand against anything, quick to take offense and attack. It's the presence of the bear you see," she said again. "The lord is walking within its presence. The people see this and flee. Don't face the bear. He will overpower you. You must use your spirit animal to be crafty. Lead the bear into a trap and take his strength from him. It's the only way to face the bear."

Johnson stared at her. *What? I have a spirit animal guiding me?* He understood everyone had one according to their beliefs. He hadn't considered it before. *What is my spirit animal? It is supposed to be crafty enough to defeat a bear.*

Johnson looked over at the procession. He was aware of each person having a spirit animal as a lifelong companion. *If a person's spirit animal gets sick he will too. If it leaves him he will die, or if it dies he will die too. So part of Lord Great Skull's power radiates from his spirit animal, the bear,* Johnson thought. *It is a far different world they live in.*

"And your spirit animal?" Johnson asked wanting to know which spirit animal was her personal spirit.

"You know mine. My spirit is the quetzal bird, the most beautiful bird in the jungle. It flies above man watching, protecting him and not letting his spirit fly away."

The great lord stopped in the court adjacent to Johnson and stared momentarily at him. "Young puppy, come here," he commanded, motioning Johnson to come forward.

"Careful," whispered Little Rabbit.

"Lord," Johnson said as he came down the steps into the courtyard.

Lord Great Skull was splattered with blood, some his own and some from his enemies. He had cuts on his chest, and his left arm was wrapped with cloth and seeping blood. In one hand he still held his war club. He was streaked with dirt. His helmet was missing and his hair dirty and messed. Blood oozed from a laceration along the side of his face. He held his head high with the arrogance of a winner. A number of the warriors with him were also bandaged and covered with dried blood, a couple limping and one being supported by two of his comrades. Behind them was a body carried on a litter.

The great lord stopped in front of Johnson and looked at the young warrior curiously. "Young puppy of Shield Jaguar, you fought well today," he said. Johnson assumed the name to be an insult referring to his close association with the king's brother. "One day soon you may become a member of my Elite Warriors."

Johnson thought quickly. The Elite Warriors were a group of high-ranking nobles who were fighters led by Lord Great Skull. Their eligibility was determined by birth. Earlier, Shield Jaguar mentioned becoming eligible for the Eagle Warrior Society. To be considered, one would have to have killed four of the enemy, and he had four kills. Evidently Lightning Sky's performance in the battle was worthy of note.

"I would be honored, Lord," he replied cautiously. "I killed two of the enemy today. Shield Jaguar said that I may be eligible for the Eagle Warrior Society."

"Rabble, that's all they are, a gang of bullies. He leads a gang of bullies. But I give them credit, they can fight. You however, might be better served fighting with your own class."

"I would be honored to give it my consideration," Johnson answered. Was he being politically correct? He wasn't sure. Lord Great Skull and Shield Jaguar were adversaries, but how far did it go? He assumed that Lightning Sky was firmly with Shield Jaguar but perhaps it best to make options appear to be open.

"That was his youngest son," Little Rabbit said after the group passed. "It was his first battle."

"The one on the litter?"

"Yes. The body will be carried from compound to compound so all the people will know of the death of the Great Lord's son. Tonight the women will cry all night as they prepare the body for burial."

§

Johnson and Little Rabbit left Shield Jaguar to get some rest. "It's sad," he said as they entered the palace courtyard. He gestured toward the wailing women who were now washing the bodies in preparation for burial in the morning.

"They will be there all night," she replied. "Everything must be done right to prepare their souls for the journey."

"Is it a difficult preparation?" Johnson asked.

"No, but it must be done carefully. Bad spirits try to steal the soul. Tortillas and peppers are wrapped and placed in the right hand of the deceased, a turkey head is placed in the left hand and a precious stone or two is hidden in the folds of the clothes so the soul has a means of bribing or bartering if need be. The body is then wrapped."

Johnson listened in amazement. He knew the process from the codex describing the Maya burial practices. But it was written in the Thirteenth Century; obviously the rituals were practiced from a much earlier period. Thinking back he knew that the turkey will lead the inner soul on its journey to the afterlife. A black dog carries the soul across a river and the tortillas compensate the dog for his assistance.

Little Rabbit continued, "The face of the deceased is covered lightly, and during the night of mourning the covering is removed from time to time and the deceased is given water on a flower to drink. Shaman from each family will visit each body and chant to keep bad spirits away. In the morning they will be taken to The Place of the Dead."

Leaving the palace, they walked past the outside walls of the compound and found a dark corner. Little Rabbit threw her arms around him holding him tight.

"I was so worried," she said. "When the runners came back and said many died in the fighting I was so scared one would be you."

"I was with Shield Jaguar and his guards," he claimed. "They protected me."

"Protect? By the god's wrath Lightning Sky, you lie to me. How can they protect you when you kill two of the enemy? That's dangerous. See that wound? It didn't get there by itself." She thumped the wounded arm with her hand and he winced. Looking distressed, she kissed the wound, hugged him again and cried, "Oh love, did I hurt you? My love should receive no pain from me."

"Can I see you tonight?" he asked hopefully. He had been waiting for months, yearning day and night to hold her in his arms again.

"I must stay with the women tonight," she replied as she laid her head on his chest. "As a priestess it is my duty to perform the rituals to guide their souls through the underworld. They need to know the way to the river and how to find the black dog. They need to know how to ward off the evil spirits who want to steal their souls.

"When will we be together?" he whispered.

"Soon my love, soon."

§

The birds were singing when Johnson awakened. The sound of crying rent the air. He had awakened twice during the night to the wails of the mourning woman. The old woman who had dressed him during the last journey into the past stood by the door waiting for him to rise. *A servant or a slave?* Johnson wondered as he looked up at her. She was small but stood proud. The mouth with missing teeth stood out. Most older people here had missing teeth. Wearing a simple, colorless cotton shift which stretched down to her calves, brief sandals and freshly combed long straight black hair, she exemplified the typical woman he saw here.

"Time to rise, my son," she said as she saw him stir. "It is going to be a busy day for you."

"Is it?" Responded Johnson.

"You have your duty to do today."

"My duty?"

"We bury the dead this morning," she replied. "The women have prepared the warriors throughout the night. This morning we send them on their journey to the afterlife."

"And my duty?" Johnson repeated.

"You and your brother will accompany the king leading the procession to The Place of the Dead."

Johnson got out of bed. The ceremonial clothes were laid out on another platform. It reminded Johnson of wearing his Sunday best. As she dressed him he noted the differences from prior clothes he had worn. A fine red cotton loincloth was wound around his waist as a base for the finely embroidered cotton kilt with a god symbol hanging in front of it. His bare chest was accented with heavy jade jewelry. She combed his hair, setting it in a swept-back fashion and placed the massive headpiece decorated with a snake's head staring forward on his head and finished the task by tying a long jaguar-skin cape around his neck which flowed over his back. "You are ready," she proclaimed proudly, stepping back to look at her work.

Stepping out the door into the inner palace courtyard, Johnson looked around. There were no fires and no cooking this morning; evidently a time of fasting.

"There you are cousin," called the king as he approached. He looked sad. Tears were welling in his eyes as he looked slowly around at the small groups of people, close family members, gathered around each body.

"It's a sad day," he said, fighting back the tears, "when we have to say goodbye to so many friends."

Johnson looked around. Across the yard he saw Little Rabbit performing some type or ritual over a body. The face cover was pulled back and she stood at the feet. She dipped a flower in a bowl of water and shook it over the body while chanting. Johnson hardly recognized her. Dressed formally, she was a different person. Her dress was made of the finest white cotton with various-colored flower patterns woven in. Over it she wore an open floor-length coat highlighted with geometric diamond patterns. Her hair was styled above her head and flowing back, held by a small headpiece with ornate feathers trailing from it. Hanging from her neck was a wide breastplate of jade stones and on her wrists wide jade wrist cuffs.

Johnson was stunned. This exotic young woman had mystifyingly transformed again. In the pageant of life's changing events now she was a priestess, dignified and apart, a companion and spokesman for the gods. Communicating with the gods, she interceded for man holding the fate of their loved one's spirits in her hands as they traveled to the afterworld. Her presence brought comfort in this time of sadness as her gentle nature assured the loved ones that all was right in the world, balance was maintained and they would meet again in a better place.

Johnson turned back to the king. "Yes it is a time of sadness," he replied as he gazed at the man. Here, talking to him, was one of the great kings of Maya history. An acclaimed warrior, he held the title of a man who took twenty captives, the highest number found in the Maya records. Obviously a man proven on the battlefield, he was also a builder, continually adding to the splendor of his city. And he was a man of compassion who cared for his people. Today was a hard day for him.

"You did well yesterday," the king said. "You take after your brother," he said, referring to Shield Jaguar.

"He's a hard man to follow," Johnson said.

"Yes," replied the king thoughtfully. "He's brash and young but he can fight. He's very good at it. But you fought well yesterday too. You are eligible to join a warrior society now, but which one? Both Shield Jaguar and Lord Great Skull want you."

What would Lightning Sky say? Johnson thought. The king wanted an answer.

"I'm giving it my consideration," replied Johnson cautiously. "But I'm leaning toward going with my brother."

"Wise choice," replied the king. "Lord Great Skull can be overpowering, but a good man to have on your side."

Shield Jaguar came out of the palace and yawned like he had just risen. He walked stiffly over to Johnson and the king. His arm was in a rope sling. "Are we ready?" he asked.

"Yes, I think so," replied the king as he motioned to a man at the end of the courtyard. People looked up as a horn sounded.

"It is time," the man called loudly, "time to go to The Place of the Dead."

The twenty bodies were placed one behind the other in a line. Two carrying poles were bound to each wrapped corpse. Four men picked up each body. The funeral procession started. In the lead was the king followed by Shield Jaguar and Lightning Sky. After them were three priests and two priestesses, Little Rabbit and the other woman who was on the pyramid when Johnson first arrived. Behind them came the bodies carried solemnly and slowly followed by a group of musicians playing melodies that were slow and sad.

At specified stations the procession stopped. The bodies were placed on the ground and the faces uncovered. Little Rabbit and the other priestess gave the corpses a drink of water by dipping a flower in a bowl of water containing floating flowers and holding it to the corpses' lips, prayers were intoned, then the procession started again.

When they arrived at The Place of the Dead, the king motioned Shield Jaguar and Lightning Sky, to sit, one on either side of him.

They took places solemnly on a low platform officiating over the funeral ritual. They sat immobile watching four men carry each body to its designated location. The graves had been dug the previous evening, each in a section used for family members. The bodies were placed beside the grave and a priest went to each one, chanting incantations praying the deceased do well on their tests in the underworld and imploring them not to take any souls of the living with them. The priestesses followed and gave each corpse a final drink from the flower dipped in the bowl.

When the final rites were completed, the priest came and stood next to the king. The king raised his hands, a horn blew a long note and in unison each body was lowered into the ground by four warriors letting them down with ropes. Everybody wailed and cried as they bid farewell to their loved ones.

§

"Beware of the wrath of Cizin the god of death, when he burns their souls to release their spirits in the journey through the underworld," screamed the dwarf. Everyone looked up the hill overlooking The Place of the Dead. A dwarf stood there with his hands cupped his mouth. Beside him was a small, twisted man holding a staff for support.

"Broken Monkey," Johnson heard the king say with a shudder.

"That fornicator," whispered Shield Jaguar. "What's he doing here?"

"He's going to demand a bribe or he'll curse the warriors' souls," the king replied.

"Give him a bribe?" Shield Jaguar exclaimed. "A spear up his ass would be better."

"And invoke the wrath of Cizin? Brother, even I don't want a god who can keep me from the afterlife mad at me. Cizin burns the souls to release their spirit. If he does it too fast the spirit can't get away. It gets caught and consumed and can't go to the afterworld."

"Cizin demands a demonstration of your reverence," screamed the dwarf and the twisted hunchback held the staff high in the air, "or your loved ones will never see peace in the afterlife and you will never see them again."

Johnson looked around at the people. A different type of crying was coming from the women now. Grief turned to desperation. They stared at the two in horror. Broken Monkey could keep their husbands and sons from the afterlife. He had the power, he was a hunchback. Everyone knew he was a companion of Mam, the god of evil. Some even say he is the god's brother.

Broken Monkey was a mean, bitter man who terrorized the community. The people believed that the god of lightning deformed the bodies of babies who's souls were not suited for this life. Crippled babies were ritually killed right after birth. His mother, not able to accept his fate, ran away with him into the jungle. She was a loving, nurturing mother and his early life with her was happy. But she died early, and at a young age he had to fend for himself. It was a hard life. No one had helped her and no one helped him.

As he became older, the hump on his back grew. Everyone believed that humpbacks were able to communicate with the gods. When he was a teen and the hump was easily seen, he learned that as he hobbled down the road and cursed people, they were afraid of him and kept their distance. One day he cursed a man who threatened him, telling him that his dog would die. That night he set out poison for the dog and the dog died.

The people said that gods had killed the dog at his command. They said that the gods listened to Broken Monkey and did his bidding. It was the first of many similar events and his dark reputation grew. The people were afraid of him and left gifts of food and clothes by their shrines to appease him. In time he learned to demand what he wanted and was given it.

"The god *Cizin* wants his due," the dwarf screamed. "Before the sun dies today, a gift must be left for him on every grave. He will consider if it is sufficient in his decision on how to burn the souls." Suddenly there was a loud boom and a cloud of smoke arose in front of the two. The people pulled back in fear. When the smoke blew away there was no one standing on the hill. They had disappeared.

The return journey to the living compounds was solemn and in absolute silence. No one spoke lest the souls of the dead find them and steal their souls to take along with them to the afterworld. When they arrived at the royal palace grounds the king said to the other two. "When the sun touches the top of the trees in the west, gather Lord Great Skull and my other counselors and come to the palace. We need to make plans."

Chapter 11

The king's chamber was dimly lit, just late afternoon light filtering through the doorway. The king, Bird Jaguar, was seated on a raised stone bench, a plate of fruit next to him. He picked up a piece and nibbled at it. The king's primary counselors and military generals, Lord Great Skull and Lord K'an Tok Wayib' *were* seated a level below him to his left. Shield Jaguar was worried as they entered the king's chamber. He had just been summoned. Since it was in the king's chambers, this would be a formal session. They would be discussing their response to the battle yesterday. The solution was easy, he thought. They had the enemy on the run. Follow them home and keep the pressure up before they could raise the proper defenses then crush them.

There was a problem though. When King Bird Jaguar had formal sessions with his brother and counselors, he was more inclined to command than to listen, but obviously Lord Great Skull had his ear and the decision had already been made.

There would be little room for negotiation. The king was the king and let no one forget it. His words were the first words, the last words and the words they would live by. The others were already there when Shield Jaguar arrived. He came up to the king, bowed appropriately and took his place to the right of the king at the foot of his bench.

"We lost twenty good men yesterday," the king opened. "Good men, friends and warriors. They will be sorely missed."

"My son included," said Lord Great Skull, a ring of sorrow in his voice, the pain of his loss gripping his body tightly in grief.

"It was only a battle yesterday," followed the king, "but it helps to restore our honor. We did well but there will be more fighting. Piedras Negras has had us under their foot for too long and they expect us to stay there. It should have been addressed long ago."

"We should follow up and attack them," Shield Jaguar said without waiting for the king to put forth his opinions.

"They are not as weak as they seem," the king answered. "That might be a trap."

"We were fortunate yesterday," Lord Great Skull added. "The gods were with us. We got a warning of their coming and had time to set up a defense. The surprise attack on their flank made the difference and gave us the victory."

"And that is why you are a good general," the king replied, praising the lord while looking straight at Shield Jaguar. "You think before you fight and that is why you win." Shield Jaguar paled, the implication obvious.

"They will expect us to attack now," replied Great Skull. "Their city is ringed by outlaying towns subservient to them which are the layers of their defense. It is their strength. We'd have to face the forces of each one, one after another."

"Then we will defeat them one after the other," followed Shield Jaguar. "Their king is not a warrior king. He likes to sit at home, build his temples and administrate." Shield Jaguar glared back at his brother.

The king smiled. He was the supreme ruler, his word was law never to be questioned, and his brother always had a jab. He was a warrior; building held little interest for him. He chuckled at the arrogance of the man. What a pair of balls he had, the balls of the jaguar. Face them head on and win or lose by sheer will and strength. That was his only strategy.

"We need to prepare well before we attack them," said the king.

"Prepare what?" Shield Jaguar snapped. "We've got them on the run. Now is the time to take them."

"They will only run behind their defense position," said Lord Great Skull, "and wait as they bleed us of warriors. That was not a large force yesterday. It was meant to feel us out. They found out we are stronger than they thought. Perhaps they will wait and see what we will do, but I think they will probe us further."

"How do you know that?" spat Shield Jaguar.

"Because young puppy, war is what I know," answered the great lord with a growl.

"And that makes you right?"

"It's his experience," answered the king. "He's been at this longer than you have. He's a fighter and be assured he's a good one. We have many victories. Lord Great Skull's counsel is valued in both peace and war."

"So we sit on our asses and wait for them to do something?" asked Shield Jaguar in frustration.

"No, we don't wait," replied the great lord. "They will be watching to see what we will do. If they find us hiding in our city they will attack again. We need to show them we are not afraid of them."

"And just how are we to do that?" replied Shield Jaguar suddenly interested.

"We go hunting. We send out hunting parties, but instead of food we hunt men. We find them, kill them if we can, or chase them home, afraid of our power."

"I'm beginning to like this," Shield Jaguar said. "I like hunting."

"Tomorrow," said the king, "we will send out three groups

of warriors into different areas. Lord Great Skull will lead his family warriors, Lord K'an Tok Wayib his family's warriors, and Shield Jaguar the Eagle Warriors."

§

"We're going hunting," Shield Jaguar said enthusiastically as he approached Lightning Sky and Smoking Squirrel who were waiting outside the king's chambers.

"Really," Lightning Sky replied, "for what?"

"Men," replied Shield Jaguar, a big grin on his face. "We hunt for men tomorrow. Lord Great Skull thinks Piedras Negras will send warriors out to probe our defenses to see if they can attack again and we are going to hunt for them."

"Sounds better than hunting the giant river rodents," said Smoking Squirrel. "Do we catch them or kill them?"

"Lord Great Skull says kill them and chase the rest home to tell their king how well we are defending our land, but if we can capture one or two I'd be for it."

Johnson was ecstatic. *Wow, accompanying a war party in the jungle, a chance for fighting an enemy again. I have been dreaming about this for the months while back at the university. I'm ready. I am a warrior now; actually I'm an Eagle Warrior. Lightning Sky had his kills and they accepted him. I can handle it. I will get to go with them at last—if I'm still here in the past. I must make a prayer to the gods, maybe an offering would be better, to let me stay at least another day.*

As they sat talking about the upcoming expedition, Lord Great Skull came out of the palace chamber followed by his scribe and assistants. His personal warriors fell in behind as his procession proceeded. When the great lord went from place to place it was always in a procession, letting everyone know his position of importance; he was the Great Lord. Only the king's entourage was more impressive.

"Hey, Great Skull," Shield Jaguar called as he watched the lords retainers scurry to assemble behind him. "Where are your balls? Did you leave them at the foot of my brother's dais again?"

"I'm not so quick to lose mine as you are, young puppy," the lord spat as he stopped in front of the three young warriors. "Knowing when to wear them is something you still have to learn."

"You can't be a winner without balls, old man. You should wear them all of the time." Shield Jaguar smirked enjoying the consternation on the other man's face.

There weren't many men who could meet Lord Great Skull's ferocity when he was on the battlefield. He held tremendous pride in the ability to lead men into battle and he was always the man in front, a warrior who wreaked devastation upon his enemies.

"When the time comes, I'll have more than enough balls to handle it," the lord spat.

"If my brother chooses to give them back to you," said Shield Jaguar.

The lord glared at him. "You have much to learn, young puppy." He paused and laughed, "But, you have potential."

§

The sun went down. There was very little activity in the palace courtyard. A state of sadness hung in the air. All of the noble houses were still in mourning and would be for a number of days. That morning the fallen warriors were buried and today was a day of fasting, smearing faces with ashes, wearing slave's shifts. The gods needed to know that life without their loved ones wasn't worth living. The wives and mothers would go to the graves every day for the cycle of a moon to talk to those on the other side and leave food and drink to sustain them while they made the journey to the afterworld.

§

It was hot. Johnson was tired. Everyone had been preoccupied with the funeral and their grief. Earlier he had slipped away and spent the day wandering around the ceremonial complex, committing it to memory. He went from temple to temple closely observing each one, trying to memorize everything he saw.

When he approached anyone, they would step aside and look at the ground as they let him pass. He could see people trembling at his presence with fear in their eyes. He was the nephew of the king and a brother to the wild prince, Shield Jaguar. Their lives could end with the flick of his finger. The king was omnipotent, his kin close. To the common man there wasn't much difference. They were cut from the same cloth.

When he went into the temples it was always the same. A priest would walk up to him, stop, then back up turning to the side. He would stand there watching and waiting in servitude. Wherever Johnson went the priest would follow. Once Johnson asked a question about which god was worshiped and whether the god resided in temple. The answer was quick and short then the priest stepped back, bowing his head, signifying the answer was complete. He appeared relieved when Johnson left.

There weren't going to be any casual encounters to be found here, nor any interviews on his part to learn how they approached the theological beliefs of their culture. The answers to his questions were responded to with curt short answers. He looked for Little Rabbit. She was a priestess, but he didn't know where she officiated. She was nowhere to be found.

As evening came, the sun went down into the otherworld where it traveled at night. Slaves lit the torches in the inner courtyard. It was sweltering, no wind for relief. Johnson, dressed casually in a loincloth and sandals, sat in front of Lightning Sky's sleeping room on the stone walkway overlooking the courtyard. Again the scientist, he quietly observed those around him. Women in small groups sat crying and consoling each other in their grief. The men sat together at the end of the courtyard in a larger group, recounting the battle, giving praise to those who had fallen. As the stories were told, each of their fallen comrades was a hero who either killed or saved someone before he was taken. No life was ever lost without reason. In this society everybody contributed.

Emerging from the darkness, Little Rabbit entered the courtyard. Seeing Lightning Sky, she came and sat down beside him saying nothing. They sat in silence. She was barefoot and wore only a plain shift coming to mid thigh. Simply dressed, she was just a girl, almost a woman, and no longer the high priestess from that morning. To Johnson her presence felt pure, like the clear water of a deep spring bubbling from the ground, affecting everything around it. The nearness of her warmed him. He felt a comfortable sensation wash over him. He felt strangely complete. She was beside him now. He had returned to the past for this.

"The souls don't want to leave," she said pensively. "They want to stay here with the people."

"And that's a problem?" he asked.

"Yes, I've implored them again and again. I've said, you must go. Follow the spirits of the turkeys we left with you and find the black dog to take you across the river to the place of comfort."

"All of them have stayed here?" he asked.

"No, but most have stayed," she replied. "The meek spirits have left but the strong ones stayed. They are together. When they are together, they can resist passing over. They must be convinced to go."

"And what can you do about it?"

"Appeal to the gods and perform the rituals."

"Rituals?" Johnson asked.

"I will spend the night in the temple, the one dedicated to my mother. When the moon is high and Venus the Evening Star has left, I will perform the rituals calling upon Chamer, a death god of the underworld for help. Just before the sun is reborn, when the light is starting to push the darkness away, there are dark shadows. The night spirits start to move from place to place looking for somewhere to hide.

"Chamer, as a skeleton dressed in white and carrying a scythe with a blade made of bone, will come from Xibalba with his monsters and hide behind the shadows trying to catch the souls. If a soul is caught, it will be eaten by the monsters and will never live among its loved ones again. They will be scared and run for the river to cross over to travel through the underworld. They will either be captured or make their way to a paradise where warriors, priests, and women who died in childbirth go. There, Chamer's monsters cannot follow."

"Will any be eaten?"

"Perhaps, if they are surprised and don't flee quickly enough."

"It's a large responsibility you have, saving the souls," Johnson said.

"It's my duty," she replied solemnly.

"It's early," she said, "and we have some time before I have to be there. Get changed and walk with me to the temple. She got up and walked to her sleeping room. When she came out a few moments later she was transformed into a priestess again, wearing a long white robe with blue borders around the neck, sleeves and hem. A small ornate headdress with inlaid jade and feathers trailing from it was on her head. With the air of a priestess, she commanded the presence of all around her.

"Why aren't you changed?" she asked. "You can't go the Great Plaza like that. Are you not nephew to the king? Royal blood runs through your veins. Never let anyone forget it."

Johnson got up slowly and entered the sleeping room. *What am I going to do? There must be a protocol on what I'm to wear, but which clothes are they? Where is the old woman who dressed me before? I need her.* There were a number of combinations of garments carefully folded on another raised bench. *How am I to decide?* Standing there looking at them, he started to shake. *It was going so well, now what?*

As he stared dumbly down at the clothes, Little Rabbit casually stepped past him and picked up a white loincloth and red shirt and gave them to him. As he changed into the clothes, she opened a box and pulled out a jade necklace and two large rings. She tied the necklace around his neck and placed the rings on his fingers. Getting his sandals, she motioned him to sit as she kneeled down and placed the sandals on his feet. Last she placed an ornate headpiece upon his head. He noted that it was smaller than the ones used for ceremonies. As he stood up she threw her arms around him, hugged him hard and said, "Now you are dressed like a noble lord, my love."

He looked at her questioningly. *Something isn't right. It is like she senses my consternation with the clothes and knows I am a fake. The others said she could see things. They said she knew what was going to happen before it did. But what did she see? She sees something, but what?*

§

Leaving the palace, they walked toward the ceremonial center. As they came to the crest of the hill they could see the great complex stretched out on a flat plane adjacent to the river. A long stairway with a row of torches ran down to it.

"Beautiful," Johnson said as he stopped to take it all in. "I think it is more beautiful at night in the torchlight."

Little Rabbit took his hand and squeezed it. "Yes it is," she replied. "Let's sit here on the stairs awhile."

They sat side by side on the top step, holding hands and admiring the view. He looked down at her, small and delicate, a vision of loveliness. She was a lovely mystery. Spellbound, he sat there enchanted with her presence and he felt pain return in his chest. Strong and sharp, it tore him back to reality. If the past trips were any indication, he would probably be back in the future tomorrow and she would be gone from him again. *Damn it all to hell. First I miss the battle because I got here too late, then I miss being intimate again with the girl who stole my heart. She has to go to a temple and chant all night because some dead men's spirits said they didn't want to go to heaven, or whenever the hell they were supposed to go. The gods must be toying with me. How could they send me back in time just to observe a funeral?*

He felt her shudder and she squeezed his hand harder.

"I know who you are," she said softly as she looked up at him carefully.

"What?"

She repeated "I know who you are. You are not Lightning Sky." She took his hand in both of hers, squeezed it and held it to her cheek.

He sat there in silence. After a while he asked,

"Why do you think I'm not Lightning Sky?"

"He loves me, but you love me differently."

"How is that?" he said cautiously.

"Before anything else, Lightning Sky loves being a warrior. Fighting and the glory of winning come first and I come second. He and Shield Jaguar are as brothers and live for war. One day, in the time of the many great wars, they will be known throughout the land of the Maya as great warriors. Fierce and courageous, they show no mercy and expect none.

"How am I different?" he asked.

"There is a gentleness in you when you come near me. You are a warrior, yes, proud and fierce and men quake in your presence. But with me you are tender and I am precious in your heart."

"And you know who I am?" he asked not sure he wanted the answer.

"I know you're not Lightning Sky, but a god; you have taken

Lightning Sky's body to be with me."

A god, she thought him a god. How could he tell her who he was and how he got here? She'd never understand. Yes he took Lightning Sky's body, and sure, he wanted to be with her. She was exotic and she had cast a spell over him. Deep down he knew that most of his wanting to return to the past was to be with her again. In her world a god taking possession of a man's body was entirely possible; in fact it was probably considered reasonably normal.

"I'm from the future," he said, "thirteen hundred years in the future."

"I know," she replied. "A god can come from any time he wants, the past or the future. Time means nothing to a god."

He sat in silence not knowing what to say. He had been found out. What was to happen now?

"I love you," she replied. "I love Lightning Sky but I love you more. You are gentle in your strength and you are a part of me."

She loves me, Johnson repeated as a warm feeling filled him. *She said she loves me,* he repeated over and over to himself not willing to release the thought. It enthralled him. He looked at her in awe as she searched his eyes for a response. He shivered violently. *This was insane. He wasn't of this world. Tomorrow he would be gone.*

"My mother told me I would fall in love with a god," she said. "Before she died, when I was a little girl, she said a god would fall in love with me and come to our world to be with me. She told me to love him with all my heart, every single minute I was with him, because there would be too few." She looked up at him holding his eyes with the innocence of a child. "I love you my god. I love you.'"

§

As they reached the bottom of the stairs, a light, misty fog rising from the river hung over the Great Plaza lending an eerie glow in the moonlight. In contrast, the pyramids, swathed in dark flickering shadows from the torches, were sharp crags rising from the primordial marsh. The ceremonial center, a rendition of the Birthplace of Man, no longer looked man-made.

"The spirits of the gods are here tonight," Little Rabbit said. "On nights such as these they come."

"And the gods, do they come too?"

"No, they cannot leave there unless summoned. But spirits, both man's and god's, travel through the night causing mischief. We must be ever vigilant."

"And you are going to summon a god here tonight. Won't that be dangerous?"

"Oh yes, the rituals must be done very carefully so the god only comes for a short time and then goes back to Xibalba with his monsters. If it isn't done right, the monsters stay here and cause bad things to happen. They steal man's belongings and hide them. They cause illness to man's spirit and even death. If they catch a man's spirit animal it may become sick. We must be very careful of the monsters."

"Come with me," she said as she grabbed his hand pulling him into the darkness beside a small pyramid. She turned, threw her arms around him and kissed him passionately. "We have only a few minutes tonight my love. Hold me. I need to feel your strength. It will carry me through the night," and she kissed him again.

"More time, more time, we need more time," she cried, her head held tightly against his chest. "The gods tease us again with the crumbs from their table. They give us no blessing, just a few stolen minutes of bliss, then hours of yearning for another few minutes. They must laugh at us."

"I have you right now," Johnson said thinking he would be pulled back to the future tonight. "It's all I'll ever have."

They stood in the darkness of the pyramid for a long time clinging to each other in desperation, reassuring the other of their feelings.

"The moon is up and Venus low in the sky," she said. "We must go." She pulled away, walking again into the light.

They walked silently past the temples until they reached the one she sought. Johnson looked up. It was known to him as Temple 11, dedicated to Lady Sak B'iyaan, the Great Shield Jaguar's third wife.

He looked at it closely. In the future not much was left of it, just a crumbled foundation. The temple was built on a low rise. It consisted of two rooms facing a small stone-paved courtyard with an inlaid design. Carved frescos lined the temple walls with intricate figures of ancients and gods painted in vivid colors.

Johnson knew that of the three temples dedicated to the great Shield Jaguar's three wives, only temple 23, Lady Xook's, maintained a vestige of its former glory. Archaeologists gave credit to its artistic beauty because he built it for his principle wife, the glory of the other temples obliterated through decay. Johnson could see Temple 11 was easily equal in craftsmanship to the great temple.

"This is your mother's temple. What was she like?" he asked referring to the third wife of the great king; a young wife, a princess from another town married to him to cement an alliance. He must have been in his eighties when she bore him children. "What was her relationship with your father the great King Shield Jaguar compared to his other wives?"

She laughed. "She was kind and loving. Since she came from another city she didn't have many friends here so she spent a lot of time with my brother and me. My father was an old man, more like a grandfather to me. He liked having a younger wife.

That's why my brother and I are here. I remember his counselors remarking about the smile on his face in the mornings and the gleam in his eye. He was something of a sensation when we were born."

"And his other wives?" Johnson asked. "How did they take it?"

Little Rabbit held her hand to her mouth and giggled. "Grandmother Xook didn't like it at all," she said smiling with the memory as she looked up at him.

"You call her grandmother. Wasn't she a wife, like your mother? That would make her a stepmother."

"Yes, but she was very old, and I was very young, so I called her grandmother. She liked that when I was a little girl. She liked me, but not my mother."

"Did she give your mother a hard time?"

"She wouldn't talk to my mother or Grandmother Eveningstar. She was the great Shield Jaguar's principle wife, who came from a great family and wouldn't let anyone forget it either. According to her, the other wives didn't count."

"Really?"

"People were scared of her. She was mean, really mean. When she wanted something everyone ran to give it to her."

"And your father?"

"I think perhaps he may have been scared of her too, at least in his later years. He gave her almost anything she wanted, I think just to get rid of her. He was a king and a deity, yet she screamed at him just as if he were anyone else."

"And the temple over there, was it dedicated to her?" he asked as he pointed to the one he knew as Temple 23. It was assumed to be, but he wanted to make sure.

"Yes, she lived there most of the time as she got older."

He looked over at the temple across the plaza highlighted in the moonlight. The theories about Lady Xook abound in the archaeological community. As principle wife to the great Shield

Jaguar she left no surviving heir, but had a major role in all ceremonial functions. It was assumed her family was politically very powerful. Bird Jaguar, the present king, and brother to Little Rabbit, was born of Lady Eveningstar, a minor wife and a princess from Calakmul.

After the great Shield Jaguar II died, it was ten years before Bird Jaguar IV ascended to the throne. In the academic community it was believed that Lady Xook and her family were powerful enough to stop his ascension. Why and how they did it, was the question.

"So the great king had problems with his wives," Johnson said with a chuckle.

She laughed as she squeezed his hand. "There is a saying, 'A man who has a house with three cooks never eats a good meal'. People say that was why the king was so thin."

"What about the present king, Bird Jaguar?"

"She hated him. He hid from her whenever he could. She never missed an opportunity to criticize him, especially after my father died."

"But she performed a ritual dedicating him as an heir with a blood sacrifice ceremony," he countered. There were stone records attesting to this.

"Oh yes, the great king insisted she perform the dedication ceremony. People still talk about that fight. She wanted to officiate in the twenty-year period-ending celebration. She claimed it was her right, as principle wife, or there would be no dedication to Bird Jaguar's succession. My father, the king, got really mad. He roared that he was the king and his word was law. And if she refused to perform the blood sacrifice for the dedication of Bird Jaguar, she would be banished to remain inside the palace for the rest of her life. He stated that there would be a dedication to his only living heir and she, as a principle wife, was going to do it and be bound to honor it after he died. Afterwards, he even put up a lintel on her temple to remind her of her obligation. She hated that too."

"Doesn't sound like she honored it," he replied in reference to King Bird Jaguar being kept from the throne for ten years.

"There are stories. When we have more time I'll tell you. The great king was only in his grave a few days and she claimed to be his incarnate spirit and that he changed his mind about Bird Jaguar and a king should be named from her family. She kept that story up until she died."

Johnson perked up. Records indicated there was an interim king after Shield Jaguar II died. Records from Piedras Negras alluded to Yoaat B'alam II who witnessed a K'atun-anniversary (period ending) in 749 A.D. It was thought he was possibly the appointed king.

"Did she get her way?" he asked.

"For a short time, her family was powerful. They commanded the warriors. Two of her brothers tried to step into the position but they didn't last. One started a war with Dos Pilas and was captured in a battle and sacrificed. The other lasted a little longer, but after she died, Bird Jaguar and Lord Great Skull killed him and two of the Xook family Ajaws. Bird Jaguar smashed his monuments. By birthright, he is king now and no one contests it. He has made many monuments to support his claim.

"And you and Shield Jaguar; how did Lady Xook treat Shield Jaguar?"

"He was too small to be a problem to her. She hated my mother but she liked me and tolerated Shield Jaguar."

"Tolerated?"

"He stood up to her, even as a small boy. He'd tell her, 'My father is a king and you are only a woman. Who are you to tell me what to do?' She'd get mad then go 'humph' and then ignore him. I think she liked his gall. She said he was like his father, the great king, when he got mad. She respected that I think."

She kissed him hard, then turned without a word and walked up the steps to the temple. It was time to call a god into the world of man.

§

Broken Monkey looked down from the top of the pyramid. He laughed softly to himself. He had been watching the two lovers for the last half hour. At first he thought it just an illicit love affair between a priestess and a warrior, an interesting diversion to watch. But when he recognized Little Rabbit he had to know more. She wasn't a simple priestess. She was the king's sister. Slowly he climbed down the dark side of the pyramid hiding in the shadows to get closer to them.

Broken Monkey often came to the ceremonial center and climbed the pyramids on dark nights. He liked those nights the best. On top of a high pyramid he would sit and watch over the temples and plaza. It was his world then, the world of the night spirits. The spirits were better than man. They didn't look at his twisted body and make him ashamed he wasn't like other men. He liked the spirits and he despised men.

Men were afraid of him and that gave him satisfaction, but not enough. He was bitter. Today everyone believed he was a companion of Mam, the god of evil. No one dared oppose him. He could call Mam's wrath down on anyone and the cruel god would send a monster to hurt or kill the antagonist's companion spirit.

He lived in a cave on a bluff overlooking the river with a dwarf who was a powerful practitioner of magic. The dwarf was his slave, they said, whom he stole from a king in the north. Broken Monkey never spoke to anyone. The dwarf spoke for him. Periodically they would come to the city and Broken Monkey would stand on a rise near the edge of the Great Plaza and the dwarf would stand before him and shout a warning, "Beware of the wrath of the gods, they send death and destruction on those who oppose them," and then he'd include something he didn't like about man for them to worry about. There were many things about men that Broken Monkey didn't like.

Slowly Broken Monkey moved into a dark shadow. He wanted to know what they were talking about. "The king's sister; what could he get from her?" he asked himself as he looked down from just above them. He sat quietly and listened.

"I know you're not Lightning Sky, but a god," he heard Little Rabbit say. *A god? Lightning Sky was a god and he's not Lightning Sky?* He strained to hear more. *She loved him she said but he wouldn't remain here for long.* It didn't make sense to him. Broken Monkey knew something unusual was happening and he had to know what it was. He watched her walk away and climb the stairs to a temple while the warrior left in the other direction. He would watch her closely now. Perhaps he had come across something he could use to his advantage.

Chapter 12

It was dark when Johnson awakened. His first thought was for Little Rabbit. It wasn't light out yet. She would still be at the temple chanting; calling the monsters of Xibalba to scare the souls of the dead warriors into leaving the world of the living. But that was thirteen hundred years ago and he was back in the future. Loss and despair gripped his heart as his body tensed with the realization.

Then he felt it. His bed was hard, very hard and there was no mattress, only a light pad. He slipped his hand under the pad and felt rock. He stretched his hand out to the wall; rock again. He wasn't in the lodge in the little town of Frontera Corozol where he booked a room. Was he in the cave? He heard a dog bark, and a child crying. No he wasn't in the cave either. Two nights had passed and he hadn't gone back. He was still here in the past with Little Rabbit. Joy filled his heart and the pain left him. He felt a smile cross his face. Maybe, he hoped, he would never go back.

Laying in bed, waiting for the sun to come up, Johnson wondered what would happen today. Shield Jaguar said they would be going hunting and their quarry would be men. At first it sounded exciting, a trek in the woods with the guys, maybe a fight. The only fight he had ever been in was the one on the first trip back in time, and remembering it honestly, he was lucky. If it weren't for Shield Jaguar, he'd be dead; assuming if his surrogate body died he would too. What did he know about fighting? He was a professor. The real Lightning Sky had been trained for war since he was a boy. Warriors didn't get that way by claiming the title. They trained at it here as well as in other ancient civilizations.

How was he going to fake it this time? And if he didn't become involved what would happen to him? He couldn't let the others attack and sit there and observe the process like the scientist he was. It wouldn't work that way.

"Okay, lazy one," the old woman said as she entered the room. "It's time to get up. The moon has left the sky to hide from the sun."

He looked out the doorway. It was still dark. Not early dawn dark, but totally dark. It was the middle of the night.

"I thought the sun was to come up before it is time to get up," he said.

"Not today. Shield Jaguar wants to be in the jungle shortly after the sun is reborn." She laid out the same warrior outfit he wore the first time he went back in time.

"Now get up my son. You can't keep the prince waiting."

As she dressed him she prattled as before. "You must be a warrior, strong and courageous. You must do honor to your family by fighting well. Aren't you a member of the Eagle Warrior Society now; one of the elite? You have four kills and Shield Jaguar is taking you with his warriors. If you are captured you must be brave and curse your captors as they torment you, and die well, bringing honor to yourself."

Did she imply torture and die well with honor in the same sentence? This is getting serious. Fear swept over him. This wasn't right. He wasn't sure he wanted to go with the war party now. *I am in the wrong place.* It was no longer a matter of faking it. In fact, faking it had nothing to do with it. He didn't belong here. *I'm not a Maya warrior; I'm a college professor, and now would be a good time to go back to the future. What have I gotten myself into?"*

"Come on brother," he heard Shield Jaguar call from the courtyard. "It's time to go. The warriors will be getting ready. We go hunting today and the prey is worthy of matching our skills."

"The prey is worthy?" Lightning Sky asked as he stepped out into the courtyard.

"We may be the prey," Shield Jaguar laughed. "They will be hunting too."

"Great," Johnson whispered under his breath.

Three large groups of two hundred warriors each were assembled on a high hill overlooking the ceremonial center; the three hunting parties. Torchlight lent a surreal quality to the gathering. Servants and slave women were passing out tortillas and peppers and there were beans for dunking the tortillas in. The warriors were congregated in small groups, eating with companions, discussing the day to come.

Johnson noted that the mood was jovial. These men looked forward to the task, hunting they called it. These warriors lived for battle. They were bred for it. For them it was what life was all about. For centuries the Maya city states were in an almost constant state of war. "Today is a good day," they said. "There may be fighting today." Sacks of food were handed out to be consumed on the expedition, enough for that day. If more were needed local community leaders would provide as commanded. A horn sounded and the men grabbed a last tortilla and assembled in groups around their leaders. It was time to go hunting.

Shield Jaguar's Eagle Warriors moved briskly toward the northeast, adjacent to the Usumacinta River. A hundred elite Eagle Warriors were at the front of the column and another hundred seasoned warriors following. Dozens of runners had been sent ahead of the main party. They would pass through the outlying communities and spread out into the jungle before the sun rose. Their job was to locate the enemy and bring word back to the main party. The jungle would be a dangerous place today.

Leaving the city, Johnson was able to observe the countryside as the sun started to rise. There were large palaces, the homes of the noble families, near the ceremonial center. As they got further away there were smaller family compounds with a few houses arranged close to one another. Children came running out to cheer the warriors. Most were predestined to be common farmers growing corn and beans, but some, a very few, would become warriors. Those who demonstrated superior skills on the ball courts found in every community might have the chance.

Further out, single small houses were built near the fields the owners worked. The noble families owned and oversaw many of the large farms. However, in the outlining areas, independent farmers raised their own crops but were subject to a large percentage paid as a tax.

Everywhere he looked there were farms with crops growing. Hundreds of thousands of people needed to be fed. It took a lot of food. He had read studies that the population had grown sharply during the Eighth Century. Trying to supply sufficient food for the increase in people put a strain on the agricultural process. The first of three great droughts, considered strong contributors to the collapse of the Maya civilization, wouldn't come for another forty years, but the strain on society being able to feed itself must have begun long before that.

Then Johnson noticed it. It wasn't very prevalent but it was there. The Maya had a strict method of farming involving crop rotation. Due to the nature of jungle soil being thin and without many nutrients, they needed to periodically let the land recuperate. Then the jungle growth was cut down and burned and the plot was planted again. There didn't appear to be enough land laying fallow. Somewhere they must be cutting corners and not giving the land enough time to recover. Short-term needs were too great. They would plant more often, but crop yields would go down instead of up. In the long run the harvests would provide less. It would only take a few years for the effect to be felt. By the time the droughts came, it might be enough to trigger the collapse of food production. Civilization couldn't support itself without food production significantly exceeding the amount of food needed to sustain it.

"Move to the side," Shield Jaguar called to the procession coming toward them. "Make way for Prince Shield Jaguar." They were on a narrow trail and there was not enough room for both groups to pass each other. One would have to stand off to the side. It wasn't going to be Shield Jaguar's procession. A contingent of armed warriors were leading a large group of barefoot men clad only in dirty loincloths who were carrying large reed baskets. Moving off the path to both sides of the trail, they stood blankly watching the prince's procession pass. The line of watchers seemed to go on forever. Johnson estimated it well over a mile long.

"Who are they?" Lightning Sky asked.

"They are slaves who carry the tribute," replied Shield Jaguar. "They are coming from San Jose Mutal with 2000 baskets of corn."

"Corn?" said Johnson," I thought tribute was cocoa and jade and such."

"At one time, yes. Now it is corn. We plant more, but people are going hungry. Menzabac, the weather god, doesn't favor us anymore. The rain gods have not given us the rain we need for the corn. Many plants die, and the ones that live give smaller ears. Chak, the god of maze, is angry at the weather god for not giving enough rain but Menzabac is too fierce and Chak too gentle. He can't convince Menzabac to give more water. Now he thinks we aren't sacrificing enough to the rain god. He wants there to be more offerings of blood. We need more captives to sacrifice. We need lots of captives. The sacrifices must be made more often so he knows we honor him. Only big sacrifices will appease him so he will send more rain."

§

The farms thinned out and then came the thick jungle. When they came to a cenote, Shield Jaguar called the warriors to a halt. "We wait here," he said to his men. "The runners will return."

"And if they find nothing?" asked Smoking Squirrel.

"Then we move another hour forward and try it again."

Runner after runner came back. "Nothing to be found," they all said. Shield Jaguar sent them out again and waited for an hour and the warriors started forward again. The warriors moved silently. Any sound might echo through the jungle. There was always the possibility the runners had missed finding their prey and they were being sought by the enemy. It was a big jungle with numerous caves, sinkholes, and rock formations to hide in. It would be easy for a large force of warriors to find a place to hide and prepare an ambush. It worked both ways.

Another hour later the war party came to a large cave and the men waited again. Johnson sat back admiring the beauty. An opening over two hundred feet high, half the size of the hill above, opened into a monstrous cavern stretching more than a hundred yards deep. A clear stream flowed over the rocky bed consisting of large hunks of limestone once part of the ceiling. *This must be a place of the gods.* He found a seat inside the entrance on a large limestone bolder overlooking the stream.

The world seemed calm and peaceful here. A jewel of creation, it should not be marred by war. He looked at the resting warriors scattered along the stream. They seemed harmless from here. His reverie was broken by a shout as a runner came in and stopped, struggling for breath as he called out something Johnson couldn't hear. Men gathered around and Johnson knew paradise briefly found was again lost. It could mean only one thing—the hunters had found their prey.

"The enemy is on its way," Shield Jaguar said to his men. He drew a map in the sand. "Here is where they are, and this is the way they are coming. We will set a trap and meet them here between these two large hills with the limestone faces."

"Let's hurry," called Smoking Squirrel. He would lead the seasoned warriors when they split the forces at the trap.

"Caution," commanded Shield Jaguar. "We need to hear from the rest of the runners. Not all are back yet."

"Caution from you?" Smoking Squirrel countered. "It's attack now and kill them all, isn't it?"

"I'm starting to listen to Lord Great Skull. He says to think before you fight. Maybe there is a better way."

"You listen to him? That's a new one," exclaimed Smoking Squirrel.

"I can't afford to go home battered and him come back victorious. He's too powerful now. The attack will come. Let's be sure it is the only group of enemy warriors out there."

Runner after runner came back except the last one. Nothing was found they said. Still Shield Jaguar waited. An hour later a man staggered in wounded and bloody. He had been hit with two spears and had lost a lot of blood. He wouldn't live much longer.

Shield Jaguar knelt beside the man and held his head up.

"Little brother," he said compassion in his eyes, "who did this to you?"

"The enemy; they wounded me but my spirit companion hid me and carried me here."

"Where are they? We will avenge you and lay your spirit to rest."

The wounded warrior's breathing was weak. "A large group of warriors are near the river where it bends twice, at least two hundred. They are moving parallel to the smaller force coming up the trail between the large hills with the limestone faces. They have runners in advance of the smaller force. I think they know you are here." The man gasped for his last breath and died.

Shield Jaguar called his warriors together. "They have set a trap for us," he said, "but they mistake who they are dealing with. We will turn their trap against them." He smoothed the sand and drew another map. "They expect that we will find the smaller force and attack it. They are waiting for us and have set up a trap When we attack the small force, they will come from behind and catch us between their forces. They plan to make the surprise attack between the two hills with limestone faces.

"They are wrong. We will attack the larger force here." He drew lines in the sand. "They have to go through this small gorge as they follow their bait. We will attack them here with one hundred-fifty men, the Eagle Warriors. It will be enough. Their smaller force will be here when they learn of the surprise," he pointed with his stick. "They will rush to help, thinking the larger force needs them. They will have to come along this stream," he drew in the sand, "and Smoking Squirrel's warriors will be hiding and attack them at the place of the big boulders. When our two hundred wins over their three hundred, songs will be sung about us for many nights."

§

Lightning Sky's breath came in rasping gasps and still he ran. Shield Jaguar was in the lead running hard, his warriors close behind. He was hunting now. His face set, hard and determined. The prey, now identified, was not to get away. Even with the hard body and conditioning of Lightning Sky, Johnson was having a hard time of it. He hadn't expected the discomfort that needed to be endured when pushed to the limit.

They ran nonstop for an hour. Pain engulfed him. His throat and lungs burned, his legs cramped in waves of pain. The pit of his stomach held an immensely hot fire radiating through his entire body. But he refused to quit. The others had to be feeling the same thing and they kept going. He must too.

Without slowing, Shield Jaguar held up his hand and the smaller party split off and headed up another path. In another quarter hour they came to a small hill and Shield Jaguar called a halt. All but four of the men stood and gasped, catching their breath as they watched the four climb the hill quickly and peer over the top. They motioned for the others to follow. Johnson reached the top and peered over. The landscape looked the same in front and behind. The rain forest always looked the same; a tangled mass of vegetation.

The four runners remained just behind the crest of the hill. The remaining warriors moved back down and out of sight. The trap was set. Then they waited.

"Just like waiting at a water hole for a deer," Shield Jaguar whispered. "When he comes to drink, if we spring quickly, we will eat good that night."

The men laid their weapons beside them. Each man came with two spears, one for throwing and one for thrusting, a war club with inset obsidian tied to his belt and a shield. First the throwing spears would be hurled at the enemy. Then the short spear would be taken up and they would charge. The short spear was preferred for close fighting.

"When it starts stay close to me," Shield Jaguar counseled him again as he did during his first fight. "My guards will protect you." Ten warriors were dedicated solely for Shield Jaguar's protection. As a royal prince he was a prime target to be taken captive. Fighting and dying was acceptable for a member of the royal family, especially a king or prince, but being taken a captive was not. There would be a loss of honor for Yaxchilan if he were captured, even if he died well.

§

A sudden burst of screaming broke the silence. Startled, a flock of parrots scattered from the nesting tree screeching as they rose. A troop of howler monkeys moving through nearby trees took up the cry, setting up a tremendous racket. One hundred fifty warriors stood up, and threw their spears. Arcing through the sky they landed amidst the enemy, killing with deadly accuracy. Mass confusion ensued as Shield Jaguar and the warriors ran down the hill, screaming at the top of their lungs and engaging the survivors with their thrusting spears.

Lightning Sky, running beside Shield Jaguar, slammed into the mass of men. His spear took the first man he faced in the chest. It stuck. He pulled, but it wouldn't come out. It was stuck. He panicked. He needed that spear. Forgetting about the fighting going on around him, Lightning Sky concentrated on pulling at the spear. A guard stepped past him spearing an oncoming warrior in the throat and hitting him with his shield throwing him backward. "The club!" he shouted backward to Lightning Sky as he grappled with the man.

Lightning Sky pulled his club and shield just as another warrior came at him. The guard was busy fighting, so were the others. He was expected to hold his own. Blocking a jarring blow with his shield, he swung the club overhand catching his opponent in the head. Another blow came, and he blocked it with the shield. His arm buckled and he fell backward to his knees. The man came in, swinging down hard. Lightning Sky rolled to the side and swung his club for the man's legs, catching him in the calf, making a cut to the bone. The man fell, and Lightning Sky swung at his head, now within range, splitting it in half.

He rose and quickly to his feet and slowly swung around

looking for further danger, but none was close. He was in a calm spot in the middle of a battle. Fighting was going on around him but only half the men were still engaged against an enemy that fought bravely, dying in the process. The surprise was total and lasted only a few minutes.

Lightning Sky started to tremble. The tremor started from deep within him sending waves of intensity which rocked his body. He took a deep breath and held it, but he couldn't stop shaking. It was over and he was still alive. His arm hurt terribly from the blows he had stopped but he was alive. He thought of the error he made with the short spear and the guard who had saved his life. Another flood of fear came sharply over him but passed quickly. *That was close, too close.*

The tremors in his gut continued as he caught Shield Jaguar's eye and held the club in the air in a victory stance. In return Jaguar Shield held up a captive by the hair. Johnson noticed the club he was holding in the air. The club didn't shake. He looked at it closely. No, it wasn't shaking. He held his hand level in front of him. It didn't shake either and he smiled. Then he broke into a broader smile. He had won again!

§

The moon was high when the warriors got back to the palace. The surprise had been total, the victory complete. Shield Jaguar had another captive to his credit, a captain of the enemy warriors, one who knew the enemy's plans. He would reveal them soon, Shield Jaguar had told them. He was looking forward to the process. Lord Great Skull's warriors had encountered the enemy too. There had been a battle and losses had been heavy but his warriors were victorious.

Lightning Sky was dead tired and went to his sleeping room as soon as they returned. *Let Shield Jaguar explain everything. He is the leader, isn't he? He is the prince and the glory is his.*

Lightning Sky was hungry and felt exhausted. *Hunger can wait, I need to sleep.* He flopped down on his sleeping pad fully clothed; blood sweat and pain accompanying him.

He was almost asleep when she came in and lay down next to him. "I was worried when you were out there. I'm so scared of losing you," she said.

"Losing me?" he replied. "Never." And he wrapped his arms around her.

"Whew, you stink," she replied drawing back. "If you want to love me tonight, you'll have to smell better than that."

"It's the warrior in me," he teased. "I'm a great warrior—another two kills today."

"I don't want a great warrior. I want a great lover, and a great lover doesn't smell like you. Come with me," she commanded.

"I need sleep," he mumbled half asleep again.

"What you need is a bath." She pulled him to his feet as she laughed at him, "and you're going to get one."

He stumbled after her as she led him out of the palace and down to the river following a secluded path, unseen from prying eyes.

"It's too far," he complained as they reached the river. "Dump me in the water here, rinse me off and let me go back and sleep."

"Not a chance, great warrior," she replied. "We're going to do this right," and she pulled him along behind her.

Stopping at a little inlet she stepped back, slipped out of her shift and said, "Strip, mighty warrior." She stepped into the little pool of knee-deep water.

He looked at the soft contours of her body in the moonlight. Need for sleep forgotten, pain put aside, he stared longingly at her. *My God, she is beautiful. The perfect woman, and she stands in her purity in front of me.* He looked down at himself. Blood covered his padded vest and ran down the front of his loincloth trailing along his leg to his foot. His hands and arms were coated in grime. He raised an arm and checked his armpit; powerfully bad. Leadenly he shed his clothes and entered the pool.

Slowly, with a soft cloth she washed him, starting with his feet and working up. As she washed each body part she kissed it and softly purred, "Your foot is clean my love," and teased, "and it's working quite properly, my fierce warrior," or "your leg is clean my love, and it too is working, my fierce warrior." When she got to his manhood, she took time cleaning it and stroking it until he got hard. She said, "you're manhood is clean my love, and before the night is over I'll find out if it is working properly. Then is the time to be a mighty warrior."

When she reached his left arm—his shield arm, she washed the dirt away and discovered the large discolored bruises. She cried in distress, "You're hurt, my love." Tears flowed down her cheeks as she looked at the arm. It looked bad.

"It will be okay," he assured her, trying not to let her know it had set up and he couldn't move it. "In a couple of days, it will be okay."

"I must go to the temple and make a sacrifice to the gods for them to heal you," she cried.

He looked down at her and squeezed her arm tightly with his right hand. She winced. His voice became hard.

"The gods had you last night. Tonight you are mine. I'd rather lose the arm than have you in a temple instead of being with me."

She pulled back and a frightened look crossed her face. She stood there bewildered, and searched into his eyes. She put her head on his chest, held it there for a long quiet moment and softly said, "Yes, my love."

Quietly, she finished bathing him, led him from the pool and toweled him dry. "Come," she said, as she led him to a grassy spot next to the pool. She lay down, beckoning him to join her. His tiredness vanished as he lay and held her in his arms. She came to him quietly, trembling and submissive only following his lead.

"Little one," he said, "don't fear me. I love you for who you are, not for what you think you should be. Come to me with your love pure, strong and demanding. It's the way I know you. It's the way I want you."

A big smile crossed her face and she hugged him fiercely. "I'm hungry for you and you can never give me enough to make me full." She hugged him tightly again. Burying herself in his arms she clung to him in desperation. Slowly she pulled back, the smile gone as she looked longingly into his eyes. A tear rolled down her cheek.

"Our time together is too short. The pain of our parting will burn me to cinders, and I'll still want more, forever hope for more and am destined to wait an eternity for more. I'm yours forever. After the sun stops shining, the moon hides forever and the gods forsake man, I'll still love you."

Johnson held her close, and brought her to him. He kissed her tenderly, the response warm and demanding until they were lost in each other. Once again childlike, she came to him with abandon, and their passion grew stronger with every kiss. Wave upon wave of pleasure enveloped each as they consumed the other, giving totally, and never getting enough, hungry for more. They reached a peak of ecstasy again and again, floating eternally, oblivious to the world around them. And when they were spent, they lay in each other's arms and soon fell into a blissful, contented sleep. The last thing he heard was, "The gods have provided another precious gift my love. For now they take joy in us."

§

Broken Monkey watched the two bathers as he sat silently on the low bluff across the river. It was a quiet night and their voices carried far. He had followed Little Rabbit when she left the temple earlier in the evening and returned to the palace. The warriors were returning from their raid. They had met resistance and the fighting had been heavy. He was sure she would meet with Lightning Sky again tonight. She would want to know how he had fared.

He sat quietly, observing the palace, looking for a way of getting inside without being seen so he could find a place to hide and listen to them. Normally climbing across the roof was the best. On the nights when they had their banquets in the courtyard he would sit on the roof and watch the eating, drinking and dancing and yearned to be part of it. Deep down inside he was angry and blamed them. It would be difficult but he could climb back down to where he could stand in a doorway. The thick palace walls made for a tunnel-like entry, and there was room to stand in it and not be seen—if the inhabitants were not watching closely.

As he contemplated the problem, Little Rabbit and Lightning Sky came out of the palace entrance. Broken Monkey was excited. This was better. He could follow them now. They would find a place to be together where they thought no one would be watching. He liked the intrigue. If he could find a way to manipulate the king's sister, he might have a measure of control over the king himself.

He blackmailed many people in Yaxchilan who regularly gave him information about affairs and plans made by the heads of the great families, sometimes even the royal court. It was the price they paid to keep others from learning about transgressions that would harm their place in the community.

They didn't know he was behind the blackmail. Broken Monkey never approached the people himself. He had his women slaves do that for him. He used the information to manipulate people to do his bidding. It gave him power over them and he liked it and wanted more.

Now he had something on the king's sister, but not enough. An affair with Lightning Sky might embarrass her for a little while, but not sufficiently to trap her. If approached by one of his women, Little Rabbit would probably have her whipped severely for her insolence. And after it blew over she would just take up where she left off. Wasn't she Shield Jaguar's sister? Those two did what they wanted and people accepted it. But he'd find something he could use because she said Lightning Sky wasn't Lightning Sky, and she loved whoever he was. Love was her weak point—or Lightning Sky's—and love could always be exploited.

Broken Monkey could see them quite plainly in the moonlight washing each other in the river. She was beautiful, pure and not ashamed of her nakedness. His desire rose. He wanted to possess her, take her from this man and have her for his own, but Shield Jaguar would find out and kill him. Being a sage or god or holy man or whatever, would make no difference. Shield Jaguar was a man who had no fear of the gods. Broken Monkey knew he considered himself destined to become a god, one who walked the earth instead of being confined to Xibalba. Yes, Shield Jaguar would kill him, and it wouldn't be an easy death.

As Little Rabbit and Lightning Sky lay in each other's arms, spent from their lovemaking, they talked. Lightning Sky told her he would soon be returning to his world. He could only stay for a short time. She cried and held him tight.

"I won't let you go," she said with tears rolling down her cheeks. "You can't leave me again."

"We have no choice," he replied holding her closer. "The gods only allow me a short time. They won't let me stay. When the drug wears off I am pulled back into the future."

"How much of the drug do you have left?" she desperately asked.

"Enough for about two, possibly three more trips, I think, but maybe not. I seem to use more each time."

"That's not enough," she said as she raised her head up and

studied his face. "Can you find more? There has to be more somewhere, or you can make more of it."

"I've tried everything I can think of. The plants you used to make it no longer exist in the future, in my time," he said as he held her tighter.

"My love, what shall we do? I've just found you. I can't lose you or I'll die." She buried her head into his chest again and held him tightly as the realization that nothing could be done set in, and she cried.

Broken Monkey smiled broadly. He knew how to get to her now. He knew her price. He would have to find a way to keep the man here if she was to do his bidding. He'd have to find out more about this drug they talked about. It was the key. He left them laying there, and climbed the steep bluff to the cave he lived in. He felt good. When he got back to the cave he would whip one of the slave girls, the younger one, until she bled and screamed and was filled with horror, then he would take her. It would be a fine finish to a very interesting night.

Chapter 13

It was dark when he opened his eyes. "We must get back to the palace, little one," he mumbled, "or your brother will discover us." He reached over to touch her. He was alone. She must have left. He floated in the twilight between sleep and wakefulness, filled with the warmth of her love and yearned to have her again. "Where are you my love? I need you," he called softly.

A hand gripped his shoulder and shook him gently. "You have returned," the old man's voice said. "You have come back to the present." Johnson opened his eyes and looked around. The cold of the cave crept in to surround him and he shivered. The old shaman moved back to the little fire for the warmth it provided, placed another stick into it and looked sadly at him. "You are in the present," he said again.

"It can't be," Johnson moaned looking blankly into the old man's eyes. "I want to go back. I need to go back," he pleaded.

"No," replied the old man. "It would never be permitted. You are not of that place. This is your world. This is where you belong. You asked the gods to show you the ancient city and the ancient ones. They have done so. Now it is time to come home."

"I can't be here. It's a mistake. Can't you see that? I must go back."

The old man sat staring into the little fire. When it died down, he got up, lit a torch from the embers and walked to the tunnel leading to the surface. He turned and looked at Johnson. "It is time to leave," he said and entered the tunnel.

Johnson looked around wildly. Little Rabbit was waiting for him. He had to find a way back. Where was the powder? He'd take more powder. It would take him back to her. Feverishly he looked around. It was in a little jar with a cork stopper so no powder escaped. The jar should be a quarter full, enough to return a couple of times yet. It was nowhere to be found.

The old man took it. The old bastard stole my powder. He wants it for himself. He wants to travel to the past to talk to the gods. Isn't he a shaman, a holy man claiming to be the spokesman of those same gods? And I'll never see Little Rabbit again. He got up and stumbled to the tunnel. *I'll kill that old bastard. He'll never use the powder. No, better yet I'll catch him and make him give it to me. Like Shield Jaguar or Lightning Sky, I'll stake him to the ground and build a small fire in the palm of his hand. Steal from me; I'll teach him. I'll get the powder back and then I won't need him anymore.*

He grabbed a torch and ran into the tunnel. He stumbled and fell, bruising a knee and cutting his hand. The torch fell and went out. Cursing, he crawled along the floor looking for it. He had to find his way back to the chamber. Without the torch he would never find his way out of the cave.

He stood up trying to get his direction. He felt his way along, walking cautiously. After what seemed an eternity he came to a dead end. *No, this isn't the way. I'll go back, but which way?* He was lost. Groping along the wall he hurried faster, back the way he had come. Suddenly the wall guiding him ended. He was at a fork. *Which way?* They both seemed the same.

His anger turned to fear. He was lost. Then fear turned to panic.

I'll never find the way out. I could die here. The old man would be long gone with the powder and it wouldn't bother him if I'm never found. He stumbled and fell, the hand hurt worse as he curled up in pain. He lay there for what seemed a long time. *Can't stop, to stop means to die, I must go on.* He started to crawl, groping in front of him. It was futile, he was lost in this labyrinth of tunnels.

Suddenly he saw a faint glow, just a promise of light. Looking at it he continued to crawl toward it. The light got brighter, and it was moving. The old man had come back. Johnson remained there on his hands and knees as the old man approached. Fear forgotten, relief filled him. He stared at the light-giving torch. He was saved.

It was night when they came out of the cave; a hot humid night with a full moon shining brightly from above. Johnson was exhausted. Relieved to be rescued, the hate and fear were gone, left behind in the cave. He was drained physically, mentally and emotionally. He weakly followed the old man to the pickup.

"The powder is yours," said the old man as he got in. He handed Johnson the jar. "The gods gave it to you. It is not my place to take it away. But you must never use it again. The gods are not to be trusted. They will deceive you and make you suffer for their pleasure. They will destroy you. Leave here and never come back. Go back to your university. That is where you belong. Don't return to Yaxchilan. There is nothing left there for you."

"I can't," Johnson whispered weakly. "You don't understand, I can't."

The old man drove Johnson back to the archaeological site. A tent was there and some food. It was just him and the ruins in the light of the full moon. Exhausted, yet with no desire for sleep, Johnson sat in the foundation of the king's palace where the inner courtyard was and envisioned it when Bird Jaguar was the king, when the prince Shield Jaguar and Little Rabbit lived there.

He went down the hill to the ceremonial center and walked through the ruins. Little was left of the once majestic city, not nearly enough to envision its glory. He came to Temple 11, where Little Rabbit called the gods into this world. There were only lines of rocks showing the location of the foundation. He came back and sat at the foot of the stairs that led up to the palace. Looking around at the ruins he sat sobbing softly and then started crying like a baby. He cried and cried until he had no more tears, then curled up into a fetal position, rocking gently and stared into the night neither seeing into the past nor the present.

§

The snow was coming down hard now. The Christmas break was over and Johnson was back at the university. He stood at the window and looked out over out the campus at the snow. About four inches coated the ground. Crushed paths of footprints led where walks had been. Students hunched against the onslaught moved from class to class. It was one of those snows which stuck to everything. The trees were starting to take on a surreal quality of white shadows against their stark barren winter branches. It was beautiful, he thought.

"You look terrible," Phoebe said as she came into the empty classroom. Saying nothing, he walked back to his desk, picked up his papers and opened his briefcase.

"I'm doing okay," he replied.

"You don't look okay, Alan. In fact you look like shit."

"I'm doing okay, Pheb."

She came over and stared at him across the desk. A worried look grew on her face. "I can see the hangover from here. It's more than a little noticeable."

"So I drank a little this weekend," he replied not looking up. "What's the big deal?"

"A little, looks more to me like a lot."

"Don't worry about it. I can handle it."

"It's starting to show on you Alan. People are beginning to notice."

"I'm working on developing a presentation to the archaeological society next spring, Pheb," he said changing the subject. "It's a difficult approach. I need to get it right."

"What will they believe?" she asked. "You say you saw a lot when you went back this time. Some of that stuff is pretty radical."

"I owe it to science to tell it all," he replied.

"Are they ready for it all?" she asked.

"Are they ready for all of what?" asked Dan as he entered the room.

"Alan's trip was rather unique," said Phoebe.

"Did you become the warrior again?" Dan asked. "When you left at Christmas, you said you would become a warrior."

"Yes Dan, I became a warrior."

"Really, what was it like?"

Johnson smiled at Dan's youthful exuberance. He felt that way once, especially on excavations. Digging with a trowel and a spoon isn't a lot of fun. He had occupied the time fantasizing about the ancient culture he was studying and what it was like. When he was lucky enough to excavate a grave and find the grave goods buried there, a whole new world of speculation opened up. How were the artifacts used by the previous owner and why were they important enough to be buried with him or her?

"Being a warrior? It was exciting Dan, but being a warrior of royal blood was a whole other world. There were hundreds of warriors, most from noble families but still many were commoners."

"Royal blood; you were royalty?" Dan asked in amazement.

"He says he was the nephew of king Bird Jaguar IV, and cousin to the prince and the next king," explained Phoebe. "That's getting pretty royal."

"We were treated special," Johnson said. "I was the cousin of Shield Jaguar III who was a prince and the half brother of the king. Both were born of the same father. Shield Jaguar III, in the eyes of the people, was nearly a deity like the king. He demanded that the people pay reverence to him. Transgressions resulted in punishment, even death.

"He is one of the most dynamic men I have ever met—a natural leader who draws people to him. He is in a struggle with the great Lord Great Skull and the king, Bird Jaguar IV, for his succession to the throne. The king is frail and appears to be weakening. He may be sick. The king has dedicated his son Chel-Te' as the next king but Shield Jaguar III advocates that he should be the next king; it is his birthright.

"His two cousins, Lightning Sky and Smoking Squirrel, were his companions and advisors; he called us his brothers. Shield Jaguar was treated like the king. People moved out of our way and stood to the side and stared as we passed. In a crowded market, word of our coming would pass ahead of us from mouth to mouth and an aisle would open to us. The three of us would pass through followed by a party of Eagle Warriors, Shield Jaguar's personal guard."

"Eagle Warriors?" Phoebe asked. "You didn't tell me about Eagle Warriors."

"They were warriors of the Eagle Society; a group of men who were superior fighters."

"Like the Aztecs?" asked Phoebe.

"Exactly. It must be a very, old tradition. Teotihuacan had their Feather Warrior almost two thousand years ago. Five hundred years ago at Chichen Itza, the Temple of the Warriors was dedicated to the Eagle and the Jaguar societies."

"Which one were you in?" asked Dan.

"There was only the Eagle Warriors during the classic period."

"So you were good on the battlefield, huh?"

"You had to kill four of the enemy; Lightning Sky killed six and he was only twenty years old when I left."

"Wow. How many did he kill in his lifetime?"

"We don't know. History holds no record of him, only the kings, heirs to the thrones, and sometimes great lords."

"And captives," added Phoebe. "Don't forget the captives."

"Captives?" asked Dan. "They were important enough to be recorded on the stone monuments?"

"If their position in society was high enough they could be. Their society was based on ritualistic war. The act of showing off high-level captives, and torturing and sacrificing them at important ceremonial events, was kind of like bragging."

"You loved it didn't you?" Phoebe injected, staring coldly at him.

"Loved what?"

"Being Lightning Sky, being a warrior."

Johnson looked thoughtfully at her as he contemplated his answer. "Yes Pheb, I loved it. I loved every minute of it. I'd go back there in a second and stay back there if I could."

"And that's what is eating at you, isn't it? You want to be back there and you can't."

"Yes, I'll admit it. I'm preoccupied with the thought. My heart is back there."

"Is that what this is all about," Phoebe asked in astonishment, "the girl?"

"Yes, the girl; of course she is part of it. I'm enchanted with her. She's an exotic beauty beyond any man's fantasy. But it is more than that. Back there I was a man among men, a warrior who was revered, and I held a high station. Quite frankly Phoebe, I deserved her."

Phoebe stared dumbly at him. "Alan, you can't be serious. It's just a dream, a figment of your imagination."

"Logic would indicate that, but I just can't buy it. It was real and she was real. Since I've come back this time, I think of her all of the time. I yearn to be with her. I want to go back there to be a part of their society where I can be with her."

"Alan, you can't."

"I know it, and it's tearing me apart inside."

"And your drinking, you know that won't take you back there."

"It puts me in a state where for a while I don't have to be here."

"And you think it helps?" she replied scornfully.

"Actually Phoebe, nothing helps."

§

The American Association of Archaeologists annual conference was in its second day. Dr. Alan Johnson had just finished presenting his paper. As the Head of the Department of Archaeology for the University of Wisconsin, he was considered an expert in New World Archaeology who specialized in the Maya Civilization.

His was the last presentation of the day. The room emptied quickly with a few laggards. Tomorrow would wind up the conference. His presentation, *Three Kings and the Dynastic Succession at Yaxchilan—an Edification*, had been met with a mixed reaction. Verbal responses of opposition to his presentation were made from the floor. Normally considered poor manners, these were openly antagonistic.

Johnson stood at the podium watching a group of attendees coming toward him. The young man who had made the out-of-place comments during his speech was the leader of the group.

"You've got to be off your rocker," were the first words from the young man. "Where did you come up with this crap?"

Johnson looked calmly at Brad Stevenson, a post-grad teaching assistant from the University of Arizona, who had worked on the Yaxchilan site learning excavation techniques with a team from his university a couple of years before. Brash and outspoken, he was gaining the reputation as a 'pain in the ass' by tenured professors.

"Actually," Johnson replied taking up the challenge. He wasn't going to take any shit from this little prick. "I pulled it out of my ass and if you can't handle yourself in a civilized manner, I'll gladly shove it up yours."

"I wouldn't doubt it came straight out of your ass," responded Stevenson.

Johnson glared back as he clenched his jaw. He set his teeth and the muscles of his neck tightened. His first response was defensive, quickly replaced by an aggressive feeling of the need to attack. *Doesn't this arrogant puppy know to stand aside and give me the proper respect? He needs to be taught a lesson.*

"Then what's your problem?" Johnson said as he fought to control his temper. "You claim to know where it came from and you've obviously assessed what you believe it to be. Case closed. Now it's time to go home to Arizona where some of the slower students actually believe you know what you're raving about."

"I've been to Yaxchilan; I've excavated there," the young man replied. "I know what happened there, and I think you're full of shit," Brad said, his voice rising.

Johnson took a step forward, his eyes narrowed, nostrils flaring. *I'll have to teach this arrogant monkey penis some manners.* Catching himself, he stopped for a second. *What's happening? I want a piece of this guy.* He looked around. He was in a large hotel meeting room, not the jungle. This was civilized society.

Slowly, he carefully answered, "You've implied that already, Brad. Have you anything new to say? I'm sure your little entourage is biting their nails waiting with baited breath for your acute perception of the world of the past."

"I know what happened at Yaxchilan. I know its history, and your crap isn't it. I wrote a thesis on the Classical Lowland

Maya."

Johnson recoiled again. *That arrogant bastard, who does he think he is?* He looked around for a weapon, something he could use to smash this young fool along the side of the head with. *Bring him to his knees. Let him kneel to me then he'd know who he's dealing with.* He stood there, angry, tense and ready. He looked around the podium. There was nothing. He looked around the room. Awareness of where he was returned again. Dazed for a moment he strove to collect his thoughts. He needed a response, a civilized response. He was a professor he reminded himself.

"Brad, you know what you have been told about what happened by people in the field that are better at this than you will ever be. You have taken their work, read it, paraphrased it, reorganized it, and spit it back just like all young graduate students, providing the same 'refreshingly new perceptions' that have been recurrently promoted by a thousand students before you. If you remember, I was on the board that reviewed it. Your focus was on Palenque and the importance of genealogy in the dynastic progression. You only researched about half the literature and your conclusions were rather shallow.

"Actually, I would have thought you would have allowed my presentation to provide a basis for an empirical rebuttal, perhaps with occasional heated rhetoric. Pile of shit or not, it should spur your student's mind out of its shell of complacent mediocrity if for no other reason than to play with the probability I may actually be correct. You disappoint me."

"Alan my friend," called Gerhardt Weber, as he lumbered up to the stage heavy-footed and puffing. "You continue to amaze me. Like my young friend Stevenson here, I don't believe a word of what you have said, but what fun we will have discussing it."

"Gerhardt, it's good to see you," greeted Johnson.

"As hard as I was on you last time," continued Gerhardt, "I think you won me over. Perhaps you will again."

"He's full of crap," repeated Stevenson again.

"And so are you most of the time Brad," Gerhardt replied. "Dr. Johnson threw down the gauntlet of another perspective. It is now our turn to analyze it and accept or reject it in the course of civil interaction and scientific analysis."

Stevenson looked around at the students following him. The response wasn't what they expected; his hero status diminished. "I don't buy it for a second," Stevenson said with bravado for the students.

"Your choice," Johnson spat, glaring at him ready to pounce.

"Come along Alan, the group is waiting for you for dinner. Jim Harper from Penn State says he is buying. You know that doesn't happen very often."

"Christmas five years ago," replied Johnson. "Remember, he proposed a new theory to the group at dinner that Curl Snout, the Teotihuacan general who defeated Tikal and killed Tiger Paw in 378 A.D., was gay."

"Oh, he had me going on that one. He got me so mad I wouldn't speak to him for a year."

"Thanks, Gerhardt," Johnson said as they left the conference hall. "I don't like that man and strangely I was ready to take him on."

"Ya ya, he is a little prick," Gerhardt said, "but he is right about one thing."

"What's that?"

"This time you *are* full of crap."

§

Johnson watched as his friends filled their plates with snacks. The hospitality room at the hotel had only a few people. The conference had just ended and most participants had returned to their rooms to freshen up, call their home or office, or just watch a little TV and catch up on world events. For years the four of them had always gotten together at conferences and discussed whatever came across their minds.

Once they put the pleasantries of catching up on each other's lives behind, they usually ended up taking a controversial presentation from the conference, and under the guise of debate tore it apart. It was a ritual they all enjoyed; gloves off, no holds barred, a 'you're full of shit' attitude and a general lack of the refined analytical protocol called for in their field. For a short time they could put their academic caution behind them. It was something they all looked forward to. Johnson knew his presentation would be the topic of discussion this afternoon. Like kids playing King of the Hill he would have to stand at the top and fend off every onslaught no matter how tough the opponent.

"You sure as hell did it this time," Jim Harper said, as he sat down on the couch and placed his plate of snacks from the hospitality table on his lap. Bill Jefferies and Gerhardt Weber followed and took chairs as they sat around a small coffee table.

"Jim, would you mind explaining yourself?" Johnson said. He looked over with a startled look on his face.

"Your presentation, *Three Kings and the Dynastic Succession at Yaxchilan—an Edification,* was rather off the wall wouldn't you say?" Responded Harper.

"Off the wall, no, I'd say it was insightful."

"A drug-induced hallucination is insightful?" asked Harper.

"I'm not so sure it was an hallucination. The more I consider it and review my field notes, I'd say it was more than an hallucination."

"Field notes," Jefferies asked, "you took field notes?"

"Yes, extensive notes as soon as I got back, I recorded everything I experienced, saw and felt. I wrote down the whole thing."

"If not an hallucination, what would you call it?" Gerhardt asked.

"I call it going back in time, but to ease your reservations or doubts, I'll concede it was a vision, an accurate vision of the past."

"Vision of the past!" Gerhardt exclaimed. "You stood up at the podium and called the king, Bird Jaguar IV, a pompous old windbag. That's a hell of a vision."

"Would calling him a shrewd politician be more to your liking?"

"It rolls off the tongue better and sounds more professional, I'll give it that," Gerhardt replied.

"He was one who never let you forget where he came from. Whenever addressing a crowd it always came out. 'I'm a descendent of the sacred leaders of my royal family. I'm a descendent of the gods', and he'd name one or two. In small company he was a contemplative man who listened to his advisors. He was careful and calculated with his decisions."

"Isn't that what a king is supposed to do? I wouldn't call it being an old windbag."

"You'd have to be there Gerhardt. He was a man who never missed an opportunity to promote himself. It probably comes from being held back ten years after his brother died before he became king."

"Speaking of him becoming king," Harper said, "you claim Bird Jaguar IV staged a coup and seized power. There is absolutely nothing in the records to support this. It's a blatant claim, Alan. You have more professional integrity than that. I just can't buy it without empirical evidence to support your conclusions."

"Jim, Lord Great Skull Zero had the power. Within his family, he controlled the largest number of warriors. Bird Jaguar needed that power. The Xook family, which claimed the rightful line descending from the First Father didn't just decide one day that now he was ready and give him the position. They tried to promote one of theirs as the king to secure the bloodline, quite unsuccessfully," countered Johnson, "by placing Yoaat B'alam II on the throne. Bird Jaguar seized the power with a coup and afterwards erased any mention of Yoaat B'alam II of the Zook family from the records."

"Alan, there is nothing to support that," Gerhardt claimed. "You are pulling this stuff straight out of your ass, vision or not ,this is pure bullshit. There is no scientific evidence for it."

"Gerhardt, think about it. He comes to power just after he marries Lady Great Skull, as a second wife, who has just bore him a male child. The royal line is now tied to the Great Skull family, not the Xook family. Then we find that Lord Great Skull is one of his chief advisors and eventually becomes a regent for the king's son when he comes to power a few years later. That's payback. Even without my testimony, deductively it is feasible. You can't deny that."

"Professionally you can't make these claims, Alan," Gerhardt said. "You can't substantiate them without some type of proof."

"Gerhardt, I've been there, I've talked to the people that witnessed these accounts."

"Alan, you've had a dream. It's time to wake up now and come back to the real world."

"I've been in the real world, Gerhardt."

"Hold it guys," Jefferies said. "We are all friends here. Alan has an interesting proposal. We need to listen to him."

"What you are telling us is preposterous," Gerhardt said as he ignored Harper. "It's pure conjecture and speculation, and poor speculation if I do say so. I've known you for a long time Alan, and you have always held my respect, but quite frankly I think you are making this all up. It might make a good fiction story, but as far as science goes, it is trash."

"Trash, you think I'm spewing trash, Gerhardt? I've been there. I've met the king and the great lords. I took the body of Lightning Sky. Smoking Squirrel and I are cousins to Shield Jaguar, brother to the king, and his closest friends. He refers to us as brothers. These bogus claims, as you call them, were told to me by Shield Jaguar III himself."

"This is the Shield Jaguar III who you claim was not Bird Jaguar's son but his half brother?" replied Gerhardt. "He is also a son born of the great Shield Jaguar II, sired when he was in his late eighties with a very young wife?"

"You got it."

"And what happened to Chel-Te', king Bird Jaguar's son?"

"I don't know. He was only a child when I was there."

"But Alan," said Gerhardt, "the record specifically indicates that Chel-Te' succeeded his father and changed his name to Shield Jaguar III. There is a lintel in Temple 33 which specifically says that Lady Great Skull Zero was the mother of Shield Jaguar a/k/a Chel-Te', which confirms Shield Jaguar as his royal name."

"I know what the record indicates, but I also know Shield Jaguar was another man, and he was not Chel-Te'."

"And he succeeded King Bird Jaguar IV; you know this?" Gerhardt asked.

"Yes, I assume that."

"Assume, you assume it?"

"The time I was there was before Shield Jaguar came to power."

"So you don't really know, not for sure, even in your dream?"

"Gerhardt, it's the only logical conclusion."

"But you don't know for sure."

"No," Johnson said, defeated.

"Look Alan," Gerhardt said, "for six generations the king's name in Yaxchilan changed from Bird Jaguar to Shield Jaguar and back with each successive generation. The name Shield Jaguar would be the next name for Chel-Te''s generation. Perhaps it indicates he is from that lineage in honor of his grandfather."

"No Gerhardt, they were different persons."

"I think you are delusional, Alan," said Gerhardt. "I don't think there was an hallucination or a vision. I think you are suffering from disillusionment."

"Gerhardt, that's crazy, if I may use the term. I know what I saw. I know what I experienced. It was real. I thought that you three, my closest colleagues, would understand and support me. I found a new way of seeing the past, interpreting a prehistoric culture. You of all people should know what a scientific breakthrough this is. The ability to experience and observe an ancient culture, the same as a contemporary one, is revolutionary."

"It's shit," Gerhardt spat. "It's pure shit. It's worse than the sensationalists claiming to be scientists who sell films on National Geographic television. They at least twist the truth, not make it up."

Johnson got red in the face and shouted, "You think I'm making all this up? You think I came here and put my professional integrity on the line by making this up? It's real and revolutionary in scientific methodology."

"Alan, you're out of your mind. It's pure rubbish," Gerhardt retorted.

"And the rest of you, do you concur with Gerhardt?" he asked as he looked from man to man.

One by one they all nodded their heads. "I'm afraid so," Jim Harper said. "Your conclusions are just too far-fetched, and the process you claim to use has no scientific justification. This presentation severely bruised your credibility, and anything like this again will probably destroy your professional career."

"Well thank you very much!" Johnson shouted as he got up and hurriedly left the room.

§

It was a humid night, hot for early May. Johnson sat on a bench beside a path on a little hill overlooking Lake Mendota, staring out over the water. Beside him on the bench was a paper bag with a bottle of gin in it. Periodically he took a long draft. His stomach was tight and he felt numb. He was tired, exhausted really, but not with the type of tiredness that would lead to sleep.

Earlier that day he had a meeting with Dr. Shuster from the Chemistry Department, and Dr. Lomas from Biology. For over a month they had been working on analyzing the drug in order to duplicate it. The biologist found that two of the plants used to make the drug were extinct and he couldn't find alternatives. The chemist worked on a potential blend of chemical compositions that were comprised in the drug, but spectra analysis indicated that they couldn't even get close. This morning they told him that their efforts were going to be discontinued.

"I thought I'd find you here. I was worried," Phoebe said as she came up the walk. "May I sit down?"

"Public bench. You're going to sit whether I like it or not," he said flatly.

"I was told you come out here in the middle of the night, but why? It's two in the morning. What are you doing out here?" she asked ignoring the slight.

He didn't respond, just continued staring out across the water.

"The drinking is getting worse, isn't it Alan?"

"Don't ride me on my drinking, Pheb. I've got a handle on it," he said as he picked up the bag and took a drink, then handed it to her.

She took a sip then opened the top of the bag looking at the level in the bottle. "From here it doesn't look too good," she replied.

"It's okay. Don't worry. I have some things to work out. When I get them fixed, things will go back to normal."

"Alan, I care about you. I don't like what I'm seeing. I don't like what you are doing to yourself."

"I'm not hurting anyone Pheb. It's my life. Right now it's a little complicated. A drink or two helps."

"Helps? Alan, how can sitting out here at two in the morning drinking from a bottle in a paper bag help?"

"I've changed Pheb, something inside of me has changed. At the conference I almost attacked a participant because he criticized me. I wanted to bring him to his knees in front of me, bleeding and begging for mercy. I actually had to fight myself to keep from doing it. I've felt that way a couple of times recently but not as strongly as this time."

"Alan, this scares me."

"I know. It scares me too. But at the same time it excites me."

"Excites you?"

"It's a powerful feeling Pheb: strength, confidence, arrogance."

They sat there without saying a word, both staring at the lake. She finally reopened the conversation.

"I've been told you often come out here late at night Alan, why?"

"The bars are closed. It's a good place for a nightcap before I head back to bed."

"I heard some of your students talking. They say you spend long hours out here by yourself, even when it's cold."

"I like it here Pheb. It's peaceful."

"Come on Alan, let me in. I know you, and I don't buy it. Your mind is too logical. Drunk or sober, you don't do something like this without a reason."

"You wouldn't understand."

"Try me."

"She comes out here."

"She? Who?"

"Little Rabbit."

"You can't be serious."

"Sometimes late at night I see her."

"Out here?"

"Yes."

"Alan, that's not possible."

"I know, but it happens. She calls to me."

"Alan, you're scaring me."

"Pheb," he said looking into her eyes, beseeching her to understand, "she calls to me. Not with words but she calls."

"And you see her?"

"Yes, sometimes, like in a mist, a vague outline, but it's her. I know it's her."

"What does she want?" Phoebe asked.

"She calls 'Come back'. That's all, 'Come back'."

"And what are you going to do? What can you do?"

"I've signed on to lead another graduate student team to Yaxchilan this summer."

"Is that wise?"

"Probably not, but what choice do I have?"

Chapter 14

Phoebe held Johnson's hand tightly as they sat together in the long thin boat, a motor launch, one of a small fleet which handled river traffic on the Usumacinta River between Mexico and Guatemala. On the Mexican side, the road to Guatemala ended at the river in Frontera Corozol, and on the Guatemalan side, the road to Mexico ended at Bethel. The towns were fifteen miles apart, so any traffic wanting to cross from one side to the other, took a boat between the towns.

"The students look so excited today, don't they?" said Phoebe.

"They're always excited when we get this close. It's the great adventure of their lifetime, a chance to be a real live archaeologist and go on an excavation. You were the same way Pheb."

"At times it seems so long ago, and other times like yesterday," replied Phoebe.

"Happy to be coming back?"

"I have work to do here. The new hieroglyphic steps are calling, 'decipher me, decipher me'."

"I've been told you're going to be on your own soon," said Johnson.

"Gerhardt Weber offered me a place on their dig down near

Tikal this fall."

"It will be good experience and having a mentor like Gerhardt would do well for your career."

"I really want to stay here at U.W. but it is a good opportunity," said Phoebe.

"Take it Pheb. Opportunities like that don't come along often. Gerhardt will be good to you."

"Are you going to be okay on this expedition?" Phoebe asked.

"I've got you as my strong supporter. How could I go wrong?"

"Can you handle another trip into the past, Alan? Look what it did to you the last time."

"Of course, but I've got the hang of it now. I'm the great warrior Lightning Sky, brother to Shield Jaguar," replied Johnson.

"I'm not talking about that," said Phoebe. "I'm talking about the girl."

"Handling it when I'm there in the past isn't the problem, Pheb. Handling it when I come back is."

"You've been dry for a month now. It could cause you to fall back."

"Thirty-three days today, Pheb, not a drink in thirty three days. I think I have a hold on it."

"Dr. Johnson," called one of the girls in the front of the boat, "there is the Guatemalan border patrol on the hill overlooking the river. We must be getting close," she said pointing to a sandbag defense position with three soldiers in it. The students waved and they waved back.

"Another ten minutes, Jan, and we'll be there," he called back.

"You've got to set them up and get the dig going before you go Alan. You owe it to them," said Phoebe.

"It will be done professionally. You can take over for the short time I'll be gone," replied Johnson.

"You never know how long, and you're exhausted for a couple of days when you get back."

"Don't worry Pheb. It will all work out," he said, "as long as I can get the shaman to help."

"Is he really essential?" Phoebe asked.

"I'm afraid so. I tried the drug back at the university, nothing, not even a good high. It's either the cave is a portal, or the ceremony is actually the catalyst, or both. I need a shaman to perform the ritual."

She studied him. "You said the old man won't help anymore."

"It may be a real problem."

§

There was a dull heavy pain in his stomach just below the navel, and his feet felt leaden as he stumbled along the path by the river. Dr. Johnson was walking in a daze, just putting one foot in front of the other, going in the right direction but not caring. It made no difference. Disbelief was slowly being pushed aside by reality. It couldn't happen this way. He had waited months, dreamed of returning, anticipated every second until the time arrived. He lived for it and now it was gone.

The old shaman declined to help him. The old man was adamant that he would not go through the ritual again. Johnson walked back to the excavation site, numb with disbelief. He had reasoned, begged and pleaded, but the old man was unrelenting. The gods were not to be bothered again, the old man exclaimed. They had provided the gift of visiting the past before, but they would not do so again.

"What am I going to do Phoebe?" he asked when he got back to camp. "He won't help."

"Perhaps he's right, Alan," she replied as she leaned back in her chair, pushing away from the table and computer she had been working on. "You have seen what it was like during the classic age, at least to a point where you believe it. I know you are caught up in this, but you said this was a scientific experiment, and from where I am sitting, it looks like you have completed it."

"But I can't Pheb," Johnson replied. He sat down across from her. "You know I can't."

"What choice do you have?"

"Maybe I can do it myself."

"You said that you thought the ritual may be what's important," Phoebe said. "Who's going to do it for you?"

"I'll do it myself. I watched the old man perform it. I'm sure I remember the sequence and what was said. I'm certain I can do it."

"Alan, this no longer goes under the heading of a scientific experiment. You're doing something altogether different now."

"Don't you see, I have to do this," he replied pleading for understanding. "We've talked about it before. I thought you were in my camp on this one."

"To help you learn about the past, yes, but this has become an obsession with you. I don't think this has anything to do with science."

"Phoebe, the context is irrelevant now," he said as he looked at her with pleading eyes. "I must return to the past. Don't you understand? I don't have any choice in this. She has called to me. I must go back."

§

He had a hard time finding the cave. It all seemed so easy when the old man led him. He found four caves before he found the right one. The hills were full of them. The whole area was comprised of limestone. Put a little underground water movement with a limestone base and let it work for a couple of million years and you have a cave. He lit a firebrand and entered the cave.

Johnson repeatedly looked at the torch to see how it was faring, wondering if it would stay lit. He was surprised to find he was afraid of the dark. The last time when he was lost, the darkness had scared him to the core, and seemed to still be affecting him.

Trembling, he moved cautiously. He was coming closer to the portal. He smiled to himself. A feeling of well-being suddenly flowed through him. He was going to see her again. Little Rabbit was waiting for him. He had seen her apparition. It called to him to come back to her.

He built the little fire just as the shaman had done. When he was finished, he laid a piece of paper next to him and laid out two lines of the powder. He would sniff it in the same manner as taking cocaine. He started to duplicate the ritual the old Shaman had performed as he lit the cigar and blew smoke in the four directions of the compass. Then he opened the little bottle of tequila and took a sip and spit it out in the same manner. Holding his hands in front of him, palms up, he chanted the words the old man used. When he was finished, he lifted the paper and strongly snorted the powder, a line in each nostril.

It was dark when he awakened with just a little wavering light. He was laying on stone. It was cold and hard. Sitting up he looked around. The little fire was there, just embers now. He was still in the cave. The powder had put him to sleep with no other effect. He stared into the embers and looked around the cave. It felt so small and miserable, just a hole in the ground, dark, cold and damp. It had led him nowhere. He laid down on the cold rock floor, his head in his arms and cried. He cried for a long time.

§

For two days Johnson wandered around the ancient site, lost. The students speculated on what was wrong. He had been so bubbly when they were en route. He couldn't wait to get there. Now he talked to no one and left Phoebe and Dan to oversee the excavation's progress. Phoebe was worried about him.

Upon his return from the cave he shared his despondency with Phoebe and Dan. They had sympathized with Johnson about his predicament, but could offer little solace.

§

"Dr. Johnson," said Dan, coming up to his field desk in the palace with another man. It was two days since Johnson had tried to perform the ritual in the cave.

"I'd like you to meet Jose Rodrigas, the new shaman of the village."

"The what?" Johnson asked as he looked up at the boy. He was only a teenager with pimples on his face.

"He's a shaman, the one who has been in training since he was a small boy. There is always a shaman in training. You taught us that in one of my first courses at the university. The traditions must be maintained. Something can always happen to one man, so the people's spiritual knowledge must be learned and kept by an assistant who will one day take over. I found the assistant and he agreed to participate in the rituals with you and see if he can open the portal you talked about."

"Is this true? You will help me?" asked Johnson.

"Si, Senior, I will help."

"And the old shaman, won't he get mad at you?"

"Si, Senior, he will be mad but he is old and tired. I am the village shaman most of the time now. He will be mad for a little while, then we will drink a little tequila and talk about the crazy Americano and what the gods are going to do with him.

"If he resists helping you and I help, then the gods know we will follow any way they want to go. It will be their decision, not ours. They are the gods. If they don't want you to go back in time, they can tell you themselves."

"Professor," Dan said, "perhaps you can get a couple of bottles of tequila for the shamen. They would like to have a drink and talk about the crazy Americano and the will of the gods."

§

Johnson and the young shaman used the old man's pickup truck to make the trip to the cave. The young man was excited to be performing the ancient ceremony. It was the first time he was to administer a ritual of this type. He and the old man had discussed it long into the evening the night before as they enjoyed their gift of tequila. His head hurt this morning.

"Senior Johnson," the young man asked, "what is it like to talk to the gods? Do they look like the pictures?"

"Well Jose, it is sort of like telepathy."

"Si, telepathy," Jose responded. After a pause—"Dr. Johnson, what is telepathy?"

"It's like talking with your mind. You don't say the words, you just feel or think them."

"So you don't know what the gods sound like?"

"No, and you can't really see them either," Johnson said.

"They are just there and you ask them to transport you to the past."

"And they do it?"

"That's about it, Jose. They do it."

"The old shaman says that you don't have much powder left and when it is gone you will not be able to go back to the past."

"That's right, only a few more trips and that is it."

"Do you like it there?" the young man asked.

"Yes," Alan paused,"yes I do. I feel very alive there. The people have become my friends, probably closer friends than I have here. I'm looking forward to seeing them again."

"I hope you do."

The road ended and they continued on foot. It seemed to take forever. Johnson was anxious. How was this trip going to go? It seemed he had waited forever for this moment. The further they got into the cave, the tenser Johnson became. *Will I have problems with the gods? They could say no. The last time they told me that since the old society was gone, there was no reason to travel to the past. They have to send me back, but to what date will it be? They were sending me to different dates in the past, sometimes years apart.*

The young shaman built the fire slowly as he thought about the ritual. He wanted to get it right. As he prepared the offerings of smoke and tequila and laid them in front of him, his hand shook. He put the powder in the tube careful not to spill any and laid it in front of him. Then he sat in meditation for a long time. Johnson sat opposite him, the fire in between.

"We're ready," he finally said as he started the ritual. Johnson noted that his voice was now strong and firm in invoking the gods to accept him, a traveler into their world.

Offerings made, petitions complete, the young shaman placed the tube of powder into Johnson's nose and blew. There was a violent jolt which felt like his head was exploding. It was the last thing he felt.

§

A cheer went up from the crowd.

"Point," shouted Shield Jaguar to the ball player. "Come on K'an-Tok', lets have another."

Johnson looked around. He was on a raised platform overlooking the small ball court in the plaza. Everyone was standing and shouting, even the king. There were four players on the court and a ball being bounced through the air between them. At each end of the court there was a line of men. Johnson looked over at the king. The king was on his feet like all the rest. Beside him was a young man almost as tall as him dressed ceremonially and as intent on the game as the older man. Shield Jaguar, Smoking Squirrel and he were further down along the platform. Good seats.

Johnson looked around. He had returned to the past during a ball game and he was sitting with the royal spectators. The court was small, only large enough for a small audience, maybe thirty people on each side. The people were packed in tight, except for the king, the young man beside him, and the queen. Spectators lined the hillside above the plaza, and the sides of the near pyramids were covered with people—not the best seats, but they could see the play.

Lightning Sky and Smoking Squirrel were on either side of Shield Jaguar. The other two were intently watching the ball as it rapidly passed from player to player. The court consisted of a flat rectangular playing area in the shape of an 'I'. The center court was about fifteen by thirty feet and had sloping side walls running its length and a back wall running a few feet above as a retainer. The players were to keep the ball in the air using only their hips and thighs. It could bounce off the sloping walls but was not to touch the ground.

There were two teams in the court below. Each team fielded two players on the court and had four goalies on the sides of the 'I' -shaped field. The players were wearing heavily padded clothes and sturdy sandals. On the right knee was a flat pad and another on the left arm. Tied around their waists were stone yokes. They helped protect the players from the hard rubber balls but also assisted in being able to control the direction and velocity of the ball.

The ball game was one of the universal underlying elements of the Maya culture for almost two thousand years. The basis of their entire theology was based on the ball game as it was played by the Hero Twins and the gods in Xibalba. Every city and town, however small, had at least one court and often there were a number of them. The teams were comprised from each noble family. There were two types of games, those for sport, and those for pageants telling the story of creation.

"Monkey turds," he heard Shield Jaguar call out, as another cheer went up from the crowd. Another point scored, obviously from the opposing team. The people continued to scream as the play continued. Johnson looked over at the king again. Something was different, but he didn't know what. He and the younger man were screaming for the same team, both intent that their favorite team player would score a point.

Then it hit him, the young man. He was a young teenager, but nevertheless a teen. He was with the king and had the same deformed elongated head indicating royalty. Chel-Te', it must be Chel-Te'. This was the king's son, but the last time he was here Chel-Te' was just a boy. This young man must be at least five years older.

He looked wildly around. This was a royal function. Where was Little Rabbit? Maybe she was here. He looked beyond the king studying every person. The only woman there appeared to be the queen sitting next to him, reserved, quietly viewing the game, distinctly apart from the crowd. No, Little Rabbit wasn't there. He looked along the veranda on the other side of Shield Jaguar and Smoking Squirrel, and then he saw two women behind them. They were obviously in their twenties and were shouting as wildly as the men. Dressed as priestesses, they were the only women on the platform.

His mind was looking for a woman-child. Little Rabbit had the vitality of youth, the body of budding womanhood and the gregarious personality of openness. When she smiled and laughed everyone around her did too. Joy followed her everywhere. For the last year he clung to the memory of her coming to him with the innocent love of a child and the passion of a woman. These two spectators were obviously women in every sense of the word.

Suddenly one of the woman stopped cheering and turned and stared at him intently, her face a mask of confusion. Then she smiled, a wide smile, and her eyes sparkled. As she looked at him her face turned soft and he could see the recognition and longing in her eyes. A tear rolled down her cheek as she turned back and quietly watched the game.

A wild cheer came up from the crowd. Johnson looked, the players had stopped playing. Everyone seemed to be talking at once. He looked around him. Smoking Squirrel looked sullen.

"Here," he said, as he took off his jade rock necklace and held it out to Shield Jaguar, "it's my favorite one."

"You'll live," Shield Jaguar responded. "If I remember right you won this from me last year. It was my favorite too."

"Perhaps you will win it again next year," Johnson said.

"My luck he'll be wearing the smaller one next time. I don't like wearing that one as much."

"It's always the same," said Little Rabbit who overheard their conversation. "Every so often when they come to the ball game they make wagers of priceless jewelry to impress the crowd. A brave cheer is heard from the winner and loud groans from the loser. But really they are only trading jewelry for the next year. One year one wins, the next year the other wins and everybody thinks they are big gamblers, men willing to put it all on the line. You guys are just a couple of fakers."

"She's your sister," Smoking Squirrel said to Shield Jaguar. "Can't you make her shut up?"

"You want to try?" was the reply. "She talks to the gods and you never know what she might ask them to do for her."

She looked at Smoking Squirrel with an exaggerated frown. "Give me a hard time and I'll turn you into a frog, young noble. What color would you like to be?"

Johnson watched as the man he knew as a fierce warrior paled.

"I like being a smoking squirrel," he replied contritely.

"I can handle that too. What color squirrel would you like to be?" Her eyes twinkled and the corners of her mouth curled up slightly in a smile.

"Perhaps if you said something nice to her," Johnson said, "she might change her mind."

"Little Rabbit looked up and him and smiled broadly. "There's an idea. Say something nice to me."

"But you're a woman," Smoking Squirrel growled. "You are supposed to serve men. We are the warriors, the masters. You are to follow our commands."

"I'll serve you, brave warrior. You decide the color and I'll pick the animal," she taunted. "Maybe a mouse would do better—a red mouse—and I'll put you in the hole in the ground that holds the king's great white snake."

Smoking Squirrel paled further, and appeared noticeably shaken. "You're pretty and a pleasant person to be around," he replied weakly.

She beamed. "You really think I'm pretty?" she asked with a radiant smile.

"Of course."

"And pleasant to be around?"

"Except when you want to turn me into a mouse."

She laughed. "Perhaps I'll leave you as you are then."

Horns trumpeted. Everyone stood in reverence as the king and his assembly left the ball court. The king was weak and had to be supported by two attendants. He walked slowly and appeared to be in pain. His son, Chel-Te', followed closely looking straight ahead acknowledging no one.

"What happened to the king?" Johnson asked Smoking Squirrel.

"His spirit is sick. The shaman says his spirit animal was wounded in a fight with a monster's spirit that got loose from Xibalba and is hurt very bad." *If his spirit animal dies, the king will die too.*

It was good to be back, Johnson thought. Listening to the

banter of friends again was comforting. He had waited a long time for this. Johnson felt at home; this was where he belonged. The group started walking toward the palace together. As they left the ball court Little Rabbit took her place behind the others with Lightning Sky.

"I've waited a very long time for you," she said. "I was afraid you wouldn't come again."

"How did you know it was me?"

"I felt you near to me at the ball game. It was a good feeling."

"The gods play tricks with me," he replied. "I don't know where in time they will send me."

"That's their way. You must make sacrifices to them and tell them what you want. Sometimes they listen."

"I want to be here, with you, forever."

"It can't be." She looked at him with a tearful frown. "My mother said it would only be for a short time. She was a very powerful seer. She was almost never wrong."

"I want to be with you tonight," he said.

She stopped walking, looked up at him, and laughed. "Then you better not drink so much at the festivities tonight."

Chapter 15

Johnson had come back during a Period Ending celebration. Every twenty years, a designated period of time ended and another time started. Dates were determined by their calendar, and events related to the festivities were recorded on stone tablets placed in the ceremonial center, a written history cast in stone.

The feast after the ball game was grandiose. The setting was in the same place overlooking the ceremonial center as it was during the first time Johnson was there, when they came back with the prisoner.

At the feast, the ball players were honored guests of the king. K'an-Tok', a high ranking noble, and Mi Kimi, a younger noble, were two of the best ball players in Yaxchilan, and renowned for their skills. Everyone in the countryside recognized and honored them. Tonight they had the privilege of sitting at the king's table across from Shield Jaguar, Smoking Squirrel and Lightning Sky. The king was in a jovial mood, carrying on an endless conversation about his building projects and what he was going to do next. Chel-Te' sat between the king and Shield Jaguar. He was sullen and mute.

"Lightning Sky, we must see more of you on construction

projects," the king said. "You have a way with the artisans. They do better when you are around."

"I do what I can," Johnson replied.

"You spend too much time being a warrior with my brother here," the king replied.

"He's an Eagle Warrior now. He's killed eight of the enemy. It's his right to be a warrior," Shield Jaguar said. He's my strong right arm, and Smoking Squirrel is my strong left arm.

"Yes, yes," replied the king, "I suppose, but he could still help the builders."

"Let Chel-Te' help," Shield Jaguar said. "He won't be much help on raids."

"One day I'll be as good a warrior as you," the youth snapped.

"I see you are more like my brother," Shield Jaguar replied. "He likes to build."

"You'll see," said the prince. "You'll see. I'll be a great warrior."

"Hey, Great Skull," Shield Jaguar called over to the next table. "We've got a great warrior here for you. He thinks he will be good enough for your Elite Guard."

"I'm sure he will," the great lord called back, a look of disdain on his face.

"You've been hanging around my brother too long," Shield Jaguar called back. "You're becoming too careful with your words."

"Enough," snapped the king. "You're disturbing my evening."

Little Rabbit came over and kissed the king on the cheek. "How are you feeling brother?" she asked. "Is the bark drink helping?"

"Sometimes," he replied. "I'm afraid my animal spirit is ready to travel to the other world."

"Do not be in a hurry. He still has some time left," she replied.

"I can feel him getting weaker," the king replied.

"You need to eat more," she admonished him. She stooped

down so her head was at his level and pointed a finger in his face. "King or no king, I command it," she laughed.

He smiled. "I no longer feel hunger, only a pain where the food should go, but for you dear sister I will try."

Johnson looked at the king. He was pale and noticeably thinner than he had been the last trip to the past. The man had decided he was going to die. Johnson knew that in primitive societies it often happened that way. The will to live and life seemed to be bound to each other; lose the will and the body dies. *How much longer does he have?*

The king clapped and the slaves started serving the meal. Everyone was talking about the games, and there were many salutes to K'an-Tok and Mi Kimi, the ball players who were the honored guests at the banquet tonight.

Johnson sat listening to the conversations. He was enjoying the meal. He hadn't realized how much he had missed it. Back at the university he was often alone, his family spread all over the country. They used to see each other on holidays, but even that was waning now.

But this was a gregarious community. Everybody knew everybody in a close social relationship, each had their place in the structure, each was part of the whole. As he watched, it occurred to him—family. This was a large family. There were hundreds of thousands of commoners living in little groups and family was obviously core to their social structure. You could see it in the housing complexes from the king's down to a simple farmer's. Families lived, worked and played together. The primary difference was the royal families were privileged. They controlled the wealth of the society, and lived at an elevated level. With privilege came the responsibility of governing, and a strict pecking order of each individual's place in society had been developed. From the king on down, all knew their position relative to the others.

Cities stood apart as separate political systems and became city states. Their leaders were considered royalty with a claim to be descended from the First Father, originator of man. They all carried the same core cultural values: the same language, a common writing system, awareness of the same creation myth, worship of the same gods, and a common calendar to record their history.

In time, rivalries developed between the cities and competition became a central theme, showing itself with ritualistic warfare. It evolved into a sort of pecking order between cities with greater kings, lesser kings and subservient kings, paying tribute and forging alliances against common enemies. Wars between the cities continuously changed their hierarchal order, all vying for the top positions.

During the latter half of the Classical Period there was a competition in building massive public structures led by the large cities that became super powers in the area. Each city seemed to try to outdo the others. They built extravagant ceremonial complexes and palaces. The late Eighth Century brought the height of building. More and larger ornate structures were built by city states throughout the Maya region of Mexico, Guatemala, Belize and Honduras.

§

It was a long celebration. Dinner was eaten slowly in courses, accompanied by loud conversations and laughter. It was a joyous occasion. As the day wore on, the king appeared more tired. He seemed to be having a hard time maintaining his composure and regal bearing. He was continually attended by Little Rabbit.

During the dinner, the sun had set. As darkness settled over the site, slaves placed torches every few feet around the courtyard. They illuminated the event and highlighted the combed pyramid, emphasizing it as a backdrop. In the plaza, away from the temples and pyramids, noble families of lesser status watched. The effect was like a well-lit stage, and they were watching a play.

After dinner the king raised his hand and the horns sounded.

"It's time for the ceremonies," said Smoking Squirrel.

"Ceremonies?" asked Johnson.

"The stars are in alignment, and it is time to celebrate. We must show the gods with dedications and sacrifices that we are thankful for another twenty-year period coming to an end. We have two captives to sacrifice today. The gods will be happy."

During the meal the horns had been trumpeting regularly. It was a call to the people to come to the ceremonial center. As they ate, the crowds continually grew larger. Thousands of torches had been set out. Hundreds of people were there to observe the ceremonies.

§

The king raised his hand again, and the horns trumpeted three times. The procession was about to begin. As the king rose from his place, Little Rabbit helped him. He held her arm as they took their place at the head of the procession. The queen and Chel-Te' followed the king. Shield Jaguar followed the king's family and the king's counselors came behind him. Lastly, high ranking nobles, the heads of the families, took their place in the line.

It was a solemn procession and the king and his entourage slowly walked to the center of the complex. The crowds of people pulled back, opening a way for the king. People bowed in reverence. Here was a demigod in their presence. Most had only seen him from a distance and had never been close to him. They were awed. A procession of musicians followed the royal party. Their horns blared, and drums were rhythmically beaten, summoning the gods into their presence. Dedications were to be made in their honor, and the gods must be there.

The king stopped at the bottom of the pyramid. It looked

steeper to him than before and he felt weak. He had to make it to the top. For his people, he had to make it.

"Help me little sister," he said to Little Rabbit. "I am a frail old man, and it's a long climb."

She looked back at Shield Jaguar and said, "Your brother is here too," as she motioned to him.

Together they assisted the king to the top of the pyramid. There awaited the high priests with two assistants and the two captives. Fear filled the captives' faces. They knew that life was about to come to an end, and their places in the afterlife in doubt. They had been tortured for weeks with their finger nails pulled out, followed by their fingers being systematically cut off.

They could no longer communicate by making the appropriate signs with their fingers as they talked. How were they going to convince the gods to let them through the underworld and through the 'place of trials' and into the 'place of comfort' with their loved ones? There was no honor in being caught on the battlefield.

The king took his place at the top of the pyramid, and with conviction, stood tall. He looked out over the sacred site at the hundreds of spectators below. They were his people, his children. Bathed in the soft light of a thousand torches, they worshiped him. His heart was filled with joy. He looked at the new buildings, many which he built. It was an old city, and his father had started the new building projects many years before, making it beautiful again. He had carried on his father's work. It would soon be up to his son to continue the work of two generations to glorify their city. It was the most beautiful city in all of the land, and his building had brought it up to the splendor that it now was.

The ceremony was to begin. The priest stood behind a stone altar and solemnly chanted prayers to the gods in the ancient tongue, thanking them for another period of prosperity, and beseeched them to continue to be kind to their people and shower them with bounty.

"The gods favor us," the king shouted weakly to the people "The gods favor us and will give us prosperity for the next twenty years."

The people cheered and cheered. It was good to have the gods favor them. They needed better harvests. There had been prosperity for many years, but there were many new children in the land. It was getting hard to feed them. There was no more farmland to be had, and crop yields were not as great as before. People were starting to go hungry. The gods must help and their king talked to the gods and they promised to help. It was cause to rejoice.

"The gods desire a sacrifice!" called out the king. "They need the sacrifice of blood to quench their thirst and their need grows. They want more than the blood of a king or queen solemnly collected and given to them. They want the blood of a man, all of his blood."

"Sacrifice! Sacrifice!" the crowd yelled. "Give the gods a sacrifice." They knew that there would be a sacrifice. It had been the talk throughout the land that they had 'gifts of men' to give the gods tonight. A double sacrifice would please the gods, and they would send them abundance. The gods were thirsty, and they paid well for their blood.

The two assistants grabbed one of the captives, dragged him to his feet and pulled him to the edge of the pyramid. They held him up for the people to see. A cheer went up. It was time. A bucket was placed in front of him and he was forced to his knees. The man shook and drew back screaming, "No!" The crowd saw his fear, and yelled louder, "Sacrifice! Sacrifice!" All eyes were on the captive, their gift to the gods. His blood paid their debt. They would be prosperous again.

The priest stepped behind the man and raised a knife of black volcanic glass. The crowd cheered louder, again chanting

"Sacrifice! Sacrifice!"

Swiftly the priest reached around the captive slicing his throat from ear to ear, and the assistants pushed his head down into a large bowl. They needed to collect all of the blood. A cheer went up from the crowd. It was a good sacrifice. While the blood ran out, the priest held his hands out over the scene and chanted again to the gods imploring them to accept their gift.

When the body was drained, the priest held the bowl high and yelled, "Blood for the gods!" and the crowd cheered again. The body of the captive was rolled down the stairs of the pyramid to be left to lay there for the night. Sometime just before sunrise it would be picked up and thrown into the river.

The second captive was brought forward and held up to the crowd. He defiantly screamed at the crowd calling them 'old women and dung eaters' and to do their worst. They screamed back at him while laughing and shaking their fists. He was a man of courage. It gave him honor even in the face of a dishonorable death. The gods might be favorable to his soul.

As the body of the second captive landed at the bottom of the pyramid, the priest held the bucket of blood high and chanted incantations. On the corner of the pyramid landing was a pyre piled high with paper. Slowly the priest poured the blood over the paper careful not to soak any spot too much. It must be done exactly right or the gods would be displeased. The blood must be burned, consumed by fire, for the gods to receive it. When the paper burned, the blood burned and the gods were happy.

Heavy white smoke curled from the fire. The priest chanted and the crowd cheered. Now the gods would be happy and be good to their people. It was a good night for a celebration.

§

At various places throughout the ceremonial center large bonfires had been made. Each family had its place on the plaza

There would be eating and drinking and dancing long into the night. The entire ceremonial complex would be a place of celebration.

Johnson stood at the edge of the courtyard containing the royal family's festivities. It was a large courtyard in front of the temple with the comb at the back and there was a small pyramid off to one side. Two large bonfires were built at either end of the courtyard and the area was ringed with torches. .

He looked out over the site. Torches were strung up the stairs of every pyramid and the faces of the temples were illuminated by their flickering light. Immersed in the glow of a thousand torches were bright spots, the bonfires and hundreds of people were congregating. Celebrating would start as soon as the king proclaimed it was time. Tonight there would be dancing with abandonment, A period ending ceremony was a celebration for the whole town, one of the big events in their evolving history.

Little Rabbit came to his side and stood there quietly watching with him. "Is it like this where you come from?" she asked.

"Sometimes, but it is different."

"Different?"

"You always have family, always family. Everybody celebrates together."

"You don't?"

"No, our families live apart. Only sometimes do we come together, usually for dinners together on special days."

"How sad," she replied. "What does one do without family? Here, not to be with your people or family is the worst thing. To be cast out, away from the people, is a punishment. Death is better."

"The king is not well?" Johnson asked, changing the subject. "I saw you helping him during the ceremony."

"No, he is not well. His time in this world is short now. His spirit animal is dying. He will follow it shortly."

"And what will happen then?"

"I'm afraid there will be a time of turmoil."

"Can you see it?" he asked knowing she had an ability to see the future. "Do you know what will happen?"

"I see only the turmoil, but I am afraid for my brother. It will be a dangerous time for him."

"Why?"

"More than one man wants to be king. Men will kill for it and the gods will just stand and watch and make bets on who wins."

"And Shield Jaguar, will he win?"

"I don't know. But he does not lose easily." She stood there staring at the bonfires in the distance, lost in thought.

§

The horns trumpeted again announcing another ceremony. A quiet came over the site. What was happening? A crowd collected in front of the king's pavilion. People climbed on the pyramids and temples to be able to see. It must be something special. There had been no rumors about a special ceremony.

Then a lone horn sounded. Two slaves carried the king's dais down from the palace and placed it in front of the pyramid at the edge of the courtyard. King Bird Jaguar IV took his son Chel-Te' by the hand and led him to the dais and instructed him to sit on it. The king and Lord Great Skull took places on either side of him. A contingent of warriors stood on either side of them.

The horn sounded again and a priest carrying a *flap staff*, the manifestation of the king's power, came slowly down a pyramid in the ceremonial plaza and walked toward the courtyard. A contingent of guards carrying torches surrounded him, the light emphasizing his entrance onto the stage as he came forward and ceremoniously handed the flap staff to the king.

Music started to play. The king and Lord Great Skull started to dance. They danced in choreographed steps coming into the center in front of the young prince. The king was holding the *flap staff*. They danced, at times each facing the other, and at other times each facing Chel-Te'.

Johnson looked on in fascination. A Flap Staff Dance. He had seen them on lintels that had been placed in the temple doorways and on the stone trees that recorded their history. It was a dance that reinforced the authority of the power of the king. But this one was special. The king would die soon and this dance was used to authorize the transfer of the king's position and authority to the young Chel-Te', but to be held and guided by Lord Great Skull.

As Johnson surveyed the ceremony trying to take it all in he noticed Shield Jaguar. He sat there at his place, his face white with fists clenched. Evidently he wasn't aware this was to happen tonight. There was a look of pure hate on the man's face. Formality dictated that he sit and watch, which implied to the people he was in concurrence with the ceremony. Lord Great Skull had outmaneuvered and trapped him. The king's dedication was law. It must be obeyed.

Anger poured off the king's brother. He was tight, concentrated, and ready to spring, just like he was before charging into battle. He glanced at Lightening Sky. "Never," he said with the guttural growl of an animal. "He'll never keep the throne."

Johnson turned back in fascination to watch the dance unfold. One of the most famous lintels known was carved in commemoration of this particular ceremony. The original was held in a private collection. The owner remained anonymous but Johnson had seen photos that had been provided of it.

As the music played, the king formally gave the *flap staff* to Lord Great Skull. The king was dying. His son was only sixteen years old. Lord Great Skull was being formally given the power to be regent to the young king. He would hold the power of the office until the young king matured. The actual power of the young king would be restricted until then. Lord Great Skull was almost a king now.

As the dance ended, the crowd cheered loudly in support of the king's decision. They knew he had a short time to live and he had provided for them. The royal line would continue and important decisions of state would be made by the man with years of experience as counselor to the king. They were not aware of his ambition.

As the cheering continued, Shield Jaguar leaned over and whispered to Smoking Squirrel and Lightning Sky, "Tomorrow when the sun is born again, we go to Bonampak," and he got up and left.

§

"Come with me," said Little Rabbit later that evening. The celebration had died down. The consumption of the fermented beverage had its effect on the people. Small groups were consumed with boisterous talk and occasionally shrieking laughter. "No one will notice our leaving."

They walked out of the palace courtyard, through a hall and into the night. Little Rabbit suddenly pulled him against a wall into a dark shadow.

"Silence," she whispered into his ear.

It was dark, and his eyes hadn't adjusted from the torchlight in the plaza to the darkness outside. He strained to see and hear what she warned him about. Slowly his eyes adjusted. In front of them were two opposing groups of warriors. The leaders stood face to face, their warriors spread out behind them.

"You won't get away with it!" Johnson heard a familiar voice say.

"And who's going to stop me? Not you!" was fired back.

It was Shield Jaguar and Lord Great Skull. Shield Jaguar had his guard of Eagle warriors behind him, and Lord Great Skull a group of his personal guard and family warriors behind him. It was a standoff.

"Do not underestimate me Great Skull. It would be a big mistake," Shield Jaguar warned.

"You're a lot of talk," spat the great lord, "just a kid with a wise-ass mouth. I have been given the power by the authority of the king, and I have the noble families on my side. You're soon going to find yourself without a place here. Chel-Te' doesn't like you and I'll be happy to be rid of you."

"I'm still brother to the king and uncle to Chel-Te'. I have royal blood and position. You may find that hard to challenge."

"Royal blood perhaps, but your position will end soon. Your brother Bird Jaguar put up with your antics. I guarantee you, Chel-Te' won't."

"And what makes you think that?" growled Shield Jaguar.

"He's not like his father," retorted the lord. "I'm sure that with my counsel he will find a way to be rid or you."

"Be very quiet," Little Rabbit whispered as she pulled Lightning Sky along the dark shadows of the wall. "We shouldn't be here. We must leave. It's dangerous."

They followed a path down to the river. She stopped at the water's edge and grabbed him around the waist. "Hold me close," she said trembling.

"You're scared," he observed. "Why? What don't I see here?"

"A time of great turmoil is coming. Many will die. It will never be the same."

"Because of what we heard?" he asked.

"Don't you understand? Both Shield Jaguar and Lord Great Skull want to be the king. The lord got the king to make him regent when he dies. He has the power. This makes him almost a king."

"But Chel-Te' is to be king. He has been dedicated," Johnson said.

"And Lord Great Skull is regent. He makes the decisions and tells Chel-Te' what to do. Chel-Te' will follow his advice without question."

"But Chel-Te' will still be the king. Won't he come of age and rule on his own? That is what the ceremony was all about."

"He will rule only for a short time," she replied. "He's arrogant and stupid. The throne will be taken from him. He has only to die and Lord Great Skull will be in a position to take over the throne. He is the regent and he commands the warriors. Who is to stop him?"

"And your brother, Shield Jaguar, is there nothing he can do?"

"I don't know. He won't give up without a fight. I see conflict and killing. I'm sure that it will be decided with blood and the loser will die."

"But history indicates that the next king is named Shield Jaguar," Johnson added from his knowledge of history.

"What's in a name?" she replied. "Kings change their names all of the time. The winner will want to be associated with my father the great Shield Jaguar II. Any one of them would take his name to convince the people he is the rightful heir."

"When will this happen?"

"Very soon, I think."

§

The river flowed slowly, gently pulling at their canoe as they made their way to the opposite shore. Little Rabbit was silent the whole time, lost in her own world. Johnson instinctively knew to leave her alone with her thoughts. She was seeing things now, a world she had never seen before, a world different than she lived in. The future was confusing, turmoil abounded. It troubled her.

"Come," she said as she took his hand, held it tight and led him through the jungle. She moved slowly, cautiously, seemingly aware of something he couldn't see. At times she stopped and waited, looking around as though she heard something.

"Is something wrong?" he asked.

"The gods are arguing tonight," she replied. "Some are on Shield Jaguar's side, others on the great lord's side. There is no peace in Xibalba."

They came to the little hill that covered the pyramid they called their special place. Quietly, they removed the brush hiding the doorway.

"My love," she said as she wrapped her arms around him, "we need to make a sacrifice to the gods tonight."

"What? I need you tonight. It's been too long," he said as he held her closer to him.

"We will be together my love, I promise you, but first we need to pay the gods their due for our time together. They are troubled tonight and when they are this way they deny man. We need their support now and during the troubling times to come or they may forsake our love and deny us the little time we have.

"Come," she said as she took his hand again and entered the small temple inside the pyramid. She lit the lamp and a soft glow radiated throughout the room. She placed the lamp on the altar, and from a bag took a necklace of jade and amber stones. Johnson stared at them. He could see they were of the finest quality fitted with gold wire and attached to a gold chain. It was the most exquisite ancient jewelry he had ever seen.

"My father's; it was the great king's favorite," she said. "He gave it to me just before he died and said that anything so beautiful should only be worn by a beautiful woman. I said I was just a little girl, but he said one day I would be a beautiful woman and I would wear it then."

"And you wear it now?"

"Oh no, I have never worn it. I've saved it for a special time. This is a special time. I offer it to the gods to bless our love."

"You've said they have forsaken us, and they will never bless our love. Will this change their minds?"

"Perhaps, but probably not in this lifetime," she replied as she lifted her face to kiss him.

They knelt before the altar as she chanted in an ancient language for a long time. Then she took a knife, and beneath the sleeping platform, deeply dug a small square hole. While chanting more words, she placed the necklace in the hole, covered it with blue sand she took out of the bag, and filled the hole with dirt. When complete, she turned back to the altar and chanted again.

"Come," she said happily as she pulled him to the sleeping platform. "It's time to complete the ritual."

Johnson held her close and felt a sensation of ecstasy enter his body. She was in his arms again, next to him, her spirit merging with his, part of his being, the way it was meant to be. He felt whole again, embracing an unfathomable joy. His life had meaning now. He was refreshed, reborn. He held her close, not willing to loosen his hold lest she leave him again.

She lay with her head on his chest and clung to him with the same fervor. They held each other for a long time as their feelings of love replaced the desperation of their situation. For a while, just a short while, nothing would be able to separate them. After a time she freed up a hand, made a fist and lightly pounded his chest.

"We've got a problem," she said.

"Yes, little one. What's our problem?"

"If you don't let me loose, I can't make love to you."

"And that's a problem?" He laughed and held her tighter.

"If I didn't need you so much I'd cast a spell on you right now," she teased.

"You have cast a spell on me. You've caused me to love you," he said as he loosened his grip and kissed her softly.

"Tonight is ours," she said. "I've waited so long. Tonight we will be one again and I'll have to hold tight to the happiness for a lifetime." She kissed him tenderly, then passionately and then with abandon. He responded until they were consumed with each other. The pent-up longing each had suffered released and in desperation they tore at each other, their need to be joined insatiable. Each gave with complete abandonment, with their total being; each taking and giving, immersed in the ecstasy of being with the other. Their love drove an unquenchable need for fulfillment. And when released, they lay clinging tightly to each other as the spasms of afterglow slowly subsided.

Later, they came together again slowly, tenderly, letting the immersion with the other consume them with a slow burning fire that clung to their souls and joined them as one forever.

§

Little Rabbit awakened; something was wrong. She stepped outside. There was no moonlight. The moon was gone.

"You must arise," she cried while shaking Johnson. "We have slept too long. Hurry, we must go quickly or we will be found out."

He got back to his sleeping room just before sunrise. The old woman was there waiting, a worried look on her face.

"You're late," she whispered hoarsely. "You must hurry or your brother will be asking questions."

"Why?" he responded. The old woman seemed to know everything that was going on.

"He wouldn't be happy knowing about you and his sister."

"No?" Johnson said.

"No, he has plans for her."

"Really?" Johnson said.

"You've had your fun. Now it's best to let her go," she advised. "It will only cause you trouble. Your brother loves you, but there is a side of him you don't want to cross."

"Really?" Johnson said again, his curiosity increasing.

"Yes, really. He's ambitious like his father. Never stand between him and his ambition. Brother or not, he'll kill you or anyone else who keeps him from getting what he wants."

"And I'm between him and his ambition?" Johnson asked sarcastically.

"He has plans for her my son, and they don't include you."

Johnson stood there ready to be dressed again. Which costume was she going to chose for him to wear this time?

"What are you waiting for?" she asked. "Get out of your banquet garments and into a loincloth and gather your weapons. You are a common warrior today out hunting for food."

§

Lightning Sky wrapped his loincloth around him, grabbed his weapons and headed toward the small hill with the big tree the flint sky god broke in two. It looked like a hunting party was sitting there. No formal costumes were worn. About half the group was there waiting for the rest to show up. The last to arrive was Smoking Squirrel.

"What took you so long?" Shield Jaguar asked Smoking Squirrel as he came up. He knew there would be questions.

"Slept late, drank too much chorte last night," Smoking Squirrel answered, as he held his head in both hands and hunched his shoulders to indicate the pain he was in.

"I thought I saw you leave with the new dancer."

"You mean the new young one with the small tits and nice legs? I didn't get much sleep either."

"You're not going to get any sleep today. We need to hurry and be gone before anyone else is awake. I need for everyone to think I went out in the jungle to cool off after last night."

"Where are we off to?" Lightning Sky asked.

"I need to talk to Chan Muwaan II. A runner went out last night asking him to meet us by the boulders along the river flowing away from his city when the sun was at its highest point."

"Why are we going to meet Chan Muwaan?" Johnson asked Smoking Squirrel as they followed Shield Jaguar out of the city.

"Perhaps he can help."

"Help?" Johnson asked. He knew of a Chan Muwaan II. He was the king of Bonampak, but his reign was later than the time that they were in. Was he the same man before he ascended to the throne?

"There will be fighting when the king dies," Smoking Squirrel said, "Shield Jaguar needs more warriors. Chan Muwaan can provide them."

"He would do that?"

"Perhaps, for a price, but you can be sure it will be a high price."

The hunting party walked along the river until just before sunrise and located the spot where canoes were waiting to take them across. It was a nice morning but the group was solemn as they entered the jungle and headed toward the city on the next river to the south.

Shield Jaguar was silent, moody. The other warriors took their cue and left him alone. When he was in this mood, he might lash out viciously at anything. Midmorning brought them to a place where they put the canoes ashore and started walking through the jungle. Shield Jaguar, in the lead, set a quick, determined pace. He was impatient.

When the sun was high in the sky, the path cut back toward the river. They came out of the jungle and there were three boulders the size of cars in the water. Another group of warriors were waiting, spread out casually around and on top of the rocks. When their approach was noticed, the men slid off the boulders into a defensive position.

"Hello, my friend Chan Muwaan," called Shield Jaguar.

From behind the line of warriors stepped the prince from

Bonampak dressed simply as another warrior. He was short and stocky; his hair was tied in the back of his head in a knot. A long scar ran down his left cheek and he had a stout black beard covering his chin. His gaze was fearsome, like a caged wild animal, accenting his coal black eyes that penetrated all he looked at.

Johnson felt caught in his glare. This was a dangerous man, arrogance radiated from him. The request to meet Shield Jaguar was really a summons. Bonampak was a vassal city of Yaxchilan. His demeanor made it known he was present but not of his own accord.

"Chan Muwaan, still hiding behind your betters I see," chided Shield Jaguar.

"I didn't see you leading the pack like a good dog should," returned Chan Muwaan. Both had guards. As princes, both were too important to travel alone and would be captured if an enemy were able to find them. The resulting prospect wasn't a good one.

The three nobles from Yaxchilan and three from Bonampak sat in a circle. The warrior guards remained at a distance out of the sound of their conversation. The two leaders made some small talk, a polite gesture of protocol of their meeting.

"Last night," Shield Jaguar finally opened, "my brother, the king, performed a Flap Staff Dance giving Lord Great Skull regent power over Chel-Te' after he dies."

Chan Muwaan looked over at the man across from him and cautiously asked, "Will that be soon?"

"Soon enough," replied Shield Jaguar. "The king is very sick. His spirit animal is dying and he will follow it."

"And what will happen to you?" asked Chan Muwaan?

"That may depend upon you my friend. Right now Lord Great Skull considers me pushed aside, relegated to a mere noble of the royal family, and that he holds the power."

"And Chel-Te', won't he be king?"

"He's just an arrogant boy filled with his own self importance. He will do whatever Great Skull tells him."

Chan Muwaan sat back and considered the situation. "And you need my help?"

"Yes, my friend. I need your help to take the throne away from Chel-Te'. If we wait, Lord Great Skull may take it. If he manages to kill Chel-Te' and me, the throne will be his."

"Your friend you say? Yaxchilan holds Bonampak as a vassal city. That doesn't make me your friend."

"You want to be king of Bonampak and your family position is tenuous at best. If I am the king, I can make that happen, or you can deal with Chel-Te' or Lord Great Skull. I think you are better dealing with me."

"Is that so?"

"Chel-Te' is a monkey's penis. Even if he supports you, He will raise Bonampak's tribute. It's how he will pay for building his temples. His father, the king, is finding it harder and harder to raise tribute for his building projects. Chel-Te' will demand more. I don't build temples, I make war."

"I thought Lord Great Skull is a good general. He will make war," Chan Muwaan replied.

"Not if Chel-Te' holds him back. He can't protect you from Piedras Negras, I can. They will be a lot harder to deal with than me."

Chan Muwaan studied the man in front of him. He had a claim to the throne at Yaxchilan but it was not the direct route. "So you want me to be your friend, you say. What would a friend do for you?"

"When the king dies, the time will be right. There will be confusion and I can take the throne. I need your warriors to help me remove Chel-Te'. If he ascends to the throne, he would have the power to stop us."

"If we don't succeed it would mean war between our two cities again and Yaxchilan is stronger."

"Not if I win. Then we become friends. Friends help each other—both ways."

"That's a big if," replied Chan Muwaan cautiously," and the warriors are not mine to give. They are my father's. I don't think he would be willing to loan them out."

"I don't need all of them. You have your Eagle Warriors the same as me. Between us there are enough of them to do the job. You will be rewarded."

"And what do you give me as a 'friend'?"

"What do you want? If it is in my power I would want to demonstrate my friendship to you."

Chan Muwaan sat and contemplated a long time. This was an opportunity. If both of them were kings he would have tremendous power being tied to Yaxchilan as a partner instead of a vassal. Would this man make it possible?

"I think I would want three things when I ascend to become king," Chan Muwaan replied. First, I want the title of *Yajaw* making me a king of Bonampak allied with Yaxchilan, not a vassal. Second, I want you to attend my ascension ceremonies giving me my new position. And third, I want your sister Little Rabbit as a wife, who will provide an heir to my throne." It was a high price.

"Done," said Shield Jaguar a slight smile twinkling in his eyes. It was what he expected. "What you desire will be yours."

Johnson sat there stunned. He had just heard Little Rabbit being bargained away for another man's kingdom. *What in the hell is Shield Jaguar doing, giving his sister away? They can't do this. I won't let them. She is Lightning Sky's woman, she is my woman.* And the old woman's words came back to him. Shield Jaguar would kill anyone who came between him and his ambition.

He looked at the two men and realized the relations were warmer between them. The deal had been made. Little Rabbit was the chattel, and each was getting what he wanted. Both would become kings, deified as all-powerful rulers, and he felt helpless.

"When do you need my help?" Chan Muwaan asked.

"When the king dies. I will send a runner for you to bring your warriors. When you get there we will take the palace while the king is being prepared for burial. There will be a state of confusion then. We must kill Chel-Te' and Lord Great Skull. Then the throne will be mine."

"They may not be easy to kill," Chan Muwaan said.

"Lord Great Skull will be looking for me to do something. He will be on his guard. Extra care will be taken to protect Chel-Te'. We must move faster than he anticipates."

"He may be ready for you."

"Then it will be a good fight."

§

"Do you trust him?" Smoking Squirrel asked as they watched the last of Chan Muwaan's men fade into the jungle.

"He knows it's in his best interest," responded Shield Jaguar.

"Not if we lose."

"We aren't going to lose," Shield Jaguar said as he gazed out over the water. He picked up a flat stone and threw, skipping it across the surface. He watched it sink and looked for another to throw, an idle activity showing he didn't want to discuss it further. Inside he was lost in thought. For a long time he continued throwing rocks.

His warriors camped beside the river where they had met the other group. It was a nice place. Shield Jaguar was not in a hurry to return to the city.

Over and over in his mind Johnson recanted the meeting between the two princes. *Little Rabbit has been given away, barter for Shield Jaguar's ambition. How dare he, and to that arrogant bastard, too.* He wanted to kill them both. With the anger came the knowledge that he had the skills to do it.

"You have to let her go," Smoking Squirrel said as they were walking along the riverbank just before sundown.

"What?"

"Little Rabbit, you have to let her go."

"You know?"

"Of course I know. I'm your brother. I see the way you look at each other and how you sneak off in the night."

"But we love each other," Johnson shot back.

"Her destiny is to become a queen," said Smoking Squirrel, "and you are just a noble; a noble with a future as counselor to a king, but still just a noble."

"And if I won't give her up?" Johnson shot back.

"Then he will kill you."

"That's the second time today someone has told me that he will kill me."

"Then it's time to listen. He loves his sister and lets her play with you. It makes her happy, but he has plans for her. She knows this and accepts it. You must too."

"He knows?" Johnson said aghast.

"Of course he does. There is very little that man doesn't know."

Chapter 16

The sound of the bubbling brook awakened him. He shivered. It was cold. Instantly Johnson knew he was back in the cave again. He had returned to his own time. *"No, no, not now, not when everything is about to happen. There is going to be a fight for the throne. Little Rabbit said the winner would take the great king's name and use it to declare his legitimacy. I never considered this. Maybe the archaeological community had interpreted the lineage of Yaxchilan correctly after all.*

He opened his eyes and looked around. "I need to go back," he told the young Shaman. "I need to go now, right now. I must be there when the king dies. I must know who wins. I must know who the next king will be."

"That is not possible, Dr. Johnson. You have just come back to this time. The gods would never allow it," the shaman replied.

"Let me talk to the gods," Johnson snapped. "Let them tell me that I can't go back."

"The old shaman told me that we will make the gods angry, they will withhold the rains, our crops will be ruined and we will go hungry."

"If the gods withhold the rain, I will send food to the village,"

Johnson said. "I will have the university help the village and provide new seed for the next crop."

"It is very dangerous for you," replied the shaman. "I feel the danger. You may never come back this time."

"I'll take my chances," Johnson pleaded. "I must know who won and how they did it."

§

Johnson could see the eyes looking at him. They were big eyes. One set of eyes appeared very sad and the other looked angry. Around the eyes were shapes, which must be the heads, Johnson thought. Forms started to come into focus, humanoid forms. Then they backed away leaving only the impression of having a body, but the eyes remained, one set sad and the other angry.

"You have come again," a voice said. "Why are you here?"

"I must return to the past," said Johnson. "I must know what happens when the king, Bird Jaguar IV of Yaxchilan, dies."

"There will be another king. There is always another king."

"But who, and how does he come to power? I must know this."

"Why? There is always another king. Who he is, is not important. He will just be a king."

"Isn't he to be descended from the First Father in Xibalba?" Johnson asked.

"Everyone is descended from the First Father."

"In my time I am a teacher," Johnson said. "I need to know what happens so I can tell those who learn from me."

"Tell them that there is always a king. When an old king dies a new king takes his place. This is the way of things."

"In my time we want to know who the new king is and how he got to become king. It is important to us. It is how we view history and the time when the people lived in this land and worshiped you, their gods."

"Where do you want to go?" asked the voice after a long silent deliberation.

"To Yaxchilan when the king, Bird Jaguar, dies."

§

His head and wrists hurt and his hands were numb. Johnson tried to move his arms. They were tied behind him and he was shackled to a wall. There was light coming through a doorway indicating it was daytime. He looked around; Smoking Squirrel was next to him and then Shield Jaguar. All were bound, sitting on the floor of a very narrow room with their backs to a wall. Two guards, spears in hand, were standing on either side of the door casually watching them.

He was back in the past again, but when? And why was he tied up? He tried to think it through but his head hurt and there was blood dripping down onto his shoulder. Obviously he had been hit in the head.

"What happened?" he whispered.

"He's awake," Smoking Squirrel said.

"What happened?" he said again.

"You're awake. We thought you would die," was Smoking Squirrel's reply. "The head wound looks bad."

"What happened?" Johnson asked a third time.

"That monkey-fornicating motherless pig's ass was waiting for us," shot back Shield Jaguar. "May the gods damn him."

"Waiting? I don't understand," Johnson said.

"Lightning Sky's head wound is bad," Smoking Squirrel said over his shoulder to Shield Jaguar, "he doesn't remember."

"Great Skull, he was waiting for us," spat Shield Jaguar. We came back from a hunt and he was waiting for us with two hundred men. It was a trap."

"I don't understand," Johnson repeated. "Why would Great Skull take us captive."

"The king is dead," said Smoking Squirrel.

"Convenient for Lord Great Skull to be so prepared," added Shield Jaguar, "just like he knew it would happen. When we got out of the canoes, they descended on us, came in from all sides. We only had twenty men with us. It wasn't even a fight, but at least you tried."

"Brave and foolish," Smoking Squirrel added. "Two hundred warriors and you pull your war club and want to take them all on. You're lucky it was only a head wound."

Johnson felt fear running through his body. *This wasn't supposed to happen. When I was here the last time, the king was close to death and Shield Jaguar was planning to pull a coup and seize the throne when the king died. Evidently it didn't work. It sounded like Lord Great Skull stopped him. Now what is going to happen? I'm certain if Lightning Sky is killed, I will die too.*

"So, are we prisoners?" asked Johnson. "Lord Great Skull's prisoners? What happens now?"

"We'll have to wait and see," said Shield Jaguar. "I don't think he would dare kill me, not before the ceremonies making Chel-Te' the king."

"And us?" Smoking Squirrel asked.

Shield Jaguar laughed. "Maybe you're not quite as important as I am." He laughed again. It was a good joke.

§

There was a smug smile on Great Skull's face as he came through the door. He had pulled it off and was ecstatic. It showed. He had stopped Shield Jaguar from seizing the throne and was in control of the situation now. He had the power now. As regent to Chel-Te', he would make the policy decisions and the little brat would sit on his throne and proclaim them to be law.

Johnson tightened up, instantly angry as the lord kicked his outstretched legs.

"Move them out of the way," the lord commanded, and kicked

them again.

As he struggled against his bonds, the angrier Johnson became; his entire being wanted to strike back, to put the arrogant bastard in his place.

Behind Lord Great Skull was his eldest son, following his father in anticipation of becoming a lord himself one day. The great lord was preparing him for that time. There was a great deal to learn about politics and affairs of state.

Lord Great Skull stopped in front of Shield Jaguar and looked down. "Well little puppy, you're not so tough now, are you?" he said.

"You monkey's ass," Shield Jaguar shot back. "I'll have you whipped to death for this, along with that sniveling little whelp you have with you." He glared at the young man with satisfaction as he watched him pull back in terror.

"You're not in any position to do anything about it," the great lord replied with a laugh. "You're mine now."

"You think so?"

"Oh yes. I have you, I have your warriors and I have your sister. You're nephew Chel-Te' will be the next king. He hates you and he listens to me. The Eagle Warriors are swearing allegiance to Chel-Te' as we speak and they will be under my banner along with the other warriors in my family. I have the power now."

"And me? You don't have me."

"You will fade into the background, a noble prince and the people will know you are out of favor with the king. In a short time you will become a passing memory in people's minds, a man who wanted to be king, but it wasn't to be. They will forget you soon enough."

"And what makes you think I will do that?"

"Your life, you brothers' lives, your sister's life, they all hang in the balance."

"You can't kill me. I am a member of the royal family. The

heads of the families would never allow it and they have the power to stop it."

"I can keep you a prisoner until they forget about you; let's say for a year or two. Then if you disappear, they will notice but will do nothing. You won't have been in the picture for a long time. It will all be in the past.

"Or, I can free you to be part of the royal family. Prostrate yourself before Chel-Te' and show the people you accept his rule. You will have position and privilege but not power. You and yours will live."

"And as a warrior?"

"You can become a warrior in my Elite Warriors under my command. It is your right by privilege of birth. You can still fight, but you cannot lead warriors again."

"You are going to command me, a royal prince? By all the gods in Xibalba, it will never happen. I'll die first!" Shield Jaguar glared at the lord, refusing to say anything more. He seethed with anger. Who did Great Skull think he was? He was a commoner, the head of a family and brother to the queen yes, but still a commoner.

"You'll have a lot of time to think about it," the great lord said and he walked out the door.

§

"He's not going to do it, is he?" said Lord Great Skull's son as they left the room.

"Do what, chose to live?" replied the great lord. "Sure he is. It will just take some time for him to come to that decision."

"But he would rather be dead."

"No, he would rather be king than dead. That is why he will accept life."

The young man looked thoughtfully at his father and realized he knew the outcome before he went in to talk to Shield Jaguar.

How did he know? There was so much to learn.

"Then isn't he too dangerous to let loose?" the young man asked.

"We will have to watch him very closely. I'm sure he will want to try something."

"Then why isn't it better to kill him right off?"

"Because he's right. The heads of the families will never allow us to just kill him. It is best if he looks like he is part of the royal family, accepting Chel-Te'. Perhaps an accident will befall him later and we will not be blamed."

"Then what?"

"Then Chel-Te' leaves no one in his bloodline when he dies."

§

"You're hurt," Little Rabbit cried as she came through the door and saw Lightning Sky's wrists. As she started to rub them with a salve made from the sap from a plant, her eyes got big and a smile crossed her face. "You're back," she whispered as she recognized Johnson. "It's a very bad time."

"I had to come," he said. "I had to know what happened when the king died."

"What happened?" she said with a scowl. "Lord Great Skull has won. He has stopped Shield Jaguar and secured the throne for Chel-Te'. That's what happened," she said loud enough for all to hear.

"Is that all?"

She looked toward the guard still at the door, then looked back and smiled. "Today it is," she said softly.

"Don't spend all of your time on him," Shield Jaguar called as he rubbed his wrists. "We need some salve on our arms too."

As she turned, Johnson saw him grin and wink at her. He was sure there was a blush when she turned back to him. *Yes, it was a close society and Shield Jaguar knows about us,* he thought.

"What happened?" Shield Jaguar asked Little Rabbit as she applied salve to his wrists.

"The king got really sick after he ate yesterday. I think there was something in his food. He died quickly. The physicians said that his spirit animal finally left him and he went to join it in the afterworld. Then suddenly Lord Great Skull's warriors were everywhere, and your Eagle Warriors were rounded up and placed in the plaza without their weapons. A few resisted and were killed."

"And Chan Muwaan," Shield Jaguar asked, "he never came?"

"No, nothing from him. I heard that his father stopped him. He was told by Lord Great Skull that if he became involved with you, Chel-Te', the rightful king of Yaxchilan, would destroy Bonampak and kill the royal family."

"And Chel-Te'?"

"He thinks that now he is a god and the king. He sits on the bench in the throne room in the palace and calls the lords to kneel to him."

"But he's not the king until Bird Jaguar is buried and off to the otherworld. The council must approve and he must be presented to the gods by the priests."

"He doesn't care. He's starting to take land from people he doesn't like, and give it to those he likes. He's making proclamations. He claims he is going to raise the tribute and build more temples."

"And what is Great Skull doing?"

"He smiles and nods at Chel-Te''s proclamations. Lord Great Skull is crafty. He has gained control of the warriors. He has the power. He will watch and wait. Chel-Te' will not be popular.

§

Chel-Te' sat in his palace and looked down from his platform at the man on his knees before him and sneered. Two guards had forced Shield Jaguar there and held him. Another one was standing behind him holding a club with embedded obsidian flakes into it. His sister, Little Rabbit, and cousins, Smoking Squirrel and Lightning Sky, were off to the side watching. Warriors restrained them.

"Well Uncle," the young king laughed, "you aren't so arrogant this morning."

Shield Jaguar looked up, anger burning in his eyes. His brother's son, the little fornicating weasel had a wild look in his eyes. He sat cross-legged, pointing a shaking finger down at Shield Jaguar, laughing hysterically.

"You aren't so big now, are you?"

Shield Jaguar glared hard at the boy-king.

"Perhaps today you will die."

Silence.

"I can make it happen. Just a flick of my finger and fire will come from the sky and strike you down," the young king proclaimed.

A slight smile curled at Shield Jaguar's lips and he emitted a soft chuckle. He looked at the young king defiantly.

"The only reason I don't do it is because Lord Great Skull here says we need you for show," Chel-Te' squeaked. "You must be part of the ascension ceremony when the gods give me their blessing. The people must see you there. They must see you pay homage to me."

Shield Jaguar looked the king in the eyes and smiled openly and the young king didn't know how to handle it. At least for now they needed him, or better stated, they needed his position. Once the people saw him subservient to the king, they still couldn't do anything to him for fear of reprisal. This king wasn't strong enough to stand up to the noble families, not if they confronted him directly.

"Do you swear allegiance to me?" Chel-Te' screamed. The guards held Shield Jaguar down and the warrior with the club raised it.

Shield Jaguar smiled openly and chuckled as he continued to look the king in the eyes.

Suddenly Lord Great Skull came from beside the king, grabbed Little Rabbit and threw her down before Shield Jaguar. He pulled out an obsidian knife and held it to her throat. The guard forced Shield Jaguar on his stomach, face pushed into the floor. "She will be first to die," the lord spat, "and then those other two you call brothers; then you and I will face the families for it. I'll feed you to the god Mar and they will be afraid to petition him in your behalf. Yes, they will be angry but you will be gone."

Lord Great Skull lowered his voice and softly said to Shield Jaguar, "and then the last of your royal line is that little weasel up there on his bench." He smiled a knowing smile.

Shield Jaguar stared at the lord. *Yes, he would do it and he would get away with it too,* he thought, a*nd all will be lost.* He raised his head to the king. "You have my allegiance," he said as he listened to the king's high-pitched cackle.

§

The night was hot, sweltering, yet Johnson was shivering. Nerves. His mind hadn't caught up to the events of the last few hours. He was reliving them over and over trying to process them. He knew what happened. Shield Jaguar didn't pull off the coup, but his mind couldn't accept it yet. Johnson kept running the events around in his head. He was scared and angry and there was no way to strike back.

It was dark and confining in the little room. Very little light was provided by a small candle on a low table by the sleeping platform. It was stuffy, and there was a guard at the door watching him. No longer bound, he was confined to Lightning Sky's sleeping room in the palace. Others could come and go, to and from the room, but he must remain inside.

His old woman had just left after bringing him some tortillas and a meat stew to eat. She spat at his guard's feet as she left, and uttered a guttural profanity. The guard raised a hand to hit her, but she drew back and threatened to put a curse on him if he did. He paled and shrank back.

Lightning Sky's old woman was a person to be feared. She had a powerful animal spirit, a wild boar with huge tusks who she claimed protected both her and Lightning Sky. She threatened anyone who would harm him with having her boar attack their spirit animal. Only Lord Great Skull, with a bear for a spirit animal, laughed at her. "We will have one dead pig for dinner if you don't put a leash on him," he would tell her and he would growl "Grrrr" as she ran away.

Johnson stared at the guard, a constant reminder of his situation. *How could this happen?* Johnson thought. *It's not supposed to happen this way. Shield Jaguar was supposed seize the throne; he was supposed to become king.* Johnson had been so sure that it would happen that way. He had staked his professional reputation on it and shouted it to the world. And he was criticized by the entire academic community for it.

We will be killed, he thought. *We will all be killed, Shield Jaguar and all his supporters, and history would record that Chel-Te 'took his regnal name of Shield Jaguar III, after his grandfather, just the way the archaeological community interpreted it.* Johnson sat staring numbly at the guard. *How could I have been so wrong?*

"Be gone!" snapped Little Rabbit to the guard as she entered the room.

"My orders are to watch Lightning Sky," was his stoic reply.

"I said be gone!" she repeated again glaring at the man.

"But...."

"But? You have the audacity to question me? I'll have you whipped within an inch of your life."

"But princess...."

"But what? Get out. I command it."

"Lord Great Skull said to keep my eyes on him."

"Lord Great Skull? He is only a servant of my brother the late king, and you are a warrior of no consequence; one of Lord Great Skull's pretty boys, a play warrior from the elite class. I am a princess of the royal family. How dare you question an order of mine? Now get out!"

The guard hurried out the door to take a position on the outside.

Johnson smiled as he listened to the dialogue. "You like getting your way," he stated with a chuckle.

"How dare he question me," she shot at him, fire still in her eyes. "No one questions me."

"Not even me?"

"Especially not you,or I'll turn you into a lizard." She broke into a grin and laughed.

"Do I get to choose the color?" he replied remembering the conversation after the ball game when she threatened Smoking Squirrel.

"No!" she turned up her nose in mock indignation. "You can only be the color I like." She ran to him and threw her arms around his neck.

"Now I command you to kiss me," she stated as she smothered his lips with hers. She kissed him hard and desperately over and over, hungry for his kisses in return.

He held her tightly like he needed to be part of her, not willing to let her go. She was in his arms now and that was all that mattered.

She pulled him down to the sleeping platform, stripping off his loin cloth. She smothered his lips with her kisses as she stroked him until he was hard, then lifted her shift, and pulled him inside of her. "I need you my love," she cried as he entered her. "Fill me with your seed," and she rhythmically consumed his manhood harder and harder until they were lost in each other.

A fire of passion consumed them spiraling higher and higher until they exploded together, lost in themselves, lost in each other. Two became one, a whole being created from their love, they held each other in desperation, never wanting to leave each others embrace.

As the passion abated Johnson felt a gnawing fear gripping him with the knowledge that he would have to give her up. He would have to remember this time, relive it over and over again. He wanted to hold her in his arms forever. But it was only these memories he could take back. It seemed so wonderful now and so little to cling to. Slowly they separated, ripping apart their intertwined being, leaving each an empty yearning, needing to have it back again.

They lay together, Little Rabbit curled up against Johnson. Johnson looked around the room. The guard was no longer there, but he had to be nearby.

"Won't the guard come back?" he asked.

"Not if he wants to live," she said flatly. "Noble or not, I would have him whipped to death."

"Wouldn't they stop you?" he asked in amazement.

"Who?"

"His people, perhaps."

"No one but the king can command me," she stated proudly. "It is my birthright."

Johnson looked closely at her. There was no bravado in her statements. For her it was a matter of fact.

§

It was time to bury the king. The gods proclaimed it must be accomplished within the second cycle of the sun after his spirit animal departed from his body. The women of his family had been preparing his body all night and placed him in his finest clothes before wrapping his body. The high priests made the appropriate sacrifices in the temples and the priestesses administered the sacred incantations over his body to prepare it for the journey through the underworld on its way to the afterlife. He must be rightly attended if his spirit would watch over the people and come again to them when he was called.

The place of the burial was prepared and waiting. The king, Bird Jaguar IV, would be laid to rest in front of his temple on the hill. The vault had been constructed months ago to the king's specifications, then sealed until it was needed. He would take many of his possessions, and two slaves would accompany him into the afterlife to serve him.

Johnson was led out of his sleeping room in the palace where he had been confined. The procession was starting to assemble. It would proceed from the palace to the tomb, just a short distance up the hill overlooking the river. A high priest would lead the way followed by Chel-Te', accompanied by the lords, and then the body of Bird Jaguar IV carried by six warriors. A contingent of twenty more warriors, ten on each side, would march as honor guard to the king.

"How have you fared?" Shield Jaguar asked as Johnson was escorted to his place in the procession. Shield Jaguar, Little Rabbit and Smoking Squirrel were already there.

"Reasonable, under the circumstances," he replied as he studied the man, looking for a reaction.

"It's time to put my brother down into his grave. I have been waiting for a long time for this, but now I feel sadness."

"For the king, or for you?" Johnson replied.

"For my brother, of course," said Shield Jaguar with a hint of a smile. "We must appear to accept this and be ever vigilant," he whispered. "Lord Great Skull will be watching and waiting for any opportunity to pounce on us," and as he looked over at the king and the great lord, a scowl grew on his face.

"You don't look like you are accepting this very well," Johnson observed.

Shield Jaguar glared at him and said nothing, his eyes radiating dark embers of hate.

§

The horns sounded twice, and the group came together in their places ready for the procession. When the horns trumpeted three times the procession slowly moved forward. Waiting outside the palace and along the route were hundreds of people loudly wailing and mourning. They came forward to place flowers on the ground in front of the procession. The royal musicians followed the group playing a sad melody with rhythmic beating of drums to call the gods into their presence. Bird Jaguar respected the gods and sacrificed to them in his life on earth. Now it was time for them to mourn him along with his people.

A hush went up as the people saw Shield Jaguar in the procession following the body of the king. Rumors had circulated that he was dead, that the king had him killed.

"See, Shield Jaguar follows the king," was told from mouth to mouth quickly informing the people of his status. "He follows Chel-Te'."

In the front of the procession, Lord Great Skull, walking just behind the king, smiled broadly. He knew what the people were saying. They thought that Shield Jaguar would be the next king, but they were wrong. When they watched him being subservient to the young king, they accepted Chel-Te'. Everything was coming into place nicely.

The stairway up to the temple on the hill was steep. Poles were fitted to the platform where Bird Jaguar was laying so the back could be pushed up to stay level with the front, as the procession went up the hill. The late king's body wouldn't be handled like a commoner, but respected every step of the way.

Johnson looked on in amazement. In his time it was common

knowledge that there was a burial in front of Temple 33 and over it was the temple's plaza. Who was interned there was not known, but Bird Jaguar was considered a possibility. Temple 33 was built by him in his honor. It was a prime location. From there you could look over the ceremonial center below and the river circling the site forming a peninsula. The view was spectacular.

The high priest waited, watching the procession reach the top of the hill. He wore a white cloth wrapped around his waist hanging down to mid thigh. On his chest was the heavy jade neckpiece, and brilliant green quetzal bird feathers flowed from his headdress. Two young priests stood behind him, one on either side.

An altar had been placed in front of the burial vault and on it lay the body of a jaguar, that would also accompany the king on his journey. The body of the king was placed in front of the altar, his platform resting on benches, just below the level of the altar. The people in the procession gathered in a semicircle to view the ceremony.

The high priest chanted incantations beseeching the gods to accompany the king's spirit through the Place of the Trials to the Place of Comfort.

"The gods," said Little Rabbit as two men wearing masks emerged from the temple, went to each side of the altar and started dancing.

"The gods?" questioned Johnson.

"Yes, Chamer is the skeleton dressed in white and carries the scythe with the blade of bone, and the other is Cum Hau. Both are death gods summoned to accompany the king during his time of trial.

Johnson looked closely. They were men with masks but to the people there they were the gods of death. They had been called because the king deserved to be accompanied by the gods during his journey.

As the high priest officiated, the musicians played, the gods performed a dance, and the people clapped. The spirit of the king was sent off with joy, knowing he would be with his ancestors and would continue to watch over his people and provide them with prosperity for all time to come.

Bird Jaguar was solemnly lowered into the grave accompanied by the two assistants to the high priest. Johnson wished he could look into the chamber and see it. He had excavated many grave sites to recover bones and grave goods hundreds of years after the burial. Most were decayed and in disarray after so long and he had to imagine how it looked when the funeral took place.

The priest waved a god effigy rattle over the jaguar while chanting incantations. The spirit of the jaguar would accompany the king, warding off any spirits that would harm him. All who saw the jaguar with him would know in life he was a king and pay homage to him. Only a king was accompanied by a jaguar in the underworld. The jaguar was lowered into the vault and a silence came over the crowd. The spirit would be moving from the body soon.

Next came the slaves, the king's servants in the next life. Fear showed in their eyes as they shook and held back. Each of the high priest's assistants took one and forced him into the vault. The king's spirit was waiting. Johnson couldn't see what happened next, but the knives they carried when they returned were dripping with blood.

As fitted stones were placed over the vault, the people held their hands over their mouths. The king's spirit started his journey and it might want to take them into the afterlife too.

§

A horn sounded twice. The funeral for Bird Jaguar was over and the coronation of the new king, Chel-Te', was about to begin. In a solemn procession, the high priest moved up to the terrace in front of the temple, turned and looked at the people. Behind him sat a finely carved stone dais waiting for the new king. The death gods had disappeared inside the temple and new gods, gods of life and prosperity, danced on either side of the dais, sanctifying it with their blessings.

Chel-Te' waited at the bottom of the stairs to be summoned by the high priest. Standing there with his face in smug anticipation, he turned his head to face Shield Jaguar as he sneered and laughed. He was to be king, and he wanted his father's brother to know it and feel the loss. He was only a mortal man after all, and he, Chel-Te', was about to be deified as a god.

Beside him, on his left, stood his mother Lady Great Skull, and at his right side, Lord Great Skull, his regent. Three groups stood to witness the event, the high lords of the realm to one side, the high nobles from the five families on the other side, and members of the royal family stood behind him.

Johnson watched as everyone took their places. He knew the temple as number 33, built and dedicated to Chel-Te''s father Bird Jaguar IV. Constructed on rising terraces, it was a long building with a high comb above the roof which made it distinct and the most beautiful building on the site. Sitting on top the hill overlooking the ceremonial plaza it could be seen from the river as the crowning jewel of the city. It was a fit place to dedicate a king.

"Why aren't you part of the coronation?" Johnson whispered to Little Rabbit as she took her place next to him. "Every time something important happiness you play a significant part in it".

"I am a seer, a priestess. I can perform ceremonies honoring the gods. I can listen and sometimes hear the gods talking. But the high priest talks to the gods and they talk back to him. Only he has this power. When he calls, the gods will come to honor Chel-Te' and support him as the king. The gods listen to him. Aj Kin the son god who protects mankind from evil and Kukulan the god of light, love and culture are here dancing and rejoicing for us. It is a great day."

"I thought you didn't want him as king?"

"I don't, but the gods do. Man must follow the will of the gods."

Johnson looked at the men in the masks who were dancing beside the dais and at Little Rabbit and the people in the ceremony. The people appeared in a state of bliss. The gods were in their presence. They had spoken. Chel-Te' was the new king. It was the gods' will for the people and it was to be their destiny.

Johnson looked over at Shield Jaguar. There was no sign of bliss over the presence of the gods from him. Only hate radiated from his face, stone cold hate. He glared at the gods. He glared at the high priest, and when he looked at Lord Great Skull Johnson could see the intensity of his hate magnify. A chill ran up Johnson's back. *This isn't over. But what can be done?* He looked closer at the man. *Yes, this man isn't going to give up.*

The horn sounded again and Chel-Te' climbed the stairs and faced the priest who was holding his hands in the air and chanting. The priest placed a hand on each shoulder and called an incantation in the air above his head imploring the gods to support their new king and bring prosperity on the land. Then he fell to his knees kissing Chel-Te''s feet. Chel-Te' stepped around the man, went to the dais and sat down with his legs crossed, and faced his people. He was now the king.

In the temple, seated right behind Chel-Te', was a life size stone statue of Bird Jaguar IV, the new king's late father. During the last years of his life he had put extensive energy promoting his son to become the next king. The people believed that his spirit now resided in the statue and that through it he saw his son ascend to the throne.

§

Solemnly the people filed up to the seated king and one by one knelt down before him in reverence. Chel-Te' sat there accepting their acts of submission, haughty and without acknowledgement. It was their duty. He wasn't the son of Bird Jaguar any more. He was the king now. He looked over the line of people waiting to pay homage to him. Which one of them would be the first to refer to him as the 'Son of the Great King' again? He was only sixteen, but he was now the king, and he would have any man severely whipped who referred to him as less.

He looked at his uncle, Lord Great Skull. The man looked smug, too smug. His father had designated the great lord as his regent. He didn't like his uncle. He didn't like the way he bossed him around. *The lord acts like he is the king now and I am still a boy.* He resented the attitude. *That won't last long,* he vowed to himself. *I am the king now and the lord is going to know it.*

The line moved slowly, each noble holding his submissive pose, seemingly wanting to be recognized. When Shield Jaguar came before the king, he went down on one knee. Chel-Te' motioned a guard to push him down. As both knees hit the floor, Chel-Te' pointed all the way, and the guard pushed Shield Jaguar's head all the way to the floor and held it there.

"Who is the king?" Chel-Te' asked.

Shield Jaguar gritted his teeth and said nothing.

"Who is the king?" Chel-Te' screeched in his high-pitched voice as his face turned red.

The guard pushed his face harder into the stone floor. "You," Shield Jaguar barely whispered.

Chel-Te' laughed, "Best not forget it or life could get very uncomfortable for you, Uncle."

§

The music played wildly and the dancers gyrated in the flickering light of the bonfires. The intoxicating fermented cocoa corn beverage was brought in buckets. Everyone was drinking and eating from platters of food that was brought by slaves. The young king sat on his bench weaving back and forth heavy with the effect of drink.

A naked young woman was dancing in front of him. With small budding breasts and the suggestion of a mound of black hair between her legs, she was just coming of age as a Maya maiden. Dancing back and forth in front of Chel-te', she wanted to catch his eye hoping to impress him. The daughter of a high-ranking noble, finding the king's favor was a desired situation for her and her family.

Her father sat at another table smiling, hoping the king would take her for the night. At sixteen, the young king needed to release his seed often, and a child from the king, even if it were not publicly acknowledged, would bring prestige to the family. He hoped her mother had counseled her well in the ways of lovemaking.

Shield Jaguar, Smoking Squirrel and Lightning Sky sat at their places, stoically watching the scene. In front of each of them was a large platter of food and a stone cup with chorte in it. None of their food or drink had been touched. Each man sat bolt upright and remained that way as the party became louder and more primal.

Shield Jaguar was required to be at the king's inauguration party, but they couldn't make him participate. His brothers supported him. The people would know he was still Shield Jaguar III, the son of the great Shield Jaguar II, Chel-Te''s grandfather.

"Think she will get him?" Smoking Squirrel asked as they watched the young dancer try to seduce the young king.

"I think he will pass out first," Lightning Sky responded. "See the way he is weaving?"

"The little prick will never get it up," Shield Jaguar stated. "Couldn't use it if he did."

"No, you don't think so?" Johnson responded.

"Nope, too small."

"I think she's a virgin," responded Smoking Squirrel. "Hers probably isn't very big either."

"You left a virgin running about?" Lightning Sky said. "That's unusual."

"His father had little balls and he has a little prick," Shield Jaguar said smugly. "I'll wager she'll still be a virgin in the morning."

"He might surprise you," called Lord Great Skull from another table. He had been watching the three of them all night. Shield Jaguar's defiance stood out. It worried him. It was being noticed by the people and would be discussed throughout the community the next day and there was nothing he could do about it. The man had gall. He had to give that to him, but he was neutralized and that is what counted. Given enough time he would be gone.

"You're sister's whelp?" Shield Jaguar retorted. "He must get the small prick from you."

"You overstep yourself," the great lord snapped.

Shield Jaguar looked at him and grinned without uttering a word. He was getting through.

Little Rabbit came and sat next to Lightning Sky, picked up a pepper off his plate and started to eat it. "You boys having fun?" she asked.

"You're the seer," Smoking Squirrel said. "Is the little king going to get laid tonight?"

"Don't worry Smoking Squirrel, she'll still be a virgin in the morning. He'll pass out first. You'll still get your chance."

Little Rabbit slipped her arm through Lightning Sky's. "Let's leave," she whispered in his ear. " We still have some time."

"Not tonight," Shield Jaguar spat as he looked angrily at her.

"Why?" she shot back, a defiant look on her face.

"Because I need him here tonight."

"Then you have me here tonight too." She gripped Johnson's arm tighter and rested her head on his shoulder. Then she looked defiantly at her brother and sat up and kissed Lightning Sky on the cheek. "And I'm no longer promised to Chan Muwaan either."

Chapter 17

The ride back to the archaeological site in the pickup truck was slow and jarring. Rains had inundated the road and it was worse than before. The shaman navigated around the washed out areas and dipped in and out of the potholes as slowly and evenly as he was able to. Johnson hardly felt the ride. His body was in the present, but his mind was in the past.

How could this have happened? Nothing had changed, everything was the same. History is what it is and the community of archaeologists had interpreted it correctly. How could I have thought differently? But who is this ancient man I am following so desperately—a figment of my imagination, a figure in a dream induced by drugs? Perhaps it's a vision of the past with a real offshoot thread, a quest for power that never materialized. I don't know. I know no more now than when I started. He was tired, frustrated and depressed

"It was all for nothing," he mumbled to Phoebe when she met the truck as it returned to the lodge. She looked quizzically at the shaman.

"He's been like this since he came back," the shaman said.

"What happened?" she asked as she took his arm and walked

back to the lodge with him.

"It was all for nothing," he said again. "Nothing changed."

Johnson looked beseechingly at her. "Phoebe, it must have been a dream, something generated by my imagination. I was so sure Shield Jaguar was going to usurp the throne. I even had the shaman send me back a second time so I could observe it happen."

"And what happened?"

"It didn't happen. Chel-Te' took the throne when his father died, just like the stone records indicate."

"You mean the king died and he just took over?" Phoebe asked. "Then what happened to this guy named Shield Jaguar who you told us would become king?"

"When the king died, he had a coup planned," Johnson responded. "He even made a deal with Chan Muwaan, the prince from Bonampak, to bring warriors to help him."

"And didn't it work?"

"It didn't even start. Lord Great Skull had him arrested as soon as the king died. Chel-Te' was crowned and Shield Jaguar knelt in subservience to him."

"You have a rich imagination Alan," Phoebe replied. "That's quite a drug you took."

"I don't see how I could have made it up, even in my subconscious," he replied.

"What other explanation is there? It all came back to what you know as an archaeologist. Think about it. Nothing in history is any different. History happened just as you knew it would. You just used the drug and your imagination and made up the story about it."

"And I bought it?"

"It looks that way." Phoebe concluded.

§

That evening after dinner Johnson again sat with the students. Dan had told them all he knew about the drug, Johnson's use of it, and the ritual with the shaman. They were interested in hearing of his experiences. Young minds, Johnson surmised, were open to new concepts, not as critical as his colleagues. It was good to have them to confide in.

They wanted to know how the ritual with the shaman was conducted. They agreed they couldn't support the actual travel-back-in-time concept, but they could support a vision. They came to the conclusion that perhaps the vision could be right. *Why not use the results of the vision as a teaching aid? They enjoy it and it made for a baseline, a place to start. I am, after all, first a teacher, and my observations push them to strive for a higher level of thinking as they contemplate the society they are studying.*

Johnson held the discussion to observations on the ancient culture, and did not delve too far into the personal aspects of his experience. His recounting of the funeral and the coronation of the king was met with numerous questions. His descriptions brought life to subjects they had studied about, but were concepts of passage rites instead of a vision of the actual happenings. He described the rituals in intricate detail.

The ball game was a hot topic of the night. Ball courts were found at all the Maya sites. It seemed that everywhere you looked there was a ball court, but no one knew exactly how the game was played. Each site, however small, had one and most sites had a number of them.

"You arrived during a ball game?" Dan asked. "Was it like our ball games?"

"Not really; volleyball would probably be the closest. I didn't see much of it. It ended right after I got there. Two players played center court, and they had to keep the ball in the air without using their hands. They wore yokes around their waists and hit the ball by swiveling their waists. Evidently the game ends when the first team achieves a set number of points."

"What about the hoop in the court?" asked Susan. Did they make it through the hoop, and was anyone sacrificed?"

"They tried for the hoop but when I was there no one made it. I don't know what would happen if someone made it through the hole in the hoop. I'm afraid we still don't know as much about the ball game as we'd like to," Johnson concluded.

"How did you feel going back to the Eighth Century?" asked another student. "Were you afraid of them finding out who you really are?"

"The first times I was scared; in fact I was terrified. But this last time I felt like I was among friends."

"And the warrior and the girl?" asked Dan, a grin on his face. "I want to finally find out about the warrior and the girl. What about them?"

The group's attention picked up.

"On this trip I was a warrior again, but I only accompanied other warriors on a trek through the jungle where the prince, Shield Jaguar III, had a meeting with Prince Chan Muwaan II of Bonampak, a nearby city that was allied with Yaxchilan. It wasn't very exciting this time."

"And the girl," Susan asked. "what of the girl, the one where the family would be mad if they knew about your being together?"

"Yes, I found her again. She is the sister of the prince, Shield Jaguar II, and a priestess in a temple there. We got together again."

"Well?" asked Susan. "What happened?"

Johnson smiled. "A man of honor should never kiss and tell."

"And you're a man of honor?"

"I'd like to think so." His eyes twinkled and he smiled at the memory. He still felt the warmth of her embrace. She was still with him now but he knew in a short time he would miss her and the pain of losing her again would return. He'd try not to let it affect his responsibilities to the students.

They continued to ask questions throughout the evening. It felt good to have the students around and enthused. It boosted his confidence. Johnson replied to their questions in his nondescript manner, careful not to speculate too deeply. He played down the court intrigue on Phoebe's advice. "Just the facts Alan, just the facts," she had told him.

§

Later in the evening Johnson asked Phoebe, "How did they take it?" They were alone walking in the moonlight along the Great Plaza, as he pointed out things of interest he had observed in his trip, and wove stories around them.

"They are still supporting the vision theory. The consensus is that your explanations of what was happening were thin, like you were pretty far from the action instead of being in the middle of it. They liked the graphic descriptions. They said that they made them think they actually saw what you saw, but the interrelationships could be something you imagined."

"So they don't believe me either?" Johnson said with disappointment.

"I think they are giving you the benefit of the doubt. At least they aren't tearing your vision down."

"And you think it is a vision too?"

"I don't know what to think, Alan. It's all so bizarre. One minute I think you actually saw all this, and the next I think your mind imagined it. I'm confused."

§

There was a light fog hanging low to the ground as Johnson walked through the Great Plaza. He couldn't sleep. The howler monkeys were making a terrific racket this morning, long before the sun came up awakening him, and he couldn't go back to sleep. He felt he had to get up and take a walk. Something was pulling at him. The sun was just starting to peek over the tree line across the river. The fog only came up to about his knees. Leaving the palace he could see the pyramids and terraces and temples. They looked like they were floating. Early rays of the emerging sun cast long shadows. The plaza looked like it was going through a rebirth, emerging from the primordial marsh of Xibalba again.

He closed his eyes and he could hear the sounds of the ceremonial center waking for the day: priests chanting early morning greetings to the gods, a woman calling potential customers while selling tortillas, a horn from the hill signaling the king had arisen, and the buzz of people talking.

Then he'd opened his eyes, and it was a cold dead place again. The fog was there and some vestige of temples, but mostly just crumbling ruins. The absence of color was most striking, just bare stones discolored by centuries of exposure to the weather.

He walked along the plaza until he came to Temple 11, where Little Rabbit said her mother lived and where she had fond memories of her father, the Great King. Only the remnants of the foundation were left. Her father had built his temple in front of Temple 11, and between it and his other wife, Lady Xook's temple. There was a small courtyard between the temples that the king and his young wife frequented with her children as a family. Johnson smiled at the thought as he walked around the foundation and let his mind wander.

It had to be a vision, he concluded, but what about Little Rabbit? The feelings were so strong that the pain hurt. His stomach felt like lead, and he walked around in a nauseated daze. How could he feel this way about a woman who lived thirteen hundred years ago, even if she did, which was now doubtful? Thinking about it rationally didn't help his pain. The pain was there and it felt very real.

Johnson walked around looking at everything. At the back of the temple there was a stone patio, a flat space constructed with a view overlooking the river. He laughed under his breath. They had a deck with a water view, choice real estate in the Eighth Century. How often did she sit here and look out over the river, he wondered as he sat on the side of the foundation overlooking the patio and watched the water. It flowed softly by, the fog still hanging along the banks.

Then it caught his eye. Something on the other side of the river was moving, shrouded in the fog, just being touched by the sun's rays. *It's a young woman,* he thought as he strained to see. She was waving. He waved back.

She was wearing a headpiece with green feathers, a priestess's headdress. The wispy fog opened. For a second he could see the white shift and the heavy green jade neckpiece. She wasn't waving; she was motioning for him to come to her.

"Little Rabbit," he cried, "is it you?" Tears welled up in his eyes. He moved forward and looked closer. The young woman continued to motion to him.

"Little Rabbit," he called again as he stumbled down the side of the terrace and ran toward the river. The fog came up and surrounded the woman as Johnson ran toward her. At the river bank he stopped and stared at the fog. "Little Rabbit, Little Rabbit," he called over and over as he strained to see through the fog. A slight breeze came up and swept the fog away. The bank on the opposite side of the river was empty.

§

"Alan, you're delusional," Phoebe responded when Johnson told her about the experience that morning. "I know you have been running around lost in your thoughts for a week now, and

I've left you your space, but this is too much. You have to get hold of yourself."

"Phoebe, it's the same as before, back in the States. Little Rabbit is calling me."

"It was just a drug-induced dream. You have to face that."

"I am facing it. You just don't understand."

"What other choice do you have? None," Phoebe responded.

"Okay Pheb I've come up with an idea. I've designed an experiment to support what I have seen. Let's take the drug together so we both go back in time. We either go to the same place together, two separate minds in the same place, or two separate minds going somewhere different. When we come back we compare notes. If we both remember the same things, there has to be something to what I have said."

"No," said Phoebe immediately. "I won't take the drug."

"Why not? I've taken it and I'm okay."

"That's a matter of opinion. You haven't been the same since the first time, not by a long shot."

"It's the scientist in me that got caught up in it. That won't happen to you. You'll just be an observer. I need you to be an independent observer, to give credit to my claims. If we both see the same thing then they have to believe us."

"Alan, this scares me. It scares the hell out of me."

"I'll be there to help you if you need it."

"You won't know who I am."

"Yes, but you will know me. You'll know I'm Lightning Sky. You only have to find out who he is, and you can give me a high sign. Then I'll know who you are."

"No, I can't Alan. I just can't."

"Don't you have a curiosity about what the past was really like? Phoebe, I am offering you the chance of a lifetime to really see the past, to see what the society was like and what Yaxchilan looked like at the height of its glory."

"Yes, but...."

"No buts, Phoebe. There is very little powder left and I want to share it with you."

§

The young shaman, Jose, was all smiles when he picked them up in the old shaman's truck. He knew Phoebe from the expedition the year prior. The idea of including her appealed to him. He believed they actually went back in time. He assured her that she would be near Alan when they arrived and there would be no problem.

"Are you excited, Miss Phoebe?" the shaman asked.

"That's hardly the way to describe it," she responded.

"To go back and see the old ones, that is a great thing," the shaman said. "The gods must care very much for you."

"I hope so," she replied as she looked beseechingly at Alan.

"It will be okay," he said.

"But what if I can't find you, or go somewhere else."

"Where else is there to go? The gods will send us back together. You know I am Lightning Sky. All you have to do is indicate who you are and I'll watch over you. What could be easier?"

"What do you expect to find?" asked Phoebe. "Your hypothesis of Shield Jaguar becoming king was wrong."

"I don't know. The society will be there, along with a political structure as before, just with different people. Chel-Te' will be the king."

"And Shield Jaguar?"

"That's the big question. What will he be doing? I don't know. He'll very likely have some official function, probably something politically visible but not very important. Lord Great Skull was opposed to letting him live but he seemed to think it was important that the people see Shield Jaguar as subservient to them."

"And what of Little Rabbit?" Phoebe asked.

"What about her?" he said with a grin.

"She can't be real."

"When I'm there she is."

"And what of me?"

"Don't worry, you'll fit in."

§

It was chilly in the cave. Phoebe switched from the sweats to the chills. During the trip in the truck she felt okay. Talking to the young shaman helped calm her, but when they started down the tunnel into the bowels of the earth, fear crept in. *What am I doing here? This is insane. Sure I trust Alan, but this goes way over the line. How could I have gotten myself caught up in this?*

She was about to turn around and run when they came to the chamber with the stream.

"It's getting close," Alan said, his face beaming. He was eager to proceed. "Pheb, you're going to love it."

"Alan, I'm rethinking all of this. I'm not sure this is right."

"You'll be okay. The shaman will take care of everything."

The shaman built the little fire and performed the ceremony as he had done before. She watched as he blew the drug up Alan's nose. The man went absolutely rigid and started to shake like he was having epileptic convulsions. Maybe he was going to die.

"No, I don't want to," she heard herself say. The shaman held her head tightly. "I really don't want to do it," she pleaded. She couldn't move, then he blew hard and she recoiled and everything went blank.

§

The first thing Phoebe saw was the woman standing at the altar chanting. She was a young woman, holding her hands out and chanting to the idol sitting there. Phoebe looked around the small room. The room was illuminated by two torches, one on either side of the altar. Very little light was coming through the door indicating that it was late in the day. The walls were covered in fresco-like paintings of what she took to be gods and underworld monsters. They looked like the ones she had seen in the books of Classical Maya. They were obviously made by a very talented artist. They looked real.

She looked again at the woman facing the altar. She was wearing a long white gown with short sleeves, and had long black hair hanging down her back. Then she looked at herself. She too was wearing a long white gown and had a stone necklace around her neck. It was obvious that a spiritual ritual was being performed by the woman in front of her and she was somehow connected to it. Perhaps she was an assistant of some type in attendance.

The ritual complete, the woman turned around. Phoebe was struck by her exquisite beauty. Her hair tumbled over her shoulders. Her dark brown eyes, complemented by a black tint, sparkled radiantly, and her lips were outlined and lightly painted with something that had a pearlescent shine.

"Come, we can return to the palace," the priestess said. Phoebe stood there dumb. What had the woman said? It was the Maya tongue. She recognized that much but not the words. She had learned a moderate amount of the local Maya dialect to use in dealing with the village people when on an excavation. Most archaeologists did, but she hadn't used the language in over a year and her skills were rusty. She just nodded her head hoping it wouldn't be noticed. The priestess walked past her and out the door.

"Oh my God," Phoebe gasped as she stepped out of the temple door. She stopped and stared. Spread out in front of her was the Great Plaza ringed with beautiful temples with people entering and exiting them. And the pyramids were striking. Many were painted bright red. They were set along a wide plaza corridor. Together they made a symmetric structure, blended together recreating the birthplace of man. Even to an untrained eye it would be obvious this was a ceremonial center.

The mainstay of the Maya culture was their tie to the place of origin, Xibalba; their progenitors the Hero Twins, the ancient gods and the assent of man. They were the people, created and watched over by the gods, and they built and dedicated this site to the gods. Alan had described it to her, but he hadn't even come close. The late afternoon sun rendered long shadows and soft light accenting their beauty. She walked down the steps and stared in awe, first at one temple then at another, each one more fascinating than the one before.

"Come along," said the priestess. "Running Deer, what is the matter with you today?"

"I'm here," Phoebe said as she came to the side of the priestess as they continued their walk up the plaza. They passed Temple 23 and she stared longingly at it. The relief paintings that had survived into her time were faded and worn, just vestiges of their former self, only suggesting their eloquence. Even from a distance she could see the bright decorations sharply in detail.

"Tomorrow we will be dedicating the altar in the new temple at the top of the hill," the priestess said. "You will have to go to the people's market and get some fragrant herbs to burn. Can you do that yet this afternoon?"

Phoebe just stared. *The priestess just said something about a market and asked if can I do something. I wish she would talk slower. Maybe I could pick it up.* She nodded in compliance. It seemed best thing to do. When she and Johnson considered this trip they hadn't considered the language barrier. Johnson speaks the Maya language that survived today in Mexico and Guatemala which is close enough to that so it isn't a problem for him. It is for me. Can I feign laryngitis and keep from talking? It would only be for a couple of days. Maybe I can pull it off. I have to find a way to get rid of this woman so I can wander around the site. There is so much to see and so little time. I have to help Johnson record details and need to memorize as much as I can.

"We need the herbs," the woman said again. "Will you go get them?"

Phoebe pointed to her neck, then grabbed it as if in pain and hoarsely whispered an inaudible, "What?"

The priestess stopped and looked closely at her. She touched Phoebe's neck. A serious look came over her face and she stared intently at Phoebe, looking at her hair, her skin, her ears, her eyes. Her observation roved back and forth then centered on her eyes and she stared into them.

"You're not Running Deer," she said very slowly. Her eyes grew big and she stepped back, "Where is Running Deer?"

Phoebe just stared back at her. *I have been found out.* Her stomach tightened up and she had to gasp for breath. *What will happen now? I understood what was said but how am I to reply? Johnson told me that in this world spirits can enter and take bodies, witches can conjure evil spells and who knows what else. What would this priestess do if she thinks an evil spirit took this woman's body? It probably won't be a very pleasant experience.*

"Running Deer will come back to you soon," Phoebe said very slowly, one word at a time searching for the words.

The priestess stood back; fear clouded her face. She continued to stare and started to tremble. It looked like she wanted to run. Then she held her arm up in the air and screamed "Guards!"

Almost instantly, six warriors surrounded them wondering what was happening, their spears pointed inward.

"She's a witch!" the priestess screamed, pointing at Phoebe as she stepped behind a guard. "She's a witch!" She peered cautiously from behind the guard.

Phoebe stiffened in fear. Fierce men surrounded her, their

spears pointed inches from her body. *Are they going to stab me?* She understood the word witch and it didn't sound good.

"I'm not a witch," Phoebe struggled to say. "I'm not a witch."

Little Rabbit continued looking around the guard and staring at her with a look of horror. *My assistant is gone and in her place is a witch, a bad spirit who could only bring harm to me. I have to do something to neutralize this creature, send it back from where it came before it causes harm, but what?*

"Take her to my mother's temple and tie her to the altar," Little Rabbit ordered. "I will deal with her tonight when the moon rises."

"No," screamed Phoebe, "you can't do this!"

Two warriors grabbed and held her. Another bowed to the priestess, talked to her for a few moments, then reverently backed away from her. They marched in procession, two holding Phoebe between them dragging her along, followed by the one who talked to the priestess. She fought. She wanted to run but they held her tight. Upon reaching the temple they strung a rope to a ring along one wall and tied Phoebe with her hands behind her so she could only sit on the floor and hurriedly left.

"No," Phoebe screamed. "Don't leave me here!" She was more terrified than she had ever been in her life. She struggled against the bindings. It was hopeless. They were unbreakable. She was a prisoner in this little dark room with no hope of rescue. *What is going to happen? Will they kill me? What has Johnson gotten me into? He said he was going to protect me. "Just give me a high sign," he said, "and I'll do the rest." Where the hell is he?* She shivered and looked around the dark chamber and started to cry.

§

The sun was about to go down behind the horizon. Johnson looked around. *Where am I? We aren't in the city center, but probably somewhere close.* He was with a large body of warriors sitting in a wooded section of rocky land overlooking a field of corn. Shield Jaguar and Smoking Squirrel were there too, talking to some men across the way.

As Johnson looked around, trying to get his bearings, a group of warriors entered the makeshift camp. Johnson recognized the leader, Chan Muwaan II. The man had a mean look about him, intense and deadly; one who would strike in a split second no matter the odds against him. Born and bred to be a warrior, destined to be a king, Johnson couldn't envision him in any other capacity.

What is he doing here? He didn't show up in support of Shield Jaguar when the king died. Johnson looked around. *Where am I? Where did the gods send me this time? Maybe it is earlier in time than before. There is a large body of warriors, all armed and painted for war, standing and watching Shield Jaguar. It appears he is their leader. But he has been stripped of the right to lead men. What are they doing here?*

"Are we ready?" Chan Muwaan asked without the formality of a polite greeting as Shield Jaguar stood up to meet him. Johnson felt the tension and obvious hostility. The prince from Bonampak wasn't about to be subservient to Shield Jaguar. He was a prince destined to become a king and Shield Jaguar only a hopeful.

"My Eagle Warriors are ready," said Shield Jaguar curtly meeting the arrogance of the man. "They wait for us near Yaxchilan. Are yours ready too?"

"They are here. They are Eagle Warriors. They are always ready," answered Chan Muwaan

Johnson looked around. *Yes, they are the Eagle Warriors. But they had been taken away from Shield Jaguar. Lord Great Skull commanded them now.*

"Together we will win, and before the sun comes up I will be the king," responded Shield Jaguar.

And then it hit him, the coup. *It was happening, not when the king died, but later; but when, what year is this? It had to be later than when it was originally planned. The question is, how much later?*

"It is a good night for this," Shield Jaguar said.

"The seer cast the sacred bones," Chan Muwaan said, "and foretold there would be a bad omen tonight."

"Bad for Chel-te'. Did he tell you that too?"

"He's not Chel-Te''s seer."

"You scared?" sneered Shield Jaguar.

"I'm scared of nothing," the man spat back, "not even you."

"Good." Shield Jaguar stood tall and looked him defiantly in the eye. "Then you are ready to capture Lord Great Skull tonight."

The man glared back at Shield Jaguar. "Then do I get to sacrifice him too?"

"Not tonight," laughed Shield Jaguar. "I need him for a time and I need him in one piece."

Johnson watched the two men. History indicated that they would both be kings someday. The bond between them as warrior kings would last a lifetime and be recorded in infamy in the battle scene painted in the Bonampak murals, a pictorial record of when they fought together. He looked again at their hostility and lack of trust and concluded they had a long way to go. Would they ever make it or would the record just imply they did?

Shield Jaguar called the men together to give last minute instructions. "Late in the night when the moon goes away we will strike," he opened. "I have garments worn by simple farmers who take their produce to market. They travel the paths late at night to set up their produce before dawn. We will go in ones and twos from village to village disguised like farmers until we get to Yaxchilan and there regroup into war parties.

"When the signal comes, Chan Muwaan's warriors will descend on Lord Great Skull's palace, capture him and subdue his warriors. Kill only as many of his guards as needed to capture him, no more. Tie the remainder up. My party will take Chel-Te"'s palace. Bring Lord Great Skull to me. My warriors will bring the rest of the lords."

§

Phoebe was shaking. It wouldn't stop. The warriors had bound her wrists tightly behind her as they tied her to the altar. She had screamed and tugged and twisted trying to get away. Fear gave her strength as she struggled until one of the men slapped her hard and she stopped, stunned by the stinging pain. He was mad and roughly pulled tighter on the ropes to let her know it.

After they left she struggled to free herself and her wrists were becoming raw. Pain cut into her each time she moved. Phoebe was more scared than she had ever been in her life. It was dark in the little room. She was alone but each time she heard something outside she cowered back against the wall shaking violently, her heart in her throat, terror tightening up her spine. *They are coming for me. They are going to kill me. They are savages and they think I am a witch.*

Outside a full moon started to rise covering the site with a soft glow. Slowly a little light filtered through the door, just enough to give life to the fresco paintings on the walls. Phoebe watched the pictures of the gods and their monsters appear to come to life. In the dim light she could see the ones closest to the door. They appeared to be entering her chamber. As the moon rose higher more light came in. She could see more monsters around the room. They were staring at her, guarding her, witnesses to her demise. Phoebe stared back at them. They were real and they were watching. She shrank back in horror. *My mind is playing tricks on me. They are just paintings of ancient gods, but they are watching me.* She heard noise outside. *Someone is coming. It is time.*

The priestess came through the door followed by three men

carrying spears. They looked fearsome, strong looking men with geometric tattoos on their faces, arms and bodies. All wore simple loincloths and sandals and something on their heads, not a hat but a headdress with an animal skull facing forward. The skulls were all the same, some type of bird skull. One had a bone through his nose and as they opened their mouths she could see their teeth were filed down into various geometric patterns. The effect was shocking. They looked gruesome and terrifying.

Their dark eyes glared at her, radiating hate mingled with fear. She was a witch and they were watchful. She might cast a spell on their spirit animal; best to kill her quickly.

Torches were lit and placed on either side of the altar. The priestess also carried a torch. The torchlight flickered off the walls and the frescos of the gods shimmered. They looked more alive now as they surrounded the group, grotesque observers of what was to happen. They were her judges and she was in a chamber of horrors. Too frightened to scream, she pushed back against the stone wall, hardly daring to breathe as she tried to get away, but it was unyielding.

The priestess stood and looked down at Phoebe for a long time. Moving from side to side she seemed to be studying her, curious, like observing a captured animal, dangerous in the wild but harmless in its cage.

"Who are you?" the priestess said very slowly, braver now with the presence of the three warriors.

"I am from the future," Phoebe said.

"Only a god can come from the future. Are you a god?"

"No," she responded her voice shaking. "I came with another who was to guide me, but I don't know where he is."

"You are a witch," the priestess said sharply, her hand pointing, finger extended, within inches of Phoebe's face. "What have you done with Running Deer?"

"No," Phoebe shouted sharply. She shook as she stared up at

the priestess. "I'm not a witch," she struggled to say. "Running Deer is safe. She will return when I leave."

"And when will that be?"

"I'm not sure. My friend has been here before. He can only stay a day or two."

The priestess lowered herself down on her haunches, eyes level to Phoebe's. She held the torch near her face and looked closer, studying her, like she was looking at something very dangerous.

"Who is your friend?" the priestess asked.

Phoebe hesitated, trying to control her shaking and collect her thoughts. She was in real trouble. Somehow, she realized, she needed to hold out until the drug wore off and she went back to her own time. She had to convince this priestess she was not a witch. Johnson had told her that Little Rabbit thought him a god and accepted the concept of a god in a man's body. Perhaps she could use that.

"My friend is a god," she said with a confidence she didn't feel. "He brought me here with him. He is a powerful god."

The priestess drew back with a shocked look on her face.

"A god, which god?" Without waiting for an answer she rocked forward close to Phoebe's face bringing the torch closer while moving her head from side to side looking from different angles like she was trying to see through her eyes into her spirit. "What are you to the god?" she asked cautiously.

"He is a powerful god from the future. He is stronger than your ancient gods," Phoebe added.

The priestess thought for a minute. "And you are you a god too?"

"No," replied Phoebe, "I am his helper."

"A helper, how do you help a god?" the priestess asked, a questioning look on her face."

"I do his bidding."

"A slave. You are his slave?" the priestess said.

"You could call me a slave," Phoebe said lifted by the thought. A slave was probably better than a witch.

"Who is this god?" It was the crucial question. Phoebe had to take a chance. The priestess was curious now. She had to keep her that way. "His name is Johnson. He is a god of learning and knowledge."

A surprised look came across the face of the priestess. "Jon-soon," she said. Her face took on a blank look as if in thought for a few moments and was suddenly replaced by a large smile. Phoebe watched the transformation as the priestess smiled and absently bit her lower lip in thought. Before Phoebe's eyes, the commanding priestess visibly softened. "Jon-soon is here again?" she asked. Her face glowed and her eyes sparkled and she took a deep breath and held it as she turned and looked out the door. Suddenly she wheeled back with a wild primal look in her eyes. "Where is he?" she shouted.

Phoebe shrunk back again at the intensity. "I don't know for sure, but the god Johnson is near here," Phoebe stuttered.

The priestess squatted lower on her haunches, arms wrapped around her legs lost in thought. She started to shake and a tear rolled down her cheek. She was visibly trying to maintain her composure. "He came back," she sobbed. "I thought he was gone forever."

Phoebe looked at the priestess, amazed at the transformation. The hard exterior of authority had dissolved and in front of her was a very emotional young woman. This had to be Little Rabbit, the woman Johnson was obsessed with.

"You are Little Rabbit," Phoebe said softly. "Johnson has told me many things about you and how he loves you."

"Free her and leave us," the priestess shouted over her shoulder. The guards jumped to obey her.

Phoebe stood up and rubbed her wrists. She intently watched Little Rabbit. *What is going to happen now? I'm not sure if I'm safe yet. Those savages are just outside the door. I can see them.* The one who appeared to be their leader stood where he could see what they were doing. *He looks angry. Given the opportunity he'll kill me in a second.*

"Jon-soon is here again," Little Rabbit repeated as she stared at Phoebe, amazement showing on her face. The smile broadened and then she turned serious. "I must go to him."

"You know where he is?" Phoebe asked.

"I think he will be with my brother and he is in great danger."

"Danger?" Phoebe replied "What type of danger?"

"It is time for my brother Shield Jaguar to claim his birthright and take his father's place as the king. They are going to attack the palace tonight and kill Chel-Te'. There will be fighting and killing. Many will die."

Chapter 18

The flaming arrow arced through the sky, the signal to attack. Obviously it would alert the king's guards. Would they give the cry or investigate first? Shield Jaguar assumed the latter. The guards would come out from their positions in the dark and look at where the arrow came from or went to. In either case they would be in the open. By the time they figured out there was danger it would be too late. Two hundred warriors had to subdue six hundred. The only way was to defeat their leaders quickly and take control.

Before the arrow hit the ground, two hundred men silently rushed the various family palaces. Shield Jaguar led fifty men into the royal palace, the residence of Chel-Te'. When they entered the large outer courtyard, many of the guards were in the open. Shield Jaguar's warriors threw their spears hitting with deadly accuracy. A cry was raised and the warriors grabbed their war clubs and charged.

In the inner courtyard, the king's guards quickly grouped in a formation in front of the door to Chel-Te''s palace, ready to face the charging warriors. Shield Jaguar smiled when he saw them. He'd spare them except they were under oath to defend the king to their death, an oath they would die for tonight. The Eagle Warriors, battle hardened veterans, charged the defense position. The king's warriors fought back bravely to the last man.

Chel-Te' watched in horror from the door in front of his chambers as his protection evaporated. He could see Shield Jaguar well guarded behind his men.   Anger over road his fear and he picked up a war club and held it forward in defense as the warriors surrounded him. A warrior slammed it out of his hands and the young king stood defenseless. His anger, suddenly gone, turned to fear as he looked at the men. He recognized them. They were supposed to be his warriors.

"Stop," he screamed. "I command you take Shield Jaguar prisoner. He is not your king, I am."

The men surrounding him smiled at the attempt, a couple laughed. "Not for long," he heard one say. "There will be no mercy from us."

Shield Jaguar stood in the courtyard, in front of the steps to the king's chamber. "Bring him here," he commanded as the men grabbed Chel-Te' and dragged him forward.

"You fornicator, you don't have the right!" screamed Chel-Te'.

"No?" spat Shield Jaguar, "tell them that." He pointed to his men. "They give me the right."

"I am the son of the great Bird Jaguar and was dedicated as heir to the throne by him and sanctioned by the gods!" screamed Chel-Te'.

"And I am Shield Jaguar III, son of the great king Shield Jaguar II. I claim my birthright tonight and the gods support me!" shouted Shield Jaguar into the air as he plunged an obsidian dagger into the heart of Chel-Te', letting him fall at his feet.

Four warriors carried the stone dais from the king's chamber onto the veranda overlooking the three steps leading down to the courtyard. Shield Jaguar climbed the stairs, sat down on the dais, crossed his legs and looked out over the courtyard. He was now the seventeenth successive king of Yoaat B'alam I's dynasty.

§

"Bring in the lords," commanded Shield Jaguar in a booming voice. Chel-Te''s body was laying prone at the bottom of the stairs in front of him. "But hold Lord Great Skull back."

Lightning Sky and Smoking Squirrel stood to either side of him, a couple of steps back. The Eagle Warriors were standing in a ring around the outside edges of the courtyard backs to the raised veranda and buildings. Torches had been placed every few feet around the perimeter.

"Kneel down," Shield Jaguar commanded the lords after they were herded in front of him, "or join him." He pointed contemptuously at the body of Chel-Te'. "I am the king now. I claim my birthright as the son of Shield Jaguar the Great."

"That is up to the Council of Lords," one of the men, the head of one of the five noble families said. "They make the decision on who is king."

Shield Jaguar motioned with his hand to come forward. Two of the Eagle Warriors grabbed the man and dragged him in front of the new king. His eyes were full of fear.

"Kill him," he said to a guard who drew a knife and slit the lord's throat. He fell next to Chel-Te'.

"Does any other of my esteemed lords want to continue the discussion?"

The men stood mute. Fear permeated the group.

"Then the Council of Lords approves," Shield Jaguar said smugly.

The men continued to stand mute.

"Now kneel," he commanded the group of lords. They all knelt except one lower-stationed noble, a young man known for his arrogance.

"And you?" Shield Jaguar asked.

"When you have been made king in accordance with our ways, and have been sanctioned by the gods in ceremony with the lords in attendance, I will kneel to you," the man replied.

Shield Jaguar motioned again to bring him forward. The man was grabbed and dragged in front of him.

"You can't do this," he screamed realizing his error. "I'll kneel, I'll kneel."

"Kill him," Shield Jaguar commanded a warrior. The warrior slit the man's throat and dropped the body beside the other two.

The rest of the lords were kneeling.

"I am the king!" he shouted. "I have the divine right. Never question me again. The penalty is death."

Shield Jaguar looked across to the other side of the courtyard's veranda where Lord Great Skull was being held.

"Bring in lord Great Skull," Shield Jaguar commanded.

The great lord was brought in escorted by four of Chan Muwaan's warriors with Chan Muwaan following. They stopped, leaving Lord Great Skull standing in front of the three bodies. Shield Jaguar sat on the raised dais above. The great lord glared at him. Death was near and he'd show him how a man should die.

"These men questioned my authority," Shield Jaguar said softly, pointing to the three men on the ground. "Do you question my authority?"

Lord Great Skull stared at Shield Jaguar, stood tall, and said. "I have served your brother and his son faithfully as their counselor and regent. Do you want me to renounce them?"

"Not at all," Shield Jaguar looked hard at the man, his long time rival. "This is between you and me. Do you question my authority?"

Lord Great Skull stole his eyes away from Shield Jaguar's intense gaze and looked around. Shield Jaguar's warriors were firmly in place. Chan Muwaan's warriors had disabled his men, and those who weren't killed were now under guard. He had no support left.

"Your authority appears to be unquestionable at the present time," the great lord spat.

"Do you question my authority, now or in the future?" Shield Jaguar growled.

Lord Great Skull looked around again. Three high-ranking men were dead at his feet. He could easily join them. Behind him knelt the remainder of the lords of Yaxchilan in subservience.

"No, you have absolute authority, now and in the future," he answered.

"Kneel to me," Shield Jaguar commanded as he pointed at the ground.

Slowly the great lord knelt, bowing his head.

Shield Jaguar looked around. "All appears to be well in my kingdom," he mused sitting a little taller. "Yes, all appears to be well. Life will go on."

"And my family," Lord Great Skull asked as he looked up expecting to be sentenced to die. "What will become of my sister, Lady Great Skull?"

"Swear allegiance to me and you will be my chief counselor," Shield Jaguar said softly.

"Chief counselor?" Lord Great Skull gasped in surprise.

"You would keep me as chief counselor after all I have done against you?"

"You only challenged a prince, an arrogant young man, but you have served your kings well. I am king now and I need to be well served. I need a strong, experienced leader at my right hand, helping me. You are a strong warrior with experience. I will make you my counselor."

"And my warriors, what is to happen to them?"

"Ha," replied Shield Jaguar with a laugh. "I think for a little while you would better serve me without them. Lightning Sky and Smoking Squirrel will take command of all the warriors of

Yaxchilan. They will be my two captains. They will take care of the warriors for you."

Lord Great Skull Zero looked sullen, defeated. His family would never rise to prominence now.

"But," continued Shield Jaguar, "you will be my general. There will be many wars. You will become known as a great general. I command you to teach my captains well. Someday they will need to be great generals."

"And my sister," he asked of Chel-Te"'s mother, the former queen of the king, Bird Jaguar.

"Take her home to your palace and keep her there inside the walls. She can come out for official functions and will fill no capacity beyond that which is necessary."

"Come, take your place," Shield Jaguar said as he held his palm out to a spot to the right of his dais. Lord Great Skull climbed the stairs, bowed again to the king and took his place sitting on the floor next to the dais.

§

Phoebe and Little Rabbit left the temple and followed the Great Plaza along the walkway between the rows of temples and pyramids.

"They are beautiful," Phoebe said slowly as she looked at the structures. A few more of the Maya words were returning for her use. She wanted to look everywhere at once. Everything was exquisite. Her concept of a pyramid was an occasional bare block structure with a little box-type temple on top. The temple complexes she was looking at here brought symmetry, color and meaning to their theology. She could feel the function in them.

"You haven't seen them in the future?" Little Rabbit asked.

"Most of them have been lost. The Maya left them and the jungle reclaimed them," Phoebe replied. "Men are trying to put them back together but it is a slow process."

"And you came here to see them?" Little Rabbit asked.

"Yes, so I can help."

They continued to walk. Several guards came up beside them. "I'm not a witch, you know," Phoebe cautiously said one of them.

"I know; you are a sister to Princess Little Rabbit," the warrior answered with a slight bow.

"They are my protectors," Little Rabbit said of the guards. "My brother insists on it. Each has vowed to protect me to his death."

"Wow," claimed Phoebe.

"And you also. I have commanded they will do the same for you. One or two of them will always be near but you probably won't see them. It is only when there is danger like tonight that they will stay beside you."

At the middle of the plaza walkway, the leader of the guards stopped them and announced they should wait here.

"We must continue," Little Rabbit commanded.

"We will wait here," the leader of the guards replied.

"Take me to the palace," she commanded louder.

"No, it is too dangerous," he said firmly.

"I am a royal princess; I command it," she spat at him, determination on her face and a note of anger in her voice.

The man paled and held his ground. "Your brother instructed me to keep you safe tonight. That is what I am doing," the warrior said firmly.

"I'll have you whipped for this insolence, a hundred lashes." she threatened. The guard paled further.

"If you command it Princess," the man replied, determination holding, "but my duty is to keep you safe and it will not be safe on top of that hill tonight, not for a while yet."

"You have six men. That is enough to protect me," she retorted.

"Shield Jaguar does not want you to be taken as a hostage," he replied sternly. "We will wait until this is over and then we will go up the steps."

Little Rabbit stood there fuming. Suddenly, they saw the burning arrow arc through the sky. As they stared up at the flaming arrow, warriors who had followed at a respectable distance formed in a tight circle around them.

"It's started," Little Rabbit said to no one in particular as she stared in the direction the arrow landed. "The attack has started." They stood there watching and listening. The night was quiet. Nothing was heard. Little Rabbit motioned the leader of the guards to come forward again.

"Why is it so quiet?" she asked.

"The surprise must be working," he said. "They should be inside the palace by now."

Then they heard the noise. Men were shouting, women were screaming. Pandemonium reigned. They waited and listened as it got louder.

"What is happening?" Phoebe asked.

"They are attacking the palace," Little Rabbit answered.

"Is this when Shield Jaguar becomes king?" Phoebe asked.

Little Rabbit looked at her. "You know he becomes king?" she asked.

"Yes, Johnson told me he would become king. He will become a great king."

A few moments later the noise died down just individuals were heard shouting. The leader of the warriors called one of the men forward and spoke to him for a moment. The man turned and ran toward the stairs going up the hill to the palace. Soon he was out of sight. They waited. It got quiet.

"We can surely go now," Little Rabbit said. "It has to be over."

"We wait," the warrior stated.

"Why?"

"It's best to know which side won first."

The man returned and told them Shield Jaguar was victorious and his warriors were securing the area. It would be safe in a little while, perhaps by morning.

"We go now," Little Rabbit said as she grabbed Phoebe's hand and headed off in the direction of the stairs. "Come along and do your duty," she called to the startled warrior.

"But Princesses...," he replied.

She stood tall and glared at him. "I will be there to witness my brother's ascension," she stated, "with or without your protection."

On the way up to the palace they were challenged. The leader and another of her guards moved in front the women. Three of Chan Muwaan's warriors had strayed from their posts and called to the priestess's group to halt.

"Move aside," commanded Little Rabbit's lead guard. "Let the king's sister through."

"I don't know her," spat the spokesman for the three challengers. You are staying right here until I say..." and a spear went through his chest, followed quickly by spears into the chests of the two that were with him. As they fell the warriors pulled out their spears and the group proceeded past them.

Phoebe was horrified. She had never seen anyone killed before. She gagged and wanted to throw up. It was so fast, so violent; it was terrifying. Woodenly, she walked forward in a fog of disbelief, looking back from time to time. She kept to Little Rabbit's side following the two guards now in front. She glanced over at Little Rabbit who claimed smugly, "They know who I am now, don't they?"

When they arrived at the palace courtyard, the guards ordered warriors aside and made room for the women, giving them a place to be able to see clearly.

"That must be Shield Jaguar," Phoebe said as she looked at the scene. "But who is on the ground in front of him?"

"Chel-Te'" said Little Rabbit.

Two more men were brought before him and killed. Phoebe

was still horrified. This couldn't be happening. The books and all her training hadn't prepared her for this. They just taught that there were kings, and wars, and sometimes sacrifices were made to honor their gods.

As she stood there in shock, she heard the king call, "Bring Lord Great Skull forward." She stared at the scene. Her horror was slowly replaced by fascination. She knew the characters. She had read about them, deciphered the stone records of them, speculated about their influence over their society's direction, and now they were in front of her, alive and touchable.

A scene in history was unfolding before her eyes. Johnson was right. There had been a coup. He had claimed that Chel-Te' and Shield Jaguar had both ruled, but Shield Jaguar prevailed and history gave credit to the wrong man.

She watched in fascination as Lord Great Skull held his head high and approached the new king. She knew this man, at least academically.

"Here's number four," said Little Rabbit referring to an addition to the pile of bodies at Shield Jaguar's feet. Little Rabbit stared in amazement when Shield Jaguar retained Lord Great Skull as chief counselor.

"What is he doing?" she exclaimed. "The man hates him and will only wait for a chance to kill him."

"He must have his reasons," Phoebe answered.

"No reason is good enough to keep that man. He should be killed like the others, right now, and be done with it. He's a conniving fox. You never know what he is up to."

Phoebe looked over at Little Rabbit. The princess's face was filled with hate. There was more to the woman than Johnson was seeing. She had a stake in Shield Jaguar's reign. How was she going to benefit?

The lords were moved to the edge of the courtyard where they could view the process. Shield Jaguar called for all the captains and second commanders of the warriors to be brought before him. Smoking Squirrel and Lightening Sky each took a group of twenty warriors and were sent to the palaces to find and bring them back.

"We have to stay close to Shield Jaguar," Little Rabbit whispered as the warrior leadership was sent for. "Until he is fully seated and in control, there may be someone who would capture me to try in some way to influence Shield Jaguar. What they might not know is that he would let them kill me before he would yield to anything, then he would find my captors and kill them and all their families."

Within a few minutes they watched a group of warriors, hands bound behind them being led into the courtyard.

"Is this all of them?" the king asked.

"There are still three of them missing," Smoking Squirrel answered. "We searched the rooms and they weren't there. They must have run." Shield Jaguar glared. He hated cowardice in any form. It was unforgivable.

"Send a group of forty warriors with Red Turtle," he shouted for everyone to hear. "Find them and bring them back and tie them to stakes in front of the palaces they were supposed to guard. Gather their children, even if they are grown men, to watch, but kill their male offspring before you kill the cowards so they can see the dishonor they have brought to their families. If they own land or property, take it and give it to the head of the family for his decision on who shall have it. Send the wives and daughters of these cowards away to outlying villages where the Sajals will decide their fate. Perhaps they can service the warriors.

"Let the executed men stay tied to the stakes in front of their palaces and rot for the period of a moon before you take them down, then throw them in the river," Shield Jaguar commanded. "Let them die a coward's death and be refused the afterlife, but place their sons properly in The Place of the Dead. They may not be allowed to live in this world, but I would not restrict them from the next. Remember my warriors," Shield Jaguar shouted loudly, "death without honor is the fate of a soldier who doesn't do his duty."

"What is happening?" Phoebe asked Little Rabbit as she watched the two men killed.

"My brother is claiming his birthright. He is the king and a god now and has to demonstrate it to the people. They must learn to fear his wrath."

Little Rabbit laughed and continued, "the best part is he won over Lord Great Skull. He thought my brother was not a worthy adversary. They don't like each other. I don't know why my brother kept him. Shield Jaguar always needled him about his opinions. He'd never show the great lord the respect demanded of his position and always told him that one day he would understand the difference between a prince and a counselor. I guess today is that day."

Shield Jaguar held up his hand and called to the priestesses to come to him.

"Follow me," Little Rabbit whispered to Phoebe. "When I kneel down next to the dais, kneel beside me. We represent the gods that support the king. The people must see us with him. I am the chief priestess of Yaxchilan now, and I am the spokesperson for the gods. You are with me and we are doing our duty."

When they walked around the veranda, the warriors stepped aside letting them pass. As Phoebe passed behind the dais to take her place, she looked at both the men standing there. One was Lightning Sky, but which one?

Shield Jaguar called Chan Muwaan forward. Phoebe saw a man strut toward them, his barrel chest puffed out. He was splattered with blood. There was a grin on his face which was half covered in a blue paint and the other half in white. An air of defiance radiated from him implying he didn't consider himself to be subordinate to the king. Who was he? The name was familiar.

"Prince Chan Muwaan," the king, Shield Jaguar, said, "You are an ally of Yaxchilan and a friend to me. In honor of our relationship I command that when you are made king of Bonampak, my sister Little Rabbit, will marry you, bonding our great cities and we will face our enemies as one."

Phoebe looked over at Little Rabbit noting the triumphant look on her face. That was it. She was betrothed to the heir to the throne of Bonampak and she was destined to become a queen.

Chapter 19

Word of the coup traveled through the land like a wildfire. Shield Jaguar had seized the throne and proclaimed himself king. The people in the noble palaces were rounded up by Shield Jaguar's Eagle Warriors and herded into their courtyards. Women held their children protectively close, men were trying to reason with their guards and find out what was happening. Everyone was talking at once. The lords of the noble families were separated and taken away. "Shield Jaguar is the king now," their guards told them.

Fear took control. Tonight people would die. He would kill those who had opposed him in the past, they said. Who would it be? Some of their husbands or fathers were obviously on his list and would be dead before morning. Will he kill them all? Fear turned to terror as the people stared back at their captors. In some places the people knew their captors and in others they were strangers. The warriors were on orders not to say a word to anyone. It caused even more fear.

Yaxchilan's captured warriors lay on the ground, face down in groups in relation to the families they were attached to. No talking was allowed. In every group two or three protested and refused to be silent. They were grabbed and brought in front of the leader of their guards and killed. No second chances were given. The captured nobles shook in fear, compliant in the knowledge they could be next.

§

The sun peeked over the trees. A new day began and Shield Jaguar was now the king. In the community of the noble families anger started to mingle with the fear. He had stripped the lords of their power, the same power they had used to keep the king, Bird Jaguar, from ascending to the throne for ten years.

The lords didn't like it. The more they thought about it the less they liked it. Before, they had to put up with Bird Jaguar, and here was his brother who claimed to be the king. He had the same tainted blood that the old king had. Many thought that the Xook family should supply the king, the same as they did before Bird Jaguar ascended.

Two high-ranking lords suggested that they do something about it. They said he had to be removed. The true royal bloodline back to the beginning was with the Xook family. It passed from generation to generation through the father's line as the blood of the kings. The line was broken with the great king Shield Jaguar II. His mother was from the Xook family, but not his father. At that time there were no male heirs to the royal family. She bore the royal blood as did her brothers, and now their descendents.

A member of the Xook family should be the king. Hadn't Bird Jaguar stolen it from them? The loins of Shield Jaguar II did not carry royal blood from his male line; neither did Bird Jaguar IV's or Shield Jaguar III's.

They had to find a way to remove him. If they could convince the warriors that they were the political leaders responsible for maintaining the connection to the First Father, it could be done. The warriors belonged to the families, didn't they? They were provided as a service to the king. Their loyalty must lay with the families. That had always been their base of power. It was only going to be some time before Shield Jaguar freed them and then they could set things straight. The two who were the most vociferous never noticed one of the Eagle Warriors listening to them.

Once again, in the early morning, the lords were brought before the new king. They stood there shaking, not knowing what he would do. The bodies still lay in the courtyard in front of his dais.

"I am told that you held a council meeting," Shield Jaguar opened, as he sat cross-legged on his dais looking down at them, "and discussed how you wanted it again to be like it was when you could tell the king what you wanted him to do, and expected it to happen."

Shield Jaguar waited for a response. The lords stood mute. "My half brother gave you too much control, and Chel-Te' was an idiot. It is time to change that."

"We were only discussing the change in leadership and how we might be of assistance," one of the instigators said.

"Come forward and tell me about it."

The man came forward and stood before king. "It was only a discussion," the man feebly replied as he looked down at the bodies in front of him.

"Why don't I feel so assured?" Shield Jaguar replied staring the man down. "And you," he pointed to another lord. "What have you to say about this discussion? Come forward and tell me how you want to be of assistance."

The man stumbled forward, knowing he and the others were being singled out for their treason. He looked down at the bodies and choked up.

"It was only a discussion between the lords," he stuttered. "We all talked about it, all of the lords did."

Shield Jaguar sat upright. "Let it be known," he said, "that I am a direct descendant of the First Father, heir of the dignified kings before me, and am deified by the gods. My position is not to be questioned either before me or behind my back. I, and I alone, decide the direction of our city and the people within. Hereafter, there will no longer be a Council of Lords. Your advice will be solicited if needed and as I see fit. Any talk of questioning my authority will be met with harshly."

He motioned with his finger to two warriors. The warriors came behind the lords, reached around, slit their throats and dumped the bodies on those laying at the king's feet.

"Now my Lords, any talk of removing me from my throne will be treason and dealt with as such. The next time, the perpetrator and his first born man child will be killed. This god is a vengeful god. He will let no man question him."

§

Runners were sent throughout the land. The lords who governed the local communities surrounding the city were summoned and brought before the king. Each in turn acknowledged his new king and pledged his allegiance to him. They had been informed about the pile of bodies stacked up in front of the king and the actions that got them there. They came before the king, shaking with fear. Were they to be next? Allegiance was quickly given without question as the king demanded.

"Come Running Deer," Little Rabbit said to Phoebe as she stood up next to Shield Jaguar. They had been kneeling next to the dais since just before dawn. The sun was almost midway into the sky. She put her hand on Shield Jaguar's shoulder and gave it a squeeze as she smiled broadly at him. "My brother no longer needs our assistance here. We will go to the temple and thank the gods for their support."

Phoebe rose shakily to her feet. Her mind felt numb. In a state of shock, she had watched the transformation of power play out. It all seemed unreal but she had watched it happen. She couldn't keep her eyes off the bodies stacked up before her. Blindly, she followed Little Rabbit out of the palace compound.

As they left, the warrior guards closed around them. The danger was not over yet. Looking at them, Phoebe felt safe for the first time since she arrived. They were sworn to protect her. Outside they passed the pile of bodies of the palace guards that had defended Chel-Te' and the other palaces.

"They are being prepared for burial this afternoon," Little Rabbit said. "There will be no mourning period. The ascension of my brother comes first. Tonight, ceremonies will be held in Shield Jaguar's honor. The king will not wait. Life goes on."

In the temple, Phoebe watched Little Rabbit perform the ritual thanking the gods. She tried to memorize it as she stood in attendance. Little Rabbit knelt before the altar, hands raised in honor. From memory she chanted the ancient words Phoebe couldn't understand. When Little Rabbit wanted anything for the ritual she would point to it and Phoebe would fetch and give it to her, then back away and stand at the side of the room.

"The gods are satisfied," she exclaimed when she was finished. "They approve of my brother as king. It is his birthright."

They left the temple and Little Rabbit motioned Phoebe to sit with her on the top step of the pyramid the temple was on. She was an intelligent and curious woman who believed a spirit could take a person's body for a time. She understood that Phoebe and Johnson came from another time, but from where was a mystery. Johnson was a god. She couldn't ask him about where he was from. Gods weren't to be questioned. It was enough to have a god love her and she love him back. Her duty was to give him pleasure and she was blessed among woman. It filled her with ecstasy. But this woman was a mere slave. And wasn't she the sister of a god now? She could command this slave as she wished, and she wanted to know more about Johnson.

"Why have you come here?" Little Rabbit asked.

"I came with the god Johnson to help him."

"Help him. How do you help him? Slaves only do the bidding of their masters."

"Johnson is a god of knowledge and learning. He is the patron of the scribes and students, counselor to kings. He came here to observe your world, learn your customs, and bring the knowledge back to teach our scholars." Phoebe laughed. "He didn't expect to find you here."

"Our time together is limited," Little Rabbit said as she sadly stared down the stairs.

"I feel your sadness," Phoebe replied. "He too is pained by this. He loves you too much."

"He does?" Little Rabbit smiled broadly. "My heart is light with happiness when I feel his love, but soon I will be the wife of Chan Muwaan II. He is a vengeful man. He loves me too, and would kill any man who approaches me. God or not, Johnson could die just by looking lustfully at me."

The two women talked about love, life, and the pleasure and pain of it until the sun was well past the high point of its journey. Phoebe learned about the elevated position and corresponding obligations Little Rabbit had as the sister to the king. Rank brought privilege and privilege brought arrogance. This woman was chosen by the gods just like her brother. Her word was beyond question now. It was easy to read her body language. Even a hint of the mildest slight brought a response. Phoebe remembered the reaction Little Rabbit had when the guards killed those men last night. They were inconsequential, dust beneath her feet.

When Little Rabbit learned that Johnson commanded Phoebe to learn all she could about the site she became her tour guide. They went to every temple, pyramid and structure in the ceremonial center. Little Rabbit recited the entire history and function of each. At the end of the day Phoebe was overwhelmed with the abundance of information she had gathered.

§

Horns sounded, and the king came out of his palace dressed in his finest royal costume with an abundance of jade jewelry, coverings of leopard skin, and an immense headdress with a feathered crown running from side to side. He stared over the group assembled before him. They were scared and this pleased him. Many of their class had been killed, and no one knew who would be next. The entire perimeter of the courtyard was ringed with Eagle Warriors lest someone seek revenge.

Shield Jaguar came down and took his place at the head of the center table. Chan Muwaan sat to his right with Little Rabbit next to him. Smoking Squirrel, Lightning Sky and Running Deer sat to his left. Solemnly he surveyed the participants: ranking lords and wives of the head families, and commanding lords of the land. They were begrudgingly there but were resigned to their fate. Shield Jaguar was king now, and a god, and they were his subjects. It was accepted as the will of the gods and life would go on.

Phoebe grinned. She knew who Johnson was now. He was sitting right next to her. She looked at him and suppressed a laugh. He looked funny in his ceremonial costume even if he was someone else. He must be wondering where she was. With all of the violence, had she been harmed? She was sure he was concerned. He kept looking around like he was trying to find something. She nudged him lightly with an elbow. When he looked down, she winked quickly hoping not to be noticed. He smiled back with relief.

"We did it, my friend," claimed Chan Muwaan II to Shield Jaguar. "We made you a king."

"Are you my friend now?" asked the king. "Yesterday you

weren't sure you wanted to be my friend."

"Yesterday you weren't a king."

"I think it has more to do with me giving you my sister," Shield Jaguar responded.

Johnson looked over at Chan Mawaan with hate for the man in his heart. *Little Rabbit, a political pawn to be given away. I despise the thought. She loves me. I should have her.* He glared at Chan Muwaan. The man looked smugly back at him. He knew, Johnson realized. He knew there was something between him and Little Rabbit.

Chan Muwaan sat with the arrogance of a victor. Little Rabbit sat demurely, watching closely. She realized the gravity of the situation.

"When I am king and she is my wife," said Chan Muwaan staring straight at Lightning Sky, "she will provide me lots of sons, like a good queen should."

Johnson paled. He wanted to reach across the table and kill the man. Rage built in him heightened by the warrior instinct. A moment and reason held him back. He set his face and gripped his hands at his sides and willed himself to remain at his place. An attack would be met with a spear from an Eagle Warrior.

"You seem tense tonight," said Chan Muwaan, pushing. "I suppose it's all of the excitement. Did you manage to kill anybody?"

It was an obvious slight.

"Friends are hard to kill when it is not necessary. Then they are no longer friends," Lightning Sky replied.

"Anyone is easy to kill," retorted Chan Muwaan. "Just stick your spear in them. You can always find another friend. "Right, Little Rabbit?" he asked as he looked at her.

"Yes my Lord," she said as she smiled at him. "It is easy for a great warrior like you to kill his enemies. Men should fear you and quake in your presence like they do for my brother."

As the night wore on, Phoebe became engrossed in the pageantry of dances and singing. Johnson noted that she paired off with Smoking Squirrel, plying him with chorte, the intoxicating drink. With a slurred voice he was happily describing everything to her in detail, much to her fascination.

How much will she remember? Johnson thought to himself. She was matching him drink for drink. He noticed as the night continued that she appeared to be more fascinated with the man than the pageantry. *Rather unprofessional*, he thought. He filled his cup again with the fermented beverage.

Johnson was feeling numb. There was a dull pain digging at his soul. He was angry and the drink didn't help. He tried to ignore her but he kept looking over at Little Rabbit who was fawning over Chan Muwaan, showering him with praise. The man was intoxicated and brash, extolling his virtues as a man and a warrior to all who would hear. Lightning Sky's anger increased as he sat listening. The obnoxious braggart deserved to die, and he wanted to be the one to kill him.

He had to get away or he'd do it. He knew he would try and the guards would kill him. But he might accomplish it and spare her from this arrogant monkey penis. She seemed to read his thoughts and glared at him with a back-and-forth shake of her head. He was stunned. She wanted this man. He was a fool. Shaking at the thought, Johnson got up and quietly left. He walked around the palaces and through the center as he tried to make sense of the turn of events with Little Rabbit. He thought she loved him but her eyes were only for Chan Muwaan.

As he passed the groups of Eagle Warriors positioned throughout the area, he was recognized as Lightning Sky, one of Shield Jaguar's captains, and was hailed by each guard unit. The groups of Eagle Warriors were staggered where they could see each other. If one unit was attacked, the cry would be made down the line like a row of dominos falling against each other. Shield

Jaguar was taking no chances.

Through his pain came comfort in the warriors' acknowledgement. He had position and power like he never imagined. That at least felt good, but soon he would be only a professor again. Life would be slow, dull, and without much meaning. Here he was alive. He could feel the blood running through his veins. In his world he was just another man who was pacing time until he died. How sad.

§

Little Rabbit came to him late in the night, slipping under his covers holding herself close, making no sound, frightened she would awaken him. He was leaving again. She knew it. Maybe he would never come back. She was betrothed now to Chan Muwaan, the Prince of Bonampak and if she was caught here she would be killed. He brother would order it. She had her duty. She lay there crying softly. Why couldn't she always be with him? The gods must hate her.

He stirred, feeling her nearness, and still asleep wrapped his arms around her, and her heart soared. She was in the womb again, warm and comfortable, the only place in the world she wanted to be. Nothing mattered except laying there where her soul belonged, bound to the soul of this man whom she loved. He stirred again and she pressed herself closer. She needed to be near, to be a part of him, one soul merging with the other. It was her place, her destiny. Hadn't the gods promised that one day they would be together forever? Why couldn't it be today? She had her duty and she would honor it. She would marry another. But the gods promised. They had to keep their promise, she told herself with all the desire she could muster, to make it happen.

"Little Rabbit, you came," he said as he awakened.

"Quiet my love. It is dangerous. If we are caught we will both be killed."

"Killed?" he asked.

"I am betrothed," she replied, "given to another man by my brother. My virtue is a matter of honor now. A silly maid can get away with anything; no one is hurt. But the one promised to a king would dishonor him if caught with another man."

"So we shouldn't be together," he mumbled. The affair took on new meaning now.

"I would die for just another night with you. Hold me my love, hold me close. I need to be near you. You will leave again soon and my heart will die, and once again I must endure the pain of having to live without you."

"You have Chan Muwaan," Johnson said angrily. "He will take care of you."

"I have my duty," she cried in anguish. "I must marry him. My brother decreed it."

"I saw you with him. You looked pretty happy about it."

"Happy to be a queen, yes. It is my rank and privilege. It is also my duty. He is a vain man, and he is in love with me. He will treat me right, but I have to treat him right too. You are my love, only you, but he will be my husband. A husband has his rights and I must obey him."

"And my rights?" Johnson asked. "What are my rights?"

"There is still time. I am not married yet. I won't marry Chan Muwaan until he becomes the king. Then I will have no choice. But until then we can be still be together. It will be dangerous, and we must be very careful, but we still have time."

"It makes no difference. The drug is almost gone. I can only make one or two more trips back here. When the powder is finished, you will be too," he replied.

"But there may be a way," she cried. She pulled herself closer to him, as fear generated a tremor within her.

"Why are you trembling, little one?" he asked. She felt comfortable in his arms as he quietly held her close, but something was wrong. She was afraid to tell him. It might make him mad.

"The gods have given us a present," she said meekly.

"They have?"

"You can stay here with me longer," she said as she drew back and looked at his face looking for a reaction.

"What?" Johnson asked. "I can stay here you say, how?"

"There is a potion. If you take it you will not leave me like you do. You can stay longer." She put her head on his chest and held him tightly. He felt the tremors going through her. It sounded too good, but something wasn't right here. She was scared and it had to do with this potion.

"Something is wrong," he said. "What aren't you telling me?"

"Broken Monkey has it," she replied.

"Satan's sage," he spat. "It comes from him?"

"Who is Satan?" she asked.

"In my time that is the name they give to the God Mar, your god of evil, Broken Monkey's buddy." He pulled back so he could see her face. "How did he come by this potion? How did he even know my need for one?"

"He sees everything. The spirits have eyes. He talks to them, and he knows things, private things about people he shouldn't know."

"And he told you that he has this potion?" Johnson looked at her closely. He had been told that Broken Monkey never talked to man, only the dwarf did.

"I was summoned to his cave," she said. "The dwarf told me he knew you were a god and wanted to stay here. He said he could make it happen and that if you take a potion he has, our time together will be longer."

"How much longer would I stay?" Johnson asked as he became intrigued with the prospect.

"He said it had to be taken on the night of a new moon and you could stay here forever. You would never go back to your world."

Johnson felt a little grin. Then he broke into a big smile. *It's possible,* he thought, *It's possible.* He pulled her close again and held her tightly. *I could be with her yet.* Then he stopped. *This is the god Mar's work. There would be a price for this; wasn't there always?*

"What does Broken Monkey get in return?" he asked.

"He wants knowledge and information," she responded. "At every new moon I have to tell him what my brother and Chan Muwaan are doing and planning. You have to tell him about the future and what will happen in our world."

"So we will spy on your brother?"

"I offered him many riches for the potion. He showed me a pile of jade and jewelry laying in a corner of his cave. He despises jewels and takes them only because men consider them important and valuable. It pains them to give him those objects. He wants information. That is what is valuable to him."

"And we are going to give it to him?" Johnson asked knowing that a person's honor was the first consideration in their culture. "Isn't that dishonorable?"

"Dishonorable," she spat, a fire growing in her eyes. "It's only a little information for what I get in return. I would sell my place in the afterlife if it would keep you here with me. That would be dishonorable."

Johnson lay there in silence, the concept swirling rapidly through his head. *If she is correct I could stay. I could be Lightning Sky, the warrior and Counselor General to Shield Jaguar III the king. And she would be mine, at least for the time before she was moved into Chan Muwaan's palace.* He chuckled to himself. The time when she had to leave to become Chan Muwaan's queen was further away than anyone thought.

He knew the future. The ascension dates were part of the archaeological record, his field of expertise. They were preserved historically on their stone tablets. It was presently somewhere around 770 to 772 A.D. and Chan Muwaan wouldn't become king for another seven years and then there would be time before the actual marriage took place. Shield Jaguar knew about Little Rabbit and him and possibly would hold off the marriage for a while. They had at least five years, perhaps more. It could be a lifetime.

They lay together for a long while, both lost in their own thoughts. Then slowly their passion awakened as they explored the sensuality of the other with the fascination of children. Lovemaking came easy, first the need, then the desperation to give all and take all, and finally the merging of two souls. When it was over he held her close once again, stroking her hair and enjoying the warmth of her face against his chest. Everything felt good. *Perhaps the gods don't hate us after all.* He chuckled at the thought and broke into a big smile.

Chapter 20

Wow," said Phoebe as she awakened in the cave. Johnson and the young shaman were sitting by the fire waiting for her to wake up. "I can't believe it!"

"Quite an experience wasn't it?" Johnson said.

"It was so real."

"That's what I've been telling you. It has to be real," he replied.

"It's so strange," Phoebe said. "Everything was so intense. Did it really happen that way? Was there a coup where Shield Jaguar seized the throne and killed Chel-Te'? Were all of those people I saw, really killed?"

"If we saw the same thing it did," Johnson responded. "I was part of the coup where Shield Jaguar killed Chel-Te' and seized power."

"Did Shield Jaguar really take power that way, by seizing it? It was so brutal."

"I believe he did. It's what I expected all along."

Phoebe suddenly sat back and looked at him. "Alan, we both saw the same thing. We couldn't have dreamed the same dream about a coup in the same location and with the same characters in the past. It's impossible, and it's impossible to travel through time. What happened?"

"I don't know Pheb. To me it was real, even more so now."

The shaman sat quietly listening. Something special had happened here and he was part of it.

"You must tell us all about it," he said. "I will gather the people in the village. They need to know of their past. They will rejoice in your journey."

Phoebe smiled at him. "It would be an honor," she replied. "I'd love to share what I have learned."

"It will never be the same Pheb," Johnson said as they arrived back to camp. "You will never be able to go back to making bland, conservative conclusions from the interpretation of your glyphs and relief carvings."

"I think I can handle it, Alan."

"You will meet the same resistance that I have. The gods have said that the knowledge would ruin me. Perhaps it will ruin you too."

"But we both took the drug and saw the same thing. How can it not be true if we saw the same thing?"

"I'm convinced, but will our colleagues be?"

"They must believe us, Alan, they must."

§

Later that evening Johnson and Phoebe sat in the ruins of the inner courtyard of the royal palace. They compared notes on what each observed and recorded them to be transcribed.

"It was horrible," said Phoebe, "the killings. I've never seen anyone killed before. I don't think I want to again."

"Just a part of the coup," Johnson replied. "The killing was necessary for Shield Jaguar to consolidate his power."

"But they were real people, Alan."

"They were pawns. He had to kill a few to let the others know he meant business."

"It was horrifying and they were so casual about it."

"That was part of their culture. It was accepted."

"I don't understand it," Phoebe answered. "Even Little Rabbit relished it. Her guards killed those men and she indicated it served them right for causing her an inconvenience."

"She was the sister of the king."

"And that makes it acceptable?"

"Yes, that makes it acceptable."

"Alan, how can you say that?"

"Because it is true. In their culture it was perfectly acceptable," he replied.

"But she gloated about it as if they were sacrificed to her."

"Weren't they?"

"Alan, what has happened to you? You're a pacifist. You always take the side of the oppressed."

"Something's changed Pheb. I'm different inside. I feel there is a strength there I've never had before," he said proudly. Yes something had changed. "I'm not the same man. I have brought some of the traits of Lightning Sky back with me."

"That's not possible," Phoebe said.

"Neither is time travel."

He was intensely aware of everything around him and continually assessed it for danger. It was the fight or flight response he reasoned and he had no intention of fleeing if the decision arose. Strange, he thought, he'd relish a fight if it came to that.

§

Johnson couldn't sleep. It was the third sleepless night in a row. The full moon was high, as he walked the ruins, lending an eerie light and deep shadows. He felt the ghosts of the ancients lurking just out of his sight. They were watching him. For the last three days Johnson had roved around the site and went for long walks in the jungle. He needed his solitude. He needed time to think. It was so different now. The jungle was preserved by the government. It was a thick tangle of growth. He knew he'd have to stay on marked trails or it would be easy to get lost. During the Eighth Century there was very little jungle unless you were far from the city center. The population was large and most of the available land was under cultivation.

His thoughts ranged over the actions of the last few days, at least the last few days when he was in the past. Shield Jaguar was a king now and Lightning Sky was a counselor and a military leader responsible for half of the warriors, and they would be going to war again soon. The forces of Yaxchilan and Bonampak, together under Shield Jaguar's command, made for a formidable force. They could subjugate the towns around them and strike heavy blows at Piedras Negras.

He was troubled. If the hunchback's potion worked, he could be part of that. The probability of it working was a long shot he thought. It was more likely he was promising it to Little Rabbit instead of providing it. But the concept that he could go back and stay and live a life of privilege and power was enticing.

But then there was Little Rabbit. He was in love. Thoughts of her were occupying more and more of his time. He knew he wanted to be with her, dangerous or not. *She is pledged to another man but the marriage will not happen for quite some time. Chan Muwaan II wouldn't ascend for another seven years or so until 776 A.D., and she will become his wife only after his ascension. A lot could happen in that time.*

The moon was up, and each night he went down to the pyramid where he had first seen Little Rabbit and sit at the bottom for hours staring at the little temple on top. He remembered how she came out of the darkness into his sight for the first time, a goddess incarnate, and called him to her. If only she were up there now.

He sat there, groggy and exhausted, watching and recounting the first time he had seen her there and his fascination. He knew he needed sleep. He was having trouble focusing, his mind wandering on its own accord, slipping in and out of consciousness. Through blurred eyes he saw a glow coming from the temple. He fought to focus on it. He could see it, just a little glow and the outline of a woman. Yes, it had to be her.

"Wait for me, Little Rabbit," he called. "Wait for me." Running wildly he slipped and fell at the base of the stairway and hurt his leg. Unable to rise and walk, he crawled up the steep steps "Wait for me," he called holding his gaze on the glow. She was there and waiting. "I am coming," he called. He reached the landing. "I'm here," he called. "I'm here."

The landing was empty, just a bright spot where the moon reflected more light than the surrounding area. "I'm here," he cried again as he sat down on the landing in despair. He was sure she had been there.

Chapter 21

Phoebe stood by the window, looking down the street. The leaves were turning on the few trees that lined the sidewalk. It would be nice to be back in Wisconsin for the fall colors. The campus was beautiful at this time of the year, cold, football weather. The fond memory of sitting in the bleachers on a Saturday afternoon with a boyfriend, a bottle of wine and a blanket wrapped around them passed through her mind. But those days were past. She had a teaching position at Penn State now and was making a serious push at finishing her doctorate. Living in an urban location was the price to be paid for a rewarding, leading-edge career.

Jim Harper, the department head of archaeology, rapped on the open door, breaking her reverie.

"Got a minute?" he asked.

"Sure Jim," she said as she turned from the window to look at him. "I just finished a class, Primitive Mesoamerican Civilizations."

"I've heard there are some lively discussions in that class."

"The upper classmen are always more fun," she said with a smile. "They can be challenging. I've got a couple of bright kids there. They keep me on my toes."

"That's what I want to talk to you about, Phoebe," he said as he took a chair in front of her desk. "It's come to my attention that some of the stuff coming out in there is a little off the cuff."

"Are you questioning my right to present the material to the class in my own way?"

"It's something that perhaps we should talk about." He motioned her to her chair. "Some of the talk is that you are proposing archaeological conclusions that don't fit with the evidence."

She sat back and looked at him hard. "This isn't high school Jim and they are not new-guy freshmen. We're past the 'digest and regurgitate' process at this level. And the evidence as you call it is subjective at best. It is my job to challenge them, make them think."

"Phoebe, you have one of the best heads I've seen in this field. That is why you are here. The strides you are making in new interpretations of the Maya writing system are phenomenal; three papers in the major anthropological journals in three years is exceptional. You're going to have the opportunity to make a tremendous contribution to science."

"So what's the problem, Jim?"

He sat back and looked at her for a long moment. With a sigh he said, "it's the Johnson influence, Phoebe. He's spouting some wild-ass stuff again, and you are getting the reputation of promoting his outlandish theories. It's going to hurt your career."

Her eyes flared with an unsettling gaze. "Alan has been my friend for years," she replied sharply, "yours too, for that matter. Of course I support him. He was my mentor. He's a brilliant scientist."

"He's becoming known as a crackpot," Harper retorted. "He claims to be able to travel back in time and become a royal personage who watches history in the making. That's not science."

"Maybe he knows what he's talking about, Jim," she spat.

"Ridiculous. How can you ever consider such an idea?"

She leaned forward, forearms on the desk, holding a pencil upright between two hands rolling it back and forth as she carefully considered her next words.

"Jim, I've been working with Alan for the last two months, over the phone, on the Internet, and there have been a couple of trips back to Wisconsin. He's working on a paper that reinforces his contentions and supports his conclusions. It's really something special."

"How can you say that, Phoebe? You, of all people know the archaeological records. You can read those damn glyphs. You're one of the few people who can and you know what they say firsthand."

"There is a wealth of lintels from Yaxchilan," she replied. "Some have been interpreted and we are working on others. But they are points in time, not a continuum and we know some are pure propaganda where the king, Bird Jaguar IV, re-wrote history to his own benefit."

"Yes, but Alan is now claiming he has proof that the dynastic line wasn't the way it was written."

"And I agree with him," she said earnestly.

"You can't be serious!"

Still cautiously choosing her words, she said, "I am. Jim, when we were there last summer, Alan designed an experiment. It was rather simple really. We would both take the drug at the same time. When the effect wore off we would compare experiences. If the experiences were different for each of us then it was only a vision, a creation of the mind. But if we experienced the same thing, there was merit in his conclusions of seeing the past."

"So you took the drug?" he asked.

"Yes," she replied slowly watching for his reaction.

"And?"

"And we both experienced the same thing, him from being a royal personage, and me from being a priestess.

"You have to be kidding!"

"No, we both saw a military coup where Shield Jaguar killed Chel-Te' and proclaimed himself king."

"That can't be. It is impossible!"

"But that is what happened, Jim. It is what we saw. Both of us saw the same thing and we did it independently. How could it have only been a dream if we both saw it at the same time?"

§

"I tell you I was there, Jim. I not only saw Shield Jaguar III seize the throne, but I helped him do it," Johnson said to his friend. There was a Big Ten football game the next day between Wisconsin and Penn State and Jim Harper, an avid supporter of his university, flew in for it. He had booked an early flight to be able to spend time with Alan Johnson, his longtime friend and colleague.

The stories coming out of U.W. Madison about the Classical Maya were unsettling. He felt he owed it to his friend to try to put the brakes on them. The man's credibility and reputation depended on it, even if there wasn't much of it left. They were in the Congress Bar. It was only half full, but within another hour it would be standing room only. The weekend had started.

"Alan, do you realize what you are saying? You actually think you went back to Mexico during the Eighth Century and participated in a military action to depose one king and replace him with another."

"Exactly," Johnson replied. "Shield Jaguar seized the palace, killed Chel-Te' and took his place. I fought by his side, and when he was king one of the first things he did was award me, Lightning Sky, the position of Honored Counselor and leader of half the warriors. My cousin Smoking Squirrel commands the other half of the warriors and holds the same position."

"But you aren't Lighting Sky."

"I was in his body, a rather good one, I'd say. I had his strength and I believe, even now, I retain some of his personal characteristics, those related to being a warrior."

"My friend, I can't believe this. You traveled to the past and became someone else, someone important?"

"He's still part of me," Johnson replied. "I brought some of him back with me. I'm not the same man, Jim. I look at things differently than I used to. I'm constantly looking for danger and there are times I want to fight, not just fight but to do a lot of harm to my opponent."

"You? Alan, I've known you for years. You've been a good friend. You're a fine man, gentle and kind. You aren't a fighter."

"I am now, Jim. I'm a warrior. In my heart I am, and courage is something I never had, but I have it now. I feel people need to address me with respect for my position. It's become very important to me, something I demand."

"Alan, I think you are suffering from delusions. I think you need help, some professional counseling, perhaps in a hospital. They can do good things for you these days."

"Help, you say," snapped Johnson, "yes I need help. What I need is to know how to live with it. Back in time I was a warrior, a brave one with many kills who was revered for his ferocity. People held me in both awe and fear.

"I have never felt as alive as I did when I was back there. I loved it, and consider it to have been the best part of my life. You have no idea how differently they lived. When I was there I really lived. The blood in my veins boiled, and I vented my anger on my enemies. They stood up to me but died anyway, and it felt good. Now we live in a civilized society where man has been forced to rein in his primal instincts. I'm being driven by some very savage ones. And you think a quiet rest will help that?"

§

That night Jim Harper called Gerhardt Weber in Chicago. "He thinks he's a warrior from the past," Harper said almost before the phone was picked up. "I don't know what to do."

"Really that bad?" Gerhardt said with a big yawn. He stared across the room at the TV. Half the show he was watching had disappeared as he dozed.

"I think he should be hospitalized," Harper followed. "He went on and on about a coup and his participation in it. He claimed to have gone back in time and witnessed Shield Jaguar III kill Chel-Te' and take his throne and he rambled about the different people he knew. He seemed to go in circles especially after he had a few drinks in him."

"He's not a drinker," Gerhardt replied. "One and a half was his limit, a teetottler; it was absolutely disgusting."

"Not today. He banged them down pretty good. The more he drank, the more belligerent he became. There were times I thought he was going to challenge me. God, he's touchy."

"Sure doesn't sound like the Johnson we know," Gerhardt answered.

"What can we do, Gerhardt?" Harper asked.

"Not much, my friend. I don't know what was in that drug he took but he brought it on himself."

"One other problem, Gerhardt."

"How could we have more, my friend? One is enough."

"He's a scientist," replied Harper. "He set up an experiment where Phoebe took the drug with him."

"So?"

"So she claims to have traveled to the past with him and saw the same things he did, but independently."

There was a long pause on the phone line before Gerhardt

responded. "I still contend it can't be done," he said.

§

The hangover was bad today. The headache wouldn't leave no matter what he took for it. *Thursday is a bad day for a hangover,* Johnson thought. *If today was Friday I could leave early and get a drink to take off the edge, but this is Thursday, and there's a departmental staff meeting in two hours.* He hoped it would be a short one. There was a little bar downtown that students didn't frequent. He'd go there after the meeting. It was a dive and the patrons weren't leading citizens but it was dark and no one bothered him. He pulled a half pint of scotch from his lower desk drawer and took a couple of good pulls at it, just enough to hold him over.

The meeting was a bore, the same thing as last month. The Chemistry Department wanted a new laboratory and they were working out how to accomplish it. Smithers from Economics came with his cost breakdown figures and argued with Nelson from the Business Department who handled accounting. It was the same every month, Smithers claimed he saw the big picture and Nelson was shortsighted, and Nelson claimed he'd run out of money before they got there.

Johnson watched the scenario play itself out with less than a casual interest and dozed off. Ms. Peabody from the English Department nudged him when it came time to vote. "Nelson," she whispered. He raised his hand at the appropriate moment. Duty done, he picked up his briefcase, time to head downtown for a drink.

"Alan, can I see you for a moment?" Dave Stron, the university president, asked as the rest filed out of the conference room.

"Sure Jim, what can I do for you?"

"We've been friends for a long time Al; I'm concerned about you."

"Okay."

"How do I say it? You're looking a little ragged lately. Is there anything I can help you with?"

"Just a few things I'm working through, Dave. They will be taken care of in no time and I'll be my old chipper self again," Johnson said with a forced smile.

"Al, let me cut to the chase. It's the drinking. It's showing, and not just a little bit."

"So I take a nip now and then," Johnson said defensively. "I can handle it."

"You're drawing attention to yourself. People are beginning to notice and they are talking about it. You are the department head of archaeology, and you are expected to be a representative of the university."

"Dave, it's not that bad. But if it will make you happier I will cut back."

"I hope so. I hate to tell you this, but there are six weeks until the end of the semester. If it isn't taken care of by then I'll have to put someone else in that position."

§

"She was the sweetest little thing," Johnson said to the two men sitting down the bar a ways. He was in a dive bar a couple of blocks off Main Street, one of those places where two blocks from the main stream was another world, a world of seedy bars, winos, rescue missions, pimps, prostitutes and drug dealers, just to name a few, not a place where he was likely to run into anyone from the university. He picked up his beer and finished it off. "Bartender, another here and a couple for my friends."

He looked back at the two men. "I loved her with my entire being." He licked his lips. They were getting numb. "Yep, just the sweetest little thing," he repeated again.

"I loved one like that once too," the short skinny man said, "she was just the sweetest little thing too."

"Here's to women," the heavyset one toasted. "You can't live with 'em, and you can't live without 'em."

"She was a high priestess," Johnson mumbled.

"That right?" said the heavyset man.

"Damn right," Johnson answered. "A real live high priestess."

"Don't find many of those," the skinny man answered.

"Nope," said Johnson, "but I found one and she was a princess too, a royal princess."

"Wow," said the heavyset guy. "A princess. You're a lucky fellow. What happened to her?"

"Her brother gave her away. He gave her to another man."

"That scumbag," the little man said.

"He sure was, and I loved her too."

"That scum bag," the little man said again.

"She didn't want to go. But she was going to become a queen, so she had to."

"So the other man got her?" the bartender said as he polished a glass. These drunks sure could spin some tales.

"And I'm going to kill him," Johnson said as he held up his bottle to the light and tried to focus on the level of the liquid in it. "I'm going take the drug and I'm going to go there and kill him."

"Really?" said the heavyset guy. "You're going to kill him?"

"It won't be easy, but I'm gonna do it."

"Yeah, how are you going to kill him?" the little man asked.

"I'll stick a spear through him, that's what I'll do," Johnson answered.

Two bikers came in, large men, leaned on the bar and ordered two beers. Leather jackets with colors on the back, dirty jeans, heavy boots and gloves without the fingers indicated they were outlaws, the one percent who wouldn't conform to society's norms or values. One had a chain hanging in a loop from his shoulder. As they moved up to the bar Johnson tensed. Shaking his head to clear it, he became alert. There was danger here. He could smell it. He noted large knives, straight blade knives in sheaths hanging from their belts, the blade slipped into their back pockets. It advertised they were felons who could not carry guns.

"Stick him with a spear. That should take care of him," the skinny guy said.

"Damn right," replied Johnson with less of a slur. "That'll show him." He pushed the fog aside and looked straight at the bikers.

"Who you gonna to stick with a spear?" one of the bikers asked as he looked over at Johnson.

"The guy who took his girl," the little one said. "Serve him right too."

"Her brother gave her to another guy," the heavyset one said. "He's a real scum bag."

The biker pushed back from the bar and walked over to Johnson, looked at him and laughed. "This puny guy? You drunks got a sense of humor. Come 'ere," he called to the other biker. "Take a look at this. This puny guy here is going to stick a spear in someone."

"He's going to kill him," the skinny guy said smugly.

The biker swatted Johnson's shoulder and laughed. "Where's your spear tough guy?"

"Don't touch me," Johnson commanded harshly, his senses sharp. He wrapped his hand around the neck of the beer bottle as it sat on the bar like he was going to pick it up and take a sip.

"Oh yeah?" the biker retorted and slapped his shoulder again. "What you gonna do about it?"

Johnson raised the bottle a couple of inches and slammed it against the bar, shattering its base. Simultaneously he swung it backhand at the biker, imbedding the jagged edges of glass in his cheek. He turned on his chair and lashed out with his foot at the other biker who jumped back and pulled his knife.

Johnson reached down and took the knife from the back

pocket of the first man who was kneeling on the floor stunned and bleeding profusely. In a fluid motion he came up and lunged, catching the standing biker's jacket and splitting it open. The man jumped back again. Johnson, overshooting him, swung a backward roundhouse with the blade extended toward the man, slicing the leather sleeve and cutting his arm to the bone. The man screamed and dropped his knife. Johnson started toward him, knife extended, and the biker turned and ran out the door.

Johnson looked at the man on the floor and stared toward the door. The bartender was reaching for something under the bar. He slammed the knife hard on the bar, handle down and the blade up and menacing. "Don't," he said. His eyes glared at the man. "Best hand it over." The bartender laid a gun on the bar. Johnson emptied it, threw the shells toward the back of the room and set the gun back on the bar. Securing the knife behind his belt, he covered it with his jacket and turned and slowly walked out the door.

§

It was dawn when the campus police came down the walk and woke him. "They must be looking for me," he thought as he shook his head and remembered what he had done. *It served the bastards right. They dared to lay a hand on me. They are lucky to be alive, if they are. I only defended myself."* He assessed the two police officers. Tension tightened his neck as he prepared for a confrontation. He wasn't going to go anywhere with them, not for a second.

"Move along," the police said. "You can't sleep out here. If you're here when we come back, we're going to cite you."

As they walked away, Johnson stared dumbly out over the lake. They no longer existed. He was hollow and empty, like yesterday, and the day before and the day before that. She hadn't come. He waited all night and she hadn't come. He knew he couldn't live like this anymore. Everything was coming down around him.

Chapter 22

The message on the phone was from Dave Stron, the president of the University of Wisconsin. Alan Johnson had not shown up for class for the last week. No one knew where he was. Did she?

"I don't know," Phoebe replied when she got through to his office. "We were close when I was in Madison, but since moving to Philadelphia, we've only talked a few times."

"It's not like him," the president said, "but he wasn't himself this semester."

"He had a lot on his mind," she replied. "It bothered him, I think."

"Well he was drinking pretty heavy and he kept saying something about having to make a decision."

"Make a decision, what type of decision?" she asked. Alan never told her about a decision he had to make.

"He never really said. Once he mentioned it was a life-changing one. That's all I know."

"Have you checked his apartment?"

"I went in with the police. It was neat and tidy. The only thing unusual were the books laying around, lots of them. He looked like he was doing a lot of reading or research."

"He's a professor. He always had books laying around. He was always referencing something."

"There were books all over the place, must have been a hundred of them. They were piled up in every room."

"Books about what?" she replied.

"That's what is strange. It seems that he was looking at everything about the Maya and lots of books on war strategy. What in the hell would an archaeology professor want with books on war strategy?"

"I wouldn't know," she replied, fear rising in her. Alan had talked about Lightning Sky being Shield Jaguar's military leader and advisor.

I know where he went; back to Mexico. It will be his last trip. There is only enough drug for one more trip. But why does he have all the books on war strategy? He will only be there for a couple of days and it will be over. Well, let him do it. He'll be back in a little while. He is always depressed when the drug wears off and he returns to the present. Since this will be the last time, he'll have to hole up someplace for a time and get it out of his system. Give him a month and he'll contact me and let me know what happened.

§

The bus from Villahermosa to Palenque was slow. It stopped every couple of miles to let someone on or off. She was so close to the site now and the damn bus was moving at a snail's pace. It was maddening.

It had been three weeks since talking to Dave Stron. Phoebe was worried and called back. No one had heard from Alan. They didn't know where he was. It would be morning before she could catch another bus to Frontera Corozol. She checked in at the hotel they normally used when they passed through. Yes, Dr. Johnson was there a month ago. They had not seen him since. At least she was on the right trail.

The trip went faster in the morning. The quickest way to Frontera was to ride in a nine-passenger van with a tour group. The van used a direct route and at the end of the road where the river is, there would be boats waiting to go to the Yaxchilan site. When the tourists found out she was an archaeologist who worked on the site it seemed there were a hundred questions. If only her students at the university had this much enthusiasm.

He was nowhere to be found. He had been at the lodge, but had left about a month ago. At the site there was no sign of him. He hadn't been there for quite a while. She went to the local village. The young shaman was relieved to see her.

"Senorita Phoebe, finally you arrive. I need your help."

"Help?" she asked, her anticipation turning dark.

"Si, Senorita. Dr. Johnson took the drug and went back to the past again. But he hasn't returned. I am worried."

"How long ago?" she asked with a shaky voice. *Something is very wrong. Johnson has been gone over a month now.*

"Too long I think," said the young shaman. "I go to the cave to see him every day and each day he becomes weaker."

The truck they took up into the hills seemed to be moving too slow. Couldn't it move any faster? She had to get there. Surely she could be of some help. The shaman said Johnson stayed in the past. How could that happen? The powder only lasted for a short time, a couple of hours in the present time corresponded to a couple of days in the past. He had been there for a month. That would be a very long time in the past.

The cave seemed colder than she remembered, a damp cold that seemed to go clear through to her bones. The deeper they went, the colder it seemed to become. *Nerves,* she shivered. *I don't want to see what happened to him.* The shaman told her Johnson was in bad shape. He was surprised he had lived this long. *Something is keeping him going. Perhaps it is the gods.*

As they entered the chamber, she could see his body laying next to the stream. There was a folded blanket under his head and he was covered with another. She went over and knelt down next to him. There was no color in his face, his cheeks were hollow, and his eye sockets deep and dark. His chest was sunken and an arm that was laying across his stomach was just some loose skin around a bone. She broke into tears and cried loudly. *This can't have happened. What went wrong?*

"I don't know what to do," the shaman said. "I think he is close to death."

"What do you do for your people?" she asked knowing the Maya religious practices were still followed here.

"I say the chants imploring the gods to be merciful and make the transition easy as they take him to the underworld for his tests to see if he is fit to continue to the Place of Comfort."

"Say the chants for him," she said. "I believe he is a Maya now. It must be close for his time there too."

She sat beside him holding his hand watching his chest slowly rise and fall with just a hint of movement. The young shaman began to chant. Both knew they were on a deathwatch. It seemed like hours later when there was a convulsion and then another and his breath expelled. The chest stopped moving. She looked for his pulse. It was gone. Dr. Alan Johnson was dead.

"He loved your people," she said as the shaman stopped chanting. "Bury him in the cave and leave a small cross over the grave. It's what he would have wanted."

It was dawn when they came out of the cave. They had been there fifteen hours. The shaman drove her back to the site. It was a quiet trip. Both were lost in their own thoughts. Before she got out, the shaman reached into the glove box and pulled out an envelope with her name on it and gave it to her.

"He said you would come. He told me to give this to you."

Tears streaked down her cheeks and she sobbed loudly as the realization hit her that he knew he wouldn't be coming back. How could he have gone back and stayed in the past? He never told her he found a way.

Phoebe held the envelope with one hand and stared at it as she wiped her eyes with the other. It was all she had left of him, the man who had been a friend, mentor and lover. She felt empty as she walked down to the center of the complex. The tourists wouldn't arrive for another hour. She had it to herself now. She knew where Johnson came when he was troubled, the place of the temple where he met Little Rabbit. He would sit for hours staring at it.

It would be the right place to open the envelope. Slowly she peeled back the flap. All that was inside was a map, with a start point, some locations to find, and an end point marked with an X, no explanation of what it was a map of. In one corner was some scribbling that looked like the notes normally put on an excavation grid map. It showed a location that was on the other side of the river in Guatemala.

Phoebe sat there staring at it blankly. What was he trying to tell her? Its lack of information meant something. Then it hit her. Only she knew the key; something was buried for her to find. Only an archaeologist would know that. The scribbling was a kind of shorthand that indicated to dig when she got to the spot where the X was.

Later that morning, when the tourists were wandering around the site, she had a boat take her across the river. The bluff over the river was the first point. It was easy to find. With a compass, she had no trouble locating the other points. There were large boulders placed there, put there by man, points that would easily last thirteen hundred years. Alan had left nothing to chance. In a couple of hours she came to a small rise, hardly a bump in the landscape. Dig on the north side, the scribbling indicated. A half hour later and three feet down she hit stone. Clearing the area she found a flat stone rolled over a doorway which she easily moved.

The room was small, and musty. It hadn't been opened for thirteen hundred years. Phoebe shone her flashlight inside and looked around. All that was there was a small altar and a raised sleeping platform. She smiled as she realized where she was. It was their secret place, Little Rabbit's and Johnson's, the place where they stole away to when they wanted to be alone and make love. She lit a candle and watched the light dance around the room. She smiled. The room took on a romantic glow. She had read his journals describing it. *Their secret place is everything he claimed—a warm cozy hideout deep in the jungle for just the two of them. No wonder he thought it was exotic. It was.*

She checked the notes and started to dig, tunneling under a corner of the altar. A foot down she hit stone and changed to excavating slowly. Whatever he left should be recovered carefully. Slowly she uncovered a stone box measuring ten by twelve inches and about four inches deep.

She opened the box. Inside, still wrapped in a disintegrating cloth, was the most beautiful necklace she had ever seen. The finest pieces of polished jade and amber were held together with golden wires looking as exquisite as the day it was made. Underneath it was a stone tablet. A big smile came across her face as she realized it was the necklace that Johnson and Little Rabbit buried as a sacrifice to the gods asking them to bless their love.

She held it up and looked closely at it. It was proof that the drug worked as he claimed. He really had managed to travel to the past. He had to have been here. They buried it together. That's the only way he could have known about it. It was the one thing his mind couldn't have conjured up.

They did it. Somehow they managed to find a way to be together. She didn't know how but they did it. She started to cry again, but the tears were different now. She knew them both, and how they loved each other, and through her pain she felt happy for them.

With a little water from her canteen, Phoebe cleaned the small limestone tablet as best she could. Looking at it closely, Phoebe saw words inscribed on it. They were in English.

I, Lightning Sky, have taken ten captives. I am the Counselor General and military commander for my brother the king, Shield Jaguar III. Our enemies run in fear and our allies pay large tribute to the great king.

I have been a fortunate man. The gods provided me many enemies to slay and a woman to love for many years before she left to do her duty and provide an heir for the royal line of Bonampak.

It is near the end of the great king's reign. All building has stopped and the fighting becomes more intense each year. The drought has been bad; many die and there is not enough food even with that taken in tribute and conquest. We have entered the time of the apocalypse when only the destructive Venus Star Wars are being waged. Soon the king, Shield Jaguar III, will die. Little Rabbit sees the future, and has said that he and I will die on the battlefield together. She has told me she and I will be together in the next life, never having to part again. The gods have promised it.

§

There was a full moon that night. Phoebe walked among the ruins. A thin wispy fog drifted in from the river. In the dim eerie light she felt like she was there again, back in the time when everything was majestic. She could visualize the terraces with the temples and the pyramids.

From a tall pyramid a young priestess looked down at her. A young warrior stood beside the priestess, holding her hand. Phoebe walked past and continued along the Great Plaza. They watched until she was out of sight. Then they looked at each other and smiled.

Historical Postscript

The last record from Yaxchilan was written in 808 A.D., ten years after Shield Jaguar III's death. The quality of the lintel was very poor, indicating the artistic representation attesting to the height of the city's glory had declined to a point of being almost nonexistent.

The entire Maya society was in the process of collapsing as warfare increased. It reads that K'inich Tatb'u Skull III, Shield Jaguar III's son and reigning king of Yaxchilan, invaded Piedras Negras and captured their king, Ruler 7, destroying their dynasty and political structure of kingly rule. It was never to rise again. The four-century-old conflict between the two kingdoms had ended. Yaxchilan was the victor.

CPSIA information can be obtained at www.ICGtesting.com
Printed in the USA
BVOW010119111012

302599BV00001B/2/P